The Slayers of Dragonhome

By John Peel

D0840980

Dragonhome Books
New York

This book is a work of fiction. Any resemblance to actual events, places or persons is entirely coincidental.

Dragonhome Books, New York
ISBN # 9780615567082

For Andrea Mountain
with gratitude

Chapter One

The world seemed to be all mud and draining rainwater to Margone as his horse tramped wearily into the small, pathetic-looking village. His cape had kept most of the storm from drenching his clothing, but his hair was soaked, and water was dripping from the tip of his nose. Thankfully, the storm was now past, though the air was still chilled. His horse *whuffed* with displeasure, and he patted its neck.

"Steady, old friend," he promised. "We'll be there soon, I'm sure. Then you'll get a good rub-down and a bucket of the best mash." *And I'll get a rest and a hot meal for once,* he added, silently, to himself. This journey seemed to have taken forever, and he was far too used to the weariness in his bones. But this part of his quest was almost completed, at least.

He looked around the sorry excuse for a village. It was barely more than a gathering of farmhouses and the various businesses that went with them. There was a smithy, with an appealing glow of a stoked fire; a tavern, which would probably have hot food and something to drink, even on a day like this; and a handful of shops, all closed, since nobody would be shopping in the height of a storm. There was nobody in the mud-filled streets, and Margone looked around, blinking his eyes as water dripped down from his sodden hair.

A movement caught his eye, and he turned his weary neck to watch a young boy - no more than eight, he judged - hurry from one of the buildings. He dodged puddles in the street to reach a small out-house, where he collected an armload of dry wood. He started back to the main house when he finally noticed the heavy horse and rider in the road. The boy stopped to stare. Obviously, in this rural community, strangers were not a common sight.

Margone smiled inwardly; it wasn't too long since he'd been very like this boy. "Good day," he called out, being careful to keep both hands in sight on the reins. Thankfully, his cloak covered the sword at his hip; he didn't want to scare the locals.

To them, he was certain, any armed rider would seem like trouble. "Well, maybe *good* isn't the right word for it."

"Hello," the boy replied, timidly. He clutched the sticks as if they might protect him.

"Maybe you can help a passing stranger," Margone suggested. "I'm looking for a place called Dragonhome - do you know of it?"

The boy stood still, silent, for a moment. Margone wondered what the place he'd named meant to the boy. Then the youngster nodded, once, abruptly. "It's out of town," he said.

Town? Margone almost laughed. This place was barely a village, and certainly nothing more. Still, to the yokels, it was probably the largest gathering they knew. "How far?" he asked.

The boy shrugged. "Couple of miles, I'd guess." He rearranged the sticks he held to free his right hand, and he pointed to the west. "That way."

"You're sure?" Margone asked.

"I've never been there," the boy admitted. "But everybody knows where it is. It's where the dragons flew from."

"Ah." Margone felt a surge of satisfaction. "The dragons..."

That seemed to perk the boy up. "Have you heard about the dragons, sir?" he asked.

"It's why I'm here," Margone said. "I have indeed heard about the dragons."

The door to the boy's house opened again, and a man stumbled out. He was a farmer, clearly, a man of soil and plants. He was dressed plainly, and obviously had little ready cash. But he had a look of concern on his rustic features, and the rider could understand this. "Can I help you, mister?" the man asked. It wasn't quite accusing, but it was far from being friendly. Again, Margone realized that strangers were not common here - or very welcome. As with many small communities, strangers almost always spelled trouble.

"I think your son already has, thank you," Margone said politely. He jerked his head toward the west. "Dragonhome lies that way, he tells me." He made it sound like a question.

"True enough," the father said. He placed his arms about the boy, drawing him into the safety of his embrace. "You headed there?"

Why else would I ask about it, idiot? Margone thought. Aloud, he said: "Yes. I have heard of the dragons."

"Story's out, then." The farmer shrugged. "I thought it might be. Drawn by curiosity, are you?"

It was really none of his business, but Margone answered anyway. "No - by my profession. I'm a Dragonslayer."

"Ah." The farmer tried to look wise. "Come to kill the beasts, then, are you?"

"Not directly - I heard that they had flown from here."

"Three years back now," the farmer agreed. He was now almost chatty. "Thank the gods they're gone - we none of us knew that the mad lord was breeding the monsters." He shuddered. "We could all of us have been murdered and eaten in our sleep."

Small loss to the Five Kingdoms if you had been, Margone thought. He made a smile appear on his face. "Most irresponsible of him, then, wasn't it? Still, it's my job to hunt them down and slay them."

The farmer scowled, his eyes pinched. "Bit young for that, aren't you?"

Margone was used to such slights; it was true enough that he was barely twenty. "But well trained," he said. "My father's family have been Dragonslayers for nigh on five hundred years. I know my job, as you know your dirt."

That was the wrong thing to say; the farmer took umbrage. "Aye," he said, slowly. "I'm of the dirt, and proud of it, too. Folks like you might look down upon us, but we're the backbone of this world. If we didn't raise food, where would the likes of you be?"

"And if we didn't kill the dragons, farmer, you'd be eaten in your sleep, remember?" Margone didn't want to sit and debate with country bumpkins. "I'll be on my way now." He inclined his head to the young boy. "My thanks for your help." He gentled the reins, and his horse slowly began to move off.

"It's in ruins, mostly," the farmer called to his back. "Fell apart a long time back. There's some shelter there, but nothing much else."

Margone didn't turn. He simply shook his head. "You're wrong about that," he said. "There's quite a lot there." He didn't elaborate; anything he said would only disturb the man, and would be spread about the village in minutes after he had left. "Thankfully, that doesn't still include dragons." He rode on, ignoring the small village behind.

He was annoyed with himself. There had been no need for him to be so abrupt with the farmer. He knew that the problem was his own - it was a fate he had come very close to sharing, and the thought of tilling the dirt and grubbing in the earth to make a living appalled him. He knew it was an honorable job, and that - as the man had reminded him - without farmers, nobody else could survive. But the thought of being condemned to such a fate chilled his soul. He had been born for better things.

Almost.

He had indeed been born to a line of Dragonslayers - but there had been no dragons for anyone to slay for more than a century. It was expensive and lengthy training to become a slayer, and when there was no obvious need for anyone to kill dragons that didn't exist... Well, he could hardly blame the peasants of his hometown for wanting to cut off the payments they were making to train him. To them, it seemed like a great waste of their hard-earned cash. But without their support, he'd have had to take up another form of life - and that meant working as a soldier for the king, or else tilling the earth as a farmer.

Then, thankfully, had come the astonishing news that there were, after all, dragons still alive. The stories varied - some said one, others a handful, and some even said a whole colony. What was most astonishing about the stories was that the dragons were said to have come from Dragonhome - the place where the Dragonslayers had gathered for their final assault years ago on the last dragons.

The dragons had flown - nobody quite knew where, but the tales were clear on that. They were no longer at Dragonhome. Which was why it had been such a surprise when the summons had issued from the place just months back. The messengers had traveled all over the Five Kingdoms, seeking the heirs of the Dragonslayers, and bidding them all come to Dragonhome. The summons had barely arrived in time to save Margone from making a new career for himself.

His father had trained Margone from birth, until his death just a year ago. It was when Hobson had died that the villagers had started grumbling about the taxes that they paid to train Margone. Nobody had dared speak up against his or her dues when his father had been alive - Hobson was not a forgiving man. Not of his son, or his wife, or of anyone. Hobson had been felled by an arrow in the forest, and nobody knew who had fired it. Nobody cared to ask, not even Margone. His father's brutality had made him many enemies, and no friends - certainly not his son.

But things had changed with his father's death, and matters had been getting very disturbing - until the news of the flight of the dragons had arrived. The talk of stopping the taxes ground to a swift halt then - the value of having a local Dragonslayer had suddenly gone up. After all, who knew if the dragons might someday come flying into their village? And, in a moment of great irony, when the summons had come for Margone to come to Dragonhome, many in the village had demanded that he ignore it and stay home to defend them!
But Margone knew he had no future at home. In months, maybe only weeks, the fears would die down and the locals would start grumbling again about how much he was costing them... No, he had decided, he would not stay and await their displeasure. He had no idea who had issued the summons - the messenger had not said, and had ridden on after delivering his brief message - but whoever it was, it did present Margone with a possible future, better than the village would offer.

And it might mean work, pay - and respect. It was worth investigating for all three reasons. He had been bred and trained to be a Dragonslayer - and slayer he would be.

But, still, he couldn't overcome his aversion to farmers.

He rode on, silently, brooding. There was only the one road, and it had to lead to the castle. His horse was tiring. He should have tried to rest it and himself back in the village, but he hadn't been able to bring himself to do it. Besides, it would have been unbearable to stop and rest when he was so close to his destination. Better to press on, and then rest.

Eventually, within an hour, he reached his goal. He reined in his steed abruptly, and studied the scene before him. It was always best to know what you were getting into.

There was no mistaking the castle. It sprawled across the land - thick, heavy and broken. It was ancient, and had known better times. From the look of things, it might know them again. Across the battlements and crooked towers, a legion of workmen was moving. There were carpenters and stonemasons, all busy with their tasks. Margone could see carts filled with hewn stones, and men getting ready to set them into place to repair holes and gaps. Teams of men were working on adding new floors where old had fallen through.

It was odd that the farmers had not known that this work was under way, otherwise surely they would have spoken of it. Something strange was happening here, but he couldn't identify it.

What was most impressive about the scene was the main gateway to the castle. It had been built clearly to create an impact, and it certainly succeeded in that. The surround to the gateway had been made into the shape of a huge dragon's head, stones shaped to mimic fangs and frills, windows placed to look like eyes. To enter the castle, one would have to ride through the mouth of the dragon. It was clever and effective, and Margone couldn't resist a smile. Whoever had built this place had known how to intimidate people.

He gentled his horse forward, toward the huge jaws of stone. The workmen must have noticed him, but they paid him no heed, continuing single-mindedly with their repairs. Margone examined the fortifications as he rode past them. This had been a great castle once, and when the repairs were complete, it would be incredibly impressive once again. Whoever had ordered this work had to be some great, rich lord. There was a lot of gold being spent on this work, and there had to be a good chance that some of that gold would be heading his way soon.

This was starting to appear more and more interesting.

He was somewhat surprised that there were no soldiers in evidence - surely a great lord would have an impressive private army? But he didn't see a single armed man until he finally reached the gateway. There was a single soldier, seated in a chair, leaning against the stones, eyes closed. His sword was sheathed, and he was clearly not prepared for combat or even guard duty.

"Soldier," Margone called out. "I seek admittance to this castle."

"Huh?" The man jerked, and his chair almost topped over. He leaped to his feet to avoid falling, and then scowled up at Margone. "What did you want to do that for?" he complained.

"Does your lord know you were sleeping on duty?" Margone asked, mildly.

"I wasn't sleeping," the soldier protested, trying to set his clothing and sword into some semblance of order. He glanced around and spotted a spear lying in the overgrown grass. He picked it up, thought for a moment and then leveled it at Margone. "I was... resting."

"If you're on guard duty, shouldn't you be guarding?" Margone asked him gently.

"What's the point of guarding?" the soldier asked. "There's nothing happening to guard against."

"Really? I thought that we were at war. I believe it's with Stormgard, but it might be Morstan or Pellow. It's hard to keep track."

"War!" The man spat on the ground. "Only the Talents are at war, and I'm not one of those."

"No, I can see you don't have any talent for anything," Margone agreed.

The soldier glared at him, obviously suspecting he was being made fun of, but unable to quite grasp how. "What do you want anyway?"

"Ah, finally - we get to the point." He smiled. "I want to see your master, whoever he may be. He sent for me."

The soldier scowled again. "If he sent for you, how come you don't know who he is?"

"Because he didn't sign the invitation." Margone was getting a little bored with playing verbal games with this idiot. He was tempted to just ride past, but there was always the chance that the moron might decide to stab him on general principles. "Would you either inform him I'm here or else tell me where I should go to find him?"

The guard seemed to be still unconvinced, but he was clearly having problems with making decisions. Margone realized that he'd better make it for the man.

"Fine, I'll go find him. Would you stand aside so I can ride through?"

"I don't think I'm supposed to do that," the soldier said.

"Then what *are* you supposed to do?" Margone asked him.

"Guard the castle."

Margone winced. He could see that this might go on forever. There had to be a way to circumvent this idiot, preferably without violence. The lord of this place might not like visitors who assaulted his men, no matter how severely they were provoked. He was about to start again when he realized there was a boy watching him with a vaguely amused expression on his face. Beside the boy was a middle-aged woman, rather stout, and looking fiercely protective. The boy was lean and dark, so he didn't appear to be her son; she was probably his keeper. Margone decided to see if he could get anywhere with the newcomer.

"Are you a little brighter than this fellow?" he asked.

"No," the youngster replied, cocking his head and examining Margone carefully. "I'm a lot brighter than him. Do you have a purpose for being here?"

"Yes - I was invited."

"Really?" The dark youth speared him with one eye. "I don't recall sending for you."

"Perhaps your father did?" Margone suggested. Obviously this boy was the son of the local lord - he had a very imperious air about him.

"I doubt that - he's been fish bait for several years now. I'm the one who makes the decisions here."

"Ah." Margone realized that he might possibly have gotten off on the wrong foot here. *This* was the lord? "Then you must be the one who sent for me."

"I repeat: I don't think so. You don't look like anyone I might have wanted to see."

"My name is Margone, son of Hobson," he introduced himself. "Dragonslayer."

The boy's eyes narrowed. "You appear to be a trifle young for a Dragonslayer."

"You appear to be a trifle young to be a lord," Margone replied.

The youngster grinned. "I'm *not* a lord," he answered. "I'm far more than that. But I *did* send for Dragonslayers, and if you are one of that dying breed, then you're welcome here. Margone, did you say?"

"Yes, more-than-lord."

The boy grinned again. "My name is Sarrow," he said. "I'll decide what you can call me later. *Lord* at the very least. You're the first of the Dragonslayers to arrive. I do hope the rest are a bit more mature than you. I really want these dragons dead, and, frankly, you don't look much up to the task."

Margone felt a prickle of anger. "I was well trained by my father. Obviously, I have no practical experience - but, then, neither have more mature Dragonslayers. There haven't been any dragons to slay for almost a century."

"Until now," Sarrow pointed out.

"Until now," Margone agreed. "But nobody seems to know where these dragons flew off to, so killing them might be a bit difficult."

Sarrow grinned again. "Oh, I know *exactly* where they've flown off to," he announced. "My sister took them."

"Your sister?" Margone was finding this conversation interesting.

"Yes." Sarrow turned to the guard. "Get back on duty, idiot - and this time stay alert. If you don't, I'll let the slayers use you for target practice. And if any more Dragonslayers turn up, send them straight in to meet me." Ignoring the fawning, scared man, Sarrow turned back to Margone. "Well, Dragonslayer - come in. I'll have someone look after your horse, and we can have a chat. If you're here, then others shouldn't be far behind. I reckon there's about two dozen of you still left. It should be sufficient for my purposes."

"Which are?"

"I want the dragons dead, of course - all of them. Wiped out." Sarrow smiled. "I will pay very well for the doing of the deed."

"Money is always welcome," Margone agreed. He clambered from his saddle so he could walk his steed into the castle grounds. "But slaying dragons is a sacred duty." He regarded the boy again. "Why did your sister take off with them?"

"She's an idiot - she's very fond of all animals, and she wants to keep them alive."

"Oh." Margone bit his lip, thoughtfully. "Then there may be a problem with her. She might get... hurt."

"I sincerely hope so," Sarrow replied. "If you do get to meet my sister, I have a very special message I'd like you to deliver from me..."

Chapter Two

"Sea Raiders!"

Melayne groaned, as she heard the cry - the third time in as many months. Even moving around at this stage in her pregnancy hurt, and she knew she was waddling as she crossed the room. If only the baby would arrive, and she could get back to being able to run and fight again. Especially now...

She could hear others running now - men to their weapons, women hurrying children to shelter. Since this was the third raid, everyone knew what they were supposed to do, and where they were supposed to be. Melayne's main task was to make sure that the women were in hiding, and prepared to defend themselves and their families should the raiders somehow break through the fighting lines. It hadn't happened yet, but there was no guarantee that this time would not be different.

Darmen's soldiers had faced the sea raiders before, but never as frequently. The Lord of Far Holme didn't have a large force - only thirty two fighters - but the Far Isles had, in the past, proven to be too distant for the raiders to strike more than once or twice a decade. And this was the third raid in as many months... The raiders were either growing bolder or more desperate for prey. Either way, it meant trouble for Darmen.

The Lord had taken the fugitives in when they had reached Far Holme three years before, and had proven himself to be a kind man. He and his wife, Perria, had welcomed them and given them shelter. Melayne couldn't bring herself to call it a home, because she felt that this was only temporary. She had often found her husband, Sander, on the cliffs, staring across the sea, back to where - she knew - Dragonhome lay. That castle had been in Sander's family for centuries, and it had really hurt him to have to abandon it. But after the dragons in his care had been discovered, there had been no other option. Dragons, by popular account, were lethal man-eaters that had to be slain. Melayne had discovered that they were in fact, nothing of the kind. While they were hardly affectionate - they were, after all, cold-blooded reptiles - they were gentle and friendly with the humans they liked. But they were young, and vulnerable, and most humans simply wanted to slaughter them. She and Sander had been unable to think of any other way of saving the dragons other than to flee with them to the Far Isles.

Their arrival had terrified the locals, but, thankfully, Lord Darmen had been willing to listen to Sander and Melayne before attacking them. When he had heard their story, he had conferred with his wife - a sturdy, sensible woman with a brood of young children - none her own. Apparently Darmen and Perria were unable to have any of their own, but they had love to spare for those of other folks. Perria had insisted that her husband welcome the strangers, and, as Melayne discovered, Darmen rarely went against his wife's wishes.

Acceptance of the dragons had been slower for the locals, but no one had been actively hostile. And when the dragons had flown against the sea raiders, the Islanders had cheered them on and finally had come to feel almost fiercely protective of the dragons.

Still, this island was not *home* - it was merely a place to live for a while.

Ysane came hurrying up as fast as she was able. She, too, was pregnant, having married Sander's guard Bantry shortly after they had arrived on Far Holme. Ysane and Bantry - much against their wishes - had ridden two of the dragons to escape, along with Sander, Melayne and Sander's young son, Corran. Ysane was Melayne's best friend and confidante, slightly stout and as blonde as Melayne was - normally - willowy and dark. Both were of an age, now 18, and both carrying babies that were near due. Ysane was leading Cassary by the hand, looking worried. Cassary, being only 2, treated the alarm as if it were an adventure.

"Sweetheart," Melayne called to her daughter, sweeping her up, and grunting with the strain.

"Momma," Cassary said, cheerfully. "Raiders!" Her eyes sparkled.

"Yes," Melayne agreed. "Now, we have to get to shelter. There will be fighting."

"Will Dadda be fighting?" Cassary asked.

"Yes," Melayne answered, as she and Ysane hurried as fast as they were able down the castle's stone corridors toward the storerooms where they were to barricade themselves in. "And so will Corran." She didn't feel happy about either fact, especially about Corran, as he was only 8. But she knew there was no stopping either male from defending their adopted country. Besides, after her, Corran was the most adept with the dragons, and she herself couldn't fight in her condition.

"I wanna fight," Cassary said, fiercely.

Melayne sighed. "One day, sweetie, you may have to. But not yet, thank the gods. Right now, it's your task to help protect me and the baby-to-be."

"Oh." Cassary considered the point. "Okay," she agreed.

"Bloodthirsty little brat," Ysane grumbled, but there was affection in her voice and eyes as she said it.

"Takes after her father," Melayne agreed.

"And her mother," Ysane commented. "Gods, if I'd known being pregnant was so darned uncomfortable, I'd never have let Bantry near me."

Melayne chuckled. "I doubt that." Her friend and the soldier were very much in love. "As I recall, you couldn't wait to -"

"Not in front of your daughter!" Ysane warned, and then laughed. "But it's still so uncomfortable!" She patted her bulbous stomach. "You in there - hurry up and come out!"

"Not today!" Melayne chided her. "We've enough trouble with a raid - we don't need a birth as well." Her own child kicked inside her, and she gasped. "Or two births," she added, warningly. "Why do the raiders have to come at the most inconvenient times?"

"They're evil," Ysane answered. They had - amazingly! - caught up with other women and children now, and Ysane started to bustle them along toward the storerooms. "And they will get what they deserve. Our husbands will see to that."

"I'm sure you're right," Melayne agreed. The previous two raids had been beaten off without severe casualties, but Melayne knew that their luck couldn't last forever. Even with dragons fighting on their side, the defenders were being exhausted by the raids. It was only a matter of time before some of the invaders made it onto land. "This time will be no different."

She hoped...

Corran had heard the watchmen's cries while he was on the cliffs. He and Ganeth had been perched on the rocks, looking out to sea themselves, searching for signs of fish. Ganeth wasn't exactly hungry, but she was a growing dragon, and her stomach needed filling quite often. It wouldn't be long before a meal would be required. Corran ran his hand across the dragon's iridescent scales, glittering purplish in the strong daylight, as they both heard the sentinel's cry.

"It looks as though we're going to be needed," he said.

Ganeth twisted her neck around in a way that would have been impossible for most creatures. Her snout opened, and her tongue flickered in and out. Then she wrinkled her nose. *They stink,* she complained. *And they've brought nothing with them to eat.* The voice wasn't audible - it was like a tickle in the back of his mind. It was a strange feeling, the more so since nobody else but Melayne could hear it. Melayne had the gift of Communication, so she could speak with any living creature. Corran had no such gift, but, somehow, he could hear what Ganeth wished.

"They didn't come to feed dragons," Corran reminded her. "They've come to raid and kill innocent, defenseless people - or so they think."

Ganeth stared at him coldly. *You humans are an unpleasant lot,* she commented. *Always killing - and not even for food. It wouldn't be so bad if you ate one another, but you just bury the bodies and let the insects and worms feast.* She licked her lips. *And it wouldn't be so bad if you tasted good, but you don't. I don't know why I like any of you.*

Corran rubbed her head, and could almost feel her purr. "But you do," he said, gently.

Well, some of you, the dragon agreed. She stretched her wings. *Well, we'd better get going. Hop on.*

With the expertise of constant practice, Corran gripped the crest of the dragon and vaulted astride her, just behind the wings. Ganeth gave a shudder of pleasure, and then rushed for the edge of the cliff. Corran held tightly as the dragon threw herself from the rocks, and into the air. For a second, his stomach rebelled, and the dragon fell. Then her strong, wide wings caught the air, and in two powerful beats she had risen again, catching the soaring currents and floating serenely in the sky.

Corran always loved flying. To be in the air, high above all the problems below, the only sound the beat of wings, the only feeling that of wind rushing past - nothing could top that experience! If only today could be simply a day for pleasure, but there was work for them to do.

The dragon rode the winds, spiraling upward, so she could get a clear view of the sea about Far Holme. There were only two good landing points for boats, though, and since one was the harbor - and defended - Corran was pretty certain the raiders would have chosen to come ashore at Craftsmans Point. In a few moments, he could see that he was correct. He was surprised to see that there were three ships, though - in the past, they had been attacked only by a single boatload of raiders.

Maybe they're learning, the dragon commented. *After all, none of the others returned.*

"I didn't think the raiders were that organized," Corran said, puzzled. "I thought they simply set sail and attacked whatever they came across."

That's not very likely, Ganeth said, and he could tell she thought he was being stupid. Ganeth meant no insult, but dragons were not at all good at hiding their feelings, and they certainly didn't worry about offending anyone. If she felt he was being dumb, she made it perfectly clear. *They have to set off from their homes with some destination in mind. They can't just sail on the off chance they'll run across something worth stealing or killing. And that means they're here deliberately. And since their last attacks failed, they've come in more force. These are probably most of the men from a single village.*

Corran had never thought about the matter like that. "So they want us for some reason, then?" he asked.

It seems logical, the dragon agreed. *Though I can't think why. The Far Isles aren't rich, so there's not much for them here.*

"And they never raided this far east in the past," Corran said, thoughtfully. "In fact, not until after *we* arrived... That can't be a coincidence."

At least you're thinking now, Ganeth said, approvingly. *Still, let's defer that until after we've dealt with these scoundrels.*

The dragon swooped downward now, riding the air currents and descending gently. Corran looked down, and could see that they had not yet been spotted. The raiders in the first ship had made land, beaching the craft. Several of the men were ashore now, and getting their gear ready for a battle. There were two of Darmen's small force of soldiers atop the cliffs, running for their lives. They had given the alarm first, of course, and were now falling back. The raiders found their retreat very amusing - even a couple of hundred feet or more in the air, Corran could make out their raucous laughter.

They wouldn't be laughing for long.

Ganeth hurtled from the sky, down to a small peak. There her claws snatched up a largish rock, and she flew on, laboring now under the extra weight. She flew over and past the beached ship, which surprised Corran.

"Aren't we going to attack them?" he asked, his head pressed alongside the dragon's skull.

Not much point - they've already reached shore, Ganeth answered. *We can do more damage elsewhere.* She had passed the second ship now. Corran could hear cries from below, and realized that they had been spotted. A couple of the raiders tried firing arrows at the dragon, but they fell far short of their intended target. Ganeth laughed to herself, and then dived toward the third ship. She released the rock from her claws while she was still more than a hundred feet above the craft.

Corran had to turn and crane his whole body to look down as the dragon swooped past, her mighty wings beating so that she rose into the sky again. The rock crashed into the ship below, just in front of the mast. It hit with such force that the deck planking splintered and sundered, and the rock kept going, virtually unslowed by the impact. It crashed through the bottom of the ship, and a plume of water gushed up like a fountain. Ganeth laughed as the ship floundered, and then began to sink. They could hear the cries of the raiders as they threw themselves overboard, and struggled to stay afloat.

They will have to let go of their armor and most of their weapons, Ganeth said with satisfaction. *Otherwise, their weight will drag the swimmers down. Those that get to the shore won't be in much shape for fighting.*

"That was brilliant," Corran enthused.

I know, Ganeth agreed. Modesty was never very strong in her. *Now, let's see what else we can do, shall we? It won't be long before my siblings arrive, and then we'll have to share the fun.*

Swooping again, Ganeth picked out a target below, one of the raiders swimming for the distant shore. With an unpleasant chuckle, she dived for the unfortunate man, and snatched him from the water, her claws gripping one of the man's arms. He gave a cry of shock as he was hauled into the air, and struggled to free himself - rather stupidly, since he was already eighty feet in the air. Ganeth laughed again, and let him go.

He hit the water almost as heavily as the stone. He sank, and did not come up again.

Ganeth went hunting for another victim...

Lord Sander rushed toward the beach with his handful of fighters right behind him. At his side, as always, was Bantry. All of his men had their weapons at the ready, and they moved in fast to attack the raiders, who were already streaming up from their landing site. Sander didn't have time to make a good count, but there had to be at least thirty - and he and his men numbered seven. It appeared to be a one-sided fight.

Until the other four dragons appeared.

Sander didn't have time to think or examine the battle after that. The first raider - a tall, hairy man wearing thick, warm furs - was upon him, howling and swinging an ax over his head. It was meant to scare him, but Sander wasn't impressed. As the man raised his ax to swing it down and chop Sander in two, Sander thrust forward with his sword, into the gap under the man's arm. The raider screamed, dropping his weapon, and blood spilled out of the wound. Sander stepped past the falling man, and with the dagger in his left hand slashed the man's throat out.

Then he was onto the second man.

Beside him, he heard Bantry howl and strike, and the other five of his warriors plowed into the attackers.

Then he focused only on the man in front of him - and the man after that, and the one after that. His muscles were sore, he was panting heavily, and sweat was flowing like a river over his skin. But no raider managed to wound him, though he killed five himself. The attackers were undisciplined, used to fighting poorly armed peasants and not real soldiers. His own troops were few, but they were professionals, and knew how to disable and kill.

And, of course, they had the dragons.

Sander didn't see much, but out of the corner of his eyes he could see dark shapes whirl from the sky, claws outstretched, seeking targets. There were screams as the invaders were ripped apart, and the sound of laughter from Brek. The male dragon was Sander's bonded friend, the only one whose thoughts he had managed to hear. Sometimes he wished he couldn't hear Brek - the dragons were not at all like humans, and they took their pleasures in very different ways to him. Drawing blood always entertained the creatures, and they all lived to hunt. And now their prey was people...

He had no idea how long the fight lasted. He kept swinging, blocking, hacking and forcing his way forward until there were no more opponents, and he realized he was standing in the surf. He panted, using his knife hand to wipe sweat from his brow, and then paused to look about him.

The beach and sea were littered with corpses. Thankfully, most of them were those of the hairy raiders, but two of his own men were down, unmoving. Bantry was beside him, laughing, and panting hard. The stocky man had blood running down his left arm, but he didn't seem to be bothered by it. His other three men were also wounded, though only slightly. It wasn't until that moment that he realized that there was pain across his chest, and he looked down.

There was a gash across his leather armor where an ax-swing must have cut into him. Blood was pooling along the cut, and he winced. It wasn't too deep, but it was unpleasant, and it *hurt.* It would probably hurt worse later. He grimaced, and surveyed the carnage.

"All dead," Bantry said, panting hard, and leaning on the pike he liked to use to fight with. "It's going to take a while to recover the bodies and burn them."

"Not our problem," Sander answered. "There will be men along soon." He examined his second in command. "You need some doctoring."

"You should talk, my lord," Bantry replied, grinning. "Melayne is going to scold me for letting you get hurt."

Sander nodded, slowly. His neck hurt when he did so. "Aye, she will that. But she'll forgive you just as fast." He looked around again. The dragons had all vanished again, and he couldn't feel Brek's thoughts. Considering the carnage the dragons had been involved with, it was probably a good thing he couldn't hear what Brek was thinking. It wasn't likely to be very pleasant. "Three ships this time..." He shook his head. "I don't like the feel of this. They're getting smarter, and better prepared with each raid." He glanced at his fallen men; their friends were pulling their bodies ashore, and would take them back to Darmen's castle. "And we lost two men this time - which we can ill afford. The next raid..." His voice trailed off.

"You're sure there will be a next raid?" Bantry asked him.

"Sure? No. Afraid? Yes." Sander sighed. "These raiders are way off their normal routes. They're coming here for a purpose, and I'm very afraid that we won't be able to stop them for very much longer..." Then he grinned, and clapped Bantry carefully on his good arm. "But let's not be morose - we won this fight, and I think we deserve a victory celebration for it. Time enough for gloom and introspection afterwards, eh? Let's go and see how our wives are doing, and get ourselves a scolding for being injured."

Together, the warriors turned and made their slow, painful way back to the castle.

Chapter Three

Melayne finished binding Sander's wound and glared at her husband. "You men," she complained. "Always fighting, always getting yourselves hurt."

"You'd have been hurt a lot worse, lady," Bantry commented, "if we hadn't fought."

"I can take care of myself," Melayne informed him. But she relented and smiled. "But I'm sure everyone else appreciates what you all did. And I do know that it was necessary. I just wish that it wasn't."

Sander looked up, sober. "You and I, and all of us. But it is necessary. I just wish I knew *why* it should be so."

Darmen patted him on his shoulder. "You're defending my land and my people," he said. "That is why it is so. These raiders would have plundered and killed otherwise."

"I know that." Sander accompanied Darmen back to the chairs that had been set up for them in the castle's conference room. It wasn't large, and there weren't many people here - Melayne and Sander, Bantry, Darmen and his wife, Perria, and Corran. The boy wasn't happy when he'd been forced to leave Ganeth outside, but there was simply not enough room inside for a growing dragon. Melayne and Perria were already seated, and the others took their chairs around the ancient oak table. Melayne gave her husband an encouraging smile as he continued his train of thought.

"There were no raids here until we arrived, were there?" he asked Darmen.

"No," the Lord agreed. "We seemed to have been spared - until now." He shrugged. "Maybe the raiders are simply having to look further for their loot these days. After all, they've been attacking the coast of Stormgard for decades - most places there are either burned out or too strongly fortified for attacks now."

"I don't think it's that simple," Sander said, sadly. "I met my wife because raiders killed her parents, and she was forced to flee. Now we're here, and here are the raiders again."

Melayne felt a chill in her heart. "You think they're after *me*?"

"I don't know," her husband admitted. "It's just an idea that came to me, but it refuses to leave again. Could it simply be a coincidence?"

"Yes," Darmen answered.

"I agree - it could be," Sander said. "But - what if it isn't? What if they're deliberately after Melayne?"

Perria stirred, and scowled. "Why would they be targeting her? And *how*? Who knows she is here?"

Sander shook his head. "I can't say. Well, Sarrow knows where she is." He looked at her. "Do you think your brother is capable of sending the raiders after you? Would he? Could he?" Melayne's stomach twisted, and not because of the baby. She had felt so protective of her younger brother all of her life - only to have discovered that some of that, at least, had been caused deliberately by him. He had the Talent of Persuasion, able to bend people to do his will. She'd been forced to do what he wished without even realizing it. And it had been unnecessary of him to do that - she would have cared for him because he was her brother, and she loved him.

But then he had revealed himself, and she had discovered, to her shock, that he didn't feel the same way about her at all. He seemed incapable of loving anyone, and thought only of using them to his own advantage. She believed it was the fault of his Talent - being able to bend people to his will had been simpler than getting them to genuinely like him.

And he had been really mad at her when she had been able to fight against his control once she realized what he was doing. He had believed that she was a danger to him.

But was he capable of trying to have her killed? She *really* didn't want to believe that of him. But she owed it to her family to think clearly about the subject - and she owed it to Darmen and Perria, too. They had taken in the refugees and given them a home and a welcome. It would be a terrible thing to have repaid them by bringing raiders to their shores.

So - *could* it be Sarrow?

"Yes, I imagine he *could* do it easily enough," she was forced to admit. "But I would like to believe that he loves me more than that."

"I'd like to believe it, too," Sander agreed, gently, clasping her hand in his. "Unfortunately, I'm not as sure of it as I'd like to be."

"Surely she's no danger to him if she stays here?" Bantry argued. "Why would he bother?"

"Two reasons," Sander replied. "First, he cannot be certain she will remain here. Second - the dragons."

Perria looked puzzled. "Does he hate the dragons so much?"

"It's not that simple," Melayne explained. She had held off talking about the subject to their hosts, but it was clear that it would have to come out now. "You know that some people become Talents and others do not?"

"Of course; we have some amongst our people, though not many."

"We discovered how Talents are created," Melayne said. "It is from dragon scales, because growing dragons shed their skins. The scales dissolve into the dirt, and somehow essences from the scales permeate into people born on the land. The stronger the concentration of dragon scales, the stronger the Talent."

"Oh." Perria was still having trouble. "But what does that have to do with Sarrow?"

"He's a very strong Talent - as am I - and he aims to stay that way. But if our dragons grow, they'll shed their scales, and that will cause more Talents to be born. Since these are new dragons, the scales will be fresher and stronger, so the Talents they cause are likely to be strong also. Sarrow is afraid that one or more of them might be strong enough to take him on - and defeat him."

"Ah." Darmen smiled his understanding. "So he wants the dragons killed in order that this won't happen."

"Exactly," Sander agreed. "That was why we had to flee with the dragons - at the time they were very weak and vulnerable. Now, thanks to your gracious hospitality, they're stronger, and would be a lot harder to kill. So Sarrow may be sending the raiders here to get the dragons. Except..." He shook his head. "That wouldn't explain why the raiders attacked your farm in the first place," he said to Melayne.

"Maybe that was simply a raid?" she suggested. "And Sarrow remembered their violence and lusts and then used them later?"

"It's possible, of course," Sander answered. "But I can't simply accept that without examining other possibilities. Think about it, Melayne - you and Sarrow are two of the strongest Talents to have appeared in a century. Is it therefore no more than coincidence that the raiders found where your parents were hiding and killed them?"

"They sacked the town, too," Melayne argued. "Perhaps they were simply after loot and slaves, and stumbled upon my parents first?"

"It's possible," he agreed. "And I can't say for certain that it wasn't so. But... I don't like coincidences, and there is other evidence."

Melayne frowned. "Such as?"

Bantry leaned forward and pulled a parchment from his tunic. He unrolled it and laid it on the table. "We searched the remaining raider ships," he said. "This was among the things we discovered."

They all bent forward to examine the parchment. Melayne could see that it was a map. It showed the southern coast of Stormgard, and the way to the Far Isles.

The promontory where her parents' farmhouse had been was marked. And so was Far Holme.

"Well," she said, slowly, "that looks pretty conclusive." She looked at the faces of her friends. "They were after me – but why?"

After a moment's puzzled silence, her husband spoke up. "We don't know, yet. But we have to try and find out."

Melayne patted her stomach. "Well, I won't be traveling for a little while. I don't think I have much longer, though, so if this can wait..."

"It can't," Sander said, firmly. "This was the third raider attack since we arrived, and I very much doubt it will be the last. This was the strongest yet, and the next is likely to be worse. Darmen lost two good men this time, and who knows how many more may die next time?" He tapped the map. "We have this, now – a way to go."

"Nothing else is marked on it," Melayne objected. "How can you have any idea where to go?"

He laid his finger on the extreme left edge. "I'd say they must have started from around this point, else why would the map start there? It's beyond the boundaries of known lands, so that's where I'll go."

Melayne glanced at him sharply. "You can't seriously be thinking of going without me?"

"I can't seriously think of taking you with me," Sander said, smiling sadly. "Our child is due soon, and I don't think a raider village would be the best place to give birth, do you?"

Ysane interrupted the argument that looked set to blaze. "Melayne, you *know* he's right. You need to be here to give birth, where the baby will be safe. Besides, do you think you can travel very far in that condition? You have trouble getting to the toilet, let alone to raider lands."

"Stop being so damned logical," Melayne growled. There was an emptiness inside her at the thought of Sander going off alone. They hadn't been parted a single day since she had met him, and the thought of waking up without him beside her hurt.

"Somebody had better be," Perria said. "There's absolutely no question of you leaving until that baby is safely delivered, and if you think there is, you'll have to deal with me."

Melayne knew when she was beaten. "Fine," she said, throwing up her hands. "Go off and get yourself killed."

"I promise to try very hard *not* to do that." Sander leaned over and kissed her cheek. "This is a scouting mission only – I have to find out who is sending the raiders after you, and why. Then we can work out a plan to stop it – together." He looked at the faces around the table. "I propose a very swift mission – just myself on Brek. Whoever is sending these men must know that there's a good chance they won't be coming back, so the raider villages may be on the alert. If we send a ship, it will be spotted, and most likely attacked. One man on a dragon may have a much better chance of getting through."

"I don't like it," Melayne said, flatly.

"Nor I, lord," Bantry argued. "It's my job to be with you."

"It's your job to stay here and protect your wife and mine," Sander answered. "There may be further raiders on the way, and Darmen is going to need all of the men and dragons we can spare to defend Far Holme." When Bantry started to argue, he added, sharply: "I *am* your Lord, and you *will* obey me! I know what I'm doing."

There was an uncomfortable moment of silence, and then Ysane sighed. "Look, there's one simple way to be sure that this is the best solution." She glanced at Sander. "Take off your gloves and touch us."

Sander went silent, rubbing his gloved hands together. Melayne knew what he must be thinking. Sander's talent was to be able to see into the future of whomever he touched. The problem was that he couldn't control *what* he would see. He had touched his first wife, Cassary, and foreseen her death. That had left him emotionally crippled for years, until he had reluctantly fallen in love with Melayne. Then he had seen their impending marriage, and this had brought him back to normal once more. Since then, however, he had rarely taken off his gloves, even with her – fear of what he might see always lurked in the back of his mind.

Ysane went on grimly: "I know, you don't want to do it. But you know we're not going to go along meekly with your plan unless we're *certain* it's the right way. And you may be our Lord, but you're also our friend. And we can be very, very stubborn." She crossed her arms as firmly as she could over her very swollen belly.

Melayne shook her head. "You know she's not going to give in," she told her husband. "Besides, I agree with her - check the future. It may be that you should wait a couple of weeks and take me with you. You know you'll stand a better chance of succeeding if I'm along."

"And I suppose you think I can't do anything without you?" he grumbled. But she could detect the resignation in his voice. "Oh, very well - if it will curtail endless arguing." He slowly pulled off his right glove. "So - who do I check on first?"

"Our baby," Melayne said, firmly. She took hold of his hand - he gave a strong jerk that she tried to ignore - and then placed it over her stomach.

"I can't read anything through cloth," he pointed out. "But I don't need to." He glanced at her, gently. "The baby will be born in three days - a boy. I can read *you* since you touched me. And I saw that you will be here, without me."

Melayne was disappointed and worried. "Without you? I don't think I can bear that."

"You will bear it because you must," he told her. "I had a strong feeling that something is to happen here, but I couldn't see what. It seems to me that you *must* be here, for some reason I cannot grasp."

"You *are* telling me the truth?" Melayne asked sharply. "You're not lying to me to keep me here?"

Sander looked hurt. "I would never lie to you," he told her. "Surely you know that?"

"Yes," she said, gently. She touched his arm, where it was clothed. "I *do* know that. I'm sorry I said anything. It's just that... being here, without you..."

"I know. And being *there,* without you..." His voice trailed off. He started to pull on his glove again, but Bantry leaned across the table and gripped his bare wrist.

"What of me?" he asked, urgently.

Sander pulled free, and then looked at his soldier. "You will be here, also," he said. "I can see that you will be needed.

There is to be…" He shook his head. "It *feels* like another attack, but it isn't raiders… I can't see it clearly. But I *can* see that you will be needed, to protect Ysane and Melayne."

"Then I stay," Bantry agreed. He put a protective arm about his wife. "I will make certain no harm comes to mothers or babies."

"I know; you're a good man." Sander stood up. "Well, I had better go and confer with the dragons now," he announced. "I'll take only Brek – the others are likely to be needed here, if you are attacked again. They are your best line of defense."

Melayne levered herself uncomfortably out of her chair. "I'd better come along with you," she said. "You can communicate with Brek, but you'll need me if you're to talk with the others."

Corran had been silent until now, but he jumped to his feet also. "I'm coming along, too," he said. "If it's anything that might affect Ganeth, then it affects me. She's my best friend."

Melayne laughed. "Maybe you need to meet more humans," she suggested.

The young boy sighed. "People are okay, I guess, but…"

"A boy's best friend is his dragon?" his father suggested, smiling. He put an arm about his son's shoulders. "Come along, then – this is a family discussion, so it is only right that you're to be included." They strode together from the room.

Melayne shook her head, and then glanced at Ysane. "Will you look after Cassary for me? I'll try not to be long."

Her friend winced. "Try not to be – I think the baby is getting quite impatient."

Nodding, Melayne hurried as fast as she could after her husband and stepson. It was very difficult getting used to being pregnant again, and she was definitely ready for this son of hers - a son! - to be born. "Are you wearing boots already?" she grumbled, feeling another kick. Sander was always right with his prophecies, so at least there were only three more days to endure - and then childbirth…

In the courtyard of the castle, the dragons were all perched on the battlements, looking inward. They were still young, by dragon standards, and fairly small – the males were almost ten feet long, the females only about eight. All five were iridescent purple, but each had highlights of other colors that flashed in the sun. Brek, the slightly oldest, had red tinges, mostly about the face and neck, down onto the belly. His brother, Shath, was more a deep orange in the same places. Tura, her own special friend, was dark greenish, and her sister Loken more black. Corran's dragon, Ganeth, had highlights of blue. In bright sunshine, the dragons were dazzling.

They were all gazing intently down at the humans, clearly aware that important matters were under way. Sander stood below them, explaining his quest to them. The dragons could understand human speech, but could not form it with their own throats and mouths. Each dragon could speak mentally to the human with whom they had bonded, but not to anyone else. Melayne, because of her Talent, could speak to all.

"So, you see," Sander concluded, "I believe we must investigate the origin of the raiders, to see why they are trying to kill Melayne."

Brek's large head peered down at her. "Yes, she must be protected," he agreed. Melayne relayed the speech to Corran. "And your path seems to be the best to take. A small party has a better chance of getting through. There will be four of us."

"Four?" Sander looked puzzled. "I had thought just the two of us."

"I know you did," Brek said. "But Ganeth and Corran must go with us."

"Corran?" Both Sander and Melayne spoke sharply at the same moment. Melayne deferred to her husband. "It is too dangerous for my son – he must stay here, where he will be safe."

"He will not be safe here," Brek stated, firmly. "If the boy stays, he will be killed. He is destined to accompany us."

Sander scowled. "What, have you turned prophet now, also? I had thought that power limited to myself."

Ganeth leaned her long neck forward. "We cannot see the future as you can," she explained. "Not with certainty. We see… patterns. That if this one thing is done, that one result will follow. And if a second thing is done, a different result is inevitable. It is difficult to see, and sometimes harder to understand. But when it comes to our bonded humans, matters are clearer. I can assure you, if Corran stays here, he will perish when the attack comes - and so will I. That future is unquestionable. But he has a chance to live if we accompany you on this quest of yours."

"A chance?" Melayne asked, sharply. She loved Corran as much as if he were her own true son. "Not a certainty?"

Brek gave a cold laugh. "The only certainty is death - it comes to us all, eventually. Corran will die - if he stays, it will be soon. If he goes, it will be later. How much later we cannot say. It may be a week, it may be a year. It may be a hundred years. But if he stays, he has less than a hundred hours. The choice must be yours."

Melayne felt devastated - *both* her husband and son to leave, without her? And with no guarantee that they would survive. How could she give them up? But - how could she not? If Corran stayed, he would die. And that must not happen.

"There is a second reason," Ganeth added, "one stronger for us. We must seek mates."

"Mates?" Melayne blinked, surprised. "But I thought… " She glanced from dragon to dragon. "I had assumed that you would mate with each other."

Tura shuddered. "Melayne, would *you* mate with *your* brother?"

"No," Melayne agreed, with passion. "Even if he wasn't a terrible brat - no. But we're human, and you're dragons. Many animals mate with their siblings."

"We can't help what lesser species do," Shath commented. "But dragons cannot do that. We need mates we are not related to. Otherwise we five shall be the end of our line."

Sander shook his head. "But you five are the last already," he said. "There are no more. And you are only alive because my grandfather rescued your eggs when your parents were slain." He looked worried. "It is hard to believe that you will allow yourselves to die as a species."

"We shall not die, if we find others," Loken stated.

"But there *are* no others," Sander argued.

"Indeed, there are none in the Five Kingdoms," Brek agreed. "But your quest takes you outside the Five Kingdoms. You do not know what may live there. There may be more dragons."

"And there might not," Sander argued.

"Perhaps," Brek agreed. "But it is our best chance. While you seek humans, we shall seek dragons."

"It is not as foolish as you may believe," Ganeth added. "You know that Talents are caused by cast-off dragon scales in the earth. Over time, the power of the scales dies out, and no more Talents will occur. That is the *real* reason humans have been killing dragons – to prevent Talents from being born." She focused her steely gaze on Melayne. "Yet both Melayne and her brother have very strong Talents – stronger than they ever suspected. This can only be because the dragon scales close to where she grew up were fresh. That means that there were dragons on that coast not too long ago. They may yet survive, somewhere further into the unknown lands, or even out to sea. We will hunt for them there – and, perhaps, find the mates we need so desperately."

Melayne reached out to stroke the dragon's snout. "That makes sense to me," she agreed. "But what did you mean that my Talent is stronger than I suspected? I can only Communicate with animals. I am very happy with my Talent, but it is not a great one."

"You are wrong," Brek said, coldly. "Your talent is Communication – not only with animals, but with people. It is very powerful." Seeing her blank stare, he sighed. "Think, woman – when you speak to people, they either take to you immediately, or dislike you intensely. This is not normal among humans – generally trust takes time. Yet people instantly know whether they are with you or against you. You find friends and enemies with equal ease. You Communicate with them. You are open, and they respond with the same openness."

Melayne was confused and uncertain. She had never considered such a possibility. Could it be that she had more strength than she knew?

Sander touched her shoulder gently. "There is truth in that," he said. "I knew from the moment I met you that I loved you. How I knew it, I couldn't say – but know it I did. And Ysane left her family to join you without a second thought, even though she loved them dearly. And Hada took an instant dislike to you when you came to Dragonhome, seeing you correctly as a challenge to her rule of my house. The dragons speak the truth – there is great power in you." He turned back to Brek. "Very well," he agreed. "I'm not happy with my son accompanying us, but I can understand that it is necessary. We shall make preparations and be ready to leave in a few days."

"Hours," corrected Brek. "There are not days to waste."

Sander shook his head, and Melayne felt another shock at the thought that he might have to go now. "I must be with my wife," he said. "She is having our child in three days. I have to be here for the birth."

"*She* has to be here for the birth," Brek stated. "You are not required. Our quest is more urgent than you seeing another of your offspring brought into this world. If we do not go, the world that your child will enter may be one of bloodshed and disaster. We *must* go."

Melayne dreaded the thought, but she could see that the dragons were quite serious in their belief. The time, at least for them, was *now*. She clutched Sander feverishly. "I wish you could be here," she said, honestly. "But it seems that we're now taking orders from dragons."

"So it does," he agreed, sadly. He stroked her hair gently. "Melayne, you know I want to be here, with you, to welcome our son into the world –"

"But it's more important that the world he enters be one he can live and grown strong in," she finished for him. "I know that, dear heart, and I know you have to go. But I shall miss you so." She clung to him desperately.

"Humans," Brek said, disgustedly. "They make such a fuss over so little."

Chapter Four

It was one of the hardest things Melayne had ever done. She stood on the battlements of Darmen's castle, watching the two flying dragons until they had faded completely from her view. Then she watched in case one might turn back for some reason. Ysane stood with her, mercifully silent. She understood that this was a time for sympathy, not words. Melayne felt empty without Sander and Corran.

Then the baby kicked again, and she grunted. She wasn't empty quite yet! She turned back to Ysane. "Life goes on," she said.

Ysane patted her own stomach. "We're proof of that," she agreed. "Though at the moment it's a slow, waddling sort of life. I wish I'd asked when my baby was to be born. It can't be very long - thank goodness."

"It's going to be busy around here in the next few days," Melayne agreed. "And we'll be the center of some of that activity. Come on, I'd better see what mischief Cassary is getting into."

Ysane grinned. "She's your daughter, all right," she observed. "If there's trouble to be found, she'll be in the thick of it."

Melayne nodded; for a two-year-old, her daughter was quite precocious, and definitely inventive. Even when she was being watched, things had a habit of getting... interesting. She and her friend headed slowly back down the stairs, one hand on the thick stone walls all the way down. Two of Darmen's soldiers followed them, mostly unobtrusively. The king was taking Sander's warnings of danger quite seriously.

They found Cassary playing happily in the room Lady Perria used for relaxation. Perria was there, sewing, with two of her maids. She looked up with a sad smile when the pregnant women entered. Perria was much older than they were, but still quite beautiful. There was a touch of silver in her hair, and a few lines on her face, but it was still very clear that Darmen had found himself a rare gem when he had married her. She had not been born on Far Holme, but on a smaller, outlying island.

"Come," the Lady said, gesturing to seats. "Sit, and talk. The men are all getting busy, preparing for the raid that Sander foresaw, but there's nothing much for us women to do except to stay out of their way and allow them to get on with it."

Melayne sank thankfully into one of the chairs. One of the maids slid a padded footstool beneath Melayne's swollen ankles. What a relief to be off her feet! She thanked the girl, and then turned to Perria. "I hate all this fighting, and I am so sorry that I brought it to your shores."

"You had no way of knowing it would happen, my dear." Perria reached across and patted her hand. "You are simply trying to do the best you can, and Darmen and I have never regretted giving all of you sanctuary here." She shook her head. "It is simply the times we live in. Mind you, I can't recall any period in history marked by too many years of peace. It seems that men are always fighting somebody, somewhere, for some reason."

"Or none," Ysane grumbled. "Some men simply seem to enjoy hurting people, taking what they have no right to, and causing terror. I am so glad our men are different - they fight to defend us, and only for that reason."

"We have good husbands," Perria agreed. "And your men have good wives. The two of you have become very dear to us." She paused a moment. "Do you think that there is a chance that you may have to leave us?"

Melayne hesitated before replying. "I have been wondering that myself," she said, eventually. "We *are* placing you in danger, and if we were gone, peace might return to your shores."

"And it might not," Perria said sharply. "The raiders might well have come here eventually, anyway. We're out of the way, but there are always those restless souls who seek to export their violence wherever they can. Besides which, even if you leave, the raiders probably wouldn't know that you had. We'd still be a target, whether you were here or not. And if you are here, at least we can help to defend you."

"I only wish I knew how they discovered where we were in the first place," Melayne said. "I had thought I'd left them far behind me."

Ysane said, hesitantly: "Sarrow knew where we were heading. He might have told them."

Melayne scowled. "Why would he do that? He may have become obsessed with his own safety, but surely he must know I would never hurt him. Besides, if he'd sent them, surely he'd have told them about the dragons? The raiders never seem to expect them."

Ysane sighed. "Melayne, your problem is that you don't seem to be able to see the evil in others. The good you can always discover, but you really have a problem understanding that there are people who are just plain rotten, through and through. And Sarrow is one of them. He's so rotten he might not even care about warning the raiders that there are dragons here."

Melayne felt a sting of indignation. "He's my *brother,*" she protested. "I can't help but love him, even if he doesn't seem to feel the same way."

"He's a *monster,*" Ysane objected. "One who will do anything he can to further his own ends. Melayne, you *know* he used his Talent to force you to protect him."

"He didn't have to do that," Melayne said. "I would have given my life to save him anyway."

"That's my point," Ysane growled. "He *didn't* have to do it - but he did it anyway. He didn't trust your love enough to allow you to be you. He had to use his power of Persuasion to force you to do his wishes. And if he couldn't even trust you then, the sister who loved him unconditionally, then what makes you think he trusts you now that he *can't* use his power on you?"

"She does have a good point," the Lady agreed. "Sarrow is suspicious and manipulative. He must be terrified of what you might do once he lost control of you. *We* know you'd never hurt your brother, but *he* doesn't know that. One thing I have learned in my life, Melayne, is that people judge others by what *they* would do in the other's place. You're so full of kindness and love that you always assume other people will be the same - and they won't. Because Sarrow is suspicious and manipulative - he will assume that you will strike back at him because that's what he would do in your place. I do not think it is beyond all possibility that he might have informed the raiders where you are."

Melayne didn't want to believe it. She had spent most of her childhood and her teen years looking after her brother, and she loved him deeply, even without being forced into it. But perhaps her friends were right, and she was misjudging her brother. She could see that he might get mad at her - he always did have a temper when he was thwarted - but she *still* couldn't accept that he would betray her or want her dead. "That's just suspicions," she replied. "Not proof."

"No," Perria agreed. "It's not proof. But it is something you should consider. Mind you," she added, changing the subject slightly, "what I can't understand is *why* the raiders are so obsessed with you. They've invested a lot of effort and lives in trying to find and slay you. Look at all of their losses. It can't simply be because of a whim. There must be a compelling reason for it."

"One that would prove Sarrow innocent," Melayne said, with some triumph in her voice. "They were after him as much as me, at least when they struck at our home. He could have had nothing to do with them then, so he most likely has nothing to do with them now. He's not likely to have made friends with people who were trying to kill him." She frowned. "You know, I had always assumed that the raiders had simply attacked my home and the village because they had stumbled upon us. Now it looks as if we were targeted - and I can't imagine why."

"Somebody has it in for you," Ysane agreed. "And they have, as the Lady said, invested a lot of time and effort in striking at you. They knew where you were three years ago, and they know where you are now. But how? And why?"

A thought occurred to Melayne. "If they have some way of finding me, then maybe they *would* know if I left Far Holme. I might be able to save everyone here by leaving."

"You can't be sure of that," Perria objected.

"It might be worth trying," Melayne said. "Ysane, maybe they have a Finder - you know, like that girl, Devra, I met. Her Talent was to be able to locate things. If the raiders have somebody like her, they could be tracking me that way. So, if I leave, they'd follow me, and you'd be safe again."

"But only if that is how they're Finding you," Perria pointed out. "Otherwise, if you leave, nothing would change, except you'd be in greater danger without your friends to help protect you." She glanced sharply at Melayne. "I do hope you're not planning anything foolish like leaving here without our knowing."

Melayne flushed - that thought had indeed occurred to her. "No," she promised. "If I go, you'll know. Besides, I'm not sure I can go anywhere in this state - and even if I did flee, it would be terribly dangerous for Cassary."

"Speaking of whom," Ysane muttered, glancing around, "where is she?"

Melayne felt a twinge of panic, which evaporated almost immediately. "Playing," she said, with a sigh, pointing. Her child was in a corner of the room with one of the dogs, scratching its stomach. Cassary did seem to have an affinity for animals - the last time she'd vanished, they had eventually found her in the kitchen, curled up under one of the tables, amidst the kitchen cat's latest litter. They had all been sleeping together. Maybe it was because of her mother's ability to talk with animals, but the child had no fear of any creature.

She would have to learn to fear man, though...

"Well, let's get back to more womanly things," Perria suggested. "I for one have had quite enough talk of raiders and battles. Let's try and focus on better subjects. I'm sure we'll have reason soon enough to be thinking of warfare again."

Melayne tried to accommodate the Lady's wishes, but it was hard for her to concentrate on sewing. It was even difficult to keep her mind on the baby, despite its frequent reminders that it was almost ready to emerge into the world. Her thoughts were centered on her husband and stepson mainly, worrying about them. She and they had never been apart for more than a few hours since she had met them, and her life seemed so hollow now they were gone. It was even worse knowing that they probably needed her aid, and she could do nothing to protect them. She was sure Sander's vision was right - but it placed a terrible strain on her. When she could spare thought from her missing loved ones, she kept returning to her own problem. Why were the raiders after her? She refused to believe that Sarrow had anything to do with them, whatever her friends might think. Sarrow was a brat, but he wasn't *evil*. He simply gave in to the temptation to use his Talent. It was out of fear for his own safety, she was certain, and not simply because he enjoyed manipulating the unsuspecting.

She even felt guilty that she had abandoned him, leaving others to look after him. After all, he *was* her brother, and that made him her responsibility. Or - was that simply his Talent influencing her still? No - it *had* to simply be her sisterly love.

Didn't it?

She was getting nowhere with her thinking - it was like walking through a maze. The same things kept coming around, and yet she couldn't get away from them. She could see no solution to her problems that didn't involve risk to the people she loved the most - as well as to herself, of course.

And what was this fresh danger that Sander had vaguely seen? Some new attack? Could they be ready for it, and strong enough to withstand it? If she had been in any direct danger, surely Sander would have seen it. But he had only vague forebodings. He had seen the death of his first wife, Cassary, several years before it had happened. That image had haunted him for years, and he had refused to open up his emotions to allow him to love anyone else - until she had come along and refused to allow him to wallow in fear and guilt any longer. If she were destined to die in the upcoming raid, he would certainly have seen that. So she was safe from death, at least. Of course, he had only seen *her* future. Nobody else was guaranteed to be safe. And even she would be threatened by something. She could understand why his Talent frustrated her husband so much - it gave him enough information to be worried, and not enough to reassure him. When he had seen the death of his first wife, for example, he had not seen beyond his terrible loss to the promise of fresh love. She could understand why he was reluctant to touch anyone with his bare hands - who knew what involuntary horror he might have thrust upon him? To be able to see the future was a dreadful burden. At least her Talent was always helpful.

She wondered about Corran, too. He was now eight years old, and almost as serious as his father. He had a Talent - that much was certain - but nobody, least of all Corran, knew what it was. It might erupt into life at any time - in fact he might have a Talent and not even be aware of it. No one had known about Sarrow's ability until almost too late. Melayne didn't know if Sarrow had even been using it consciously. Corran had always been shielded from the world by his father - his son was the only link he had left to Cassary, the first wife he had loved so much. Even though Melayne knew her husband was very happy in his second marriage, he would always have an empty place in his heart that only Cassary could have filled. That was simply the way he was.

How would Corran be able to handle this adventure with his father? She didn't know. He was always self-sufficient, but unworldly. She had to chuckle mentally at that thought, though. Talk about unworldly! When she had fled with Sarrow, she had been even more sheltered than Corran. She had been forced to learn on the road, and, frankly, her own naivete had been appalling. It was more than a miracle she hadn't died. She had succeeded in some struggles simply because she wasn't aware that she could fail. Thankfully, though, she had always met people and animals who helped her. Her first real friend had been the wolf cub, Greyn, who had helped her tremendously. She still missed his odd outlook on life and his fierce devotion to her. After him had been Devra and Corri - two of the first Talents she had ever met. They had been forced to train for the King's army together. Melayne had accidentally freed them all without really knowing what she was doing, and those friends had taken their own path to seek their own fate. Then she had run across Ysane and Bantry - thank all the powers that those two were still with her! Truer, braver friends she could never have found. The dragons, of course - they were alien, and their thoughts were not human, but they were her friends, and they were loyal to her. And, now, Darmen and Perria.

She had a great deal to be thankful for. Even with danger hovering uncertainly in her future, she had been given great blessings. It was now up to her to make certain that she did her best to preserve them all.

Melayne had been paying only the vaguest attention to the chatter of the other two women, but now she jerked back to reality as she saw a startled expression cross Ysane's face. "What's wrong?" she asked, sharply.

"I think my time has come," Ysane said, flushing. "The baby's decided it wants to be born..."

Perria threw her sewing aside, and jumped to her feet. To one of the maids, she snapped: "Get the doctor!" To the other: "Take Cassary and keep her out of the way." She spun around to Melayne. "Don't just sit there, mouth open, girl! We have a baby on the way!"

Chapter Five

The first day of flying was almost pure fun. Corran had clung happily to Ganeth's neck as the dragon's mighty wings had carried them together through the sky. They were several hundred feet in the air for the most part, though Ganeth enjoyed swooping down closer to the waves from time to time simply for the joy of it. Brek and Sander had stayed aloft, not joining in this sport.

For several hours, as Far Holme shrank and then faded into nothingness behind them, the only thing below them was the sea. Gray, choppy waters roiled in the wake of winds. From time to time, fish flickered from the sea and then dove back into the depths. Other than that, it was as if they were flying in an unchanging world.

Finally, though, a sliver of land appeared in the north. The dragons altered their flight slightly to parallel the thin wedge of land. "We don't want any humans there to see us," Ganeth explained to Corran. "It's best for us all to stay invisible." That made perfect sense, though Corran was a little unhappy with the thought of missing the sight of a land new to him.

The dragons swooped down to scoop fish from the water for their mid-day meal. Corran and his father had brought along several days' supplies of food and water, of which they ate and drank sparingly on the wing. For further long hours, the dragons' great wings beat at the air, taking them ever westward. The sun was starting to sink toward the horizon when Ganeth and Brek made a final pass at the ocean, and rose with large fish in each of their front legs. They then spun about, flying northwest. The land grew larger, and the dragons scanned the coastline carefully for any signs of humans. When both agreed there were none, they soared in to settle on the cliff top. Ganeth gave a sigh of great relief. "That was more exercise than I needed," she complained. As soon as Corran hopped off her back, the dragon began scratching herself, like a dog with fleas.

Corran's legs were wobbly after a day on the dragon's back, and it took a few minutes of walking before they returned to normal. Then he aided his father in searching for dry, dead wood in the trees that fringed the cliffs. Soon Sander had a small fire blazing away, with one of the fish sliced into steaks and cooking away. The dragons, always liking their meat fresh, simply gobbled down their own portions and promptly fell asleep.

Eating their own fish later with their knives, Corran and his father leaned back against the trunks of adjacent trees and simply enjoyed the growing twilight. Soon the stars blinked into being. Corran could hear the waves crashing against the rocks below, and found it a relaxing noise. The slight stench of seaweed reached his nose, mingled with the scent of cooked fish and slightly pungent dragons. This was actually quite fun - even if the purpose behind it was serious. It was like going on a camping trip - alone with his father.

He glanced at Sander. His father was staring off toward the east, his eyes hooded in shadow, despite the light of the fire, which was dying down now they had no further need of it. The night was warm, so they wouldn't need blankets, either.

"Do you miss Melayne?" Corran asked, softly.

His father jerked slightly, and then turned his head to face his son. "Yes," he admitted. He reached out and laid a hand on Corran's shoulder. "It's good being here with you, but I do miss your step-mother."

"So do I," Corran agreed. "I really like her." He didn't care for most females, but Melayne was not most females. She was so different, so full of life and laughter. She'd happily join in his games, or read him stories, or just simply sit with him quietly. He didn't remember his own mother, and Melayne was the closest female friend he had. He also missed his little sister, Cassary. She was just getting to the interesting age where she was exploring the world and her abilities, and could start joining Corran in his games.

He wondered if he had another brother or sister yet. He was glad to be away from all the fuss that was associated with birthing a child, but it would have been nice to have seen the squalling little latest addition to the family. Now he'd have to wait until he got back again.

"I'm sure she misses the both of us, too," his father said. "You know how emotional she can get. I hope she's coping."

"She *always* copes," Corran said proudly.

Sander laughed. "Yes, she does. She's the most amazing person." Then he turned sober. "I only wish I knew what danger is lurking for her. I feel so guilty, leaving her at a time like this."

"That's typical of a human," Ganeth commented, without opening her eyes. "Worrying over what can't be helped."

"We can't help worrying," Corran protested. "We love Melayne."

"So do we," Ganeth pointed out. "But it doesn't mean we expend useless energy and make ourselves sick worrying about her - especially when there's nothing we can do about it. Whatever will happen, will happen. We must do what we can where we can. You two would be better advised to think like dragons."

Corran sighed. As much as he liked the dragons, they could be very hard to understand at times.

Eventually, they all settled down to sleep. Sander wondered about standing watch. "We don't know if there are people around," he said. "And there's no way of knowing how they'd react if they stumbled across a pair of sleeping dragons."

"You think we'd *let* them?" Brek scoffed. "Our ears are ten times as sensitive as yours. Our sense of smell is a thousand times better. Even asleep, we'd know if humans were approaching. Get your rest, and don't worry."

"There are times," Sander muttered, "when I think dragons have way too much arrogance."

"At least we have something to be arrogant about," Brek answered. "We're not weak and feeble, like humans."

"You were, once," Sander reminded him. "I had to look after you, remember?"

"And almost killed us," Brek said. "If Melayne hadn't come along and been able to speak to us, we'd have starved to death. Do you wish to take credit for that?"

"Dragons," Sander muttered again, darkly.

They all slept through the night, and ate a quick breakfast in the morning before taking to the air again. Corran was a little sore from spending so much time astride Ganeth the previous day, but other than that was rested. Once again, the dragons flew out to sea, and then parallel to the coastline, keeping it barely in sight. The dragons, of course, insisted that with their far superior eyesight, they could see every detail of the far-off cliffs and beaches.

Shortly after a mid-air lunch, the dragons wheeled and started to approach the coast. "We're getting close to the spot marked on the map where Melayne was raised," Ganeth explained.

Corran was curious about this. Melayne was from Stormgard, one of the Five Kingdoms. It had been at war with Farrowholme, where he had been born, ever since he had been born. He had always wondered what an enemy country would be like. Melayne had told him that it was exactly like Farrowholme in most respects, except that it was ruled by another king. Corran couldn't see why that made much of a difference, and he'd always suspected that there must be more to it than that. After all, why would two countries fight simply because they had different kings?

But as the dragons flew closer to land, he saw that Stormgard didn't seem to be very different from his home. The same sort of cliffs and hills, the same kinds of rivers and forests. If he hadn't been told, he would have assumed he was back in Farrowholme again. Maybe Melayne was right, and all the differences between the two warring Kingdoms didn't amount to much at all.

There was no sign of any people. The dragons flew low over the water now, so they couldn't be seen at any great distance, and they winged their way into a river estuary.

"The farmhouse of Melayne's family isn't far inland," Sander called. "It should be on the left bank any moment now."

Corran peered intently down, but it was the dragons who spotted the tiny building first, of course. They wheeled around and then swooped in to land in the wreckage of what had once been a field of crops. Neglected for several years, it was now mostly overgrown with weeds. Only small fences and some neatly planted rows of food plants showed it had ever been otherwise.

Just ahead of them was a small farmhouse - well, the ruins of one. It had been made of local stone, but the roof had been burned, and then caved in. The door was smashed down, and the windows shattered. Fire had rushed through the building, leaving nothing much inside but bits of charred furniture and the empty stone walls. There had been a central room with a cooking fireplace, and then three other rooms. One of them must have been Melayne's room, but there was no way of knowing which. Ashes, dirt and insects were all that could be made out now. Corran and Sander walked gingerly through the house in silence as the dragons went off on their own.

"It's terrible what human beings will do to one another," Sander finally said. "It's a good job the dragons aren't here, or they'd have something caustic to say, I'm sure."

"They'd be right, too," Corran said. "The raiders did this - and for what? Melayne's family wasn't rich, or anything. There was little enough to steal except food. Yet they killed Melayne's parents and burned down their house."

"Yes." Sander frowned, and then moved to the door. "But I don't see the bodies here. You wait by the house - I'm going to have a look around. Melayne said she hadn't dared to come back and bury them, and that they had been killed just outside the door."

Despite his father's instructions, Corran followed. There was no sign of the bodies outside, which was definitely odd. The raiders certainly wouldn't have bothered to bury them. The two of them trailed around the wreckage of the home.

In the rear, in a small field, were two neat graves.

"Maybe somebody came from the village?" Corran guessed.

His father shook his head. "That was raided and burned, too. If anyone had survived, they'd hardly have bothered to come here when there was so much to do in the village."

"Maybe the King's Men buried them?"

"Maybe," Sander agreed, but Corran could hear the doubt in his voice. "But they would have been chasing down the raiders. They are soldiers, not undertakers. Still, *somebody* obviously cared enough to bury them. I wonder who."

Ganeth flopped down to a landing beside them. "Typically human, and very wasteful of food," she commented.

"We humans bury our dead, not eat them," Corran said. Even the thought was disgusting. "What do dragons do?"

"Well, considering that none of the five of us have died yet, that's hard to say," Ganeth answered. "But I suspect we'd eat them. Why waste good meat?" She didn't wait for a reply. "Tell your father we have found something that you two should see. Follow me down to the cove." The dragon set off at a brisk trot. The two humans followed.

There was a pathway from the farm down to the sea. Melayne had told Corran many times how she had always loved to sit beside the sea, just to hear the waves crashing and the sea birds calling. She still did that on Far Holme. Corran thought it was kind of dull, just sitting in the sun, but Melayne was a lot older than him - ten whole years - and he knew old people did funny things sometimes.

There was a small dip between the cliffs as they approached the sea, and Corran could spot the waters ahead. Then they came out onto a pebbly beach. Large rocks lined the area, but this was a sheltered bay, where a ship could land with ease.

The raider ship had clearly done that. It still lay there, mostly submerged, only about ten feet from the shore. It was a crumbled wreck, burned and ruined. What wood was visible had been charred by flames, and the mast was merely a stump.

"The King's Men caught the raiders!" Corran said, excitedly. "They didn't get away with their foul deeds."

"I doubt very much that the King's Men did this, either," his father said softly. "They were heading this way days after the raid. The sea wolves wouldn't have waited around that long. They always strike and retreat within hours."

"Then who could have done this to them?" Corran asked, puzzled.

"Perhaps the same people who buried Melayne's parents," mused Sander. "Whoever they were." He looked down at his son. "Wait here," he instructed. He took off his cloak and sword, and handed them to Corran. Then he waded out into the water, and swam to the wrecked boat. Corran waited and watched while his father clambered aboard the creaking ruin and looked about. After a few minutes, Sander dived overboard and swam back to land.

Shaking himself, Sander claimed back his cloak and sword. "They were killed on board," he said, puzzled. "Most were seated, ready to row. There were also at least twenty captives, chained in the hold. There's not much left but bones now, but that's quite clear."

That's quite odd, Ganeth commented. *Those men were warriors - if they were attacked and killed, they wouldn't have been in their seats.*

"No," Sander agreed, when Corran relayed this comment. "Ganeth is quite correct - those men would have had their weapons drawn, and died fighting their attackers."

"Then why didn't they?" asked Corran, confused.

Because, Ganeth explained, *they knew and trusted whoever killed them.*

That made no sense at all to Corran. "You mean they were killed by other raiders?"

"No," Sander said, slowly. "Other raiders wouldn't have bothered to go up and bury Melayne's parents. There's only one thing that makes any sense to me of all of this. The raiders were killed by a Fire Caster."

Corran had never considered that, but he realized how much sense it would make. "It would have had to be a very powerful Talent to do this," he said, quietly.

"Yes," his father agreed.

"Somebody from the village, maybe?" Corran suggested.

"I hardly think so," his father objected. "Whoever did this burned the captives from the village, too. He or she would hardly have killed their friends."

You allow human beings too much compassion, Ganeth objected. *Talents only survive in your society if they remain hidden. If the Fire Caster had to show their power, the Talent might have killed all witnesses. Even friends.*

Corran shuddered at the thought - but had to admit that the dragon had a good point. The Seekers were sent by the Kings to discover all Talents and enroll them in their armies. Melayne had discovered that this was in order that the Talents might fight and kill one another. People with no Talents hated those born with the gifts, and were glad to send them off to die. It was why Sander had kept Corran isolated in Dragonhome so long - for fear that his own Talent would lead to Corran being taken off to war. The Seeker had discovered Corran had a strong Talent, but it hadn't yet manifested itself, and Corran had no idea what it might possibly be.

"Perhaps you are right," Sander said. "People can sometimes do truly horrible things."

“They do many horrible things,” Brek said, coldly. “Come with me - there is something else you must see.”

The dragon led them back toward the farm, and then aside to the banks of the river that ran nearby. Melayne's father had made small canals to help irrigate the fields and they had to step across a number of these channels - now choked with weeds. They came to a flat area where Ganeth was digging. She was nose-down, her strong claws hurling dirt like a dog after a buried object. Corran thought it one of the oddest things he'd ever seen her do.

"What's this about?" Sander asked.

"Another human secret," Brek answered. When Sander reported this comment to his son, he added: "He sounded rather angry."

"He is angry," Ganeth called to Corran. "Come and see what was buried here."

The two humans edged past the dragon and peered into the pit she had dug. She had unearthed a number of bones - definitely not human, they were far too large for that. Then Corran glimpsed scales, and understood.

"A dragon," he breathed.

A mature one, Ganeth answered. *Slaughtered, and then buried here.*

Sander scowled. "I don't understand."

Humans kill dragons, Ganeth said. *What's not to understand?*

"I'm so sorry," Corran said, stroking Ganeth's neck. "It's just that they're so scared of you. You're so big and powerful, and we're so small and helpless in comparison."

"I can understand the killing," Sander said. "As you said, humans kill dragons. But why bury it afterward? Why not leave it to be scavenged?"

Perhaps the humans didn't want a rotting dragon in their field? Brek suggested.

"Maybe." Sander was clearly not convinced. "In that case, why not burn it? No, there was something more in mind here."

Corran tried to understand, and then something did occur to him. "Talents are born with their gifts because of dragon scales," he said, slowly, working out the idea. "And they absorb dragon scales from the scales being buried and then absorbed into the water and the earth, and then going into the plants people eat."

"Correct," Ganeth answered.

"Well, maybe whoever buried the dragon knew that," Corran suggested. "In which case -"

"They buried the dragon *deliberately* so that children born here would be Talents," his father finished, with a proud grin.

"Corran, I think that's the answer. And that means that someone *wanted* Melayne and her brothers to be Talents."

Strong Talents, Brek added. *This is a mature dragon. Its scales would have been highly potent. And the dragon was buried close to the water, ensuring maximum absorption.*

"Which raises the question of whether this was done after the dragon was killed," Sander said, "or whether the dragon was slain *precisely* so it could be buried. Opportunism, or planning?"

The dragons were silent for a few moments. Then Ganeth started to clean her dirty claws. *Either way,* she said, *there have been humans here working on some plan. Strong humans, to be able to kill a mature dragon. And our Melayne would appear to be integral to this plan. You would seem to be quite correct, friend Sander - Melayne is likely to be in very grave danger.*

"Yes," Sander said, slowly. "And we have no idea who is behind all of this yet. Until we know who has been doing all of this, we cannot protect her."

Corran felt a stab of fear. He loved Melayne, and he was desperately afraid that something bad might be happening to her right at this moment - while they were unable to help her.

Chapter Six

Melayne looked across at Ysane, who was propped up in bed, nursing her new son. Bantry, beaming as proudly as if he had miraculously given birth himself, hovered nervously at the far side of the bed. Lady Perria sat beside Melayne, and several maids bustled about the room, doing whatever tasks they felt were crucial for the well-being of the Island's latest inhabitant.

"Do you have a name picked out yet?" Perria asked, her eyes crinkled with humor as she gazed fondly at the small infant.

"Yes, milady," Bantry said, quickly. "We've decided to name him Falma, after Ysane's brother."

"That's a good name," the Lady said approvingly. "And a fine decision to name him for a family member. We'll have to see if we can't get word back to the owner of the name that he's now an uncle. Your parents would probably like to hear news of their grandchild, too, I should imagine."

"Yes, they'd be very pleased to hear," Ysane said, before Bantry could jump in again. "My folks always loved children. It's a shame they couldn't be here. Mind you, the way my mother fusses, perhaps it's better this way. She'd have everyone running all ways after all manner of useless things. She likes to feel wanted and useful."

"Don't we all?" Melayne asked. "And all I can do is sit here like a lump, waiting for my time for birthing." She winced as the baby gave another kick. "Which is only a day or so away now. I'm not surprised that this one is a boy, also - it's a troublemaker even before birth." Bantry, the only male in the room, didn't seem to catch the insult. He was back to staring admiringly at his son. "Yours was an easy birth," she added, to Ysane.

"If I'd known it was going to be so simple, I'd have had children sooner," the blonde girl answered. Then, seeing the stricken look on her husband's face, she couldn't keep her own straight longer. She reached over to pat his hand. "But never with anyone else, of course."

Perria smiled again. "So, you aim to have a lot more, then?"

"Well, *if* Bantry will cooperate..."

Melayne chuckled. "I haven't heard him complain about bedding you yet..."

Poor Bantry's face had gone quite red. He wasn't used to women joking about such things - he didn't usually stay with them much. He was a conscientious soldier and took his duties quite seriously. No doubt he'd be back on guard duty in the morning. But this day he was taking the time to be with his wife and child. Taking pity on him, Melayne changed the subject to one he would be more comfortable discussing.

"Are the lookouts all at their posts?"

It took him a moment to realize she was addressing him, and then he blinked and tore his eyes away from his son. "Uh, yes, lady. At least, they'd better be. I know I'm not there to oversee them, but they're good lads, and take their duties seriously. Especially since the last attack. They'll give fair warning of any invaders."

"Only human," a fresh voice called, from the window. Melayne turned to see a large, dark crow alight on the sill and fold its wings. "Can't see far. Not like a bird."

Melayne was the only one who understood what it was saying, of course. One of the maids whirled around. "Dirty bird!" she cried, and started toward the window making shushing motions with her hands.

"It's all right, Channy," Melayne called quickly. "The crow is a friend, and an extra lookout on my behalf."

"Good thing I am," the bird grunted, pecking at its feathers after lice. "Men miss things. I don't."

"Have you come here to tell me anything useful?" Melayne asked. "Or is it simply so that you can complain about people, and boast of crow's prowess?"

"News," the bird said, finally. Crows were like that - they had to get in their opinions first, before getting to the gist of things. Melayne understood this, and knew that rushing it would be useless. "Boat on the way from the west. Not the usual ones."

Melayne informed the others of this news. "Our friend seems to think it's not the regular supply run," she informed Bantry. "It's still out of sight from anyone of the land, but our good friend crow flies high."

"And has excellent vision," the crow added, proudly. "Tell them that." Melayne did so.

Bantry looked at the crow, then at his wife and son, then at the door. "Sorry, love," he told Ysane. "I'd better go see to the men. We may be having a fight on our hands quite soon."

"Be off with you then," Ysane said. "Go and keep this land safe for our son." Bantry nodded, and then bolted. Ysane turned to Melayne, clearly worried. "You think this means trouble?"

"Normally, I wouldn't be sure," Melayne replied. "But Sander's prophecy was pretty clear that there was going to be a real problem. It's hard to believe that this isn't it. You'll be okay here with the maids, I'm sure. I'm going to have to go and see if I can help out."

"I'll inform my husband," Perria said, standing. "Even if this is a false alarm, we'd better have the men ready. And if it isn't... Well, it's an eventful day." She smiled down at Ysane. "Falma is a beautiful boy," she said, approvingly. "I only hope he grows up to be as brave as his father and as loving as his mother."

"Right now, I'd be happy to know that he just grows up," Ysane said, sadly. She glanced down at the infant, who seemed firmly attached to her left breast. "This is some world you've arrived in, my love."

Melayne had to agree - it seemed as if troubles were never-ending, and fighting almost inevitable. Why couldn't they all be left in peace, to live their lives without hurting anyone - or being hurt by anyone? She shook her head, and looked at the crow. "Will you fly back?" she asked him. "See if those sharp, vigilant eyes of yours can count the men on the ship, and see if they are armed."

The crow preened itself proudly. "Of course!" he agreed. "My eyes see all there is to see. I will watch and report." He spread his black wings and dived outward from his perch.

Melayne patted her friend on the arm, and then walked as quickly as she could to the door. One of the maids held it open, and then closed it firmly after her. Melayne was relieved to know her friend would have assistance. If only she, too, could rest! Her feet and legs hurt from carrying the baby's extra weight, and she was so ungainly in descending the stairs. She clung to the rail and the wall as she made her slow way down to the main floor of the keep. She would need to see to the dogs, and get more of her animal friends out to spy on the newcomers. The crow could be trusted to report back, and it was likely to have accurate information, thankfully. It wasn't as giddy or flighty as some of the other birds. But, though it could report numbers of men, it couldn't tell what was in their hearts.

Was this another invasion? Sander had said that it was unlikely to be raiders again - at least, so soon - but who else might it be? Perhaps they were innocent voyagers - but it would be foolish to live with that assumption. They must be prepared to fight, and if it turned out to be unnecessary, then everyone could breathe a sigh of relief and stand down. But Melayne felt a grim certainty that this was the menace her husband had foreseen. If only she knew what kind of a menace it was...

Eventually, she made it downstairs again. She stood, panting, holding the wall for support. If only this had happened *after* she had given birth! She felt so bloated and ineffectual right now. But she would do her best, as she had always attempted. The upcoming fight might be won or lost by her actions. Much as she longed for a quiet life, she realized she was doomed to always be active. That was her fate.

She waddled slowly out into the courtyard. Darmen was already there with his wife, and they were readying their soldiers, sending them to reinforce the watchtowers. The dogs were milling around, naturally, catching the excitement, but unable to understand it until Melayne arrived to explain matters. Tongues lolling, eyes bright, they listened impatiently as she gave them orders. As each was sent to help out, they gave a cheerful bark, and then shot off to their assigned posts. Some were on patrol, others - the largest and strongest, were to help in any fighting. Even an experienced warrior could be distracted by a dog snapping at his heels. And some of the dogs were quite able enough to take down even an armed fighter.

A second of her lookout crows spun down from out of the sky and landed atop a small wall beside Melayne. It cocked its head at her and winked. "Lots of activity," it commented. "Much getting done?"

"Much *better* be getting done," Melayne said, watching the soldiers rushing to their posts, and maids hurrying the children into safety. "How are you, my friend?"

"Can't complain," the crow said, cheerfully enough. "Well, could complain, but won't. You'll complain, though. Boat on way. More troubles, more fighting, more people being annoying."

"Yes, one of your brothers already told me," Melayne answered. "In the west."

"Oh?" the crow asked, sarcastically. "Did I mention west?" He shook his head. "Don't remember saying west. Certainly not when boat is in north."

"North?" Melayne was chilled, clean through to the baby. "There's a *second* boat?"

"If there's one in west, yes." The crow preened. "*My* boat is in north."

"Oh, heavens," Melayne muttered. "This is news I could have done without."

"You want me to forget it?" the crow asked.

"No," Melayne said, hastily. "I didn't mean it like that." Crows were so literal! "Could you go back and keep an eye on it? This complicates everything."

"People always complicate things," the crow complained. "Not like birds - everything simple with birds. No raids, no fighting - except one on one. People crazy." he shrugged. "I'll watch." He flew off again.

More worried than ever, Melayne moved as fast as she could around the courtyard until she caught sight of Bantry. He was sending out a patrol to reinforce the watchers on the west.

Puffing hard, she managed to reach him as he started in on another of the small groups of men.

"We have real trouble," she said. "There's *two* ships, coming from different directions. The second is to the north."

Bantry winced and shook his head. "These raiders are learning from their mistakes. Still, there's no good landing beaches in the north, so they'll have to swing around the island. That should help a bit."

"Unless they've coordinated their arrival with the first ship," Melayne pointed out. "This is definitely going to be a fight. I'd better get the dragons."

"Right," Bantry agreed. "I'll see if I can spare a few men for the north shore, to keep an eye on the new arrivals." Muttering to himself, he turned back to the soldiers he was sending out.

Melayne moved back into the center of the courtyard. The baby kicked again, and she felt pain in her stomach. Of all the times for another raid, and for her husband to be absent! Still, everyone would do what they could. Melayne sent out a call to her dragon, Tura. She had no idea where she and the remaining two - Shath and Loken - were, but they were probably off catching fish.

Coming! came Tura's mental reply. The dragon had sensed Melayne's urgency, and was hurrying as fast as her wings would carry her. Melayne leaned against the low wall, wishing she could lie down and rest, and knowing that wasn't a possibility for quite some time now.

Tura came into a landing a moment later, furling her wings and pressing up against Melayne. "You should be resting," the dragon complained. "Your child will hatch soon."

"I don't have the luxury of resting," Melayne told her friend. "There are two ships full of raiders approaching the island. We're in for another fight, and I suspect this won't be as easy as the last."

"Humans!" Tura snorted. "I'm getting quite tired of killing these marauders. Why won't they ever leave us alone?"

"I'm afraid it looks as though they're after me for some reason," Melayne said. She explained what had been discussed earlier, as she hugged the sinuous neck of her friend.

"They probably know how wonderful you are, and want you all for themselves," Tura said.

"Flatterer!"

"They know *something* about you that even you don't," the dragon said. "They either want you - or want you dead. Given the previous attacks, I'd say dead is more likely."

"So would I," Melayne reluctantly agreed. "And I don't have a clue as to why."

The dragon showed long fangs in a form of a grin. "I'll try and capture one alive so we can ask him," she said. "Trust me, I can make a human talk."

Melayne didn't want to know what her friend had in mind. "Are you, Shath and Loken able to fight again?"

"Of course - we protect our humans. Speaking of whom, I understand Ysane has had her hatchling."

"Yes, a boy."

Tura nodded. "Loken will be pleased. As soon as this is all over, we shall have to see the child. I hope, right now, it's being protected."

"Of course."

"Fine." Tura spread her wings. "We shall be ready." Beating her wings, she launched into the air. The draft from her passage almost toppled Melayne.

Well, she'd done about all she could. Now came the waiting.

Uh-oh... And the need to go to the privy. The baby was always pressing down on her bladder...

Tura flew high, and called to her brother and sister. They had been fishing - they were all growing dragons, and needed a hundred pounds or more of fresh flesh a day. But they spun up and away from their quest to join her in the air. High above Far Holme, Tura explained the latest problem.

"Don't these humans *ever* stop fighting?" Shath complained. "I can understand fighting for a nest, or for hatchlings, or even to get a mate. But these humans fight for any and no reasons."

"We shall never understand them," Tura agreed. "But it is enough that *our* humans are in danger, and need us to protect them."

"It is enough," Loken agreed. "No one will hurt my Ysane while I have breath left in me and claws with which to fight."

"Then let us examine the ships," Tura suggested. "Perhaps we can damage them while they are out to sea, too far from land for the raiders to reach."

Shath gave a snort. "I hope their drowning won't pollute the fish," he complained.

"Few fish eat humans," Tura pointed out. "They find human flesh as unpalatable as we do."

"We do not know yet that these new humans are foes," Loken pointed out. "It may be that they are traders - or even simply voyagers who have lost their way. It would not be right to attack before we know their intent."

Shath snorted again. "They're *humans*," he pointed out. "We can hardly go wrong if we assume that they have bad intentions. But you are right - we should not become as quick to judge as they are themselves."

By unspoken agreement, Tura led the flight. Riding the air currents with leisurely flaps of their wings, the three dragons took just a few minutes to intercept the incoming craft as it approached Far Holme from the west. From high above, the boat looked innocent enough. Tura judged that it would touch land in about twenty human minutes.

Then she felt a wave of unease. She flared her nostrils, catching the faintest scent of something extremely disturbing. "I am going down for a closer look," she informed her siblings. "Stay high - something does not feel right about this."

"I sense it also," Loken agreed. "Be wary, sister."

Tura angled downwards, dropping in a lazy spiral toward the boat below. Her sharp eyes could make out men on the decks and in the riggings, taking in the sails that would soon no longer be required. She had been spotted, she knew, but from this height they might well mistake her for a large bird. In a few moments, they would know better.

Her disquiet grew with each passing second. There was a sharp tang of *something* in her sensitive nostrils, but it was elusive to place. It was a smell she should know, and yet... She was barely a hundred feet above the craft now, and the humans had most definitely seen and recognized her for a dragon. The sailors had scrambled down from the rigging, and there were armed men on the deck of the craft. Armed and armored, she realized - these were fighting men, ready for action. So they *were* raiders, though they didn't look like any she had previously seen. These were not barbarians of the sea, but soldiers in metal. Melayne had told tales of these kinds of men, people she called *knights*. But knights fought from horseback, not the decks of ships. And there was no smell of horses from the ship, only -

And now she recognized the smell, almost too late! She beat her wings, striving to clutch a rising air current and make her way aloft again.

The stench was of dragons' blood.

These men were not knights - they were dragon slayers... Her wings beat fast, as she reversed her downward spiral, and began to rise again. One of the humans on the deck had some sort of contrivance in his hands, and brought it up, pointing it toward her. She didn't know what it was, but she could recognize a threat in it. Pushing her strength as much as possible, she was rising slowly.

Too slowly.

The man on the ship did something, and a part of his weapon flew up through the air. Tura strove to avoid its path, but she was trapped by the thermal currents she was attempting to ride. Vainly, she twisted her body.

The missile slammed into her body, just below her fore left leg. There was a moment of terrible pain, and then her left wing started to droop. She no longer had the strength or skill to rise. In fact, through pain-hazed eyes, she could see that she was dropping -

Down, toward the boat. No doubt the slayer was readying his terrible weapon for another shot. But Tura didn't have the strength to rise, to fly upward to safety. Her whole world at the moment was pain, and it was difficult for her to think.

Then she realized that she didn't have to get out of range vertically - she could fly faster and easier toward the land, even with this burning missile in her body. Abruptly, she changed direction, and flew down lower, catching the rising thermals from the warmth of the sea. This unexpected move undoubtedly saved her life. A second missile whistled through the air, barely missing her head. It was followed by a third, but this one struck at a poor angle. She felt the pain of the blow, and knew she had been injured again. But the missile didn't penetrate, instead falling away, trailing drops of her precious blood.

And then she was out of range, flying with all of her remaining strength toward Far Holme and - at least temporary - safety.

Her siblings had seen her distress, and they flew down to intercept her once they were well out of range of the hunters on the ship.

"Humans!" Shath screamed in fury.

"How badly injured are you?" Loken asked, concerned and worried.

"I think I have the strength to make the land," Tura gasped. "Loken, fly on ahead and tell Melayne I need help. She will know what to do."

"I know what to do," Shath snapped, ominously. "These new humans seek our blood, but it will be their own that they will be swimming in soon enough." His wings beat strongly, and he headed toward land. Even though her mind was dulled by the throbbing of the pain, Tura knew what he was thinking - of getting rocks and dropping them onto the ship from above. As long as he stayed out of range of the missiles, he could do damage. But the ship would strike land soon, so it was unlikely he'd be able to do crippling harm.

Meanwhile, all she could do was focus on flying. Her wings hurt, her body was racked with jagged bolts of pain, and it was getting hard even to breathe. She had never been injured before, and she didn't know how to cope - or even if she *could* cope. Her only hope was Melayne - if she could make it back before her strength gave out...

Melayne was looking out to sea, but hills cut off the approach of the ship, so she didn't know there was anything wrong until Loken shot across the hills and swooped to a frantic landing in the courtyard.

"Tura is wounded," the dragon gasped. "The ship is filled with soldiers - dragon slayers. This time it is *us* they are after, and not you."

"Tura!" Melayne felt a stab of anguish for her special friend. "How badly is she hurt?"

"I don't know," Loken admitted. "She is having trouble flying, and she has lost much blood. I believe she can make it to the land, but hardly beyond that. You must come and help, now!"

"Of course." Melayne looked around, worried. "Are you able to bear me that far? I am a lot heavier than normal, carrying my child."

"I am strong, and the need is urgent. I will manage." Loken lowered herself, and Melayne somehow threw herself across the dragon's back. It was difficult, thanks to her huge belly, but she *had* to help her friend. Then she realized that none of the other humans knew what was happening.

"Wait," she ordered, as Loken prepared to fly. She gestured for one of the sentries to come, and he hurried over. "Tell Bantry that the ships are filled with dragon slayers," she said. "They are very dangerous and determined. Do not think that they will spare any humans that may be in their path." The man nodded, and hurried off with his message. Melayne stroked Loken's black head. "Now, fly, as swiftly as you can, to your sister."

The dragon needed no further urging. Great wings beat, and she rose - somewhat unsteadily - into the air, and then aimed herself at the hills. Melayne urged her on mentally, terrified that Tura's strength might have failed her, and that she had fallen into the sea.

But when they cleared the hills, Melayne saw with slight relief that Tura had made it most of the way back. She was in the surf by the cliffs, her left wing hanging at an odd angle. As Loken drew closer to her sister, Melayne could make out the shape of a large arrow buried in Tura's chest, close to her left front leg. There was blood, fresh and clotting, around it, and blood was still dripping into the water.

Loken swooped in to a landing, throwing sand and spray into the air as she skidded to rest beside her sister. Terrified for her friend, Melayne slid from the dragon's back and into the spume beside Tura.

"How badly injured are you?" she asked, anxiously.

"It's not as bad as it looks," Tura gasped, giving the lie to her words. "The missile hurts, but the bleeding will stop now that I'm no longer using my wing. With a little rest, I should be able to walk back to the castle."

"You're not walking anywhere yet," Melayne said firmly. She winced as she gently examined the wound. The arrow was of hammered iron, forged specifically to penetrate a dragon's tough hide, and fired with much force. There was at least six inches of razor-sharp metal lodged in Tura's muscle, and the blood bubbling slowly out was dark and thick. It didn't seem to be a mortal wound, but it was clearly very serious. Melayne was almost frantic with worry. What could she do to help here? Loken gave a snarl, and glared out to sea. Melayne followed the dragon's gaze and stiffened with shock. Though the dragonslayers' ship was still about ten minutes away, it had launched a smaller boat. In this, two sailors struggled mightily to row toward the shore, and there was a third person in the boat. He was clad in heavy armor, and had a large sword slung across his back.

In his hands was a crossbow, fitted with another of the metal bolts, and he was preparing to fire. His target this time was Loken. The dragon started to spread her wings, and Melayne cried out.

"No! If you try to fly, he'll have a perfect shot. Stay low."

Thankfully, Loken's sense overcame her panic and anger, and she huddled down. Melayne glanced about, seeking inspiration. She saw a bunch of gulls high up, on the lookout - as always - for food.

"Brothers and sisters!" she called to them, urgently. "Please help us! This human is seeking to harm us."

The gulls - surprised to being addressed - came lower, calling raucously as they did so. "Humans!" "Dragons!" "Humans!" "Dragons!"

"Help us, please," Melayne begged them. Gulls were difficult to persuade, their main focus being their own bellies. They had never had any trouble from the dragons, though, and in fact often followed them when they fished, hoping to pick up scraps. Melayne could only pray that this would influence the birds.

Thankfully, it did. Screaming their threats, they dive-bombed the men in the boat, releasing their foul-smelling body wastes. The sailors lost their rhythm as they were pelted, but the man in armor was hardly affected until the boat started to rock. Then he gave a cry, and struggled to remain upright.

That gave Melayne another idea - if he were to fall into the sea, he could hardly stay afloat, let alone attack them. Quickly, she called to the fish, hoping that there would be some large enough to batter the boat. She was immediately disappointed - the dragons had eaten most of the larger fish, and the smaller ones couldn't affect the boat. Now what?
Another idea came to her, and she asked the swiftest of the fish to leap across the boat. In moments, a veritable hail of shimmering bodies leaped from the water, shot through the air and back into the sea. Most passed harmlessly, but a few came close enough to the sailors' faces to panic them again. The boat

started to shake, and then the waves caught it badly, and overturned it.

With a cry, the dragonslayer fell into the water, followed moments later by both sailors. Melayne felt a moment of exhilaration as the boat capsized, but her joy was promptly dashed.

The slayer stood up. The water was only about five feet deep at that point, Even in his armor, he couldn't drown. He still held his bow, but the bolt was lost. Still, he managed to pull a fresh one from a quiver slung across his back, and fitted it into the bow.

Scared that he was targeting Loken, Melayne started to turn to tell the dragon to move. It was only at the last second that she realized she'd read his target wrong. The bow sang, and the bolt flew.

There was a terrible pain in her side, and she looked down to see the point of the arrow slash through her flesh. Her own blood sprayed, and the pain and shock overwhelmed her. She collapsed to the sands, unconscious.

Chapter Seven

Loken roared in fury as she saw Melayne hit by the arrow and then fall onto the sand, bleeding heavily. Her first instinct was to attack the monster who had hurt the girl, and her blood-lust almost overcame her. Then she realized that if Melayne didn't get medical help, she might bleed to death in a very short while. Hissing with fury and frustration, the dragon gripped Melayne's still form in her claws, spread her wings and launched herself into the air. She could only pray that the strain on Melayne's wound that this caused would not be fatal. She was the only hope now of saving Melayne's life.

On the beach, Tura was in terrible pain, but she was still conscious. She had tried to act bravely for the sake of Melayne, but her wound was agonizing. She had to have the arrow removed, and she needed help to staunch the bleeding. But her fear and anger over what the slayer had done to Melayne helped her to suppress her pain. Loken couldn't attack the slayer, but *she* could.

Summoning all of her strength, she whirled around and launched herself at the attacker. He was struggling to get yet another bolt from his quiver into position to fire again, but she had startled him by moving. He had been expecting a simple shot, and that easy target was no longer there. He stood in the waves some forty feet from the shore, but that was only a single leap away.

Her good front claw fastened about the arm with the bow, and she contracted it, heavily. The armor saved the man's arm, but the bow was crushed and useless. Her weight slammed into the startled man, and he fell backward.

Tura didn't need to fight him. She simply rested atop him, trying to ignore the fresh damage she'd done to herself by her actions. The slayer, held down underwater by her weight and that of his own heavy armor, struggled for a few moments. Then he went abruptly limp. Since this might be a trick to regain his freedom, Tura didn't move for several more minutes. In her condition, anyway, moving was not an attractive idea. Then, when she was convinced the man had drowned, she slid off his corpse and staggered back toward the beach, where she collapsed.

The two sailors, soaked and terrified, staggered up after her, but as far as they could manage down the sands. She glared in their direction, but realized that they would be no menace to her. She licked at her wound, lost in her pain and fear.

The whole attack had lasted less than ten minutes so far. One slayer was dead, but she was badly injured, and she had no idea whether Melayne was even still alive.

Things were definitely not going well.

Bantry was in a panic; he was a soldier, used to following orders, generally those of Lord Sander, who always seemed to have a plan. Now here he was, with several of Lord Darmen's men, and a horrible situation facing him. Raiders were attacking the island, and they had already shot one of the dragons, and maybe even killed Melayne. When he had the time, he knew he'd be filled with fury and pity for Melayne, but the only thing he could think now was that Ysane and their son were in deadly danger. If only he was smarter! If only he was a better soldier! But he wasn't, and it was all up to him. If he messed up now, everyone he loved might die.

The lone soldier in the boat was probably dead - Tura had managed to take him out. The two sailors who had made it to land so far were no threat - they had no weapons, and they were both coughing up sea water. He could ignore them.

That left the ship that was still drawing closer to land - and then the second ship beyond that one... He didn't have a clue how many fighting men that meant facing, but there was no other option. He couldn't think of a clever plan, as he knew either Sander or Melayne might. All he could think was to defend his wife and child - and all of the other innocents on this island.

The closest ship was now within a few hundred yards of the beach. There was no way to stop the fighters on its deck from reaching the strand. And with only a handful of men, he could hardly face them down. But there was only one way up from the beach, and the invaders would have to come that way. Bantry barked out quick orders, deploying his men to cover the top of the path. He glanced at the fighters on the ship, and saw that they were all in heavy armor. That made no sense at all to him - raiders depended on speed and surprise for their attacks, and wore minimal protection. These men were ready to hold a siege on a castle, and they had the definite air of professionals.

This wasn't a repeat of the attack a few days ago - it was by a completely different set of men with a different purpose in mind.

Shath had arrived by now, his own dragon. Bantry had never imagined he could feel affection for such a creature, but they were bonded, and he knew the male dragon was a brave and loyal companion. The dragon's long neck bent as he looked down at the new arrivals.

"They are dragon slayers," he informed Bantry. "Their purpose here is to kill us all."

"How can you be sure?" Bantry asked, feeling a stab of pain for his friend. "You can't have ever seen a dragon slayer before."

"Their weapons carry the stench of dragon's blood," Shath replied. "They have been used to kill my kind for many centuries. There is no mistaking the scent of dragons."

"No, I don't suppose there is." Bantry shaded his eyes and studied the fighters. "There must be a dozen of them."

"Thirteen left," the dragon stated. "Tura killed one, and she is badly wounded herself. We must get help to her."

Bantry felt terrible. "My men and I can't go down to her," he said. "We'd be cut down in the open. We have to fight them from ambush. And if you try - they have their bows and those lethal bolts. All we can do is to hope they try and come up here first. We might be able to hold them off."

"No," Shath said with absolute certainty. "They are fanatics. They will kill Tura before they try to come up here. All they wish is to slay dragons, and she is such an easy target. I would go to her aid, but that would be suicide. I am terribly afraid my sister is doomed."

Margone steeled himself as the ship's bow hit the sand, and the vessel shuddered. They had reached the island at last, and the first of his foes lay before him, barely a hundred yards away. It was his first glimpse of a true dragon, and he knew he should be excited and ready for the kill - but all he felt at this moment was anger. He glared at Beltran, who was leading the slayers. "We are here to kill dragons," he snarled. "Yet Pomas shot a *girl*. That is not honorable."

Beltran - tall, dark and sweating inside his armor, glowered down at Margone. "Honorable? She was trying to kill Pomas - she was *defending* a dragon! We will kill anyone who gets in our way, you fool. And if you aren't prepared to fight and die as bravely as Pomas, then you are our enemy, too."

Margone's fury was growing. He had trained with Beltran, Pomas and the others. He had known that they were committed - as he was - to slaying dragons. But never had he imagined that they would attack people, too. He still believed in the honor of his profession, and that they were *defending* human beings. That Pomas had shot a girl - and a pregnant one at that - appalled him, no matter what the provocation. But this was not the time to be fighting with his leader - not with the dragon waiting on the shore. After the dragon here was dead - and any others on this blighted island - *then* would come the accounting. "I am with you," he hissed. "Fighting *dragons*, not women."

"Then you had best hope there are no more she-witches like that one," Beltran answered. He held up his sword, sunlight dancing from the highly polished blade. "To land, my brave companions!" He gestured at the fallen dragon. "There is the first of our foes! Kill it! Let us all show our true mettle!"

With a roar of support, all of the slayers lumbered out of the ship and into the water. It was barely a foot deep, but the weight of their armor caused the men to sink several inches into the underlying sand. Together they slurped their way onto the dry beach.

The dragon hissed, rearing up a little, as they approached. Margone forgot his qualms at this moment. Here, now, was what he had trained all of his life to do - here, before him, snarling defiance, was a dragon. His first...

He moved forward with the others, his sword drawn, panting. He was excited, apprehensive, scared and heady all at once. *Now* he was doing what he was born to do, trained to do. *Now* he would truly be a dragon slayer!

Something flickered in his vision, and then a heavy weight slammed into his chest, knocking him flat to the sands. He gave a *whuff* as all of his breath fled his body. Dazed and sick, he lay there, chest heaving, fighting to take in another breath. His eyes were blurry, but he could see that all of his companions were also down, somehow. He started to try to rise, but a sharp voice snapped: "Don't!" Someone placed a booted foot of his chest and shoved him back into the sand. He felt the sword being wrenched from his numbed hand, and heard it being tossed aside.

His first coherent thought was that another dragon must have attacked them, maybe defending its mate. Then, as his mind started to work again, he realized that this was not what had happened.

People had attacked him. Actually, not even people - it looked as though they were *children*. His eyes were working again, even if he couldn't quite believe what he was seeing. A young girl - maybe 15 or so - was falling slowly from the sky. She had a cape, and shoulder-length blonde hair, and was carrying a tree branch that she tossed aside a moment before she touched gently down beside him.

Margone finally realized what had happened to him. This flying girl must have hit him with that branch, and knocked the wind out of him. By the look of things, she'd done the same with a number of the other slayers, too. Without getting up, he tried to examine the other children. They were all fairly young, one only about 10, and nobody older that a sullen-looking dark-haired girl who couldn't be a day over 18. She was the one who'd spoken to him, and she appeared to be in charge of these kids.

They were disarming all of the slayers, throwing their weapons aside. Beltran snarled as his bow was ripped from his fingers, and he tried to rise. The sullen girl kicked his chest, hard.

"Don't try it. Timon over there is a pretty skilled Fire Caster, and you're dressed all in metal. If he wanted, he could cook you in seconds."

"We're only here after the dragons!" Beltran snapped. "We won't hurt anyone who doesn't get in our way."

The girl laughed. "You won't hurt *anyone*, period." Her scowl returned. "You've done enough damage already - you've hurt my friend, Melayne. And if she dies as a result of your asinine attack, I promise that all of you will do, too. And that it will take a long time for death to free you from your pains."

"She was *defending* a dragon!" Beltran growled.

"Yes, well, she does that sort of thing." The girl turned away from him, and studied the fallen dragon. One of the boys had gone to it, and appeared to be checking out its wound. "How is she?"

The youngster looked up. "In a bad way - the arrow's deep in her chest muscle. It doesn't seem to have hit any vital organ, but she's lost a lot of blood."

"Can you stop the bleeding?" The girl looked worried. "I don't mean to be cruel, but Melayne needs us more than the dragon does right now."

The boy nodded, and turned his attention back to the dragon.

It was starting to make some sort of sense to Margone now. These youths were Talents, and they had beaten the slayers using their special abilities. One could fly, another cast fire. The boy seemed to be able to heal. So far, that he could understand. What he *didn't* understand was what they were doing here. All Talents were conscripted into the army as soon as their powers were known, and sent to the borders to fight in the wars. They shouldn't be anywhere within hundreds of miles of this small island!

Unless, maybe, the Talents out here on the Far Isles didn't get sent to the wars... Maybe the local lord withheld them all for his own purposes?

And, anyway, why were all these crazy kids defending dragons? Didn't they understand the gravity of the situation? How evil dragons were? Maybe these idiots thought of the dragons as some sort of pets?

"Listen to me," he called to the sullen girl a she started to move away. "Don't you understand how essential it is that we kill the dragons? You shouldn't be interfering with us. We're doing a vital job. Okay, I don't think that our man should have hurt this girl, but he made a judgment call in a very dangerous situation and -"

The girl pointed at him. "Shut it, now, or I'll forget that I'm a lady and kick the crap out of you. The only thing essential right now is that we save Melayne's life. You bastards hurt her, and your own lives are hanging by the same thread that hers is. So shut up and pray that she survives. Because if she doesn't, you surely won't either."

She broke off as several soldiers came running over. Their leader was a large young man, definitely from peasant stock, and he looked worried. "Thank you for your help!" he exclaimed. "I still don't believe what I saw. I'm Bantry, and I'm in charge here - well, sort of."

"Yeah, well, hello, and get out of my way," the girl snapped. "Where did that dragon take Melayne?"

"To the castle, I imagine," Bantry replied. He looked confused. "You know her?"

"Of course I know her, you moron," the girl sighed. "She's the reason we're here. I knew she needed help. But we were too late to intercept these killers at sea."

"The second ship!" Bantry exclaimed. "Then that was you, not their reinforcements."

"Bright boy. Look, we can explain it all to you later in nauseating detail. Right now, your men can help my team here to disarm these thugs and then throw them into the dungeons or wherever. Meanwhile, you can take Hovin and me to Melayne.

He's a healer, and the way things looked when we arrived, she is really going to need his help."

"Oh, yes, right," the soldier agreed. He started issuing orders, and his soldiers fanned out, collecting the discarded weapons.

Margone couldn't understand it. What was *wrong* with these people? They were acting as if he and the slayers were the villains here, and the dragons some sort of victims. Were they all insane? He wondered if there was any chance that he could break free, and maybe grab a weapon and kill at least the wounded monster. But there was the Fire Caster to watch them, and who knew what other Talents. This had seemed to have been such a simple task - how could it have gone so disastrously wrong?

And what would happen to them now?

Chapter Eight

Melayne's entire world was pain. She struggled to stay conscious as she hung in the dragon's grasp. She could feel her lifeblood draining out of the wound in her stomach, could feel the cold metal of the bolt in her side. But, mostly, she could feel only the agony this caused. A dark wash of pain almost sent her spinning into oblivion, but she clutched grimly at the shreds of consciousness left her.

My baby! she cried to herself. *My baby*!

Had he been hit by the arrow? She struggled to try and find out, but pain overrode any efforts she could make. She couldn't feel her child, she couldn't feel her body. She could feel only pain.

Despite her best efforts, she blacked out for a short while. When awareness returned to her, it was still washed over by pain. She was now lying on her back, and she could make out voices around her, and hands moving to help her. Someone had a cloth over her side, trying to staunch the loss of blood. Someone else - probably Darmen's physician, was probing her distended stomach. She felt the pressure of his hands, shifting the pain about.

"My baby," she gasped, struggling not to scream.

The physician glanced down at her. "I don't know," he told her. "It's hard to be certain in all of this mess." She tried to look down, but the hurt was too great, and she fell back, screaming inwardly. She lost consciousness again.

When awareness returned the next time, the pain had lessened slightly. There was a faint breeze across her skin, and she was amazed that she could feel anything that wasn't pain. She realized that she was naked, and that someone was washing blood off her. The physician was still there, as were a number of other people. There was a thin lad, too, with an unruly mop of chestnut hair, who was probing her stomach gently with his hands. His touch felt oddly comforting, but she didn't recognize him.

"If you're a pervert," she gasped, "as soon as I'm better, I'll beat the daylights out of you. Or, if I die, I'll haunt you."

He gave a crooked grin. "I'm not much of a pervert," he assured her. "I'm a Healer. I've seen better and worse bodies already in my life. Stop talking, and let me work."

Melayne wished she could, but there was too much that she simply had to know. "My baby?" she asked him. "Is my baby safe?"

"Safe?" He bit at his lower lip, and then shook his head. "No. But not dead, either," he added, hastily, when he saw how agitated she was about this news. "Your own wound is much more serious."

"Forget about me," Melayne ordered him, through clenched teeth. "Save my baby."

"I can't," he told her. "If you die, the baby will die. If you live, the baby may live. I have to heal your wound first. So settle back, and let me concentrate." He bent back over her swollen side, his hands moving in a gentle rotating fashion.

"The battle?" she called out. "The dragons?"

"Will you shut up and let the kid work?" a voice she knew but couldn't place growled at her. "He can't concentrate with all the noise you're making." The owner of the voice moved into her line of sight, and Melayne gasped. It took her pain-riddled mind a few seconds to recognize the scowling face.

"Devra!" This was her friend from the army training school, the one who had led the Talents off to safety. "What are you doing here?"

"Trying to save your life, as always." Devra shook her head. "Listen, the dragons are mostly okay. One is wounded, but should live - as long as Hovin finishes work on you and gets back to her. I've got everything in hand, and I'll explain it all later. Just shut up and let him work, okay? Or do I have to punch your lights out?"

"No, I'll be good," Melayne promised. She settled back quietly. At least the dragons were safe! And if Devra said things were in hand, she knew she could trust her old friend. The Talent was grouchy, but very efficient. It was a huge worry off her shoulders, and she could force herself to be quiet.

But not to relax, of course. There was still a world of pain within her, and she still could not feel her child. It had stopped kicking, and she knew with a numbing certainty that there was a good chance that she had lost the poor thing before it had ever had a chance at independent life. But giving into despair was the worst thing she could do, so she had to act as if she believed that all was well.

Hovin was sweating now as he focused his healing abilities on her side. Melayne sneaked a look, and saw that there was a hole just above her left hip, the place from which the arrow had been pulled. There was still blood caked about it - dark and rich, and, she realized, part of the supply to her unborn child. A pang of horror shot through her, overcoming even the pain for a moment. Had her baby bled to death in the womb? As she watched, Hovin's skills were closing the wound slowly. The pain was starting to die away - he must be using his ability to block it for her. She could feel her tortured lungs gasping for air, and her heart beating fast and hard. She was clutching to consciousness very thinly.

Finally, though, the wound was closed, and she saw Ysane dart forward to wash off the remaining blood. Her friend looked scared and drawn, and Melayne knew the blonde girl was terrified for Melayne. She reached out to touch Ysane's hand, and Ysane gave her a wan smile.

Hovin moved to look down at her again. "Your wound is closed," he told her. "But you've lost a lot of blood, and I can't do much about that. Rest is the only thing that will help there, and a lot of food and care."

"The baby," she insisted, clutching his healing hands.

"That is next." He took a deep breath. "I will have to induce labor, so you will give birth. I don't know if the baby is alive or dead yet. There's no movement, and the umbilical may have been severed. It doesn't look good, but there is still hope." He paused a moment. "Whatever happens, this will not be pleasant for you."

"I don't give a damn about that," Melayne growled. "Do whatever you can and must for my child."

He nodded, looking very grave for one so young. He couldn't be more than 14! "Of course I shall. Just try and stay as calm as possible, please. I'm starting work now."

Melayne nodded, even though it hurt to move her head. The only thing that mattered right now was the child. He couldn't be dead, not after all of this. He couldn't!

Cassary's birth had been relatively easy. There had been pain, of course, but the labor had been short, and the birth relatively simple. This was not the case now.

The Healer moved to her side again, and pressed his hands gently across Melayne's pelvis. "It begins," he said, softly. Melayne felt a sharp, stabbing pain, though different from before. This one started inside her womb, and seemed to explode outwards. She gave a cry, and felt the contractions begin. Her muscles that had just been healed screamed with pain, and she knew she was howling, but couldn't stop herself. Labor had begun, and her body was now working to expel the fetus - live or dead.

She couldn't focus on worrying about the baby now. Her world was pain again, even if of a different sort. Contractions wracked her, and she felt somebody grip her hand. She clutched back, glad of support.

It seemed to take forever, but then the baby moved. Melayne felt a surge of hope until she realized it was because the contractions were forcing it from her body. "I see the head," Hovin called, gently. "You're doing well. Keep going."

Melayne didn't need any encouragement. Her body seemed to be working automatically, freed from her conscious control. The baby slid out, and Hovin and the physician caught it. Melayne gave a great cry, and then fell back, barely conscious.

"It's a boy," the physician called out. She could hear the sound of a slap, but there was no cry that would show that the baby was alive and breathing. A second slap, but still no comforting noise.

"My child!" Melayne called, terrified that the boy was dead.

"He lives," Hovin informed her. "He lives. But there may be damage - he makes no sounds at all." Then he reached out with his healing hands and pressed them to her temples. "Now - sleep."

And Melayne lost all thought.

She woke later, and much of the pain had subsided. There was still ache in her stomach, but that was most likely due to the after-effects of birth. Her fingers sought the hole in her side made by the arrow. The skin there was tender, and the muscle beneath hurt, but the gap was gone, and so was most of the monstrous pain.

With a sigh, she opened her eyes, and glanced around the room. It was her own room, hers and Sander's. She felt a pang as she recalled that he was gone, and that there was no telling when he would be back. There were people with her, but the important one she couldn't see. "My baby," she called. "Where is my baby?"

Ysane's laugh cheered her, and her friend dipped into a small cradle at the side of the bed, and brought out a tiny bundle, which she handed over. Melayne clutched at the silent baby, who looked calmly back at her. There was a ring of dark hair atop the baby's crown, and he had the most piercing, ice-blue eyes Melayne had ever seen. But he was unnaturally silent, even as Melayne clutched the child to her breast. The baby began to feed, and Melayne finally could spare her attention for the others present.

There was Ysane, of course, grinning happily, and Lady Perria. There were two servant girls, and finally two old familiar faces, one of which Melayne had been afraid she'd been hallucinating. For a moment, there was a rare smile on Devra's face before it was wiped away by the more customary scowl. Beside her, Corri was beaming.

"You'll be demanding explanations, no doubt," Devra grumbled.

"I'd rather have news first," Melayne said. "The raiders - what has happened?"

"They' re all captured," Devra replied. "My Talents rounded them up, and they're waiting until you're strong enough to deliver judgment on them."

"Why me?" asked Melayne, puzzled. She gestured toward Perria. "This is the home and land of Lord Darmen and Perria - they are the ones who should have the say in this matter."

Perria shook her head. "No, dear - they are not simple raiders - they are *dragon slayers*. They came here to slaughter your friends, so the judgment is yours. And, perhaps, the dragons, too."

"Oh." Memories came flooding back to Melayne. "Tura! How is she!" Her friend had been badly injured, and a pang of guilt that she hadn't even thought about her until now consumed Melayne."

"Hovin - our healer - is with her now," Devra replied. "She's like you - stubborn, opinionated and she's lost a lot of blood. But, like you, with a little rest she should recover."

"Luckily we arrived in time," Corri added, unable to contain her excitement any longer.

"Luck had nothing to do with it," Devra complained. "It was planning - *my* planning."

It was starting to make some sort of sense to Melayne now. "The second ship, the one we thought to be reinforcements for the raiders - that was yours."

"Indeed it was," Devra agreed.

"But how did you know you were needed? And which side to help? I mean, there were dragons, and you've never seen them before."

Devra gave a tight smile. "My Talent is Finding, don't forget. Well, after we left you, the Talents decided I'd be their leader -"

"It was the only way to make sure she wouldn't complain about the leader," Corri said to Melayne in a stage whisper. "Make her it."

Devra pretended she'd heard nothing. "So I Found them a home - a small island off the coast of Stormgard. It was uninhabited, but fertile, and we settled in. The past three years, the community has been growing, and we keep having new Talents join us. Word has gotten out about us, so they drift in."

"Don't you have trouble from regular people?" Ysane asked. "I mean, a lot of them are prejudiced against Talents."

Devra shrugged. "We're far away from even the closest neighbors. Besides, who in their right mind would want to attack a bunch of Fire Casters, Flyers and so forth? So we're mostly left in peace."

"Mostly," Corri echoed. "That means five fights over those three years. All of which, of course, we won."

Devra sighed theatrically. "It was getting dull. So a month back I decided to Find out where we were most needed. I received an image of you, and this island. So I put together a team, and we headed out here. And we reached the place in perfect time, just as the slayers attacked."

"It was almost fun," Corri added. "I found a nice, hefty log and simply plowed into the slayers. They were all dressed in really heavy armor, so one blow, and they went down and couldn't get up again." She grinned. "They might be able to fight dragons, but not Talents!"

"Anyway, as I said, they're all under guard," Devra concluded. "I'd warned them that if you died, they would die - slowly. But I didn't promise them they'd live if you did, so feel free to massacre the lot of them."

"But how did you know to defend the dragons?" Melayne asked.

"Oh, come on!" Devra cast her eyes upward. "There were *dragons*, and I knew you were in trouble. There was only one side you could possibly be on - that of the underdogs. Melayne, you *never* change."

Melayne reached out and grasped Devra's hand. "Nor do you, thankfully. You're always so practical."

Devra looked slightly embarrassed, but she didn't let go of Melayne's hand. "Well, one of us has to be."

The baby had finished nursing, and had fallen silently asleep. Melayne looked down at her, worried. "And my baby?" she asked. "How is he?"

Devra glanced at Ysane, who frowned slightly. "He *seems* to be well," the blonde girl finally said. "But... he never utters a sound. He hasn't cried at all since his birth. The physician doesn't know if he is fine or not. He's never experienced anything like it."

Melayne, concerned, looked at Devra. "And your Healer, Hovin?" she asked. "Does he have anything to say?"

"Only that there is nothing wrong with him that he can cure." Devra scowled. "The child is silent, but, well, who needs a screaming babe around anyway? Maybe it's a blessing."

"Maybe he is injured," Melayne said. She looked down at her baby with love and concern. "The blood supply to him was interrupted before he was born. I have heard that this may cause brain damage."

"It can," Perria agreed. "But neither our physician or the Healer can detect anything wrong. If the boy was injured, it is in a subtle way."

"Maybe he'll grow out of it?" Ysane suggested hopefully. "In a few days, he might be bawling his lungs out, and then you'll miss these days."

"Perhaps." Melayne wasn't at all certain. There was just too much unknown about all of this, and there was no way of asking the child. Its mind might be damaged, and he might never grow up normal. *Not my child*! Melayne whispered to herself. That couldn't happen to *her* baby; her child was *perfect*.

And perfectly silent.

It didn't bode well. But at least the child was alive. And it was time to think about naming him.

And to think of other things. "Cassary?" she asked Ysane. "And your son? Are they well."

"Cassary is with the other children, playing happily," Ysane reported. "And Falma is probably screaming for his next feeding, so I'd better go and see." She came over and touched Melayne's shoulder. "But I *had* to be sure you were well."

"I know." Melayne smiled. "Thank you, Ysane, for all your care."

"This is getting too sickly for me," Devra muttered. "And if you start thanking *me* next, *I'll* be the one screaming."

Perria started to motion them all to move. "I think that's quite enough for now. Melayne needs her rest - she's been through a lot. Let's leave her in peace."

One of the servant girls took the baby. Melayne started to protest, but the girl shook her head. "He's only going into the cradle, milady," the girl explained. "He'll be right beside you as you rest. It wouldn't do for you to turn over in your sleep and suffocate the poor thing, would it?"

"No," agreed Melayne. "Not after all this effort, it wouldn't. Thank you." She was suddenly overwhelmed by everything, and found herself drifting back to sleep again.

It was two days before Melayne could get out of bed. In her time of enforced rest, she held and fed her baby. The boy was apparently alert, but never once did anyone hear him make a sound. Several of the serving girls found this uncanny - no one could ever recall a child that never cried. Some felt it was a sign of ill-omen. Melayne could only pray that it wasn't a sign of brain damage. She desperately loved the child, but every time she saw the boy's calm face, it was like another shaft through her side. She would never have imagined wishing for a baby to scream!

Cassary almost made up for it. She was now two years old, and *very* vocal. She chattered away, sometimes in the imaginary languages of childhood, often in perfectly formed words and small sentences. And she howled at the top of her lungs whenever even minor things upset her. Two more dissimilar children could hardly be imagined.

Ysane was an angel. She had completely recovered from her own childbirth, and cheerfully took charge of both of Melayne's children when her friend needed rest. She even nursed the baby alongside Falma. Falma was a normal boy - crying and needing food and changing at all hours of the day. Or, more often, the night. Even when he needed to be changed, Melayne's baby was silent and still.

The physician tried to decide if there was any brain damage. He held a candle over his face, and moved it from side to side. The silent boy's eyes followed it readily enough. "There's little more I can do at this age," he said, sadly. "He sees the world, but seems unwilling or unable to interact with it. He may be normal and merely different. Or..."

Hovin came frequently to see both mother and son. He proclaimed Melayne almost completely cured. "Your weakness is because you lost a lot of blood," he informed her. "Once your body has regenerated what was lost, you should be fine - though I'd take it easy for a while, just to be certain." The child, though, puzzled him. "I can find nothing wrong," he said, exasperated. "But I do not know if my Healing extends to matters of the mind. His body works well - he eats, and sleeps and eliminates waste regularly as any baby. But his mind - I cannot reach his mind at all. It may be that it is fine, and simply quiet. Or it may be damaged. Only time will tell."

And time, of course, passed extremely slowly, especially when one was confined to bed. Melayne was frustrated and scared, and unable to do much of anything at all. At least Tura seemed to be well. Hovin reported that she, too, was resting. The other dragons were hunting fish for her, and she was recovering slowly from her own wound.

"I'm not as adept at Healing dragons," Hovin apologized. "But Tura seems to be fine. She won't be able to fly for a month, at least, but other than that, she's doing well."

Melayne wanted to go see her friend, but was forbidden. She was tempted to rebel against the order, but knew she was still weak. If she were to collapse on the way, as seemed likely, her enforced bed-rest would be extended. Galling as it was she endured two days in her bed.

The third day, both the physician and Hovin reluctantly agreed to her getting up, as long as she was never alone. The first thing Melayne insisted on was a bath - she felt horribly dirty after all she had been through. One of the serving girls was originally told to look after her, but Corri insisted on helping instead. She helped Melayne to bathe, and kept up a running chatter the whole time. Corri was so excited to be back with Melayne again, and she had a lot of news about people that Melayne had never met that she insisted on sharing. Much of it

Melayne simply let wash over her, as the water did. It was wonderful to see and hear her old friend again. And Corri seemed to have blossomed a lot from the shy young girl in the army training camp. She was bubbly, happy and outgoing - obviously because her new life-style agreed with her. She was completely devoted to Devra, and fiercely loyal to her leader. Devra seemed to be as cranky as ever, but Melayne had always been able to see that this was simply a front she presented to the world. Devra had been hit hard by her family's betrayal in giving her up to the King's Seekers, and by the way her friends had abandoned her. It had taken her a while to trust anyone again. But it was clear that she was a strong-willed and capable leader, and filled with love for those she lead. But she covered this all up with her air of annoyed aggression - which seemed to fool no one, especially not Corri, who just acted as if Devra were all sweetness and light. Possibly the only person in the world who thought that Devra cared about nobody and nothing was Devra herself.

The bath and the chatter were eventually finished, and Melayne dressed carefully. Lady Perria had loaned her a gorgeous robe of green, which looked both expensive and regal. She added a small band of gold over her hair and a short dagger at her side.

"Should be a sword," Devra complained. "When you sit in judgment, you want the prisoners to know what their end can be."

"They'll know it soon enough," Melayne promised. "And you're the only woman I know able to wear a sword without looking uncomfortable."

"You need more practice with one, then."

"Perhaps so; but a dagger will do me for now." Melayne walked slowly and carefully to the main hall. Lord Darmen had set up three of the most impressive chairs he owned, and they were tall, ornate, carved affairs that looked very like thrones. He and Perria sat stonily in two of them. Melayne was led to the third, set in the center, and slightly forward. Here she sat, calmly and coldly.

The prisoners were led in by Bantry, their hands tied in front of them. All looked as if they hadn't slept for days, and several were bandaged. Devra had refused to allow Hovin to tend to them, and the physician had sent only his assistant. There were an even dozen of the would-be dragonslayers, and Melayne surveyed them frostily. Most were in their third decade of life, but one seemed to barely be older than her.

But all seemed defiant and angry. And all had intended to slay her dragon friends.

"This is the hall of my justice," Lord Darmen said, in a strong, clear voice. "You have invaded my lands and harmed my people. Your lives are all forfeit. You are alive now only because you have to answer to one with a better claim against your miserable lives than my own." He turned to face Melayne. "This is now your hall of justice. Speak with these men if you wish, and sentence them as you see fit. I hand all claims of vengeance and justice to you now. These are your prisoners, and no longer mine, Melayne of Dragonhome."

With a terrible cry, one of the prisoners threw himself forward, face twisted into a snarl, his hands reaching for Melayne's throat.

Chapter Nine

Melayne jerked back from the attack, and felt her healing side complain. Before she could react, Bantry had leapt from his post and slammed into the crazed man. The prisoner went down, but struggled to rise again, to reach Melayne.

He was clearly intent on killing her. But why? And why now, when he couldn't possibly reach her?

Bantry drew his sword, seeking to stop the man permanently. The slayer didn't even seem to notice. He simply snarled and struggled to get free. Bantry prepared to strike.

"No!" Melayne cried.

"He wants to kill you, my lady," Bantry gasped, still trying to subdue the man. Two of the guards had reached them now, and one grabbed the prisoner's hands - which were still bound - and the other his feet, holding him down. Bantry sat up, panting.

"I don't think he can help himself," Melayne said, slowly. The young man had a glazed look in his eyes, and his face was still twisted into a snarl of pure hatred. "It happened when he heard Darmen mention my name..." And then she understood. "Sarrow..."

"I don't understand," Darmen said. "Let us kill the youth - it is the only way to protect you."

"No. He can't help himself." The more Melayne studied him, the more certain she was that this was her brother's doing. "My brother's talent is Persuasion - he can make people do things they normally wouldn't. I think he's given this boy an order to kill me. He only went crazy when he heard my name." She stood up and walked toward the struggling youth. The guards held him tight, and he screamed in frustration. Melayne bent to look him in the eyes. "I am Melayne of Dragonhome," she said, slowly. "What must you do?"

"I must kill you!" The slayer struggled again to get free, but couldn't manage it.

"Who told you to do this?"

"Lord Sarrow," he gasped. "I *must* deliver his message to you. I must!"

"Some message," Darmen growled. "He's ordered the boy to slay you, Melayne. We *have* to kill him - I don't think he'll ever stop trying to murder you."

"Not as long as he's under my brother's influence," she agreed. "But perhaps I can do something about it." The dragons had told her she was more powerful than she had imagined, and the dragons usually knew what they were talking about... Perhaps she could use her Talent of Communication to get through to the young man behind the orders, the young man who hadn't seemed so lethal. "Look at me," she ordered him, and willed with all of her heart to get through to him. "You don't need to obey that order. You don't *wish* to obey it - do you?"

"No," the slayer gasped. "I am... I am..." He shook his head, as if to clear his thoughts. "I don't..." He stopped struggling. "I don't want to harm you. But I was *ordered...*"

"The order is cancelled," Melayne told him, gently. Then to the guards: "Let him up."

"He could be faking it," Bantry argued.

"The state he was in, he had no room for any thoughts like that," Melayne said. "His mind is now his own again. I've managed to break my brother's orders." She was somewhat startled that it had been so simple, really - she had simply Communicated with the man behind the orders, and the orders had fallen away like melting snow. "He can now answer for the actions he took willingly. Place him back with the others." The guards obeyed, and the young slayer stumbled back to join his companions. Melayne returned to her judgment seat and took her place again.

She looked over the twelve would-be slayers with anger, frustration and a coldness in her heart. These men, these *fools,* had wished to kill her dragon friends - and one of them *had* injured Tura. They deserved to be punished, and she could see that they expected to be punished. But, first, she needed information. And, to be honest with herself, she was stalling, hoping for inspiration. She didn't want to sentence anyone to die, not even this scum.

It was time to see if the dragons were right again when they had said her Talent for Communication was as strong as they claimed. These men were, for the most part, scared and defiant, and would normally not be very communicative. She reached out to them with all of her power, and then started to speak, slowly and clearly.

"You came here to kill, and it is only because of the strength and courage of my friends that your mission failed. You invaded the lands of Lord Darmen, and you threatened his people. Can any of you think of a reason why you should not be sentenced to die for these crimes."

"Crimes?" Their spokesman moved forward slightly. "We are not the ones who have committed crimes here! *You* are the ones! You have kept and protected dragons, the sworn enemies of humans. You should all be wiped from the face of this world, your land burned and salted and even your names blotted out forever. You have betrayed all human beings by your unholy and unnatural defense of dragons."

"I see." Melayne looked from stern face to stern face. The man's comments had strengthened their resolve, it appeared. All, that was, except for the youngest, the one who had attacked her. He appeared to be ill at ease, and wouldn't meet her gaze. "What of you?" she asked, softly, reaching out to him. "Is that how you feel?"

"I don't know!" he blurted out. "We were told how wicked you all are, protecting and raising dragons. And surely that must be so! Dragons are our enemies, and they must all be destroyed."

"But..." Melayne prompted, knowing there would be more.

"But..." He hung his head again. "It was never our intent to harm anyone but dragons. When you were shot, I was angry and ashamed. Especially as you were with child." He looked up. "How is the child, by the way? Did it survive?" His concern seemed genuine, and he had lost completely all of his previous anger.

"Well, at least *one* of you has some decent human emotions left," Melayne said. "The child lives, though I cannot be certain that he is well. And *that* is another crime you would be charged with, were it not that the perpetrator has already died."

"He did as he was instructed," the spokesman growled. "We are all as guilty of the deed as he."

Melayne stared at the man coldly. "Well, at least you confess to your crimes."

"They are not crimes!" the man insisted. "They were honorable actions, and we would all do the same again."

"Would you?" Melayne asked, wonderingly. She looked at the youngest slayer. "Would *you*?"

"I..." He faltered. "I do not know. I am no longer certain that our cause is just." He glared defiantly at his leader. "I *do* know that some of our actions were not."

"Then there is hope for you, at least," Melayne decided. The young man appeared sincere and honest, and the anger didn't burn inside him that she could feel in all of the rest.

"Because he is willing to turn traitor?" their leader asked.

"Because he can admit that he might be wrong." Melayne stared at the hardened man in front of her. "Admitting that you might be wrong is the first step on the road to discovery. If you cannot admit that little, then there is no hope that you will ever walk straight. Can none of the others of you say the same? Not that you *were* wrong, but that you *might* be wrong?" She looked from stony face to stony face and sighed. "No, I can see that it is impossible for you. You are all lost - too lost to even know you are lost. And I'm at a loss to know what to do with you. You *deserve* death, but I cannot bring myself to stoop so low as to order it." Then an idea occurred to her and she brightened. "Wait... You came here to slay dragons, did you not?"

"You know we did," the man growled.

"Then it is only fitting that the dragons pronounce judgment on you, isn't it?" Melayne clapped her hands. "Bantry, lead the prisoners into the courtyard. Everyone, this trial is being moved outside so that the would-be victims might attend."

"Dragons?" For the first time, the slayer seemed not so self-assured. "You will feed us to the dragons?"

"Of course not - you'd give them indigestion." Melayne rose to her feet, still feeling a little weak. "But they should have some say in what we do with you."

"Dragons?" The man looked scared. "They are not intelligent."

"They've a damned sight more brains than you lot have," Bantry said, poking him firmly with the business end of his spear. "One of them is a good friend of mine."

"You're insane. All of you. Believing a dragon can think!"

"Outside," Bantry repeated. He and his soldiers started the prisoners moving.

Melayne started walking, and Devra and Corri fell in alongside her, each taking an elbow. "What's this?" she asked. "I don't need help."

"Stop being so damned proud, and accept what we offer," Devra grumbled. "You'll fall down inside twenty paces if we don't hold you up, and you know it." She glared at one of the servants. "You, girl - bring a chair for Melayne." The girl rushed to obey.

Melayne knew she would not win this argument - and, truthfully, she was glad of the aid. She was still ill, and she knew Devra was correct. With the help of her friends, she made it into the courtyard, and then half-fell into the chair that had been provided. As soon as everyone else was present, she sent out a mental summons for the three dragons.

Shath and Loken flew down from the sky, the beat of their wings raising dust as they settled to either side of her. Tura had already been in the yard, and she moved slowly over to lie at Melayne's feet. Melayne leaned forward and stroked her friend's scaly head. Tura's tongue flickered out to touch her hand, and then withdrew.

"I'm glad you're doing well," Melayne whispered to her.

"And I you," Tura agreed.

Straightening, Melayne looked over the line of the would-be slayers. Now she could see fear in their eyes, even that of the youngest one. Well, she could only imagine how she must seem to them - seated in the yard, flanked by dragons and with a third curled about her feet. This had to be terrifying to them - the more so since they had no idea what to expect.

Truth be told, *she* didn't know what to expect, either. "These are those who you came here to kill," Melayne said is a strong voice. "Tura you wounded - but Shath and Loken are whole. None of you would stand a chance against them, not without your weapons. And yet I can see in your faces that you would still try."

"It is our task," their leader replied. "From childhood, each of us has been raised to slay dragons."

"Why?" Melayne asked.

The man seemed confused. "What?"

"Why?" she repeated. "You say you have been trained to slay dragons, but do any of you know *why* this is so?"

"I am Beltran, son of Hargar," their leader said, proudly. "I am the seventh generation of my family to slay dragons. That is why I do this."

"That's not a reason, it's just a stupid excuse," Melayne said, firmly. "I am Melayne, daughter of nobody important, and I help all those who need it. *Why* do you think dragons should die?"

"Because they're *dragons*!" Beltran exclaimed. "What more reason need there be?"

Devra sighed. "You're not going to be able to reason with him," she pointed out. "I don't know why you even bother."

"Because she can never give up," Corri answered. "It's the way she is - she's trying to save these men, even if they don't want it." She glanced at the closest dragon - Shath - and shivered slightly. "Even knowing they're Melayne's friends and won't hurt us, I'm still a bit scared."

"You're always scared," Devra said, dismissively.

"Peace," Melayne muttered. She tried again. "These dragons have never harmed anyone. In fact, they've helped us here with fishing, and they defend these lands as bravely as any man does. There is not a person on this island who would hurt one of them, and not one person they would willingly allow harm to come to in their turn."

Beltran looked around the ring of faces and saw that this was so. "You're mad, all of you! Dragons must be killed!"

Melayne moved to speak again, but Tura raised her head. "No," she said. "It is no use. Their minds are closed. They were bred to slay dragons, and if they do not slay, then their lives have no meaning. They will have lived without purpose. They cannot accept that their view of reality is wrong. They cannot change." Her gaze fell on the young man. "All but him. In him I sense confusion and the potential for change. He is not entirely certain of his way, and may be able to admit to his flaws and alter them."

Melayne repeated all of this for the benefit of the humans present. "So," she said, finally, to Tura, "what are we to do with them? Should they die?"

"No," the dragon replied. "They are sick, and it would be wrong to kill the sick. But they must be isolated, so they can have no chance of harming us. There is a small island, some twenty miles to the east - if they had grain and shelter, they could farm there. Alone."

Melayne again translated for the sake of the prisoners. "The dragons," she pointed out, "do not even wish to kill *you*, and they have every reason to desire it. I'm sure you won't see this as their having more mercy than you, but it is so. We will give you everything you will need to be farmers on that island, and then you will be left there. It will be up to you after that if you survive or not. If you can't learn new ways, then you will die."

"We are not farmers!" Beltran exclaimed angrily.

"Then *become* farmers!" Melayne yelled back. "At least they have purpose!" She waved her hand in dismissal, and Bantry started to lead the men away. Then Melayne gestured. "Not the youngest," she said. "He is to come to me."

The youth paused, and then slowly walked closer to Melayne, eyeing the dragons nervously the whole time. "What is your name?" she asked him.

"Margone," the young man replied. "Son of Hobson." He gave a weak laugh. "All of my life, I have been glad I was not son of a farmer, and forced to work the land. Now, it seems, I am to become what I always looked down upon."

Melayne smiled. "It might be appropriate, at that. You should never think yourself better than any other person. You do not know their hearts, or their true worth - or even your own. Farmers have great worth, for without them none of us would eat. Yet - we are not all called to be farmers."

"You are a great lady," Margone answered. "It is easy for you to say that. You *are* better than everyone else."

"I am no lady, great or otherwise," Melayne snapped. "I am the daughter of a poor farmer, who was slain by raiders. I am a nobody, made a lady only because I married a Lord. I am no better than any of the serving girls you see here."

Devra laughed at that. "And, you know," she told the would-be slayer, "she genuinely believes that. She is the only person here who can't see her own true worth."

Melayne scowled at her friend. "Will you leave this to me?" she asked. "You're just confusing the boy."

"Oh, yes, it's all my fault," Devra said, mockingly. "Well, get on with trying to set him straight, then."

Margone looked astonished. "You allow her to talk to you like that?" he asked Melayne.

"Of course I do - she may be idiotic, but she's my friend."

Margone shook his head. "Friend to dragons, and friends with females who sass you? Truly, Lady, you are a strange one."

"Hey, I think you *are* getting through to him," Devra muttered.

Melayne glared at her friend, and then turned to the youth again. "You admit that you may have been in error?" she demanded.

"Yes," he replied, not meeting her eyes. "I am ashamed that you were hurt."

"And what of the dragons?"

He glanced quickly at Tura, and then away. "I am afraid of them."

"So you should be." Melayne twisted in her chair - she knew she needed to lie down again, and wouldn't last much longer. "But what do you feel about them? Do you still think that they need to be destroyed?"

He struggled uncomfortably with himself. "I do not know," he finally said. "I have always been told that they must. I have been raised and trained to kill them. And yet..." He looked up, finally, at Shath, whose cold eyes looked back at him. "They do not seem to be killers. You say they are friends, to both you and the people here. This is not how I ever imagined them. I have always believed that they were monsters, who should be destroyed. And Sarrow urged me on this path, and it seemed right."

"Sarrow?" Melayne hissed, sitting up straighter in the chair. "Yes, I'd almost forgotten about him in all of this. There will have to be an accounting with my brother."

"Brother?" Margone blinked. "I had forgotten he was your brother. I thought of him only as the Lord of Dragonhome."

"He is not the Lord of Dragonhome," Melayne replied. "My husband is Lord there. And my children are heirs to Dragonhome." Suddenly things were starting to make a little more sense to Melayne. But she was feeling tired, and knew that it would be foolish to allow this to go on. "We will speak more of this, but now I need to rest. You will not go with the others - you will stay here and learn the truth about the dragons - and about people." She glanced around, and saw Devra trying to hide a grin. "I'm tempted to put him in your care," she warned the girl. "But he's being punished enough already." Then she smiled. "Corri - can I entrust him to you? Will you make sure he behaves himself? And will you try and make him see his errors?"

Corri jumped. "Me? But I'm scared of dragons myself!"

"Which makes you perfect to teach him - you can learn about them together. Tura is stuck here for the time being - she can't fly until her muscles heal. I'll assign the pair of you to looking after her." She gave Margone a hard stare. "And she will decide if you're learning anything from all of this. Now, will you give me your parole? Will you promise not to harm anyone on this island? And that includes dragons."

"You would trust me?" he asked her, clearly amazed.

"I would trust you." She didn't feel any need to explain that her Talent would reveal if he were lying to her.

"She's crazy like that," Devra muttered in a stage whisper.

"Then I will give my promise," he agreed.

"Good." Melayne sighed, and looked up at Devra. "All right - I'll go quietly back to bed now. But I'll need a hand."

"About time you admitted it."

Chapter Ten

It made no difference to Corran that they had been flying for days, getting further west - it still gave him a thrill to be on Ganeth's back and aloft. He wished his own Talent was that of Flying, but he knew that it wasn't. He had tried so often to jump into the air and simply stay there - and failed every time. He had always imagined that, one day, he would jump up, and not fall back almost immediately. But that was all it was - imagination. But flying astride a dragon was a very good second-best.

The sea-fronting cliffs and rocks near where Melayne had grown up had gotten taller and wilder as they flew on. The coast they were paralleling now was too inhospitable for anyone to live. There had been no sign of towns or even isolated farms for a couple of days now. Of course, that might also be because they were getting closer to the land of the Raiders, and they might have attacked anyone living close to this coast.

The dragons flew down to land atop the cliffs so they could rest their wings for a while. Corran and his father jumped down, and both stretched. It was a little tiring riding on dragons' backs!

Sander gestured off to the east a little. "We passed a small river just back there," he said. "It might be a good idea to fill our water pouches while we have the chance. Besides which," he added, grinning, "my backside is a little sore, and a short walk will probably help."

We'll wait here for you, Ganeth said. *I could do with a short nap.*

Corran waved, and then set off with his father. The ground was uneven and rocky. Little other than moss and a tough, wiry sea-grass grew here. There were sea birds circling, as always, and he spotted the swift dart of some small animal in the grass from time to time. But there were no signs that people had ever walked this way, much less settled. It seemed to be desolate and abandoned. The two of them strode along in silence, Sander obviously as loath to speak as his son. Corran realized he was probably thinking of Melayne and missing her terribly. He could understand that, as he felt the same way.

The river was only a five-minute walk, and it provided a little sound at last as it hurried over rocks toward the waiting sea. Its pathway had scored deeply into the cliffs, so they had to climb down some twenty feet to reach the level where they could fill their skins. Corran splashed some of the cool water on his face and took a deep drink. It felt good.

"How much further do we have to go?" he asked his father, as they both sat on rocks, gazing into the distance.

His father shrugged. "Maybe another day, maybe less. It's hard to be certain - the map isn't very detailed, and when there's no villages or farms, it's hard to be certain just how far you've gone. But it won't be long now."

"What will we do then?" Corran asked.

"Improvise - as always." Sander ruffled his son's hair. "Hopefully we'll know what to do when the time comes. Since we don't know what to expect, it's difficult to make plans."

Corran nodded. Then he asked something that was uppermost on his mind. "Do you think that Melayne and Cassary are all right?"

"I can only hope and pray that they are." Sander sighed, and closed his eyes. "I wish my Talent could tell me, but it can't. I know we did the right thing, but sometimes the right thing can be a hard path."

Corran nodded. "I miss them both so much," he confessed.

"So do I," his father assured him. "But we're doing this so that they might both be safer. And that makes this temporary parting a little easier to bear." He stood up, and slung the water pouch over his shoulder. "Well, let's get back to the dragons, shall we?"

"Right." Corran followed his father back up the rocks to the cliff walk, and then back to where they had left the dragons. Neither was there.

Sander frowned slightly. "What's gotten into that pair now?" he wondered aloud. "They said they'd wait for us here."

"Maybe they got hungry?" Corran suggested. "It's easier for them to fish if they don't have to carry us. Or they might have seen a deer, or something, and gone hunting."

"This isn't deer country," Sander said. "Goats, perhaps..." He shrugged. "Well, I'm sure they won't be long. Maybe we'd better get a little food ourselves while we have the chance. I think I've still got some dried meat."

Corran made a face. The meat was tough and much of the taste had fled. But it kept them going when there was no time to hunt and cook, and he accepted a strip and began chewing at it. It took a lot of chewing before it could be swallowed.

After an hour, his father began to get restless. He had taken to pacing up and down, and staring out to sea. Corran followed his gaze, hoping to see the dark shapes of the dragons, but there were only the raucous sea birds.

"Wherever could they have gotten to?" his father muttered. Then he made a decision. "Well, there's no point whatsoever in lounging about here lazily all day. Let's start walking - the dragons will be able to track us when they come back. Anyway, after all that flying, a little walking will do us good, I'm sure."

Corran nodded, and fell into step beside his father. They set off following the coast. Far below them, waves crashed onto the rocks, and there was a scent of salt in the tangy air. The going was fairly easy, as there were only a few scrub trees. Sometimes they had to skirt fields of rocks, but mostly there was just the sea-grass underfoot. For two hours or so, they walked, crossing the occasional stream. Those crossings were the only things that slowed them, because each stream had cut deeply into the rocks, and they were forced to descend to the level of the water, and then climb the far side back up again.

Both of them looked frequently over their shoulders, hoping to see the dragons. They saw no sign of the missing creatures, and Corran was starting to worry. The dragons were tough, and could generally look after themselves. There were no animals Corran knew of that could harm them. But where *were* they? It was the uncertainty that was the most disturbing.

Nothing they knew of could hurt the dragons - but what about something they *didn't* know of? This was a strange, alien country, and Corran had no idea what kind of creatures might live here.

Creatures that hunted and killed dragons, maybe?

He was worried about Ganeth, and the longer she was gone, the more he worried. And he was certain his father felt the same way about the missing Brek. But neither of them said a word, as if they both felt that by speaking their fears out loud, those fears might somehow be made to come true.

It was late afternoon by now, and time when they would normally have started to look for somewhere to camp for the night. Sander didn't suggest stopping, so neither did Corran. His legs were getting tired, but he didn't want to let his father down by begging for a rest. Besides, if they stopped now, they would have to talk about the missing dragons, and Corran was trying to avoid that. So, he suspected, was his father.

Finally though, his father called a halt. They were in a small valley, and there was a little stream trickling down toward the sea, and they could use it for fresh water. While Corran fetched wood for a fire, his father managed to catch a couple of small fish. He was gutting them ready for cook when Corran staggered back with as big a bundle of firewood as he could manage. Together, mostly in silence, they built and lit a small fire, and then skewered the fish and left them to cook. Sander kept looking up at the sky as they worked, and Corran knew that the missing dragons were weighing heavily on his mind.

Darkness was falling by the time the fish were cooked and flaky enough to eat. Using their knives and "plates" of large leaves, the two of them ate their silent meal. Afterward, they washed their sticky hands in the stream. Corran was exhausted from his efforts, and knew he should sleep. But he was too worried about Ganeth to think about sleep.

"I'm sure they're both fine," his father said, quietly. "They're tough, and they're smart."

"They're *missing*," Corran replied.

"Yes," his father agreed. "And we don't know why. That's the worst of it. But we have to believe that they can handle anything they come up against. They've been delayed from returning to us for unknown reasons, and we'll just have to do without them until they turn up again. Our mission is important, and we'll continue the hunt for the raider village in the morning, whether the dragons return or not. Agreed?"

"Agreed," Corran said, sighing. "But I'm not happy."

"Nor am I," his father replied. "The missing dragons are an added problem we really didn't need. But they may turn up in the morning, and we'll discover why they were gone so long. Right now, I think we both need sleep. We've gotten lazy, riding dragons, and all that walking has tired us both out."

Corran nodded, and settled down to sleep. He used his pack as a pillow, and covered himself with the small blanket he'd packed. Thankfully it wasn't a cold night. He noticed that his father had killed the fire as soon as the cooking was done - no doubt worried that the smoke might be seen by any roaming natives. They couldn't be far from the raiders' base now, so they might run into people any time.

It was difficult for him to fall asleep, though. He was so worried about Ganeth. Since he'd first met his dragon, they'd barely been apart more than a few hours. And, back at the castle, even when he slept he knew she was down in the courtyard. Now he had no idea where she was, why she was missing - or even if she was still alive. He was missing Melayne and Cassary so much, but he was missing Ganeth the most.

But he was eight years old now, and son of the Lord of Dragonhome. He was too big to cry and worry like a child. He had to help his father out on this quest, not be another burden. As worried as he was, he knew his father had to be even more worried - he was bound to be missing Melayne and Cassary even more than his son did, and he had to think about the raiders, and keeping the Far Isles protected. There was a lot of responsibility tied to being Lord Sander. And it was up to him to help his father out. No matter how scared he felt, he would do that.

He would be a good son.

Eventually, troubled and unsettled, he managed to fall into a light sleep. He woke in the morning feeling dragged out and still tired. And there was still no sign of the dragons.

They refilled their water skins in the stream, and munched on jerky for breakfast as they set off again. Neither of them mentioned the dragons, though it was obviously troubling his father as much as it bothered Corran. But there was nothing they could do about it - they had no clue as to where the dragons were, and no way to track them. All they could do was to hope and trust.

And walk.

By mid-afternoon, they must have covered several miles, and Corran was getting tired through and through. Every muscle ached, and he was more depressed than he could ever have imagined. He almost walked into his father when Sander stopped suddenly.

"People."

They were walking through a small copse of trees - Corran had no idea of their names, but they had large, five-fingered leaves, and there were dense bushes along their way, so they were pretty well hidden. But now that his father had spoken, Corran could see that there were figures ahead. The two of them were at the top of a small hill, and below them were cleared fields, where vegetables were growing in neat lines. And, among the rows, there were a number of people, all working away.

There was something odd about them, and Corran studied them carefully. They were dressed in leather and cloth, mostly in drab colors, and they were of both sexes - or, at least, long-haired and short-haired together.

"They're all children," his father said, softly, and Corran realized what he had been trying to work out. Now he could see that there were boys and girls there, some as young as five or six, and none older than about twelve. "Where are the adults?" Sander asked himself. Corran could see none.

"Maybe in their village?" he suggested. "These fields must be on the outskirts. It's probably over the next hill."

"Yes," his father agreed. "That's good thinking. But if I were their parents, I'd have at least one armed man here to guard the children - from wild animals, if not from other people."

They stayed hidden, watching the pastoral scene below them carefully. But all the children did was to weed the long rows of growths. It was getting late in the afternoon before anyone else appeared. Then it was an elderly man and a woman probably in her twenties. The old man had a sword strapped to his side, but the woman wasn't armed. She called out to the children, who gathered up their tools and then followed, wearily, back down the path that led around the next hill.

"Supper time," Corran said, rather enviously. His father hadn't caught them anything fresh, and they couldn't build a fire this close to the hidden village, so it would probably be more jerky for their own supper. He was getting *really* sick of that dried, tough meat.

"Yes." His father rubbed his chin. "There's something very odd about all of this - not that everything so far has exactly made sense. I'm going to have to do a little thinking." He glanced about. "There's a small clearing back there where we can sleep tonight. No fire and no cooking, I'm afraid," he said, confirming Corran's suspicions. "We can't risk being discovered."

It was an even worse camp than the previous nights. Not only were there still no dragons, but neither was there fresh food. Corran chewed his dried meat without enthusiasm, and then managed to eventually fall asleep.

In the morning, he woke alone. Terrified that something had happened to his father too, Corran almost called out aloud, before realizing how dangerous that might be. Instead, he jumped to his feet, and then sighed with relief. His father was at the edge of the copse, staring down at the fields below. The sun had to have been up an hour or so, but there was still a little chill in the air.

Corran moved silently to join his father, who gave him a brief hug and gestured down the hill. The children were already at work in the fields again.

"They arrived a short while ago, again accompanied by only a woman and an old man," Sander said softly. "Then the adults left the children here alone..." He shook his head. "This *must* be the raider village - but where are the men?"

"Maybe they're out raiding?" Corran suggested. "Or working on getting their boats ready?"

"Maybe," his father agreed. "But I *have* to know." He turned to face Corran. "There's only one answer - I'm going to go to the village myself, telling them I'm a traveler, and ask for hospitality."

Corran was startled. "But they might kill you!"

"Why would they do that?" his father asked, reasonably. "One man can't be much of a threat to them. I don't think there's much risk involved with the idea."

"I'm coming with you," Corran said.

"No, you're not," Sander answered. His voice was quiet, but firm. "I don't *think* they will harm me, but I can't be certain. And I won't allow them to harm you. I want you to go back a few miles, and wait. I'll see what I can find out, and try and slip away and find you again. You stay hidden, and wait until you see me - alone, mind you."

"I don't want to be alone!" Corran said, unhappily. He knew he was sounding like a child, but he couldn't help it. He'd lost everyone else, and he couldn't bear the thought of being separated from his father, too. "I want to come with you. I don't care if it's dangerous."

"I do." Sander gripped Corran's arms. "I *have* to do this, and you have to do as I tell you. If anything should happen to me, it will be up to *you* to carry on with the mission." He took all the remaining jerky from his pack and gave it to Corran. "I know you've got to be getting sick of this, but it will keep you alive for a week or more. I shouldn't be gone that long, but... just in case. I'll join you as soon as I can."

"And if you *don't*?" Corran asked. He didn't want to consider that possibility, but he didn't have any choice.

"Then it's up to you to carry on the mission," he said. "If the dragons arrive while I'm gone, don't let Brek come looking for me, understand? It might cause problems. If I don't come back in a week, you do what you think is best. I'll trust you to be brave and clever enough to work out what that must be. But stay away from this place for a few days - I'll claim that I've been traveling alone, but the raiders might well check to see if that's true." He gave Corran a big hug. "Now - off you go. I'll give you an hour's start before I go down there."

"I don't want to go," Corran said, fighting back his fears and tears. "But I *will* go, because I know it's the right thing to do. I'll miss you, though."

"Don't worry," his father assured him. "I'll be with you within the week. I promise."

But he wasn't.

Chapter Eleven

Melayne smiled down at Cassary, who was staring in fascination at her baby brother. The as-yet-unnamed child had finished his milk, and was sleeping in Melayne's arms. For a moment, Melayne felt a wave of satisfaction wash over her, and she allowed herself a few minutes to enjoy the feeling. Then she allowed reality to intrude once more, as she called for one of the serving girls to take the baby. No matter how domestic things might seem from moment to moment, the truth was that nothing now was normal.

Thankfully, she had the servants and Ysane to look after her children. Much as Melayne wanted to simply be a mother right now, she didn't have that luxury. She tidied herself up, and then went in search of Corri and the would-be dragon slayer, Margone. She had to take her time, as her side was still very sore, and she was not yet recovered from the loss of so much blood. Devra, fussing and snapping, accompanied her, complaining all the way.

"When did you get to be such a mother hen?" Melayne asked her friend. Despite her words, she felt very grateful.

"Since I was put in charge of escaping Talents by some idiotic dreamer," Devra replied. "Oh, right - that was you. So it's your own fault I'm like this. Live with it."

"I might have known it was my doing," Melayne said, hiding her smile. "Everything that's happening around here seems to be my fault."

"Nice of you to take the blame," Devra said. "But I think a few other people are at fault, too. The raiders have to answer for their own actions."

"But they're only here because of me," Melayne pointed out. "As are the dragon slayers. It's all my doing."

"Crap," Devra replied. "You're just being yourself. That insane brother of yours sent the slayers here. It's *his* fault, not yours. And the raiders made a decision to come after you. I'll agree that you do seem to be the current center of the Universe, but that's not exactly your fault. Besides, knowing you, you're planning on doing something stupid about it all."

Melayne smiled. "I'm glad I'll have your support, then."

"Support?" Devra snorted. "I don't know what you have in mind, but I'll bet you I'm against it, because it will be suicidal, crazy and heroic. And I dislike all of those things."

"You needn't worry," Melayne assured her. "I don't have any plans - yet. This is a fact-finding mission right now."

They had reached the courtyard now. Normally, it would be a bustling place, with servants and workers at their various labors. But today it was almost deserted - except for the dragon resting beside the wall, and the two humans with her. Melayne's pulse quickening as she saw her friend Tura, and she almost managed a respectable walking pace getting to the dragon. She had a large patch over the spot where the great bolt had pierced her, and there was evidence of some swelling. Other than that, she looked as if she were almost back to normal. Her head came down, and Melayne rubbed it, happily.

"I am so glad to see that you're feeling better," she said. "I was so worried about you."

"And I of you," Tura replied. "How is your hatchling? Do you have a name for him yet?"

Melayne shook her head. "I cannot name the boy until his father returns. It's a decision we must take together. Meanwhile, there is much to be done."

She turned to Corri and Margone, and wrinkled her nose. "Uh, Corri... I don't know how to tell you..."

"You *stink,*" Devra said. She never had a problem broaching delicate matters.

Corri laughed. "It's the fish," she explained. "Tura can't hunt, so Margone and I have been feeding her fish." She sniffed her hands. "Yes, it *is* kind of stinky."

Melayne couldn't help laughing herself. Corri had that effect on most people; even Devra was fighting back a twitch at the ends of her mouth. "I'm glad that you're looking after her." She looked at Margone. The would-be slayer seemed to be stricken with shyness. "And how are you doing?" she asked him. "Do you still want to slaughter dragons?"

He blushed, and looked toward the dirt. "No, my lady. I'm finding Tura to be... less menacing than I had been led to believe. And Corri has been looking after me well."

"I think they may be wanting to breed," Tura said, helpfully. Melayne was glad that none of the others could understand the dragon's speech. But she looked at Margone and then at Corri. Yes, there *did* seem to be some sort of mutual interest there...

"Good." Melayne glanced about, hoping to find somewhere to sit. Devra had anticipated her need, and had dragged over a bale of hay.

"You might get straws in your backside," she commented. "But it will make sure you don't stay here too long."

"Thank you." Melayne sat down, relieved. She was doing her best, but her energy levels were low. She'd last longer now, and there was so much to do. She turned back to Margone. "Now, it's time for you to tell us about this dragon slaying business, and about my brother. First of all, is he well?"

"Yes," Margone replied. "He's very well. He's taken over Dragonhome, as I told you before. And he gave me a verbal message to deliver to you, as well as the... more physical one." He winced as he said this, obviously still unhappy about attacking her.

"Indeed?" She patted his hand gently, to show that she bore him no ill will - and that his news pleased her. Despite everything, she was glad that her brother was fine. "And what would that be?"

"He told me to tell you that you will never know peace again until all of the dragons were dead. He said to offer you terms of surrender." He glanced at Tura. "They include the death of all five dragons."

"He would know that I would never agree," Melayne answered.

"Yes, he did say that. His actual words were 'she's not bright enough to accept my mercy'." Devra growled in her throat at this, and Margone flushed. "I'm only repeating what he said - it's not my sentiment."

Melayne smiled. "It's quite close to hers, though," she commented. "She thinks I don't take enough care for myself."

"She may be right, lady," the would-be slayer said. "But your brother said to tell you that he will spare your life only if you surrender. Otherwise he will give orders to have you slain."

"The bastard," Devra spat. Her hand went to her sword. "There's only one reply to that."

"Which Margone cannot deliver," Melayne said. She touched her friend's hand. "Peace. Sarrow is still only a child, and reacts from fear. He would never harm me."

Devra rolled her eyes. "He doesn't have to do it personally - he gave these slayers orders to kill you, you idiot. And they almost did." She glared at Margone - clearly, she had not yet forgiven him.

"Yes," Margone added, flushing. "This is true. We *were* told to kill you if you did not surrender. And I wasn't even given that choice - I was to kill you whatever you said."

"No." Melayne shook her head, firmly. "Sarrow gave that order knowing it could never be carried out. He would never wish me harm."

"See what I mean?" Devra growled. "Melayne and reality are not on speaking terms. She insists on believing the best of that filthy brother of hers."

Margone nodded his understanding. "It is a mistake," he agreed. "The boy truly wishes her dead."

"No!" Melayne wouldn't even contemplate the possibility. They were wrong - they *had* to be. Sarrow would never want her harmed, let alone dead. "He knew that I would defeat you all," she decided. "That there was no chance you would ever be able to carry out his order."

"Lady," Margone said, slowly. "I wish that were true. But it is not. As soon as I knew you were his sister, there was a compulsion in me to strike out at you. Corri told me that your brother has the Talent of Persuasion - that he can compel obedience. As it is, the compulsion only left me when I talked with you."

Tura's tongue darted. "It is your own Talent," she explained. "Your ability to Communicate got through to the youth, and made him aware of his true feelings. Your ability can counter that of your brother - he weaves spells to compel, while you force the truth."

"I hope that is so," Melayne answered. "If I can counter his Talent, then we have a way to defeat him without harming him."

Corri's eyes widened. "Melayne, aren't you *listening*? Sarrow wants you dead, and he won't stop until he achieves that goal - unless you stop him first."

"It won't come to that," Melayne insisted.

Devra sighed. "It's no use, Corri," she said. "She's in flat denial. None of us are getting through to her. We may as well change the subject." She turned to Margone. "So, Sarrow called you thirteen dragon slayers together, and sent all of you off here? Does that mean that the thirteen of you are all the slayers there are?"

"Not exactly." Margone thought for a moment. "You have to understand that there was once a sort of brotherhood of dragon slayers, when there were more dragons about. It tends to be a family thing. My father trained me, and he was trained by his father, and so on. I don't think anybody is quite certain how many there are still around. It's a strenuous, dedicated training, so my village had to support my father and me. It wasn't a popular task, especially since there hadn't been any dragons around for so long. Some of the slayer lines probably died out over the generations. And it's not a profession that's affected by politics - a slayer from Morstan, for example, might have been called on to fight a dragon in Vester. Nobody cared what country he was from - it was the killing of dragons that mattered most." He gave Tura a gentle stroke. "Sorry, but that's the way things were."

"I'm not offended," Tura answered. "You're only humans, and you didn't know any better."

"I don't think that's true," Devra said, once Melayne had passed along the dragon's comments. "I think somebody knew very well that Talents are caused by dragon's shed scales, and they were trying to eradicate the Talents by destroying the source of the scales. This legend about them killing and eating people was spread to justify their slaughter, and to fool the slayers into thinking they were protecting humans."

"That might be so," agreed Margone. "I was always told that dragons were evil, malicious creatures that had to be destroyed." He glanced at Tura. "I'm learning very differently now that I've actually met a dragon. Anyway, my point is that nobody knows quite how many dragon slayers are left in the world. Sarrow sent out invitations to all he could trace, offering money and a chance to be useful again. When I left, there were more still arriving."

Melayne felt chilled. "More?" she asked. "How many more?"

"I don't know. We thirteen were just the first arrivals. Sarrow had bought and equipped a ship, and we were sent as the front-runners, and promised money and glory. We thought we were doing the right thing."

"Yeah, you were humanity's little golden boys," Devra growled. "But how many more were there when you left?"

"About twenty," Margone replied. "But, like I say, more were arriving all of the time."

Melayne was very glad she was sitting down. She felt faint at this news. "At least twenty more?" she asked, dazed.
"At least."

"We're in deep trouble," Devra announced. "If more slayers are on their way, I don't know how long we can hold them off. We're down to two fighting dragons, and even my Talents might not be able to fight so many men."

"Then we can't let them get here," Corri said firmly. "We know where they are right now - at Dragonhome. So why don't we go and stop them there?"

"Hello?" Devra yelled. "You think it will be easier to fight them when *they* are the ones in a castle? Even a half-demolished one?"

"Well, I wasn't thinking of *fighting* them exactly," Corri answered, blushing a bit. "I was thinking we might be able to persuade them to stop this insane crusade of theirs."

"Persuade them *how*?" Devra demanded. "They're on a holy mission, and on top of that they're being mind-controlled by Sarrow. Even if we could talk to them - which I doubt he'd allow - he can simply override their common sense by ordering them to attack anyway."

"I don't want to add to the problem," Margone said, hesitantly. "But I should tell you that Dragonhome isn't such a wreck any more. Sarrow's had workmen going over the place for the past couple of years. He's built back the outer walls and restored a lot of the defenses. By now, it's probably one of the toughest castles in all Farrowholme."

"Oh, wonderful," Devra growled. "This just keeps getting better and better. An army of slayers controlled by a mad kid in a working castle. Why don't we just surrender now?"

"We don't surrender," Melayne said firmly. "Ever."

Devra sighed. "I *knew* you'd say that," she complained. "The worse the odds, the more committed you are to the fight." she spread her hands. "So, do you have a plan?"

"I like Corri's idea," Melayne admitted. "We go there and talk them out of it."

"Am I the only one who thinks this is insane?" Devra demanded.

"No," Margone answered. "I agree with you - it won't work."

"Finally, someone with brains - and it has to be one of the enemy." Devra shook her head. "Melayne, I love you, but you're crazy."

"No," Melayne assured her. "Tura said that my Talent counters Sarrow's. If that's right, then his control over the slayers can be broken."

"*If* it's true," Devra said. "You haven't tried it on anyone but wimpy boy here yet. No offense, but I'd like something a bit stronger than the word of a dragon that you can stop him. Besides, that only stops Sarrow's influence. These slayers don't need any extra encouragement to come here anyway on their quest to slaughter dragons. Like kid slayer here said, they see it as their holy business. And you aren't going to just talk them out of it. At least, not before they kill you. And, besides, there's no way *you're* going on this mission. If it's a suicide mission, that's *my* job. You're a mother now - you have *two* kids that need you right here. You're going nowhere."

"I'm sorry, Devra, truly I am," Melayne replied. Her heart hurt at the thought, but she knew she was right. "I want almost more than anything to stay here and look after Cassary and my son. I wish that were possible - but it isn't. This force of slayers will certainly be headed this way soon - if there's not another bunch already under way. They will attack this island, and there will be more fighting and more deaths - because of me. If I weren't here, Darmen and his people wouldn't be in danger. So the best thing I can do for my children is to go and strike at the threat facing them. I have to do it for them, and for Darmen, and for the dragons. I *wish* I could stay here - truly I do - but I *can't*. I have to go up against Sarrow and his army. I know you're going to argue and howl and threaten, but my decision is final. I'm the only one who can make it, and I'm the only one who can stop Sarrow, if the dragons are right."

"They could be wrong," Devra pointed out.

"They could," Melayne agreed. "But it's all we have to go on right now. Whether you approve or not, I'm going back to Dragonhome."

Devra threw up her hands and sighed dramatically. "Great! Nursing mom and baby go off to war. That's brilliant!"

"My baby won't be going," Melayne answered. "Ysane will be staying here, and I'm going to leave my children with her. She's already nursing, so she'll be able to handle my son, too. And Cassary already loves her. So that's one problem solved."

"Only one," Devra snapped. "I can't begin to count how many others there are remaing."

Corri put her hand on her friend's arm. "Give it up," she suggested. "You *know* you're not going to win any argument with Melayne. She'll agree with every point you make - and then just do what she aims to anyway. You know that."

"Of course I know that!" Devra shouted. "But I have to at least *try* and make her see sense - for the first time in her life."

Melayne smiled. "I know you mean it for the best," she said. "But I've made my decision, and that's that. I am going to Dragonhome."

Devra gave another loud sigh. "Well, I'll be bringing the Talents along - maybe we'll be of some help."

"Yes," Corri agreed. "We won't let you go into this fight alone. And, for once, don't even *think* of arguing. Devra can be even more stubborn than you are - and that's not easy."

"I wouldn't dream of turning down your help," Melayne said, feeling warm from the offer. These were good people, and brave. She was proud that they were her friends. "This isn't going to be a simple task, so I'm going to need you along, I'm sure."

"I'm coming, too," Margone said.

"No, you're not," Devra said firmly. "Which part of *you're our prisoner* sounds like we're friends and allies?"

"I'm not your enemy," Margone insisted. "Since I've been helping to look after Tura, I've come to see that I've been in the wrong. This is partly my fault, and it's up to me to help resolve it. Besides, the decision isn't yours - it's Melayne's."

Devra whirled to face Melayne. "Don't you dare agree with him!" she insisted. "This whole business is mad enough without bringing along a potential traitor. Once he's off this island, who knows which side he'll decide he's on? And if he's with us, he'll be able to betray our strengths and weaknesses to Sarrow."

"He won't be a traitor," Melayne said. "I believe him."

"Of course you do," Devra yelled. "You believe in the best of everyone. But we can't take a chance."

"I've made my mind up."

Devra threw up her hands again. "Why do I bother?" she asked.

"I was wondering that," Corri said, grinning. "You know you always lose when you argue with Melayne. She can out-stubborn you. And that's no mean achievement."

Devra gave her a scowl. "You only just got through saying I can out-stubborn her."

Corri shrugged. "It's a tough call."

Devra turned back to Melayne. "All right - what's the plan? You do have a plan, right? You're not just thinking of marching up to the gate of the castle and demanding to speak to your brother, are you?"

Melayne shrugged. "Actually, yes, that's about as far as I've gotten."

"Oh, brother." Devra rolled her eyes. "I *really* have to come with you - you need someone with a few brains to help out here. Do you seriously think your brother would allow you into the castle?"

"Yes," Melayne answered. "I don't think he'd be able to resist gloating to my face what his plans are."

Devra paused a moment. "You know, you could be right there. And maybe we can take advantage of that." She considered, and then grinned. "Okay, Melayne - you call the shots, I know. But I'm the general here, right? You *will* listen to me? And pay attention, not just dismiss my thoughts out of hand?"

"I would never just dismiss anything you say," Melayne protested.

"No, you'd simply ignore me when I say something you don't like." Devra turned to Corri. "You'd better make sure the ship's ready to sail - I have a strong suspicion that her mightiness here aims to set off in the very near future."

"I wish it could be today," Melayne said. "But I'm practical - it had better be tomorrow." Her face fell. "I'd better not leave it longer than that - I don't know how I'm going to be able to say goodbye to my children as it is. If I wait longer, I might never want to go."

"And that's a bad thing?" Devra grumbled. "You know, we Talents could probably take that place apart without you having to be there."

"There are three things wrong with that idea," Melayne said. "First, it's my battle, and not yours. Second, I don't want the place demolished - it's my husband's home. I'd kind of like to give it back to him. And, third, you wouldn't last a second against Sarrow's Talent. He'd convince you to turn on each other and protect him."

"Only if we gave him a chance to open his mouth," growled Devra.

Melayne's eyes opened wide. "I don't want him hurt!"

"Of course you don't," Devra complained. "But can you seriously think of another way of stopping him? All he has to do is talk."

"Cut out his tongue?" Margone suggested.

Devra looked at him in surprise. "You know, maybe I was wrong about you - maybe you *do* have something you can do for us."

Melayne glared at them both. "That's enough of that. He's my kid brother, and I won't have him harmed."

"He's a real menace, and he won't hesitate to have you killed," Devra pointed out. "You're the only person we know of who can stop him - and he already knows that. He won't feel safe again while you're alive. He might let you into Dragonhome in order to gloat - but you have to be very clear on one point. There is absolutely no way he will ever allow you to walk out of there again."

Chapter Twelve

Sander made his way down the hill toward the field where the raider children were working. He was glad that Corran hadn't put up a fight over his plan, and had gone off to wait for his return. He wasn't too certain that what he had in mind would work, and he didn't want to expose his son to further danger. If the dragons hadn't insisted, he would never have allowed Corran along on this mission anyway.

The dragons... He wished he knew what had happened to them. It wasn't like Brek or Ganeth to desert them - but they were, after all, dragons. What made sense to them might not be so obvious to humans. He could only hope that both of them were well; he couldn't imagine anything that might be able to harm two dragons, even small ones.

He forced himself to forget about them for the moment. This was pleasant enough countryside, and from what he could see the crops were growing well. It was very domestic for a village of raiders. He'd expected to see warriors training, and ships being prepared for battle, not a bunch of children weeding crops. Of course, maybe in the village itself those activities were going on. He wouldn't know until he got there.

If he was allowed to get there.

One of the children paused in his work, and stared. He had caught sight of Sander approaching, and clearly didn't know what to make of it for the moment. He looked to be no older than Corran, thin and wiry, with a mat of thick blond hair. He called out something, and the others stopped working and followed his gaze. Sander kept walking down toward them, and gave them a cheery wave. Several of the children leaped to their feet, and a couple took off down the path that had to lead to the village. The others moved together in a protective huddle. One boy - perhaps twelve years old - drew a sword that was really too big for him to handle and stood in front of the others, obviously aiming to protect them.

Sander had arrived at the edge of the field now, and he carefully kept both hands in sight, well away from his own sword. These were children, and probably scared; there was no need to panic them. If they attacked him, he might have to hurt some of them, and that wouldn't help with what he had in mind. "Hello," he called out, walking forward slowly. "I'm a traveler, hungry and thirsty. I wonder if I might rest and refresh myself a while?"

The boy with the sword moved forward slightly. He needed both hands to hold the weapon up, and it shook unsteadily in his grip - more from its weight than the boy's fear, Sander suspected. "Who are you?" he demanded. His accent was a little thick, but intelligible.

"I told you, I'm a traveler. My name is Sander. This is the first village I've seen in days, and I'd like to just rest and maybe buy a little food." He looked around. The other children were in a protective group, but there was no sign of fear on their faces. Some looked concerned, others angry, but none of them showed fear. "I won't harm you."

"Darned right about that," the boy agreed. "You try and go for your sword and I'll gut you."

Sander very much doubted that - the boy was having trouble holding his sword, and he'd not be able to put up a good fight with it. He raised his hands again. "Easy, boy," he said gently. "I've no wish to fight anyone."

"What kind of a warrior are you?" the boy asked. There was puzzlement and scorn in his voice.

"The kind who doesn't like to hurt children," Sander replied.

"I'm not a child!" the boy snapped. "I'm twelve years old and a man."

"My apologies," Sander said. He didn't want to make the youth his enemy. "Do you have a name, then, man?"

"Kappo," the youngster said, sullenly. "Son of Rokar." The name meant nothing to Sander, but the boy obviously seemed to think it should. Sander assumed he was a raider chief or the equivalent. That was why his son was in charge of looking after the other children.

"Son of Rokar, I would like to talk with your father," Sander said.

"He wouldn't talk with a man like you," Kappo said scornfully. "He wouldn't talk with any man who is not prepared to fight."

"I'm prepared to fight," Sander said gently. "But not with children, and not with the son of Rokar. And not with men, unless provoked. I'm a gentle sort of man."

"That's no sort of man at all," Kappo answered. "A man must always be prepared to fight."

"I'm prepared," Sander assured him. "But not without need. And here there is no need. I am not come as an enemy, but to rest and visit."

"Gut him, Kappo," one of the other boys suggested.

"Yes," a girl agreed. "He's crazy."

Kappo looked as if he was seriously considering their advice. Fortunately, he didn't get the chance to make up his mind. There was the sound of a horn from further down the pathway. Sander couldn't see anyone, nor the village that had to be around there somewhere. The trees were too thick, and the path was not straight. But, clearly, people were coming from the village. Hopefully the adults would be a little more sensible and easier to talk to. These children seemed quite bloodthirsty and very suspicious.

Was it just them, he wondered, or was everyone here like this? And what would happen when the men of the village arrived? Would they listen, or would they condemn him as the children had, without thought? Maybe this hadn't been such a good idea, after all...

He could hear people approaching, and then, from around the bend in the pathway, came the child who had run for help, eagerly leading two new people - both clearly adults. They looked like the ones he'd seen the previous evening - an elderly man and a younger woman, probably in her mid-twenties. She wore a long dress of warm-looking material, and he wore a hide jacket over pants and a thick shirt. He had to be at least sixty, and he walked with a limp - but quickly, as if he'd had a long time to get used to it.

He carried his sword unsheathed also, and he looked better prepared to use it. The woman carried a long staff that looked to be more for fighting than support.

Sander stood easily, trying to project harmlessness. If a fight began, people were likely to get hurt, and he had no real wish to harm anyone. Plus, he'd hardly earn their cooperation or loosen their tongues by killing a few of them. So he kept his hands in clear sight, away from his sword.

"He's my captive," Kappo announced quickly.

"I'm nobody's captive," Sander said. "I'm just a traveler, looking to rest and buy food."

"You're a fool," the man growled. "There are no travelers. Whatever you are, you'll be dead soon."

"I don't mean anyone any harm," Sander said, gently. "I am just passing through."

"You'll pass no further," the man said. "Here you'll die."

Sander scowled. "I've never met less friendly people. What is wrong with you?"

" We stick together," the man announced. "All outsiders are our enemies."

"I'm not your enemy - unless you make me so." Sander looked from scowling face to scowling face. The children were staying their distance, but not even on the face of the youngest child was there any sort of kindness. He glared at the man. "Are you in charge of this inhospitable village?"

"For the moment," the man answered. He held his sword ready, but didn't seem to be an immediate threat. Sander was more worried about the woman, who was inching toward him, her staff firmly in her grasp. If she got close enough, a hefty swing from it might do some damage.

He looked her in the eyes. "No closer," he suggested.

"I'm not afraid of you," she spat.

"No, I can see that you aren't. And you have no reason to be, as long as you don't try and attack me." He looked around.

"What is wrong with you all? Don't you have any concept of hospitality?"

"We look after our own," the man said. "Not strangers."

Sander realized he'd get nothing from any of these people like this. They were too suspicious, too antagonistic. But what could he do? He had to find out what was going on in this place - why the Raiders were after Melayne, and what their purpose was. But it was clear that nobody here was going to talk to him. "Very well," he said. "If that is how you feel, I shall go on to the next village. Perhaps they will be more welcoming."

"I wouldn't count on it," the old man growled. "They're three days walk from here, and they, too, follow the Burning God."

"Who?"

"As I thought." The man spat on the ground again. "A heretic."

"Heretic or stranger, it makes little difference," Kappo said. "Let's gut him now." He moved closer, as did the old man. That was quite enough. Sander drew his own sword, and stood ready. "I don't want to fight," he said, gently. "But I will defend myself if I must."

The old man limped forward, and swung his broadsword. It was a skilled blow from a man who had clearly trained as a warrior in his day. If he'd been thirty years younger, it would have been a killing blow. But now, his limp and bone-ache in his shoulder conspired to rob the move of much of its skill. Sander moved aside, and as the sword whistled harmlessly past him, he struck out at the man with the butt of his own weapon. He caught the old man in his aching shoulder. With a cry of pain, his attacker dropped his sword and collapsed to the ground.

Sander caught the flicker of movement from the corner of his eye as Kappo attacked. As he'd suspected, though, the sword was too heavy for the boy to use with any skill. Still, even a blow from the blade, no matter how skillessly delivered, would cut. Sander moved out of the way of the blow, and poised to strike back.

But Kappo was just a boy, and Sander had no real desire to hurt the child. The second of delay proved to be his undoing. He didn't even see the blow from the woman's staff that slammed across the back of his knees and sent him tumbling to the ground. He did see - but couldn't block - the second, which crashed painfully into his right arm. He felt fire along his muscles, and his grip loosened on his sword.

The third blow stopped just short of crushing his throat. The woman stood, one foot on his heaving chest, the end of her staff just an inch above his larynx. "One move from you, and I kill you," she hissed. Sander stayed perfectly still, trying to ignore the pain in his right arm.

"He's mine," Kappo cried, recovering and moving closer.

"No," the woman said. "I am the one who bested him - he is *mine*." She glared at the old man, obviously daring him to disagree. "That is my right. He is mine, and I say he does not die."

"Thank you," Sander said.

She glared down at him. "Don't thank me - you may regret that I spared you. You are my slave, and you will work for me. That is all you are, and all you will do, from this moment on. Do you understand?"

Sander did. If he argued, she would crush his throat with one blow, and he would not be able to stop her. On the other hand, if he were her captive, then perhaps she'd actually talk to him. It might be the best way to learn what was happening in this village. "I understand," he said.

"Good." She glanced around. One of the other boys had picked up Sander's sword, and the old man had recovered his own. "I will let you up, but if you try to fight further, you will be killed. If you do not do exactly what I tell you, you will be killed. Do you understand?"

"Yes."

She took her foot from his chest and moved the staff aside. "Then get to your feet, stranger."

"My name is Sander," he told her, as he rose, rather painfully.

"I'm not interested. You are simply my slave. You will obey orders or -"

"I will die. Yes, I understood that part." He looked around the circling villagers. As before, there were no gazes that were less than antagonistic. Most were contemptuous. "Well, what are your orders?"

"You will come with us," the woman said. "To the village. Tomar will watch you, as will I."

"Do you have a name?" he asked her.

"Everyone has a name. I am your owner now, and you will call me Lady."

"As you wish - Lady." She gestured him forward, and Tomar limped ahead of him, clutching his sword fiercely - but not using the arm that Sander had hit.

The woman moved behind Sander, her staff held ready to strike if need be. She glanced back at Kappo and the other children. "You have your work to do," she growled. "Get back to it. We shall deal with the stranger."

Kappo scowled. "I found him," he protested.

"And I bested him - not you." The woman glared. "Back to your work - *child*."

Kappo glared at her sullenly, but held his tongue. That was probably wise - Sander was sure she could beat the boy easily if he pushed for a fight. It was clear that Kappo knew this also - and deeply resented the fact. After a moment, he moved back toward the field; the other children followed behind. The woman tapped Sander, none too gently, with her staff. Sander got the message, and moved off after the old man.

As they walked the path, Sander examined the pair of them. The man had once been a warrior, that was clear. The limp was no doubt due to a battle wound, as there were several scars visible in areas of exposed skin. He'd been through many battles before reaching this age. He had known how to handle his sword, and if his shoulder and leg had not betrayed him, he could have been a real problem to fight.

The woman, too, was clearly a fighter. He could see that she was slender, and that her muscles were as hard as any man's.

Without that suspicious scowl on her face she might have been pretty enough. She couldn't have been in more than her mid-twenties, but she looked ten years older. Life here was clearly not soft.

The pathway ran about half a mile, and then came out above a river. This had cut a deep ravine down to the sea over the centuries, and the pathway now led downward. Along the near side of the river was the village. The houses were of sturdy wood, some painted in places, but most plain. He counted about thirty in view, many of them with small paddocks. He could see cows and a few wiry horses. There were people, too - not a lot, considering the size of the village - maybe twenty or so. There were more than forty houses and one building much larger and more ornate than the rest that he assumed acted as a sort of community meeting place or church.

As they drew nearer, some of the villagers stopped to look at the approaching trio. Sander saw that they were all like his captors - either older men with evidence of injuries received in fighting, or else women. Some of the latter were old, but many were about the age of the woman behind him. Two of the women were pregnant, and he felt a terrible pang as he thought of Melayne.

Conspicuous by their absence were any younger men. There wasn't a single man under fifty to be seen.
The river was wide and slow moving as it crawled the last couple of miles to the sea. There were jetties built out into the water, but only a handful of small fishing vessels, none built for more than about five men. Or, in this case, more likely women. There was certainly anchorage for larger vessels, as the water looked clear and deep. This had to be the village that the Raiders who had attacked Far Holme.

And, suddenly, he understood why there were no men to be seen.

"Are all your men at sea?" he asked his captor. She glared at him, but didn't reply, simply urging him on with a gesture. "Off raiding some helpless foreign land and slaughtering innocents?" he added, hoping to provoke a response.

It did, but from Tomar. The old man half-turned and glowered at him. "They are on the business of the Burning God."

"So this Burning God of yours is the one who wants women and children murdered? Sounds like a real nice sort of god."

"You're a heretic," Tomar said, spitting. "Otherwise you'd have known about the Burning God."

So that ignorance had helped to give him away. Well, it hardly mattered - it was clear from the "welcome" he had received that any outsider was considered an enemy here. "Tell me about him," Sander suggested.

"There's no need for outsiders to understand him," the woman said, angrily. "He's not for the likes of you."

"But it's his will that sent your men away," Sander said. "And maybe this time, they won't ever return."

"They always return," the woman answered, but he could detect an edge of fear in her voice. He realized that this was a constant possibility in the lives of these people - that their men might someday never come home.

As they wouldn't; Sander had helped to kill them all. He felt an irrational flush of guilt, which he killed immediately. The men from this village had died because they had attacked what they had believed to be helpless victims. They had *deserved* death - even if it had left their wives widows and their children orphans. Now might not be the best time to mention this, however.

"They do the will of the Burning God," Tomar stated. "The God will keep them safe."

"This Burning God..." Sander said slowly, as another thought occurred to him. "Does he fling fire about from time to time?"

"We do not speak of him with outsiders," the woman said firmly.

"Only," Sander went on, "I passed a Raider ship a few days back. Everyone aboard it had been burned to death. Just the sort of death that an annoyed deity might have sprung on them."

The woman whipped up her staff, and slammed him across the back with it. Sander stumbled and fell, his back a field of pain. "Blasphemer!" she yelled. "The Burning God would not punish us! We serve his will."

"Well, *somebody* burned them all to death," Sander replied, gasping. His eyes refused to focus, and he was trembling from the agony in his muscles. "Your Burning God just seemed like a good candidate."

He'd gone too far. The woman raised her staff, ready to batter him again. He didn't have the strength to fight back - or to even stand. To his surprise, Tomar moved between him and the furious woman.

"Enough, Magga," he said, roughly. "What's the point of beating a slave to death? He can do no work if he's dead."

Sander was surprised by the rescue, but it did make sense not to slaughter a slave. Without young men, this village would need all the able-bodied help it could get. It made perfect sense to keep him alive, and to force him to work.

Which might not be as bad as it sounded. People here wouldn't watch what they said around a lowly slave. If he paid attention, he might be able to learn more as a slave than he would have done as a guest. Of course, to make any use of what he learned, he'd have to somehow escape from these people. And, right now, he didn't have any idea how he might go about that.

The woman, Magga, hesitated, and then nodded. "You're right, Tomar - killing him would be pointless. Working him to death makes better sense." She glared down at Sander. "And I aim to do just that."

Obviously there was no lenient treatment of slaves here...

Chapter Thirteen

A surprising amount of progress had been made very quickly for her trip. Melayne's head was still in a bit of a whirl. Once her decision had been made - and Devra had argued against it every step of the way - the Talents and Darmen's men had gotten together to implement the decision. The Talents' ship had been brought ashore and given a thorough examination by the locals. A little work had been needed before it had been declared sound enough for another voyage. Melayne didn't envy the men who had been set to work scraping the shellfish off the hull. Then provisions for the three-day crossing had been loaded, and the ship readied to sail again.

Meanwhile, Melayne had considered who was to go with them, and who would remain. Ysane had agreed without a moment's thought to take care of Cassary and the baby. "I've put on enough weight while I was pregnant with Falma," she told her friend. "I've milk enough for two, and certainly love enough for three. Don't you worry about either of them." Then her face fell. "I just wish I could be coming with you, Melayne. You might need me."

Melayne was touched, and she laid her hand gently over Ysane's. "I need far more the knowledge that my children are safe," she said. "It will enable me to focus on the mission at hand. There is no other person in this world I would entrust my children to - and I will have absolute certainty that they will be safe with you. Ysane, with Sander and Corran gone, I *must* have my children safe."

"I understand. And they will be." Ysane smiled. "So, you'll be taking Bantry, though? He'll fight like a lion."

"No, Bantry stays." Melayne held up a hand before Ysane could protest. "Aside from the fact that you need him, this island does. He's the best fighter left here now that Sander is gone. I'm praying that once I've left the raids will cease - but in case I'm wrong, I want Far Holme as strongly protected as it can be. For the same reason, the dragons will be staying."

"They're not going to like that."

"No, they're not." Melayne knew she was going to have to have a fight with the dragons over that decision. "But, again, aside from the fact that I need them here to protect you, the children and Darmen and his people - well, if they go along with us, they'll be targets. Aside from the fact that every human on the mainland will want them dead, they'll prevent us from moving about unchallenged. It's important that we get to Dragonhome as swiftly as we can, and taking dragons along will be counterproductive. They are staying, no matter what they may think."

They thought a lot, and said more. Tura led the arguments, even though she was unable to travel herself. "Shath and Loken will protect you," she insisted.

"They might *wish* to," Melayne answered. "But they will draw unwanted attention to us, and they will be targets for the next batch of dragonslayers. I will be safer if they stay here. Tura, I *know* you all want to protect me - but you protect me best by doing this my way."

Eventually, despite their fears and wishes, the dragons reluctantly agreed to remain behind. Melayne had forced them to promise that they wouldn't simply wait and follow along after her. Shath and Loken had been reluctant to promise this, confirming for Melayne that this had been their secondary plan. Eventually, though, they had given their word to remain in the Far Islands and not to follow.

And that left only Devra to argue with - and she would be much harder to convince. Melayne asked around about her, and finally tracked her to the kitchen, where Devra was organizing the supplies they'd need for the trip. The Talent looked up as Melayne entered, and almost managed a smile.

"Just the person," she said briskly. "I'm getting the food together we'll need, and it would help if I knew how many I was planning for."

Melayne winced. Straight to the point she'd been hoping to broach slowly and carefully. Oh well! "Four, I guess."

"Four?" Devra looked stunned.

"You, me, Corri and Margone," Melayne answered.

Devra stared at her coldly. "Four people?" she repeated. "We're going to attack Sarrow with just *four people*?"

"No." Melayne shook her head. "I thought I'd made that clear - we are *not* attacking Sarrow. We're going to talk to him. If we took more people along, he'd likely think we *were* there to attack him. With just the four of us, he'll know that's not the case."

"Are you insane?" Devra yelled. The kitchen help all paused to stare in their direction, and Devra glared back at them. "What? You don't have work to do, so you're eavesdropping on a private conversation?"

"I hardly think they're eavesdropping," Melayne pointed out. "I think they can hear you perfectly clearly back in Farrowholme."

"That's not the point." Devra's glares had sent most of the servants scurrying back to work. "The point is that this is a private conversation."

"Maybe we should go somewhere alone where you can yell, then?" Melayne suggested.

"Good idea." Devra grabbed her arm and hurried her from the kitchen. As they walked, she ranted. "Let's see if I can get this through your thick skull: Sarrow has orders out for his men to kill you on sight. The only reason this first batch of slayers didn't get you is that they didn't know who you were until after they were captured. And even then, they almost managed to kill you. Arrow in the stomach - you do remember that bit, don't you?"

"I'll never be able to forget it," Melayne promised. She was still sore, and the simple thought of it sent chills rushing through her body.

"Well, next time he's going to try harder, and he'll have lots more men around to use. You're going to be a pincushion, you moron. We need to take along our own army."

"Don't be impractical," Melayne begged. "We don't *have* an army. Darmen needs all of his men here to protect his people - I can't take any of them. And you only brought a handful of

Talents. Anyway, we don't have the supplies for an army on the march, even if we had an army. And it would move too slowly. What we have to do is to get to Dragonhome quickly and settle this affair before it gets out of hand. And the less of us there are, the faster we can travel. So - four is perfect."

"Before it gets out of hand?" Devra repeated. "Melayne, Sarrow's sending men to slay the dragons and kill you. He's taken over Dragonhome and rebuilding it as a fortress. I'd say it's *already* out of hand."

"Then it's up to us to contain it. As I said, fast and lean - so, again, the smaller the group, the better. See, even you have to agree with that."

Devra looked ready to scream. "I can't guarantee your safety with so few people. Especially since one of them could actually be on Sarrow's side and is just lying to you so he can betray you." She clearly still didn't trust Margone.

"He's not lying," Melayne said firmly. "My Talent ensures that he couldn't do that. He's not a bad person, he's just been misguided in the past. Now he's starting to understand which side he should really be on."

"Well, Sarrow's not going to be happy to discover that you can reclaim people from his clutches. If he sees Margone with us, he'll know you can undo his Talent of Persuasion."

"That's fine - he's bound to discover that anyway. If he understands it from the start, then -"

"Then he'll be more determined to kill you, you idiot," Devra growled. "Don't forget, the reason he's doing most of this is to feel safe. If he knows you can counter his commands that's going to make him feel very unsafe indeed. He's bound to take that out on you."

"All right," Melayne said. "Let's say for the moment that you're completely correct. What would be your solution to all of this?"

"Mine?"

"Yes." Melayne smiled gently. "You don't like my plan - so what's yours? How would you handle this?"

"I'd get a bloody army!" Devra yelled.

"From where?" Melayne countered. "With what? You have to pay an army, and then you have to equip them, and arrange for supplies. That would take lots of money - which we don't have. Lots of men - which we don't have. And lots of time - which we don't have. Any more bright ideas?"

Devra squirmed. "Just because I don't have a better idea doesn't mean yours is a good one."

"It's the only one we've got," Melayne said firmly. "It's what I'm going with. If you don't think it will work and would rather not come along, then I'll understand."

"Not come along?" Devra looked offended. "I've got to come along - who else will look after your stupid hide?"

"Then stop complaining," Melayne said. "Four people - now you can organize the supplies properly. We'll be taking horses, so you can pack for a few extra days after we land."

Devra glared at her again. "I don't know how I let you talk me into these things," she said, darkly. "But I promise you this - if you get me killed, I'm coming back to haunt you."

"I wouldn't have it any other way." Melayne grinned. "You'd probably make a really good ghost, you know - rattling chains and haunting people would be just the sort of thing you're good at."

"And I may soon get some practice in." She sighed and shook her head. "Melayne, I don't know how you do it. Despite my best efforts, you always win every argument we have."

"Then maybe you should stop arguing with me and just do what I suggest from the start."

"And miss all the fun parts?" Devra grinned. "Are you *sure* your Talent isn't really Persuasion? It might explain a lot..." She waved a hand. "Well, if all you'll let me do is pack food, I'm going to make absolutely certain it's the best damned food you'll ever have."

Melayne watched her leave with affection. Despite all her complaints and protests, Devra was nowhere near as ornery as she tried to pretend. And she knew the girl was someone she could depend on, utterly and always. Once again, she felt that she really didn't deserve such good friends as she had.

All of the activity, of course, was partly a cover for her bottled-up emotions. She was dreading the moment when she had to leave. She had no option, she knew, but leaving Cassary and the baby was going to be the hardest thing she had ever done. Allowing Sander and Corran to go on their own quest had been bad enough - she had real trouble sleeping without Sander next to her in bed - but to leave her children...!

Cassary was solemnly wise, despite her few years, and she seemed to understand when Melayne explained to her that she had to leave on a trip. "You have to be brave, sweetheart," Melayne told her.

"I am brave," Cassary replied, looking stubborn.

"I know you are," Melayne said, smiling. "And I need you to help auntie Ysane to look after the baby."

"I will," her daughter promised. "Can I hold him?"

"Probably not for a little while," Melayne replied. "But you can sit with him."

Cassary nodded. "I will."

Melayne gave her daughter a hug. This was so hard... Ysane, however, had everything organized, obviously hoping to minimize Melayne's separation pains. She insisted on moving the baby's cradle into her own room, next to Falma's. "Have to be certain they'll get along," she insisted.

"Ysane, they're *babies*," Melayne growled. "Do you think they're going to start fighting each other?"

"They're boys," Ysane replied. "Who can tell?"

"Liar," Melayne said, without any rancor. "You just want to get me used to not having the baby around, don't you?"

"So? It seems like a good idea. You're going to have to leave him anyway, so let's get you used to it slowly." Falma abruptly started howling. "Feeding time, I guess." Ysane looked down at Melayne's child, who looked back at her, soundlessly. "Doesn't he ever cry for food?"

Melayne felt another stabbing pain in her soul. "Ysane, he doesn't cry for *anything*. Since he was born, he's been silent." She was trying not to let her fears get the better of her, but she knew she could be honest with her friend. "I'm scared that his mind was damaged when I was shot. It's not natural for babies not to cry - not even when he's hungry."

Ysane had started Falma suckling. She watched as Melayne picked up her baby and attached him to a nipple. "He's eating," she pointed out.

"He has a good appetite," Melayne agreed. "But he's so silent."

"Don't complain - I'm still getting used to being woken up all night long."

"But there must be something wrong with him," Melayne said, her voice soft and terrified.

"Nonsense. He seems healthy enough, and the doctors say he's fine. Even that Talent, Hovin, can't detect anything wrong. Maybe he's just a naturally quiet child."

"Ysane, this baby is *unnaturally* quiet."

"If there's anything really wrong with him, we'll find it out," the blonde girl said firmly. "We have the best people here, and they all will do their utmost for your child. So stop worrying. And, incidentally, isn't it time you *named* him? We can't just call him *baby* all his life."

Melayne shook her head. "I won't name him alone - it has to be a joint decision with Sander."

Ysane sighed and looked down at the child. "Then I guess he's going to be *baby* for a while, since both of his parents are off a-questing."

"Don't remind me." Melayne felt chilled again.

"It has to be done," Ysane said, softly. "Even I agree to that. You don't have to like it, but you really have no choice. Darmen's been really good to us, and we can't allow all of these people to keep invading his land because of us."

"Because of *me*, you mean," Melayne said. "I know. I *have* to go. But it won't be easy."

Ysane stroked Melayne's hair. "If it was easy, *anyone* could do it. Because it's hard, it has to be you. You're the most wonderful and smart person I've ever met. You'll sort this out, somehow."

"I just wish I had your faith in me. I feel so inadequate."

"Then *stop*. You'll sort out Sarrow, you'll stop the slayers and you'll return for your children and the rest of us. I *know* that - and I don't care what you think. That's simply the way it will be."

Melayne smiled at her friend. "Oh, Ysane, I am *so* glad that I know you. You do wonders for my spirits."

"That's me - spirit girl." Ysane grinned, and then grimaced. "Ouch." She looked down at Falma, who was sucking greedily. "You little brat - that hurt. Do you think he's teething already?"

"Not unless he's *really* precocious," Melayne answered. "Maybe he's just got really, really hard gums." They spent the next twenty minutes talking babies and feeding their children. Despite her fears, it felt good. Melayne was still bothered by the silence from her child, but Ysane was right - he seemed happy enough, and his eyes were bright and alert, and he did seem to be well.

If only he would *scream* or cry, instead of lying there solemnly.

Her last task before going to bed was to visit Tura. Thankfully, there was further sign of improvement in the dragon, which meant at least one bright spot in her current sea of problems. Melayne cuddled down beside her dragon, careful not to stress the wound. Tura's long neck bent, and the dragon's head nuzzled her.

"You're upset, I know," Tura said, gently. "And I understand why."

"Oh, Tura," Melayne breathed. "I don't know if I can do this. Leave you. Leave my children, my friends."

"Nonsense." Tura glared at her. "You know very well that in the morning you will get on that ship and sail off to face your brother. There's simply nothing else that you can do. And you will be brave as you go, because that's the sort of person you are. You can't let your hatchlings see you upset, so you'll do it with a smile on your face, even if it might slip at any moment. I *know* you, child - and I know that is what you will do because that is what you *must* do. You must trust those of us you leave behind to do the best we can, also. Don't worry about me - I shall heal. I feel stronger every day - and you know that I cannot lie to you. And your children will do well. Ysane is a good person, and caring, and will look after them as well as she does her own hatchling. You *must* believe that - because you cannot go up against your brother and his army if you are worrying yourself sick over us. You *must* trust, and you *must* act. That is all there is to it."

"I wish that was all there was to it," Melayne agreed. "But I simply can't overcome my fears by trust."

"You humans are so frail," the dragon murmured. "Not only to external troubles, but internal ones also. We dragons are not like that - when we make a decision, we accept it, and we get on with matters. You should be more like us."

"I wish I could be. But we humans are constantly fighting our fears, no matter how much faith we have."

Tura's snout tweaked in what Melayne was almost certain was amusement. "It's a very silly system; you should stop doing it."

Melayne cuddled the long head. "Oh, Tura, I shall miss you."

"And I you." The dragon sniffed. "But I shall not worry about it. You will return triumphant, or else not. Worrying will not aid you, and it will only impair me, so I shall not indulge in it. I shall focus on recovering, so that as soon as possible I shall be at fighting strength. If you do not need my strength - well, then, nothing will be lost. But if you should, I shall be prepared. Is that not a much better way of living than worrying?"

"Yes," Melayne agreed. "Yes, it is. And I wish I could do it myself. I'm sure I'd be a stronger person for it."

"You are already the strongest human being I have ever known," Tura replied. "Perhaps it is good that you have a weakness - otherwise you might prove to be insufferable."

Melayne couldn't help but laugh. "Oh, Tura - you do help me so."

"It is what friends are for, is it not?" the dragon asked. "Now, in the interests of improving your efficiency, I believe you require rest. And also shared time with your children, before you are forced to leave them in the care of your best friend." A large dragonish eye stared into her face. "Without doubts, and without fears."

"I shall try," Melayne promised. But to herself she added: *And I shall fail...*

Chapter Fourteen

Corran was worried about his father. He was also slightly hungry - the jerky was tough, and not really filling - and he was wishing he had something else to eat. And, to be perfectly honest, he was *bored*. He'd obeyed his father's wishes and stayed away from the raider settlement for the past two days, but it was *dull* just waiting and waiting when nothing was happening. There was still no sign of the dragons, and now he didn't even have his father to be with.

None of which was at all a good excuse for what he was doing, of course. He was disobeying his father's instructions and heading back toward the settlement. His father had been sure he wasn't going to be killed by the raiders - but Corran was by no means as certain. They were killers, after all, and no matter how clever Lord Sander might be, things could always go wrong. What if his father was tied up and waiting to be executed? He might be needing Corran's help...

Of course, if he *didn't*, then father was likely to be very mad with him...

But he simply *couldn't* sit around and do nothing. It left his worries and fears much too much spare time to give him horrible visions about what might have happened to his father - and the two dragons. Knowing nothing about either meant he was scared for both. So he needed to know *something*. Since he didn't have a clue where the dragons were, or why they hadn't returned, that left only his father. Corran knew where Sander had to be - if he hadn't been killed - and checking up on him would only require patience and skill. Corran wasn't certain he had the skill, but he had plenty of time to carefully check the village.

So he came to the copse of trees where he had parted from his father two days before and looked down at the fields below. As before, there were children his age and younger toiling away. Obviously growing vegetables was a long, hard business! He was glad he wasn't a farmer, because he was certain he'd never have the patience to do such a chore. The youngsters were simply going through the rows of crops, pulling out weeds, and making sure the right plants were growing strongly. It seemed even more dull than sitting around chewing tough jerky.

On the far side of the fields was the pathway to the settlement. If he swung around through the edge of the woods, staying in the shade, he should be able to get near to the pathway without being seen. The children were giving their attention to their chores, so there was no reason for any of them to look in his direction. So, slowly and carefully, avoiding any dead branches he might step on - which would make a loud noise in this still air - he worked his way through the woods, always watching the fields. He was in no great hurry, and taking his time meant he was less likely to give himself away, so he moved slowly. At one point an older girl came into the fields and handed out cups of what he assumed was water. That reminded him to take a small drink from his water flask. Other than that, there seemed to be nothing happening.

Which was certainly a good thing. He reached the pathway shortly before the girl left again. From careful concealment, he watched her walk back to the village. She was about fourteen, he guessed, and her clothes were thick but a little faded, and obviously old. Her long hair was tied back, and she didn't look back once as she strode back to the village with her water jug. Corran slipped through the trees, watching as she moved away. He was certain the pathway was the one he needed now, and could afford to take his time. He stayed about twenty feet inside the woods, so that the pathway was only marginally visible to him. If anyone else were to come along, he'd be able to hide without trouble. The girl was out of sight within moments, and he relaxed. He was doing this very well, he thought. Father would be proud of him - except, if he found out that Corran had done this, he was much more likely to be mad at him.

Corran missed his father. Until Melayne had come along, there had been no other person he felt close to. He was so glad that Melayne was his stepmother, because he felt very comfortable and safe with her. Maybe not like he would have been had his real mother lived, but very similar, he was sure. He missed Melayne, and the dragons, and everyone he'd left behind on Far Holme. Then he felt annoyed at himself for such a weakness - that was no way for a *man* to behave! Well, perhaps he wasn't a man yet, but he was eight, and he was heir to Dragonhome, and Lord Sander's son, and he had to be strong.

Then he came to a sudden halt, and panic flooded through him.

The girl was standing in the woods directly ahead of him, staring at him, and adjusting her long skirt. Her face was flushed, and Corran realized he'd made a terrible blunder, lost in his thoughts. She must have stepped into the woods to pee... and then spotted him.

Now he was in serious trouble, because she had seen him, and her mouth was opening to scream for help... He'd let his father down, and he was going to get captured, all because he'd let this girl *see* him!

If only she *couldn't* see him!

That was dumb, of course, because she obviously could. He'd ruined *everything*, and was about to be captured and wreck his father's plans.

Only...

The girl frowned, and closed her mouth. Then she blinked, and looked around.

"That's odd," she muttered. "I could have *sworn*..." She shook her head, and looked around again, and then finished adjusting her skirt. She picked up the water jug she'd laid beneath a tree, and slung it across her shoulders. "The next thing you know, I'll be seeing firedrakes..." Spinning around, she walked off, back toward the path.

Corran didn't move. He simply stood still, shocked. *She hadn't seen him!*

Well, no - she *had* seen him - and then she *hadn't*. She had thought she had been seeing things... Which made no sense at all. What had just happened? It was like he'd suddenly...

And then he *knew*. Finally, crazily, his Talent had appeared! His father had told him years ago that he had shown signs of having a strong Talent, but that nobody was sure what it was. That was the only explanation! His Talent was Invisibility! Excitement flooded through him, and he forgot his quest as he exulted in his newfound ability. He could become Invisible! How incredible was that? He could play tricks on people, and they'd never be able to see who had done it... And, right now, he could become the greatest spy in existence - he could go anywhere, and never be seen!

This was so awesome! He was Invisible!

Then a squirrel looked at him, squawked, and shot up a tree.

Corran's excitement died. He *wasn't* invisible any more. The squirrel had definitely seen him - but the girl hadn't. No, wait, the girl *had* seen him, and then he'd wished she couldn't and *then* she didn't. Maybe he was only invisible if he kept thinking about it?

Or, maybe, he wasn't actually *invisible*. After all, he had been able to see his body all the time, even when the girl couldn't. So it wasn't that he had vanished. Maybe he could just make it so that people couldn't see him. Or, maybe, simply not notice him.

He had a vague memory about something like that from a book he and Melayne had once read. It had been a collection of stories about Talents. He'd asked her about Talents once, and he'd wondered what possible powers he might have. And Melayne had found a book filled with stories about Talents and their adventures, and had helped him to read it. It had been written a long time ago, before Talents had been seen as dangerous, and to be killed off. And there had been a story, he was sure, about a boy who had been able to make himself Unseen.

That was it - Unseen!

That was the power.

The book had been annoying, though, he remembered. It was one of those whose author seemed to think that every story for children had to have a moral to it, and some of them were really, really obvious. But it had been the only collection that had stories about Talents at all, so they had endured the nonsense. Corran remembered that the story had been about a boy who was Unseen, but he was a bad boy. He had hated to do as he was told, and used his Talent to be mischievous and to get out of doing his chores and such. He particularly used it when it was bath night, so he never had to take a bath. And, as a result, he discovered that he might well be Unseen, but he wasn't Unsmelled, and his parents had been able to find and catch him, and force him to take a bath.

It had been a very silly story - but there *was* an important lesson to learn from it. He was Unseen, but people could still *hear* him if he made a noise. They might think it was just their imagination - but they might not. Especially if they knew that being Unseen was a Talent. So he would still have to be pretty careful - but he had an advantage now that he knew what his Talent was. With luck, he could slip into the village and find his father without anyone being any the wiser...

He walked carefully through the woods, following the line of the path. He considered just using the path, which would certainly be faster and easier, but realized that it was just too dangerous. He didn't yet know if his Talent operated on more than one person at a time, and if he ran into two people, that might be more than he could handle. It was safer for now to stick to staying hidden, and experiment with the limits of his Talent later, when he was safer.

It wasn't long before he saw the settlement below him. There were surprisingly nice houses lining the sides of a river, and steep cliffs guarding the way down to the water. He could see a jetty lunging out into the river, but the ship that was supposed to dock there was missing.

It was undoubtedly the one sunk back at the Far Isles. Corran felt deep satisfaction at that. These horrible people had tried to kill Melayne, and instead they'd suffered what they had planned for her. It served them right.

He watched, carefully, from hiding. There didn't seem to be a lot of activity going on in the village. Every now and then a woman would come out of a house to collect water, or sticks, or to hang laundry. Sometimes an old man, or one who was crippled, would walk between the houses. But there were no young, strong men at all to be seen. Had *everyone* left the village as a raider? Was that why there were no young men?

One odd thing Corran could see intrigued him, and he crept closer to get a better look at it. It was a large framework made of wood, positioned over a fire that several of the older men kept smoking. When he moved closer, Corran could see that there were lots of fish on the framework, being smoked. He realized that it was so that the food would be preserved, and could be kept for when there were no fish to catch. The same was obviously being done with the vegetables and fruits from the fields. He'd seen similar things done back at Darmen's castle, readying supplies for the winter.

Then he saw his father! He had to keep himself from crying out, both in pleasure and alarm. Sander looked a bit tired, but other than that he seemed fine.

If you didn't count the ropes that bound his ankles together. They were only about eighteen inches long, so Sander was forced to walk with a sort of shuffling gait. Corran realized it was to prevent his father from running away - if he tried to flee, even an old man could outrun him. Corran forced himself to watch, angrily, as his father carrying wood for the fires over to the old men who watched the smoking. He couldn't hear what was said, but he saw his father drop the load he had and then move off, shuffling, to fetch more.

His father was a *slave* here! Sander, Lord of Dragonhome, a mere slave! Anger boiled up inside Corran. He wanted to rush down and free his father - but he knew that would cause trouble. The other men in the village might be old, or lame, but they all had swords or long knives at their waists, and they would cut down his father at the slightest hint of trouble, he knew. So he had to be more subtle.

The first thing he needed to do was to let his father know he was here, and that he had discovered what his Talent was at last. Then he could sneak into one of the houses and find and take some sort of a weapon to help Sander to escape. Then, together, they would get the bonds of his father's legs and flee. It seemed like a good plan, so Corran watched his father carefully. Sander was getting the wood from a small pile under a sort of awning at the side of one of the houses. That gave Corran an idea - if he could sneak closer and somehow set fire to the wood that was left, it would burn the house as well. That would be a good distraction when they needed to flee the village. It was a shame that the houses were all spread out, though - probably to prevent fires from spreading, since the houses were all made from wood. If they'd been closer, he might have had a chance to burn down the whole village, which would serve these horrible people right.

Still, now he had a plan. He moved slowly and carefully closer to the woodpile, watching his father being forced to carry armloads of the wood to the fish smokers. All the time, Corran kept a watchful eye on the other houses. He knew his power worked close-up, but he wasn't sure how far its influence extended. If a woman coming from a house saw him at a distance, he might not be able to become Unseen. So he still had to hide and sneak down, just in case. His Talent was a good one, but until he knew its limitations, he had to be careful. Finally, though, he made it.

Of course, he reached the woodpile when his father had just left it, so he had to be patient just a short while longer. It seemed like forever, though, before Sander reappeared, ready for another load of the wood. Corran winced - his father looked so tired and filthy from carrying the wood, and he hobbled along because of the hobbles around his ankles.

"Father!" he called, as loudly as he dared. He couldn't risk being heard.

But it was loud enough. Sander's head jerked around, questing. Corran moved slightly from where he was hiding behind the pile of wood. Sander's eyes opened wide with alarm, and he shuffled forward as fast as he could. "What are you doing here?" he breathed. "I told you to wait and hide."

"I *am* hiding." Corran felt a little annoyed that his father didn't seem to be pleased to see him. "Better than I ever imagined."

"You've got to get out of here," his father snapped. "If they see you -"

"They won't," Corran interrupted him. "I've discovered my Talent at last - I can become Unseen."

"Unseen?" That gave his father pause. "You're sure?"

There was one way to prove it. Corran moved into the open, but still where only his father could see him. Then he willed himself Unseen.

Sander's face was quite comical. He stared at where he *knew* Corran was, and looked extremely confused. He shook his head and then looked again. "Corran?" he called, hesitantly. Then he shook his head a second time. "I must be imagining things," he muttered. "I could have sworn..."

Corran stopped using his Talent. His father jumped as Corran must have appeared to have suddenly become visible. "Told you." He grinned happily.

"Yes." Sander looked confused for a moment. "Your Talent is quite powerful," he admitted. "Even though I *knew* I had been talking to you, when you turned Unseen, I was quite convinced that you had been no more than a figment of my imagination..."

"That's excellent!" Corran said, grinning. "It means even if someone sees me, if I go Unseen, then they'll believe that they didn't see me."

"It certainly seems that way," Sander agreed. "But don't start getting careless because of it."

"I won't," Corran promised. "But now I *can* do it, I can rescue you."

"No," Sander said, "not yet."

Corran frowned. "Whyever not? Surely you don't *like* being a slave?"

Sander shook his head. "Certainly not - it's a horrible thing to be. But I came here to find out what is going on, and I haven't yet discovered it. It looks as if all of the young men in this village went raiding, and none of them will ever come back, of course. I think the whole place is going to die out soon. Maybe they'll last the winter, but without strong men in the spring to plant the crops, I doubt they'll live another year."

"Good," said Corran. "It serves them right - they've killed so many other people."

"It's not quite that simple," Sander said. "True, the raiders were evil, and true, their families supported their terrible lifestyle. But... there are children here, and infants and babies, and they haven't done anything wrong. But they will all die, too, if the village doesn't survive. I don't like that thought much." A pained expression passed over his face. "I wonder if Melayne has had our child yet?" He shook his head. "One problem at a time." He looked firmly at Corran. "Anyway, I don't understand why the village sent all of their young men off raiding; it simply doesn't make sense that they wouldn't have kept *some* behind. The woman who thinks she owns me, Magga, spoke of a Burning God, and said they're doing his will. But she won't talk more of him, at least yet. I'm sure there's a reason here, but I can't figure it out."

"What does it matter?" Corran asked him, confused. "*These* people will never become raiders again, so Far Holme is safe."

"No, it isn't," his father said sadly. "There are other villages along this coast, and any of them might be next to turn raider. I have to find out *why* these people did what they did, and *who* gave them the map with Melayne's homes marked upon it. And *why* this person wants Melayne dead so badly. No, we can't leave yet. I must stay and find the answers."

"I don't like it," Corran complained. "Look at what they've done to you."

"I know." Sander sighed. "But now you know your Talent, we have an advantage. I want you to stay hidden, but come back here every afternoon to talk to me. That way, when I'm ready to escape, you'll be able to help me. Will you do that?"

Corran's chest swelled with pride. Father *needed* him, and his new Talent! "Of course I will," he promised. "It'll be easier to wait now," he added, honestly. "Now I know I can help."

"Good." Sander glanced around as he heard footsteps. "You'd better go now - I think they've decided I'm a lazy slave and have come to check up on me."

"They won't hurt you, will they?" Corran asked anxiously.

"No - they need me to be able to work. Off you go now." Corran nodded, and ducked behind the woodpile. He heard somebody approaching, and then an old man's voice.

"What do you think you're doing?" he cried. "You're supposed to be working, not resting!"

"I can work better if I rest from time to time," Sander snapped back. "You'll kill me with overwork if you don't allow me a break now and then. Is that what you want to happen?"

"You're awfully mouthy for a slave," the old man growled. "When I was in my prime, you'd never have dared speak to me like that."

"I'm right, and you know it," Sander said. "I don't think Magga would appreciate your working her slave to death, do you?"

"Magga doesn't give the orders around here," the old man snarled. "You can't hide behind her petticoats, you know."

"Maybe you should tell *her* that?" Sander suggested. "Maybe then you'll limp in *both* legs." There was the sound of wood being picked up. "Anyway, I'm rested now, and ready to work again. So there's no problem, is there?"

"You're insolent for a slave."

"Only *you* say I'm a slave - I say I'm a free man, held captive for the time being. I shan't be here forever. And you had better not get in my way when it's time for me to leave."

"I've a mind to whip you!"

A woman's voice broke in on the argument. Corran realized it had to be the woman, Magga, who was his father's owner. "You haven't a mind at all, Tomar. He's my slave, and you won't touch him without asking my permission first."

"Thank you," Sander said.

There was the sound of a slap. "Don't think I'm taking your side against one of my own," Magga warned. "If there's any whipping to be done around here, I'm capable of performing it myself - and don't you ever forget that."

"Trust me," Sander said, softly. "I won't."

There was the sound of the three of them moving away. Corran waited for a few moments - both to make certain he wouldn't be spotted leaving, and to let his anger die down. How *dare* that evil woman hit his father? She would have to pay... Then he sprinted for the trees, and another long day in hiding. But it would be endurable now - he had spoken to his father, and they had a plan.

And he had his Talent to work on...

Chapter Fifteen

After three years on Far Holme, Melayne had almost forgotten how busy and noisy civilization could be. She and Sarrow had lived, until three years ago, with their parents in an isolated farm, and had gone into the local village maybe twice a year. Even now, she was still not used to having many people around her, much as she had adapted to a very different life style.

It was bad enough on the docks of Rivermouth. As their own ship had approached harbor, Melayne had been astonished at the number of other boats in the port.

"Fishing vessels," the captain had told her in his terse manner. "Unloading."

That explained the incredible flock of seagulls swarming all over the skies and water, and their deafening cries. Fishermen were lopping heads off the fish and gutting them before throwing them into salted barrels. Gulls screamed at one another as they fought for these precious tidbits. The fishermen seemed to take it all in their stride, but to Melayne it was an overwhelming cacophony of greed and maliciousness. Sometimes being able to communicate with animals was not an advantage. She tried to close her ears to the raucous voices of the greedy, fighting birds.

And to those of the people ashore. Fishermen and merchants were yelling offers, counter-offers and acceptances to one another. Wives were screaming at their husbands, and children were simply screaming. The captain saw her pained expression and twisted his face into something vaguely resembling a grin. "That's why I like to be at sea," he commented. It was probably the most words he had spoken to her in a single sentence.

He brought the ship in to an empty berth with his usual skill, and his men quickly tied it up, before running out the planks to allow the passengers and their horses ashore. As they were leaving, the captain wandered over to Melayne.

"Want me to wait?" he asked.

"I don't know how long we'll be," she said. "It might be weeks, and it could be months. I don't think you could stand the noise that long."

"Probably not," he agreed, lighting up his smoky pipe. "Send for me, then."

"I will." She clasped his hand. "Thank you, captain."

He nodded. "Luck," he offered, and then stood at the plank, watching his passengers leave. Melayne waved, and he nodded a final time before turning away, presumably to start out again.

Devra, naturally, led the way through the throng, her hands firmly on the reins of her steed, which was whickering nervously because of all the activity and noise. Melayne and the others followed her lead, Melayne speaking softly to Fleetfoot, her own mount, to keep him calm. He liked the crowds as little as she did.

Thankfully, once they were away from the dock area, the noise and crowds thinned out, and they entered the narrow, winding streets of Rivermouth itself. The houses all seemed to be built far too close together, and to lean at alarming angles. Here there were more people, all bent on making the maximum possible noise, it seemed. Neighbors screeched at each other from windows and street. Vendors hawked their wares from small carts - large ones would never be able to navigate this maze of alleyways and streets. Beggars howled for coins, and children ran wild as rats. Devra steered their way unerring, of course, thanks to her own Talent of Finding. Without her aid, Melayne was certain they'd have been lost forever in this mad warren of passageways.

She saw several scrawny, dirty-looking men paying attention as they passed by. She didn't need to be able to read their minds to know what they were thinking - a party of three young women and one man had to look appealling as targets to anyone with a larcenous mind. Margone kept his hand on the hilt of his sword, though, and that seemed to discourage any action upon such thoughts - that and the filthy try-it-and-see-what-happens look fixed on Devra's face.

Dogs and cats slunk through the streets, all occupied with their own thoughts and purposes; Melayne decided against questioning any. Aside from anything else, if the townsfolk suspected that the travelers were Talents, they'd undoubtedly call in the local King's Men to arrest them. Besides, she doubted that animals who lived in this madhouse would know anything worthwhile anyway. They seemed to be entirely occupied in questing for food or mates, or escaping pursuit. One laughing dog ran through their legs carrying a string of greasy-looking sausages that Melayne wouldn't have eaten no matter how starved she might be. Of course, she was a vegetarian, but even to a ravenous carnivore those sausages had to look revolting.

It seemed like forever, but it was probably no more than an hour before they approached the town gates and the exit from this madhouse. Melayne noted that there were thick walls some eight feet tall surrounding the town on all but the seaward side, and that there was only the one set of gates leading in and out, manned by soldiers. It implied that there was potential trouble from the surrounding countryside, and that the heavy gates were barred at night to prevent unauthorized entry.

The checkpoint was crowded, and they had to wait in line. There were a dozen or more armed soldiers checking everyone who entered or left. Melayne watched as they searched any carts, checking contents of the cart against invoices the owners carried. Each carter had to pass over a certain number of coins.

"Taxes," Margone explained, seeing her puzzled expression. "The town fathers take their share of the profits."

"But they haven't sold anything yet," Melayne said. "How can there be any profits?"

Margone grinned. "There are *always* profits for the town fathers. It's up to the merchants whether they make anything or not."

It sounded like a horrible system to Melayne, but it wasn't her place to criticize what she didn't understand. "Fine - that explains the bottleneck coming in. But what are they checking people leaving for?"

"Gold, precious stones, anything that can be taxed."

Melayne was confused. "But wouldn't they be taxed coming *into* the town?"

"Of course. But it's different people leaving with them, so there's a second tax." Margone smiled at her. "I can see you don't have a grasping kind of mind."

"It sounds like a terrible system. Why do the people stand for it?"

"Because the town fathers pay the soldiers, and they enforce the laws. The people have no option but to pay up or leave town."

"I'd leave town," Melayne said, firmly.

"If you're a merchant, you don't have that option," Margone explained. "They need lots of people to be able to sell their goods. So they *have* to stay. And other people stay because there's safety in large numbers. There are bands of ex-King's Men who prey on travelers, you know. Some of them even raid small villages. Then there are simple thieves and cutthroats who'll attack anyone in the woods they think they can beat. No, there's security in towns, even if it's expensive."

"That's horrible," Melayne decided. "It should be dealt with."

Margone laughed. "Yes, that sounds like the response I'd expect from you - you have so much compassion. But it's simply the way life is, and people don't adapt well to change."

"Perhaps they ought to," Melayne said darkly. "Once my husband gets Dragonhome back again, I'm going to see to it that there are a few changes made."

"Good luck," Margone offered. His tone suggested he didn't think she'd be able to manage it. Melayne would have argued further, but they had finally reached the front of the line.

"Anything to declare?" asked the bored soldier at the gate. He glanced uncuriously at Margone. Margone gestured toward Devra, who glowered at the man.

"Travelers," she said, briefly. "Just what you see."

"What's in the saddlebags?" the soldier asked.

"Supplies," Devra answered. "We've a four day ride ahead of us."

The man tapped one of the bags. "Open it up."

Devra looked as if she were about to argue, but Margone laid a gentle hand on her shoulder and shook his head. Instead she sighed, and unlaced the bags. The soldier poked about inside for a moment, then gestured her to close it.

"The four of you together?"

"That's right," Devra said.

"That's four kopas," the guard said.

"For what?" Devra growled.

"To leave town. We have to get paid, you know." His sleepy look was rapidly vanishing, and a couple of the men lazing behind him were starting to look in their direction. The last thing they needed was to attract attention. Somebody might remember seeing a flight of dragons a few years back, and recall Melayne as one of the riders. She carried a small purse in case of need, so she took out four of the copper coins.

"Here," she said, handing them over.

The soldier's eyes narrowed. "How much have you got in there?" he demanded.

"None of your business," Devra snapped. "That's our money."

"There's a tax on how much you carry," the soldier said. "So, show me what you've got in there."

"You've got your fee," Melayne said, gently. "Now let us pass."

The soldier glared at her. "We make our money taking what we wish," he said. "And I want more. We have the weapons, and we'll take whatever I decide is enough." Then he looked puzzled, and then startled. He clearly hadn't meant to say that. Melayne realized it was her Talent of Communication at play again - she had unwittingly forced him to tell the truth. Her Talent was starting to get a little scary.

"You've got all you're getting," Devra said. "Back off."

The people behind them in the line had started talking now, realizing that the soldiers were clearly aiming to take from them as much as they could extort. They were muttering now, but the guards could clearly see that the situation was looking as though it might get out of hand. It seemed nobody seriously questioned the "taxes" that they levied on people. Three more soldiers stepped forward, hands on their swords.

"Do as you're told," the gate guard snapped. "Tell us what you have in that purse."

"*Our* money," Melayne said, firmly. "There's no more for you." So much for not drawing attention to themselves...

"Oh, I am *so* glad we're doing this inconspicuously," Devra grumbled.

"You want them to cheat us - and everyone else?" Melayne asked.

"This isn't cheating," the guard said. "It's taxes. It's perfectly legal - and we can back it up with force if needed, girl."

By now, everyone in the gateway area seemed to be watching them. Melayne knew they were supposed to not be drawing attention, but she simply couldn't allow this to continue. She was not about to let herself be robbed by these soldiers, and saw no reason why they should be robbing anyone else, either. Still, she made one final effort to stop things escalating. "I don't see any notice posted as to what the tax rates are. If they aren't posted, how are we to know what's right?"

"Because I'm telling you," the guard said.

"You're lying," Melayne reminded him.

"So what if I am?" The guard realized he was having trouble with his tongue, but he had no such problems with his hands. He drew his sword. "You pay the rate I tell you, or suffer the consequences."

Devra sighed. "Then I guess we suffer," she said. She concentrated a moment, and then punched him, once, hard. The guard fell down, unconscious. "One advantage of being able to find anything," she said. "Found his weak spot."

Naturally, the other guards weren't going to allow their authority to be flouted like that. Four more of them moved forward, swords whistling from their sheaths. Margone drew his own weapon, and moved to block their approach.

"There's no need," Melayne said. "I can handle them without hurting them too much." Margone gave her an incredulous stare, and didn't move. Well, he hadn't really seen her in action, and didn't understand her abilities.

There was a small flock of sheep milling in the area, ready to be taken to slaughter. Melayne focused on them. "Wolves," she growled, in a low voice. Sheep weren't too bright, so there was no point in asking for their help. The word *wolves*, though, panicked them instantly. They dashed about, getting in the way of the guards, as well as pretty much everyone else present. Bleating wildly, they ran this way and that, trying to push through the crowds to flee the non-existent wolves.

Then Melayne spoke to the pigeons who were after any stray food they could find. "Please," she called, "will you help? I just want you to let loose on the men with helmets." It didn't take much encouragement - pigeons didn't have big brains, and they liked the idea of getting back at some of the humans who were constantly trying to drive them away. Happily, they let fly with runny white excrement, taking great delight in aiming for the faces of the guards.

Finally, she spoke to the horses - those of the men coming in as well as those in her line. "Please," she asked, "will you help cause confusion?" Horses were far smarter than the other animals, and they often had a fine sense of humor. Causing trouble appealed to them, and they started to mill about, ignoring the commands of their owners, and getting in everyone's way.

The whole gateway simply descended into chaos. Seeing the soldiers being attacked, the people who had been waiting to pay their taxes seized their opportunity to get away without having to pay anything. Those coming into the city rushed past the startled guards, hurrying their wagons and supplies, and those leaving did the same. The guards attempted to stop the non-payers, but were completely confused. They couldn't decide whether to try and extort money, attack Melayne, dodge the pigeons, try to round up the sheep or simply avoid the horses who seemed intent on stamping on their feet or kicking them.

Devra grabbed Melayne's arm. "I think it's time we left," she said firmly. Melayne was forced to agree - she'd done as much as she could for the moment, and somebody was going to take charge soon and put a stop to this. She followed Devra, and Corri and Margone followed them.

Once through the gate, the confusion lessened. Now there was room, people were hurrying away in varying directions, and Melayne and the others could mount their steeds. Melayne glanced back, and heard the beleaguered guards calling for reinforcements.

"They'll be after us," Devra said. "They won't dare allow us to defy them, or this taxpayer revolt might spread." She shook her head. "Honestly, I don't know how you manage to cause such chaos wherever you go."

"I only do what I believe is right," Melayne protested.

"And you do it very well," Margone said, grinning. "You were right - you didn't need me to fight for you. I'm beginning to see why your brother is so worried about you. You're far more dangerous than you appear."

Corri laughed. "Wait till she really gets mad - then you'll see what she's capable of!" She spurred on her horse. "This is almost as much fun as flying."

They rode together, slowly at first as they moved through the crowds, and then faster as the people thinned out. Margone glanced back, and scowled.

"There are mounted guards coming after us. I guess they didn't like us not paying their bill."

"Stop trying to be funny," Devra growled, "and just ride. They out-number us, and we could be in trouble."

Melayne wasn't the world's best horsewoman - in fact she'd ridden only a few times before - but being able to speak to Fleetfoot really helped. Her steed kept giving her advice on her posture, and when to lean, and when to clutch with her knees. Margone was a splendid rider, of course, since that was one of the things he'd practiced since he was a child. Both Devra and

Corri were decent riders, since they'd been trained by the King's Men when they'd been conscripted into the Talent army. So they managed a fairly good speed. Despite that, as Melayne chanced a quick look over her shoulder, the soldiers were catching up. They, of course, were far better trained horsemen.

"We may have to stop and fight," Margone called, after a glance back of his own. "They're gaining on us."

"Wonderful," Devra complained. "Just what we needed. There's a dozen of them, and no crowds or sheep out here to get in their way."

Melayne felt a twinge of guilt for her actions. She'd placed them all in danger simply to save paying over a few coins. Would she ever learn to tolerate petty evils? Probably not, if she were honest with herself. It still galled her that the soldiers had been cheating everyone simply because they had the power to do so. That wasn't right, and should never be tolerated.

On the other hand, getting everyone killed as a result wasn't too bright.

The road they were on now entered a fairly thick wood. The pathway was pretty clear, so they didn't need to slow down, and obviously led through the thickets - the main way into and out of Rivermouth. But here in the woods, maybe there were animals who might be able to help them. Melayne called out to any within hearing for aid. She had absolutely no idea if any would hear, or if they would respond if they did hear.

She could hear the hoof beats of the pursuing soldiers now, and chanced another quick look back. The men were now less than a hundred yards back, and one of them had unslung a bow and was fitting an arrow to it. Melayne really didn't think that he'd be able to hit any of them at such a distance, but she knew they were in greater danger.

"Bowman," she called to the others. They all glanced back. Devra looked around for a way off the road they traveled, but it was as straight as the arrow that would soon be fired at them. There was nowhere to hide.

There was a whistle as the arrow whirled past, finally embedding itself in a tree. No one had been hit, but the chances that they would be increased with every passing moment. Melayne was panting for breath, as was Fleetfoot. They wouldn't be able to keep up this pace for much longer - they weren't riding racehorses.

"We'd be better off stopping and facing them," Margone called. Melayne could barely hear his voice.

"If they have archers, they'll just stay back and shoot us," Devra pointed out. "They don't seem the sort to give people a sporting chance."

Melayne agreed with that thought - and realized that she'd placed everyone in deadly danger because of her actions. She *really* had to start learning when to pick her fights...

Assuming, of course, this wasn't her last fight...

She knew it was her decision what to do, and it scared her. If she chose wrong, they would all die. She'd never see Sander, or Corran, or her babies again. And the others must all have similar thoughts about similar people they would all leave behind. It was a horrible responsibility, but it was hers. She'd brought them all to this point in time, after all, in her desire to deal with her brother.

More arrows flew past them, each one getting closer. The archers would find the range soon, and then they would hit flesh. There was only one thing that Melayne could think of doing, so she called out: "Off the horses, and into the trees." She reined in as she called out, and jumped down from Fleetfoot, throwing herself between the trees. "Stay," she ordered the horse. "They aren't likely to harm you." An arrow slammed into the tree beside her, barely inches from her face, as she ducked back. The others joined her, abandoning their mounts and taking to whatever cover they could find. It didn't take a genius to see that this was going to end very badly.

Then a dark shape hurtled from the bushes, slamming into the horse of the patrol leader. The steed screamed in fear, and reared. The man kept his seat only by dropping his weapons and clutching the reins desperately. Further shapes threw themselves from the woods and into the now-milling soldiers.

The horses were going crazy with fear, shying and bucking and wanting only to run.

Melayne seized her chance, adding to the confusion by screaming out to the horses to flee for their lives. It took her a few seconds to realize that the long, tearing, snarling shapes were wolves, but the horses knew it first. They turned and bolted, heedless of what their riders wished. The wolves ran beside them, growling low and snapping at the horse's ankles. One of the wolves detached himself from the pursuit and came loping back, a decidedly silly grin on his face, his tongue lolling out.

"So," he called out, "how was *that*, Melayne?"

Melayne felt the blood rushing to her head, and she dropped to her knees to cradle his head gently in her hands. "Greyn?" she asked, in disbelief. "Greyn? Is that really you?"

"Who else?" he asked, laughing. "I heard your cry for help, and I *knew* it was you - in trouble, as always, and needing my help to get you out of it. So I brought my pack."

Melayne had a thousand questions she wanted to ask him, but she was beaten to the mark by Margone. "So," he called out, "I'm taking it that you know this wolf?"

"Yes," she said, happily. "He's one of my oldest and dearest friends. His name is Greyn." Some of the other wolves were starting to return now, all of them looking exceedingly pleased with themselves. Melayne examined her friend, who had been barely more than a cub when she'd been forced to leave him behind three years ago. Now he was fully grown, and fleshed out. "You are so handsome," she told him.

"Thank you." He accepted the compliment as his due. "These are my pack-mates," he informed her. "And my cubs."

"They're *yours*?" Melayne looked around, and could see the similarities in their faces - especially the merry twinkles in their eyes. "You have a mate?"

"Oh, yes. I haven't been bored while I was waiting for you to return, you know." He laughed again. "I stayed around because I just knew you'd get yourself into trouble again one of these days and need me to save you."

"So you have," Melayne said, laughing happily. She felt better than she had in weeks. "It's so good to see you again. And not just because you saved our lives, either."

Greyn looked at the other humans. "So, is this your pack now?" he asked. "Whatever happened to that bratty brother of yours?"

"These are my pack, yes," Melayne agreed. "Well, some of them. I, too, have a mate, but he is off on a quest of his own."

Greyn sniffed her. "Ah! You have cubs, too - I can tell. The scent is unmistakable. Are they near here?"

Melayne had to explain everything to her friend. As she did so, the other humans collected their own horses. The animals were nervous, being this close to the pack, but Margone proved to be excellent with them, and calmed them down. Melayne broke off speaking with Greyn long enough to help calm the horses by assuring them that the wolves would not harm them. Greyn didn't seem at all surprised by any of her tale, and listened through, his expression mischievous, his tail flapping. "Well," he said when she'd finished, "it's a good thing I waited for you, isn't it?"

"It certainly is," Melayne agreed. "Oh, Greyn, I've missed you so much." She gave him a big hug. The wolf laughed, and turned back to his pack - his children.

"Now," he said, "you see that your sire wasn't as crazy as he seemed to be when he told you all that he had a human sister. This is Melayne - and I want all of you to do whatever she asks of you, whenever she asks it. She is my sister and my friend."

Finally - something good! Melayne felt wonderful again.

At least for the moment.

Chapter Sixteen

They put several more miles between themselves and any possible pursuit before resting. Greyn's pack had spread out about them, and Greyn assured Melayne that the soldiers had all fled back to Rivermouth. When they rested, Melayne sat on a fallen tree trunk, hugging Greyn's furry head tightly, so glad to see him again. Aside from the occasional comments that he was having trouble breathing, the wolf seemed to be happy enough to put up with this indignity.

Devra, as usual, was scowling. "Well, so much for a low-key approach to this mission," she sighed. "That story will get around faster than you'd imagine possible - people actually standing up to the tax thieves and getting away with it. You'll be a folk hero in days. And everyone in Farrowholme will know that *somebody* special is here. If the story beats us back to Dragonhome, then Sarrow is bound to suspect the truth."

"We'll be traveling faster than any rumors could," Corri objected.

"*Nothing* travels faster than rumors," Devra stated. "But I suppose we really can't blame Melayne - we all know what she's like."

Melayne smiled slightly. "Thanks, I think. But it was my fault. I simply couldn't bear the thought of everyone being so blatantly robbed."

"Those people have stood it for years," Margone said. "If they're willing to stand for it, why shouldn't you look the other way?"

"Because *they* don't have the power to stop it - and I do." Melayne ran her hands through Greyn's thick fur. Nothing could upset her right now.

"You can't right every wrong in this world," Devra objected. "Aside from the fact it'll wear you out, there's always more."

"Then I'll just have to keep on fighting," Melayne said.

Devra rolled her eyes. "Right, let's try this one more time. We're on a *secret* mission to sneak into the country undetected and get to your brother before he knows we're here. Fighting every injustice on the way will not only delay us, but it'll give him advance warning that we're coming, and enable him to set a trap. You *do* understand that?"

"Perfectly," Melayne agreed, not at all disturbed. "However, Sarrow already knows I'm coming."

"And how can he know that?" Devra demanded.

"Because he knows *me*. If his first slayers didn't kill me, he *knows* I'll be coming after him. Sarrow is careful, and he's really concerned about his own safety - he's simply got to have planned on my surviving, and worked something out accordingly."

"Like what?" Devra asked.

Melayne shrugged. "I haven't a clue. I can't think the way he does; it's just not in my nature."

Margone laughed. "Well, let's see if the rest of us can sink down to his level, then. If it were me, and I was so concerned about Melayne's powers, I'd have spies out everywhere, ears to the ground, eyes peeled, looking and listening for any sign she was around."

"Including in Rivermouth," Corri agreed brightly. "That's the logical place for her to come ashore."

"So, undoubtedly," Margone continued, "there was probably some agent of his there who is even now getting word to him that something odd happened in port today. Sarrow probably can't be *certain* that it's you, but I wouldn't take odds against him assuming it was, just to be on the safe side. I know I would."

"There you go, then," Melayne said, cheerfully. "Then there's no overwhelming need for us to hide now, is there? We can just act normally the rest of the way there."

"*Normally* for you," Devra said darkly, "is certain to mean trouble. Even if he does suspect you're on your way, he'll hardly expect us to be such a small, fast party. He'll be expecting an invasion force, and that's probably what his spies will be on the alert for."

"Why would he expect an invasion?" Corri asked.

"Because that's what he would do - it's what he's already *done*, using the slayers, isn't it? That's how he thinks." Devra considered her own line of thought for a moment. "Which means that we might still be able to surprise him. He'll be expecting armed soldiers, not a mere handful of Talents. As far as he knows, we're still off on our own, looking for our place to live. And he certainly won't expect one of his own slayers to have switched sides on him."

"True enough," Margone agreed. "He doesn't know yet that your power can overcome his," he added to Melayne. "He's got to assume that I'm still obeying his commands, and not thinking for myself. And even if he somehow thought that, how would he ever expect that a dragonslayer would change sides and want to now protect them? I think Devra's right, and we do have a few advantages over him."

"My point, though," Devra said, looking pleased that he'd agreed with her, "is that this advantage is only ours as long as we don't give ourselves away by using our own Talents in public. So, despite everything, we still need to try and stay low-key." She gave Greyn a glare. "And I'm not sure being followed around by a pack of wolves is exactly inconspicuous."

"Is she always like this?" Greyn asked Melayne.

"Always."

Greyn gave a barking laugh. "Well, I'm not leaving your side," he said. "I don't care what she thinks. But humans won't spot the rest of the pack unless I want them to - they'll stay *inconspicuous*." He laughed again.

Melayne passed along his message to the others. Devra didn't seem convinced, but Corri and Margone seemed fine with his assurances. Melayne glanced across to where Fleetfoot and the other mounts were grazing. "Are you four ready to move on?" she asked.

Fleetfoot whinnied. "Ready and eager," he confirmed.

"Time to go," Melayne told the others. "Maybe we can outrun rumors and spies, after all."

They set off again, at a more leisurely pace to spare the horses. True to his word, Greyn's pack was nowhere to be seen, though the wolf himself was very visible. He loped along beside Melayne, clearly very happy to be back with her again. For her own part, Melayne felt much better now that her old friend was once more beside her. She had missed him the past three years, and now at least *something* felt right in her world. There was still a huge gap in her heart because of her husband and children, and there was the anxiety over her brother. But having Greyn back - well, it made the hurt lessen.

They rode on steadily until almost dark, and then Greyn howled out to his pack. After a quick response from some far-flung wolves, he reported to Melayne: "There's a small stream off to the left about half a mile. Good camping, fine place for the night."

They found the spot without trouble, and settled down to cook their evening meal. Greyn took off to hunt his own supper, disliking cooked food. Corri whipped up a vegetable stew in deference to Melayne, but the others all added meat to their bowls once it was served. After the meal, the four of them sat for a while, wrapped in blankets as it was getting quite cool, and talked about nothing much. Margone told them of his days training to be a dragonslayer, and Corri spoke about her life in a village in Farrowholme, before the King's Men came for all Talents, and she was conscripted into the army. Melayne was surprised to hear that the bubbly blonde girl had four sisters and two older brothers - and that only three of them had been Talents.

"It seems odd," Margone said, puzzled. "I mean, your family lived in the same village all of their lives, and yet only half the children became Talents. Why were the others spared?"

"Spared?" Devra scowled. "You make it sound like we've got some sort of a disease."

"Well, that's the general opinion, isn't it?" Melayne asked. "That's why the normal folk all distrust us, and why we're sent off to fight in these stupid wars, designed only to kill Talents."

"That's backward thinking," Devra stated. "We didn't ask for our Talents - we were born with them. They're as natural to us as anything else we can do. We're as *normal* as anyone else - we just have an extra skill, that's all."

"I've never really known any talents before," Margone said, slowly. "I mean, I did know a couple back home, but didn't know that they were Talents. As soon as the Seekers came, they were taken off to war. I understand from what Melayne told me that Talents are caused by living where dragon scales have leached chemicals into the soil. So I was wondering - are Talents passed along to children?" He glanced at Melayne. "Your husband is a Talent, and so is his son. You're a Talent - so will your two babies be Talents also?"

Corri grinned. "With all those dragons around them? I should think they'll be the strongest Talents ever known."

"But what about the children of other Talents?" Margone persisted. "I mean, if you had children, would they be Talents? And would they be Flying? Or something else?"

"We don't know," Devra answered. "The Kings tend not to let Talents reach the age where they can even have children. The idea is to kill us all off so we're no threat to their despotic power. Sander's the only person I know who's a Talent with a child old enough to demonstrate a Talent of his own."

"That's horrible," Margone said. "I mean, this wholesale slaughter of the Talents. I didn't know what was happening - I was always told that the Talents were fighting to save our country against invaders."

Devra snorted. "That's a myth concocted by the rulers of this world. What parent would ever agree to give up any child if they knew it was simply going to be killed? They only allow the King's Men to take their offspring because they believe it's to save their country."

"It's horrible," Margone repeated.

"Yes," Melayne said, softly. "It is. And it will be stopped." She sighed, and looked at Devra. "You're right - it looks like my impractical crusades will last the rest of my life."

"Which will be extremely short if you don't pick your battles more carefully," Devra pointed out.

Melayne shook her head. "I'm not picking any battles," she replied. "They seem to be choosing me."

At that moment, Greyn drifted back into the camp, looking satisfied. He'd obviously been feeding. He flopped down beside Melayne and started to scratch. "The pack will stay alert tonight," he reported. "If anyone comes near, they'll let me know. You can sleep without fear tonight."

"Thank you. I guess it is time we were resting." Melayne settled down, and Greyn snuggled in beside her. His furry body was quite warm, which Melayne welcomed.

Greyn laughed. "You humans need more fur," he informed her. "It's a good job I have plenty."

Melayne smiled. It felt so good having him back again. If only... She fought back her fears for her children, and for Sander and Corran. She had to believe that they were fine, and that she was doing the right thing.

She *had* to.

Somehow, she managed to sleep, though she tossed and turned all night. She awoke a few times, panting, knowing she'd had terrible dreams, but unable to recall them. Probably that was as well - she didn't need anything else to worry about.

Dawn had broken when she awakened the last time. Greyn was missing, she discovered, and she sat up, looking around the peaceful camp. The others were still sleeping, and she rose quietly, so as not to disturb them. She moved out of sight to perform her morning ablutions. As she came back into camp, Greyn came hurtling back, panting loudly.

"Melayne," he called out. "Men are coming. Armed men. They're about an hour away. We have to get moving. Now!"

Chapter Sixteen

"How did they manage to keep up with us?" Margone asked, still rather sleepy. He and the others were packing their horses quickly. "I thought we'd lost them yesterday."

"These men aren't behind us," the wolf snapped. "They're in front of us."

Melayne stopped loading, confused. "In *front* of us? They're not from Rivermouth, then?"

"No," Greyn said. "These are different men. But they're still armed, and they're heading right for us."

"That doesn't make any sense," Melayne said. "Where are these men coming from?"

"Your brother, most likely," Devra growled. "I told you he must have had spies in the port - they must have contacted more men to intercept us."

"That's possible, I suppose," Melayne agreed, doubtfully. "But *how* did they find out just where we are?"

"He must be using Talents," Corri said. "There's no other way for anyone to have found us."

"That sounds about right," Melayne agreed. "In which case, what's the point in trying to run for it? If a Talent can find us here, he or she could find us anywhere."

"You want to make a stand here and fight them?" Devra asked. She glanced around. "I suppose it's defendable in a pinch."

Melayne sighed. "Will you *please* stop thinking of fighting all the time? We may not need to fight anyone."

"Well, I suppose we could always surrender," Devra agreed sarcastically. "That's assuming they are at all interested in letting us surrender. They may have orders to simply kill us."

"But we don't know that," Melayne argued. "We don't even know these men are from my brother."

"Who else would send armed men after us?" Margone asked.

"We don't even know that they want to fight or capture us," Melayne said. "Maybe they're looking for someone else. Or perhaps they're here to help us."

"Oh, right, *that's* likely," Devra scoffed. "Melayne, look at your history - armed men and you don't exactly get along."

"Maybe this is the exception," Melayne said. "I don't think we should make a run for it. I think we should meet them on the way, and see what they want."

Devra screamed and threw her hands into the air. "Melayne, you are without a doubt the most pig-headed, stupid, optimistic idiot I have ever run into in my life!"

Corri grinned. "Yes, but she's often right. Maybe she is this time, too."

"I might have known you'd take her side," Devra growled. She glared at Margone. "What about you? You think we should volunteer to be massacred?"

Margone shrugged. "I'm just along to try and help out," he said. "But Melayne is in charge, so I follow her orders. If she says we meet these warriors..." He shrugged again.

"Is everyone in this world crazy but me?" Devra muttered to herself. "Fine. Let's go and get killed. At least I won't have to listen to any more stupid plans."

Melayne smiled at her friend. "It's not that bad," she said, gently. "Greyn will have his pack out, ready. If these men mean us harm, I'm sure we can stop them with the help of the wolves. They won't be expecting that."

"If these men are from your brother," Devra warned her, "he'll have told them to watch out for animals. Sarrow knows your powers."

"I'm sure we'll be fine," Melayne said. "Besides, aren't you even the slightest bit curious to find out how they discovered us? If they're using Talents, maybe we can get them to come over to our side."

"She's got a point there," Margone agreed.

"And I don't, of course," Devra grumbled. "Well, once you've been hacked to pieces, don't complain to me."

They finished loading their horses, and Melayne led the way toward the approaching men. Despite her plan, Melayne wasn't at all certain that Devra was completely wrong. She knew that the other girl was right in many ways - she *was* pig-headed and overly optimistic. But living her life in constant fear didn't seem like a good move, and they didn't *know* that these people were enemies.

Of course, in Farrowholme, friends seemed to be in short supply.

Melayne knew she could be leading her friends to disaster and death, and that worried her. But Greyn seemed to be confident his pack could remain unseen, and there were always ways for Melayne to act if fighting was necessary. She could spook the soldiers' horses, for example, which would give them an advantage.

Provided the men didn't attack them on sight...

Melayne shook her head: she'd made her decision, and there was no point in worrying about it now. If these men had found her once, they could do it again. Running away wouldn't help much in the long run. She simply had to have the courage of her convictions. But it would have been easier if three other people's lives didn't depend on her being right.

Why did she always have to make such terrible decisions? She'd been born on a small, isolated farm and had never looked to do anything great with her life. She had always believed she'd simply marry another small farmer and have children and grow old being a nobody. Instead, here she was, leading a fight for her own and her friends' lives, forced to take on injustice and evil far too often. She'd married a Lord, and he was off on his own quest. She'd inherited responsibility for five young dragons and far too many lives. It simply wasn't fair! She was no hero out of fable, ready to fight giants, find unicorns or save the world. She was just a young woman with a Talent who had no option but to do what she believed was right.

Her introspection ceased as Greyn barked a warning that they were getting close to the riders. Then he faded into the forest, though she knew he would not be far off.

They came to a small clearing, and Melayne had them rein in and wait. Fleetfoot and the other horses whinnied and danced back and forth, knowing that trouble was approaching. Melayne licked her lips, but her mouth had gone dry. She glanced at her friends. Corri seemed to be at ease, but she was poised ready to Fly at a second's notice. Devra and Margone had hands close to their weapons. Melayne's palms were slick with sweat; everything depended on the next few moments.

Then they heard the sound of the approaching riders, hooves thundering along the pathway. A moment later, the men came through the trees, reining in their horses and staring at the four waiting people.

They were King's Men, and there was a Seeker at their head. Melayne counted a dozen of them as they held their steeds in check. At their rear was a young man, possible twelve or thirteen years old. He had a shock of dirty blond hair and a slight smile on his face. Melayne was certain he was the Talent who had tracked them.

"I am Melayne," she said, clearly. "Lady of Dragonhome. I believe you may be looking for me."

The Seeker moved his steed forward. "Indeed we are," he agreed. None of the soldiers had made a move toward their weapons, which was a reasonably good sign. Unless it meant that they felt confident that Melayne's party was simply no threat to them. "You are summoned to the presence of King Juska."

"Really?" Melayne was interested - she hadn't been expecting anything like this at all. Still, it might be a problem. "I'm actually in a bit of a hurry right now. Perhaps I could call in on him after I've finished my business."

The Seeker glared at her. "He is the King. He is not used to being kept waiting."

"Perhaps he'd better get used to it," Melayne replied. "It happens to all of us. As I said, we're in a bit of a hurry right now."

The Seeker glanced at the soldier closest to him, and nodded slightly. The armed men all reached for their swords, though they didn't draw them. Their leader smiled slightly.

"I'm rather afraid I must insist. We would be in serious trouble if we returned without you. The King is not a patient man."

"He isn't?" Melayne inclined her head slightly. "Dear me. Just a moment, then." She turned in her saddle to face her friends. "Well, what does everyone think? Should we accept their... kind invitation?"

Devra glowered. "I don't think we need to be bothered by distractions," she said. "I'd say we decline."

Corri frowned slightly. "It might be a little... unpleasant if we do," she pointed out. "And I really don't think killing these men would be a good way to stay inconspicuous."

"Killing *us*?" the Seeker barked. "I don't think you understand - these are some of Juska's best troops."

"I'm sure they are," Melayne agreed sweetly. "He wouldn't send just *anybody* to invite us to see him, would he?" She ignored them again, and turned back to Margone. "What do you think?"

"Corri's right - a fight now would be awfully conspicuous." He looked alert, and ready for action, though. Melayne was touched that he was willing to trust her enough to risk his life for her. But perhaps conflict was not inevitable.

She turned back to the Seeker. "As long as it's not too far out of our way," she decided, "I suppose we could spare a little time."

"The King's hunting party is but an hour from here," the Seeker replied.

"And it is on the way toward Dragonhome," the captain added. "So you wouldn't be losing any time at all, would you?" He seemed to be quite amused by the idea that she had considered fighting them.

"Well, that's all right then," Melayne said brightly. She smiled at the men. "Lead on."

The Seeker whirled his horse and led the way. Melayne noted that the armed men fell in alongside herself and her friends. The captain and the young boy flanked her on either side. Behind her, she heard Devra grumble, "I knew she wouldn't listen to me..." She couldn't help grinning. One of these times she'd better do what Devra advised, or the other girl might start getting really annoyed with her.

"Were you *really* thinking of fighting us?" the captain asked. He was a young man, no more than twenty-four, she guessed, and he seemed both self-assured and amused by the notion that one man and three young women might take on his entire party.

"I don't like fighting," Melayne answered. "So it wouldn't have been my first choice." She gave him a steady look. "But if we *had* decided to fight, we would have won."

"I admire your confidence," the soldier answered. "If not your judgment. The Seeker is correct - we *are* some of his majesty's best troops."

"Then it would have been rather embarrassing when you lost, wouldn't it?" Melayne replied. "So it's a good thing for you it didn't come to a clash of arms."

The captain scowled, having lost a little of his good humor. "Just because you're *Talents,* don't think you're superior to us." He tapped his sword. "A length of cold steel will still kill you."

Melayne was annoyed herself by his arrogance. "Only if you get a chance to draw it," she informed him. "If you *really* wish to push the issue, I'll fight you. But I'd advise against it. If you win, your King will be most annoyed if you injure or kill me to prove your... virility. And if you lose, then your men won't respect you. I really don't see how provoking me is in your best interests."

The captain considered what she had said for a moment, and clearly realized she was right. With a growl, he pulled his horse away from her, gesturing one of his men to take his place and watch her, while he moved forward to join the Seeker.

The young Talent on her right chuckled softly. "I think you've made an enemy there," he said softly. "The captain is a very vain man when it comes to his fighting skills."

"Yes, I got that impression," Melayne agreed. "I take it you're the one who led this party to us."

"Yes." The youth grinned again. "My name is Batten. I'm a Seer."

"Really?" Melayne smiled back. "My husband has the ability to See the future, too."

"You don't look old enough to be married," Batten told her.

"Thank you for the compliment, but I'm not merely married but the mother of two children." Melayne studied him with interest. "You keep very bad company."

He shrugged. "I haven't had much choice - to date. When King Juska found out my Talent, he forced me into his personal service."

"No wars for you, eh?" Melayne smiled. "He must find you very useful - being able to see the future."

"Oh, I can't see the future," Batten said cheerfully. "I see only the consequences of actions or decisions. So the King will tell me what he plans, and I'll tell him if it will work or not."

"That's still very useful," Melayne said. "I wish I could be sure that the consequences of my actions will work out well."

Batten laughed. "But you go ahead with them, even though you don't know," he told her. "That I've Seen. You're very brave."

"I wish I was," Melayne said. "I'm not, really. I just do what I have to do, and hope I have the courage to go through with it." She studied him again. "Can you tell me what the outcome of my going with you will be?"

"Yes," he answered. "If you really want to know. Not every detail, of course - just what the direct result of your decision will be." He gave her a rather sly look. "For example, when I told the King about your arrival, he was most interested."

"You told him? He didn't know about us, then?"

"No." Batten looked smug. "He had asked me for a good place to go hunting, and I recommended the spot where he is because I could see that you were coming this way. Then I told him you were on your way - free Talents in his land, in defiance of the law - and he wanted to know if he should kill you or talk to you."

"Really?" Melayne was intrigued now. "And I take it that you advised talk?"

"Yes, of course. I told him it would be best to talk." His mouth twitched slightly. "Of course, he didn't ask *who* it was best for, and I didn't tell him."

"Are you planning to betray him?" Melayne asked, softly, so that the soldiers couldn't hear.

"I plan to betray no one," he said, striving to look very virtuous. "And I *always* tell the truth about what I see with my Talent. But the truth can be... quite complicated, and I do so like to simplify things." He gave her another grin. "If you want to know what will happen, you merely have to ask me, and I'll tell you."

"And you'll tell me just as much of the truth as you want me to know," Melayne added, starting to understand this youth.

Batten laughed happily. "Exactly! I see you're catching on rather more quickly than Juska has."

Melayne nodded, slowly. "You're a very dangerous young man, aren't you?"

Batten looked smug again. "I can be."

"And this is a very dangerous game you're playing," she informed him. "You could get yourself hurt - or killed."

He shook his head. "No. I can guarantee you that quite emphatically - I will come out of this business much improved. Of course, I can't say the same for everyone involved." His eyes twinkled again. "Are you sure you wouldn't like me to tell your future?"

Melayne considered his offer carefully, and then shook her head. "I suspect I might do better if I didn't listen to you too much."

Batten laughed. "Like I said, you're learning a lot faster than the King. But you *know* I can't lie to you, of course - that's a part of your Talent."

"And how exactly do you know what my Talent is?" Melayne asked.

"Because I can See the consequences of your using it. So you know I *have* to tell you the truth - which means that you can trust me." He grinned. "Simple, isn't it? And I give you my solemn word that I am doing nothing that will hurt you or your cause in any way." He looked smug again. "So - now do you trust me?"

He was right - she *did* know that he was telling the truth. But... She shook her head. "I know that often the best way to tell a lie is to shade the truth. So everything you are telling me could be the truth - and I could still end up getting hurt because you've left a convenient little detail out."

Batten laughed again. "Oh, you're so suspicious, aren't you? I thought that was Devra's job."

"I'm trying to take her advice a little more often," Melayne replied.

"Good luck." Batten gave her a mocking salute, and moved away from her side. Devra swiftly took his place.

"So - what was that about?" she demanded. Melayne filled her in, and Devra scowled. "Is he really on our side?" she asked. "It would make sense - he's a Talent, after all, just like us."

"Oh, he's a Talent all right," Melayne agreed. "But he's not like us. He's very cynical and manipulative, and he's using his gift to alter events to his own advantage. The problem is that I don't know what he's ultimately got in mind - so what we're doing right now might actually be the best possible thing. Or it may be only the best possible thing *for him.*"

"There are days," Devra admitted, "when I'm glad I'm not the leader. This is one of them. Good luck making any sense of that kid. Mind you, I don't see what the point is of having a Seer if you daren't use his powers."

"Would you trust him?" Melayne shot back.

"Not a chance," Devra admitted, giving one of her rare smiles. "Like I said, there are days when I'm glad to be only second in command."

Melayne spent the rest of the ride trying to fathom what she should do. She knew she was on dangerous ground here, with so many people involved having their own agendas. But what was best to do? In the end she could only conclude that all she could do was what she always did - try and do the right thing, and trust that matters would work out fine. It might sound to Devra to be hopelessly optimistic - and perhaps it was - but it was the only way Melayne knew how to behave.

They finally arrived at the King's hunting camp in slightly less than the promised hour. It was some camp - Juska obviously didn't believe in traveling light. There were at least twenty tents, several of them quite large. Naturally the largest and grandest had to be the King's, and it was to this one that the Seeker led them. There were men everywhere - some clearly nobles, others soldiers and others the men in charge of the hounds and other aspects of the hunt. There were no women present, Melayne noted - obviously hunting was an activity reserved only for men. There were more than a dozen wagons, too, clearly the transport for the tents and accessories.

There was a large chair set up outside the great tent - almost a throne - and a man lounging casually in it who was obviously the King. His clothing was ornate, with floral designs picked out on his tunic and trews in gold thread. A large cloak was slung across his back, a deep green in color, with more elaborate stitching. His hands were gloved, and on his right wrist sat a large falcon.

As they drew closer and dismounted, Melayne could make out details of the King himself. He was past middle age, with a stout waistline and jowls forming at his cheeks, showing he indulged too much in rich foods and drinks. His hair was dark, but thinning, and he had a neatly trimmed beard that was flecked with white. His eyes burned hungrily - but for what? As he saw the party arrive, he stood up and shook his wrist slightly. On cue, the falcon spread its wings and leaped for the sky. It gave a triumphant cry and shot upward. Melayne glanced after it, and saw that beaters had frightened pigeons from the nearby woods. Crying in terror as they saw their mortal enemy, the birds panicked. The falcon folded its wings slightly, and dove down toward its prey. Vicious claws slashed out, and one of the pigeons was caught and slaughtered instantly, dropping lifeless to the ground not twenty feet from the amused King.

Melayne was appalled. She looked from the fallen bird to the King, to the falcon, which had swooped back and landed lightly on the King's upraised right arm. "Is *this* your idea of hunting?" she demanded, loudly.

"It is great sport, isn't it?" Juska asked, amused.

"It's disgusting," Melayne told him, firmly. She glared at the falcon. "Do you enjoy that?" she asked the bird.

"It is my life," the falcon answered simply. "I kill, I eat. What else is there?"

"To kill for yourself, so you can eat - that is the way of nature," Melayne agreed. "To kill to amuse an aging man who watches murder done - that is quite another. Are you happy here?"

"I kill," the falcon replied. "I eat. What else is there?" The bird was clearly not a deep thinker.

"You can come with me and discover the answer to that if you wish," Melayne informed him.

Juska cleared his throat. "So, Batten was right - you *do* speak with animals and birds. Most interesting. Though rather rude, since I am king, and I sent for you to speak with me, not my hunting falcon."

"Oh, I'll speak with you," Melayne said. She gestured around the camp. "Is all of this to gather food, or is it to enjoy the death of helpless animals?"

"Is there a difference?" asked the King, bored. He handed off the falcon to an aide, and sat down again.

"Yes," Melayne replied. "I will allow hunting for food - but not for sport. This must stop. Now."

Juska's eyes glittered dangerously. "You are not here to tell *me* what to do, woman. You are here so that I can tell *you* what you must do."

Devra stepped forward. "You have to forgive her, your rotundity; she's never met a King before, and doesn't understand how to behave toward them."

"Yes, she *does* have the look of a peasant about her," one of the King's courtiers said. He was a tall man, dark and intense, probably less than thirty.

"That's because I was born a peasant," Melayne said. "It doesn't bother me, and if it offends you, there's nothing I can do about it."

"And yet," the King said smoothly, "you are a peasant no longer, are you? I hear that you're married to the Lord of Dragonhome - which makes you his Lady."

"That's true," Melayne agreed. "Strange things happen in life."

"And, as Lord Sander holds his title under service to me, then that means you, too, owe me your allegiance." The King scratched his beard and stared at her.

"Does it?" Melayne shrugged. "I'm a bit choosy about whom I serve."

The dark courtier stepped forward, hand on his sword hilt. Melayne glanced at him, and he snarled: "Speak gently to the King, woman, or else I'll give you a taste of cold steel."

"And your name is....?" she prompted.

"I am Lord Aleksar," he said, proudly.

"Good. I like to know the names of my enemies." Melayne turned back to the King. "Well, this is all delaying me from my journey," she said. "I'm assuming you had some point in sending for me?"

"Indeed I do," Juska agreed. He looked at her coolly. "You don't seem very formidable to me."

Melayne shrugged. "No, I don't suppose I do. But that's not why I'm here, is it?"

"No." The King smiled, widely. "I want you to go to Dragonhome for me."

Chapter Seventeen

Melayne couldn't help laughing. "Well, that's exactly where we were heading anyway, before you sent your... kind invitation to visit with you."

"I'm aware of that," the King stated. "However..." He glanced at Lord Aleksar. "I heard some disturbing stories about that place a few months ago, and sent some of my agents there to investigate what is happening. They never returned. I sent more. They didn't return, either. I sent a small company of armed men after them -"

"Let me guess, "Devra broke in. "They're now missing, too?"

"Correct." Juska looked from one girl to the other. "That disturbs me. I don't like secrets - at least, not ones I'm not in on. I wish to know what is happening at Dragonhome, and if it is a threat to my kingdom. If it is, I want it destroyed. Since none of my men seem capable of solving the problem, I thought I would ask you to settle it for me. After all, as Lady of Dragonhome, you do have a vested interest in reclaiming it, I am sure."

"I do," Melayne agreed. "But since you knew I was heading there anyway, I still don't see why you wished to see me. Nothing in what you've told me is news to me, and it certainly won't help me in my quest. So, again - why am I here?"

"I suspect treason at Dragonhome, girl," the King growled. "And that cannot be tolerated. You are off to deal with it - most inadequately prepared, it seems to me. Frankly, I would imagine whatever is there will slaughter you."

"I've been trying to tell her that," Devra commented. "But I've had no luck, and I doubt you'll do any better."

The King glowered at Devra, but continued to address Melayne. "However, there is a chance that you're not quite what you appear to be. My Seer there -" he gestured casually at Batten "- tells me that you have a good likelihood of succeeding in your mission, and the boy is hardly ever wrong."

"I did say she has a good chance of success if nothing changes," Batten pointed out. "Of course, things change all of the time."

"Quite." Juska leaned forward, intently. "So let us say that you do somehow defeat this menace that my men cannot. You and your husband - also a Talent, I am informed - will then be in possession of Dragonhome again. This is, of course, against the law. All Talents must report to fight in my army. Any that don't are guilty of treason." He glanced at all of the small party. "So you're all already technically traitors, and it is within my power to have you all executed."

"Really?" asked Melayne, mildly. "Do you intend to attempt it?" She sounded casual, but she was prepared to fight, if she had to. Still, none of the soldiers had made a move toward any weapons, though Aleksar looked as if he wished he could.

"I have an offer to make," the King said. "It doesn't aid me at all if you kill whoever is responsible for whatever is happening at Dragonhome and if you simply replace him as another traitor. But if you were my sworn representative... then I should have the advantage."

"I see." And Melayne did. It was quite clever, really. "If we fail, you've lost nothing, and if we succeed, you stand to gain a good deal." She smiled. "I can see that this would be to your advantage; but why would it be to *mine*?"

Juska smiled; he seemed confident that he was winning the point. "As I pointed out, technically you, your husband and your friends are already traitors. But I can forgive that, officially, and appoint you to Dragonhome as Lord and Lady without fear of charges. If you swear to become my bondwoman, to serve my interests and to be true to my commands, then I will confirm your right to the land and lieges of Dragonhome. And to your children and heirs, too."

"Ah." Melayne understood now. "And my children?"

"What about your children?" Juska asked.

"They are Talents also. Would you spare them from service in your army?"

The king considered for a moment. "That could be arranged, yes. Do we then have an agreement?"

Melayne let her anger flow. "We do *not*!" she roared, furiously. "Do you think I am so selfish as to make a deal with you that helps only me and my own needs?" She gestured at Devra and Corri. "These people are my *friends*, and it's your will that they go off and fight in a fake war simply to destroy them. Do you think I would ignore that?"

Devra chuckled. "She's beautiful when she's angry, isn't she?" she asked Margone.

"She's *dangerous* when she's angry," the slayer replied.

"That too."

The king seemed to be taken aback by her reply, and then he, too, grew angry. "You stupid girl!" he snarled. "I'm offering you legitimacy, and freedom. You turn that down?"

"You pompous windbag!" Melayne told him, striving to hold her temper in check. "You have no *right* to offer me anything. I'm not your subject - I wasn't even *born* in Farrowholme - and I don't accept your right to order me in any way, shape or form. You may be king right now, but that can change."

"You're speaking treason," Aleksar snapped, stepping forward, hand on sword hilt.

"According to your king, I'm already guilty of treason simply because I'm still alive." Melayne glared at both men. "And that is unacceptable." She strode forward, to stand close to the king. "Now you will hear *my* terms."

The king rose to his feet, shaking with anger. "*You* do not give terms to *me*!" he screamed. "I am the King! You will obey *my* orders, and not the other way around."

Melayne was so mad, she could hardly think straight. "You were wondering what made me so dangerous, weren't you?" she asked, her voice so soft it hardly carried to any other person. "Well, I think it's high time that you found out the answer." She whirled to face Aleksar. "You - have you taken Juska's oath of allegiance?"

"Of course I have," Aleksar replied.

Melayne smiled tightly. She looked back at the King. "My Talent is Communication," she said, coldly. "I don't merely speak with animals - I speak with *people*, too, and they must tell me the truth - whether they wish it or not." Aleksar started to look nervous and his hand strayed toward his sword hilt again. "You'd better not finish that move," Melayne told him. "Not if you want to ever be able to use that hand again."

"You're just a young girl," Aleksar growled. "You can't possibly possess the power that you claim. This is all a bluff."

"If you really believe that," Melayne challenged him, "then try and draw your sword."

She had backed him into a corner, she knew, and she understood that he would lose face before the King and his men if he didn't accept her challenge. Her eyes flickered from his hand to the falcon, who immediately started to get interested. Aleksar wasn't *certain* she could do as she'd threatened, so he took another few seconds to act.

His hand went to his sword hilt.

Melayne whistled, and the falcon launched himself immediately. In a flurry of wings and with a loud cry, the bird struck. Aleksar screamed, and fell back, his hand dripping blood from three deep wounds along its back. So fast had the action been that nobody else even had the chance to move. The falcon circled, then came to light on the pommel of Fleetfoot's saddle. "I like you," he shrilled at Melayne. "This is more fun than killing birds."

"Stay alert," she advised the bird. "There may be more of your sort of fun to come." The bird settled, happily, and Melayne turned back to the men. One of Aleksar's servants had hurried forward to bandage his wounded hand. "Now," Melayne said, gently, "do I need to hurt anyone else, or will you start listening for a change?"

"I have my archers," Juska said. "You can't turn that traitorous bird loose on all of them."

Melayne shook her head in sorrow. "How many more of your men must be maimed before you'll listen to me?" she asked. "I have no wish to harm anyone, but I will do whatever I must to protect my people." She gave a growl of frustration. "Let me give you another demonstration of what I can do. Remember, people must always tell me the truth if I wish them to." She turned back to Aleksar, whose face was riddled with pain. "You said you swore allegiance to Juska - now, tell us... did you *mean* it?"

Sweat started to crawl down the man's forehead. "I swore to serve the King," he said.

"That's no answer - swearing is just words unless you mean to abide by them. A man without honor will swear to anything - and then be an oath breaker. So, I ask again - do you intend to fully be loyal to Juska?"

Aleksar tried to keep his mouth shut, and the strain showed even greater agony on the man's face. "I will be loyal," he grated, finally, "as long as it suits me to be."

"Ah," Melayne said, smiling dangerously. "And then what will you do?"

Aleksar fought to keep silent - and failed. "If I am sure I have the support... I will kill the King and seize his throne."

Juska's face showed shock, horror, and finally anger. "He plans *treason*," he said in a cold, furious voice.

"Of course he does," Melayne informed the King. "And so, I'll wager, do most of your loyal lords. When you rule through fear instead of through wisdom, you cannot expect loyalty. Those close to you will covet your power, and will seize it the first chance they get. Aleksar is no different from any of the minions you have about you. So, from this moment forward, you will live knowing that any man in your court may wish you dead - and may aim to do something about it. You will never have another restful night. You will never be able to turn your back safely on any man. And it will only get worse for you, not better." She could see the haunted look of fear in his eyes. "I think you are beginning to understand the extent of my power," she said. "Now, let me drive the point home with you and all of your men." She looked around the circle of lords and servants and soldiers. None of them had taken a step. All looked uncertain, as well they should.

"Greyn," she called.

Instantly, there were several blurs of motion. The largest of these threw himself onto the King, knocking him from his throne and standing, teeth bared, drool dripping, above the prone, terrified monarch. Other wolves took down the closest of the soldiers and anyone else who made a motion toward a sword. None of them struck to kill, but their terrifying effect was certainly not minimized by that fact.

Melayne looked down at the trembling Juska. "Not only can you never trust any of your subjects - neither can you trust any of the animals about you. Any of them might be my spy - or my assassin. Every sparrow, every rat - even the cockroaches in your walls might be working for me. If you ever do anything I disapprove of again, I will hear of it, and I will act. And you have seen that I can do it.

"Now - you will listen to my terms." She waited and looked down at the King.

His eyes were fixed on Greyn's long, sharp teeth, inches from his face. "Call him off," he begged. "I will listen to anything you say. But call him off!"

"Am I worrying him?" Greyn asked, lightly.

"I think you are," Melayne replied, with a smile. "Perhaps you'd better let him up."

Greyn considered for a moment. "Very well," he agreed. He started to jump off the King's body when he had a sudden thought. He lifted his back leg and let a stream of hot urine flow down the King's robes. *Then* he leaped aside, and waited, head cocked.

Melayne had great difficulty keeping a straight face as the dripping monarch staggered to his feet. Devra didn't bother - she laughed openly. Corri couldn't help sniggering, and even Margone's face showed traces of humor.

"Now," Melayne said, firmly, as the other wolves also allowed their victims to rise, "you will listen, and you will take what I say to heart. First, the war must stop. No more Talents are to be sent to their deaths. The King's Men and the Seekers will stop looking for them, and they will be allowed to live their lives in peace, with their families."

Juska's face blanched. "I... cannot possibly do that," he said.

"That is not negotiable," she informed him. "You are only King because I now allow it. If you will not do as I tell you, I will replace you with someone more reasonable." Greyn growled, soft and low, and the King collapsed back onto his throne in a panic.

"It's not that!" he cried. "I would do it if I could, I swear it! But it's not just me - the other four Kings are committed to the wars as well. If I were to stop my troops fighting, those of the other nations will simply attack Farrowholme."

Melayne hadn't considered this. "Not immediately," she finally decided. "They might suspect a trick or a trap. They'd want to be certain they would be safe. And if this damnable war is ever to end, then it must begin somewhere. And I say it starts with you. You will order your troops to stop fighting, and recall and dismiss them. All Talents are to be freed to return home. If any of them *wish* to serve you, they may - but they are not to be forced to do so."

"If I do that, Farrowholme is doomed," the King wailed.

"You fool!" Devra yelled. "Don't you understand - Melayne isn't just going to stop *you*? She's going to stop the whole war. You're just the first step - Vester, Morstan, Pellow and Stormgard will follow your lead, because she'll give their monarchs precisely the same choice you're getting. They won't be able to attack you, you moron."

Melayne hadn't actually thought it through that far yet, but she could see that this was exactly what her course of action must be. She gave Devra a grateful smile. "So, that disposes of that problem," she said, cheerily. "Now, my other condition. You will cease hunting for sport immediately. Hunting is to be allowed only to put food on your tables. Slaying helpless animals as a form of amusement will cease. That, too, is not negotiable." She glared around the whole hunting camp. "If I hear from my animal friends that anyone is hunting them merely for trophies or a sick love of killing - that person will receive my vengeance. You had better all hear this and heed it." She looked back at the King. "On those terms, I promise you that you will be safe from any actions by me. And, unlike the men who take your oaths with reservations in their hearts, I swear truthfully. If you stop the war from this country and free the Talents and if you stop hunting as a sport, then I will be loyal. You need never fear treason from me or mine." She pointed a stern finger at his quivering face. "If you do not do these things, then I shall destroy you - and any who stand with you. That is your only option. Now - what is your answer?"

Juska stared at her, fear etched on his pale face. Then he looked around at his men - men had had always believed were loyal to him, and men whom he now could never again trust. He glanced at the horses, the hunting dogs, and the birds... and Melayne could see that he understood he would never, ever have a moment's peace again. Then he looked back at her.

"You have destroyed me," he whispered.

"No." Melayne shook her head. "You have destroyed yourself. I have simply exposed your folly for all to see and understand." She glared around the sullen, hostile faces. "Look around you at your… subjects. They are all considering whether you deserve their loyalty and respect," she informed the King. "And I am certain they are all thinking that their answer should be no. But consider this," she told them all. "If you do decide that Juska is a fool and helpless - which of you is any better?" She gestured at Aleksar. "Him? His right hand will never be able to grip a sword again. Him?" She gestured at another lord at random. "Is he any likelier to be able to stop me? What I have done to Juska and Aleksar I can do to any of you, if the need should arise. All of you should remember that before you do anything rash."

Aleksar gritted his teeth, fighting back the pain in his hand. "You are a monster," he hissed.

"No," Melayne answered. "You misunderstand. I am only doing what I must do to free people from your twisted desires and lusts for power. *You* are the monsters, and I am going to free this country from the grip of the fear that you hold it in. You've gotten away with your cruelties and whims for far too long. Now you will be held accountable - every last one of you. If any of you behaves in a decent, honorable way, then I will be happy to call that man a friend. But if any of you use your positions to exploit other people, I will call you my enemy. And you have seen what I can do to my enemies.

"I did not ask for this to happen," she continued. "I do not seek to dominate anyone. But I cannot allow this rampant abuse to continue any longer, not while there is a breath left in my body. It will stop, and it will stop *now*. Anyone who cannot accept this will have to face the consequences of their actions." She turned back to Juska. "So - do we understand one another? Will you do as I demand, or shall I find another King?"

Juska shook, his whole body trembling. He had almost no dignity left to him. His pride had been shattered, his nerve broken. "You have destroyed me," he repeated.

"It is your own fault," Melayne informed him. "You wished to bully me, and you have discovered that I am more powerful than you could ever have been. The difference between us is that I use my power to help others - not myself. Now, chose."

Juska's shoulders sagged, and he fell forward in his seat. "I will do as you wish," he agreed. "As long as I am able. It may not be long."

Melayne looked around the sea of hostile faces that ringed the throne. "No," she agreed, "I do not believe it will be for long. Your tyranny is almost at its end, and you will pay the price for all of the fear and distrust you have bred. But whoever seeks to take your place had better understand that it doesn't matter to me who the King is - if he does not do as I wish, I will destroy him just as certainly as I have destroyed you." She turned to her companions. "And now, I think we have been delayed quite long enough. We are still on a quest, and time is wasting." The falcon flew up from Fleetfoot's saddle so she could grip it and swing herself astride. Devra, Corri and Margone followed her lead. Greyn and his pack slipped back into the woods.

Melayne looked at the cold, scared eyes of the King's men. "In case any of you consider it, don't even dream of having archers target us as we ride away. I am completely out of patience now, and any man who takes up arms against us I will have killed. And I will do the same to the man who gives any orders to injure us. I trust you understand that I mean exactly what I am saying." Without waiting for any response, she whirled Fleetfoot about and rode away.

Devra fell in beside her. "Well," she said softly, "that was the most fun I've had in a long time. I think Juska peed himself as well."

Melayne sighed. "I didn't enjoy doing that," she confessed. "I simply could see no alternative."

"It was very effective," Devra assured her. "I don't even have to look back to know not one of them is going to try and stop us."

Margone and Corri joined them. The slayer shook his head. "It is not us who are in danger now," he said. "I do not think Juska will live long enough to see us again."

"Nor do I," Devra agreed, cheerfully. "That pack of jackals will be all over him now he's been exposed as powerless. And it couldn't happen to a more deserving man."

"Perhaps not," Melayne said. "But I still feel guilty. He will have died because of me."

"No," Corri said, firmly. "It is his own actions that have led to this, as you said. He abused all of those men while they and he thought he had the power to do so. You simply exposed him for what he is. Now they will get their revenge."

"It's very ugly," Melayne said.

"That's the human race for you," Greyn muttered, running alongside Fleetfoot. "You sure are an ugly lot."

Melayne was inclined to agree with him.

Chapter Eighteen

The last few days had been hard for Sander. He was no stranger to hard work, but the manual labor that Magga had put him to was strenuous, and the old man, Tomar, had seized every chance he could to mock and complain about the slave's worthless abilities. The children, led by Kappo, had spat on him, thrown stinking vegetables and hurled curses at him.

How could these people *live* with themselves? Sander was no idealist - he knew how cruel and uncaring some people could be from harsh experience - but he had never imagined a whole village as steeped in unpleasant people as this one had turned out to be. There was not a single person in the whole community - which numbered less than a hundred people, two thirds of which were children - who ever gave him a kind word or even a gentle look. How could so many people have become so casually evil?

The only bright point for him had been that Corran had managed to sneak into the village each day to see him. Corran was getting much better with his Talent now, through practice, and with care could even sneak up on deer without being detected.

Now Sander was hauling water for Magga. She had had him build a large fire, and was boiling up wash-water. Each trip from the fire down to the river took him ten minutes, and she complained bitterly about the length of time it took him, and how little water he could carry. Finally, he could take the constant carping no more.

"Then why didn't you build the fire closer to the blasted river?" he yelled at her. "It would have saved a lot of time."

She had been using a large wooden spoon-like implement to stir the clothing she was washing, and she whirled around, hitting him across the shoulders with the tool. "Mind your tongue!" she cried. "No slave of mine will speak to me like that."

"You've never had a slave before me," he growled back. "And if I were to stay here, you wouldn't have me for long, either, the poor way you treat me."

"Oh?" she asked, sarcastically. "Are you going somewhere?"

"Out of here, as soon as I please," he informed her.

She snorted her scorn. "You think you can escape from here?"

"I could have escaped any time I felt like it," Sander said simply. He didn't mention, of course, that Corran was waiting beside the house, with a knife that would swiftly cut the bonds that hobbled Sander's feet.

"Oh? Then why did you stay?" Magga asked, scornfully. "Do you enjoy my company so much?"

"I don't enjoy your company at all," he admitted. "But I had hoped to try and understand you people - and, I must confess, I've not been able to manage it at all. I understand you less now than I did when I came here."

Magga shrugged. "What's to understand? We simply seek to survive, like everyone."

"Not like everyone," he said. "Most people don't send their men off to loot, burn, steal and kill. Most people work for themselves, and don't make their visitors into their slaves. Most people laugh and sing, and enjoy themselves."

"Most people don't live in these barren lands," she growled.

"Barren?" He shook his head. "I've been in the fields - they're filled with abundant grains and vegetables. The river and sea are filled with fish that even your old men catch without trouble. And there's plenty of wild deer in the forests for meat. You could all live well enough without ever leaving this village."

She spat at his feet. "And what kind of a life is *that* for a real man?" she asked, scornfully. "A man must fight, and defeat his enemies to be a man."

"You wouldn't *have* any enemies if you didn't pick fights with them," Sander snapped.

"A man's blood must stir if he is to be strong," she said. "Didn't your father teach you that? My husband, my Jemmie, *he* would never have consented to live as a slave. He'd have died first."

"He's dead anyway," Sander informed her, coldly angry. She whacked him with the spoon again. "Liar! He and the other men will return soon, with great wealth and more slaves. Then we shall feast, and rejoice. There will be plenty of song and dance then - aye, and plenty more slaves to share the work with you."

"You fool," he told her. "Jemmie and his friends are *dead*. None of them will ever return. There'll be no spoils for you and no other poor souls bound and helpless as your slaves. There will only be winter and summer, spring and fall, all without men."

She hit him again and again. "You can't know that!" she screamed. "You're saying that to try and curse them! But the Burning God won't hear you - he hears only the prayers of his faithful believers!"

"He hears *no* prayers," Sander informed her. "The men *are* dead - I know because I fought them when they came to Far Holme. My men and I slew them, and sank their ship. They will never return because the fishes are devouring their bodies."

Magga went pale. "You *lie*!" she screamed, hitting out blindly with the stick.

Sander had had quite enough of this. He had learned virtually nothing from his days of captivity. Magga and the others had treated him with contempt, and refused for the most part to speak with him except in curses and foul language. His plan was a failure, so it was time to try something new. He beckoned to Corran, who ran across, knife at the ready.

"What are you doing?" Magga screeched. From her point of view, Sander's hobbles were suddenly broken apart, and a sword suddenly appeared from nowhere in his hand. She couldn't see Corran, of course, so this must have looked like witchcraft to her.

"I told you I could be free whenever I wished," Sander said. "I've decided that there's nothing more to be learned from such obnoxious people, and will now take my leave of you." Magga raised the spoon to strike again, but Sander raised the sword.

"I may well have been the man who killed your husband," he said. "I do not wish to leave your children orphans, but I shall if you provoke me further. Now, we shall talk, you and I, and you will tell me what I wish to know."

"I'll tell you *nothing,*" she said with scorn, defiantly throwing the spoon aside. Corran had to jump aside to avoid being accidentally hit. "You're a slave, and you will be punished for this."

"When the men come home, I'm sure," Sander said, exasperated. "I tell you, they will never be home. You will have to survive as you now are - old men, women and children. There will be no more spoils, no more slaves. There will only be loneliness and misery and finally death. There will be no joy, no feasting, and no song. Your husbands and older youths are all dead, and this village will have to come to terms with that fact."

"You lie!" she snarled. "The Burning God promised that they would have success, and you are not stronger than a god."

"Your god is as powerless as your wishes for your men to return," he said. "They are dead, and you are all alone. You will hurt no more outsiders, raid no more villages."

"Even if what you say is true," Magga growled, "and I do not say that it is, but even if it were true, and the men were all dead - well, then, our sons will grow up soon enough, strong and brave, and *they* will go off raiding in their turn. And *then* we will have riches and slaves again."

"You fool!" he said, scornfully. "That is how you would train your sons? To rob and murder and enslave the innocent?"

"It is their destiny," she said, proudly. "It is our way of life."

"Then it is a way of life that will stop," he vowed. "I swear to you on this Burning God you place so much faith in that your men are dead. And I further swear that if a single raiding ship ever again leaves this place, I shall not simply destroy it, but return here and wipe this village from the face of the earth." He pointed the sword at her. "You will all learn to behave, or I shall force you to. The choice is yours."

"You?" she cried, scornfully. "Slave, you have a high opinion of yourself!"

"Not of myself alone," he told her, "but of my son, and my wife, and all of the people that I call my friends. We have had enough of your raiding, and will take no more. If you will not stop, then I swear to you that we will stop you."

"You cannot do that," Magga said.

"I will show you a little of what I can do," he told her. "Corran, I think we had better teach these people a lesson that they will never forget."

"Who are you speaking to?" she demanded, suddenly worried. "Have you taken leave of your senses? There is nobody else here." Then she squealed, as Corran slapped her, hard, on the arm. "What did that?"

"The person you don't believe is here," he informed her. "The one you cannot see."

"That is impossible," she said, whirling around and laying about her with her flailing hands. "People cannot become invisible."

Something suddenly occurred to Sander. He thought for a moment and realized then that he had discovered something significant. "You have no Talents," he said, slowly. "None of your children are Talents."

"What are you talking about?" Magga asked. "Are you crazy? Has the Burning God afflicted you with madness?"

No Talents... He smiled. "Many of my people have powers that you cannot even begin to dream of," he told her. "I have the ability to see the future. My son has the power to become invisible. My wife can speak to all animals. We are all Talents. And, as a result, you are as feeble and helpless before us as a baby is before an armed Raider. *This* is what your people must come to understand. That we *do* have the power to destroy you, to wipe this filthy village from the face of the earth, if we so wish. You must learn to live in peace - or you will simply cease to live."

"You *are* crazy!" Magga gasped. She made a hand gesture, obviously meant to ward off ill-fortune. "The God has touched you."

"Not yet, he hasn't," said a dry voice from the doorway to the hut. Sander whipped around, expecting to see one of the men from the village, and to have a fight on his hands. Instead, he saw a lone man, standing, leaning on the doorframe with his arms crossed and an amused look on his face. He had a shock of dark hair, but what was most striking about his appearance was that his face was a mass of thin scars, marring what would otherwise have been a handsome face.

Magga gave a shriek - it was hard to tell whether it was of terror or delight - and threw herself face down on the hut's filthy floor. "The Burning God!" she exclaimed. "Spare me, merciful one."

Well, that saved Sander one question. He looked at the figure skeptically. "You don't look much like a god to me," he said, gently.

The man grinned. "That's because you don't know me like these, my people," he replied. He crossed the room and nudged Magga with a toe. "Oh, do get up - you're getting that dress quite filthy. Not that it was much to look at anyway" He looked back at Sander. "I've tried to teach them the rudiments of cleanliness, but as you can see, it's an uphill battle."

"Yes, I've noticed that they're not very susceptible to new ideas." So far, Corran had stayed silent, so Sander realized he had an advantage here - the "god" had showed no signs of having seen his son, so obviously Corran's Talent was still working fine.

"That's true. I've wished that they were brighter, but -" the man spread his hands "- you have to work with whatever materials come your way, don't you?"

Sander's eyes narrowed. "I'm not inclined to believe that your... visit is exactly coincidental," he said, warily. "I assume you're here because of me?"

The other laughed. "My, you *do* have a high opinion of yourself, don't you? As a matter of fact, no, it's not you, exactly, I'm here for. Nor that invisible son of yours, either." Sander couldn't prevent a look of surprise crossing his face fleetingly, and the other man laughed. "Yes, I know all about Corran - I knew his Talent before you did."

"Ah." Sander was beginning to understand. "You're a Talent, and you have other Talents with you - a Seer, perhaps?"

"Exactly." The Talent laughed again. "Oh, it's so nice dealing with an intelligent man again. You have no idea how hard it is for me to try to think down to the level of these savages. I can see we're going to get along fine - even without the aid of my Seer."

Magga had managed to climb to her knees, and she was looking from him to Sander in confusion. "My Lord," she said, pitifully, "are you not going to destroy this wretched slave of mine for his blasphemies?"

The man looked down at her in contempt. "No, I'm not. I'm not even going to destroy him because he's dangerous. He's of greater use to me alive than you or any of your pathetic people."

Sander raised an eyebrow. "For these people's god, you're not terribly kind to them."

"They don't appreciate kindness," the other man said. "I'd have thought your captivity would have taught you that by now. They appreciate only power, and I have more than enough of that." He glanced at Magga again. "Get on your feet and go and fetch Tomar and the others. It's time I had another chat with you all." He lashed out with his foot, kicking her in the ribs. "Go on, get along with you."

Terrified, Magga did as she had been instructed, and bolted from the hut. Her god turned to Sander again. "Now, perhaps you and Corran would like to accompany me? What I have to say to these idiots will be of great interest to you also." He smiled. "And, Corran - there's no need for you to remain Unseen. My Seer knows where you are every second, and I can blast you down any moment I wish. So don't play games with me."

Corran looked to his father for advice. Sander realized that the other man was undoubtedly telling the truth. He seemed casually certain of his own power, which might well be a weakness. There was no need to provoke a display of strength - yet. "Do as he says," Sander ordered his son. He could see no difference, of course, but Corran had obviously stopped using his Talent. The other man beamed at him.

"Nice to see you," he said, cheerfully. "You're a good-looking young fellow - no need to hide a face like that. Well, let's get along, shall we? I have so much to do before we leave this place." He gestured toward the still-open door.

"You're leaving, are you?" Sander asked.

"And you two are coming with me. Relax, you'll like this next part - it'll scratch your itch for revenge on these Raiders."

Outside, the villagers were starting to gather. There were also a dozen or so people Sander didn't recognize. They were obviously with the Burning God, because the locals all threw themselves face down in the dirt and the newcomers alone remained standing. Sander didn't have a clue what this Talent was up to, so he stayed quiet. He held Corran firmly, close to his side. Despite the Burning God's apparent joviality, there was a definite air of danger about his casual assumption of his own strength. Corran seemed to be sensing it, too, for his muscles were all tensed.

"What are we going to do?" he whispered.

"I think our best bet is to just watch and wait," Sander told his son. "I think we're about to learn some of what I've been wanting to know."

"Did someone go for those brats of yours in the fields?" the Burning God asked Magga, once he'd discovered which of the prone women she was.

"Yes, Lord," she replied.

"Fine," he said. "Once they get here, we can really get started. In the meantime, though, I wish you'd all get up - I hate staring at the backs of your heads. It's difficult enough to tell you apart when I'm staring at your miserable faces."

"Yes, Lord," Tomar said. It wasn't easy for him to make it to his feet, and some of the other older people had similar problems. Eventually, though, they were all standing. Sander could see that they were all terrified. He was puzzled - he knew that Talents had to be scary to people who'd never seen one before, but this reaction seemed quite extreme to him. And... a Talent who was claiming to be a god? Was he simply manipulative or actually insane enough to believe he actually *was* a god?

The villagers stood clumped together, watching, waiting. Finally, a stream of the children appeared on the pathway to the fields. All of them were excited and terrified in about equal measure. Their voices died down, and they slipped silently in amongst the older folks.

The Talent glanced at a young woman in his party, and the woman nodded. So *she* was the Seer! Sander caught her eye, and she grinned, shyly, at him. She was quite pretty, with short-cropped blonde hair. One shoulder was slightly lower than the other was, though, and Sander realized she'd been injured at one time. He turned his attention back to the Burning God, though - clearly something interesting was about to happen.

"I am Kander, the Burning God!" the Talent said, stepping several paces forward, away from Sander and Corran. "Behold!" Corran gasped, and even Sander was shocked. The man had suddenly become a living fire. Sander backed away from the blazing heat, and the villagers all moaned, and fell forward on the ground again. Sander tried to look through cracks in his eyelids, but the light was too great. He could barely make out a figure inside the tower of flame, and then a familiar laughter broke out.

"I am Kander, the Burning God!" the flame repeated. Clearly, Kander was unaffected by the raging fire that should have destroyed any living being - even a Fire Caster. "And I am *really* unhappy with the lot of you."

Kander? Sander scowled as he tried to remember where he'd heard that name before. Kander...

He straightened up slightly. He was still unable to look on the Burning God directly. Through the shield of one hand, he said: "Melayne had a brother named Kander - a Fire-Caster."

"She still has," the blazing figure replied. "And how is my young sister?"

Chapter Nineteen

Sander simply didn't know what to say. Melayne had spoken of the older brother she had barely known - he was two years older than her, and had been taken by the King's Men when she was five. That had prompted her parents to flee and then hide out in a remote shoreline of Stormgard to protect their other two children. None of them had ever heard a word again about Kander.

"She thought you dead in the wars long ago," he managed to say, still protecting his eyes as best he could.

"Natural enough," the Burning God answered. "I was *supposed* to have died - but I didn't. My scars are the result of my ordeals, but Poth saved my life."

"Poth?"

"Me," said the pretty blonde Seer. "My Talent told me that my future would be linked with his, and that we would do great things together. I was able to help him when he was badly injured, and nursed him back to health. After that, we fled the war zone, and Kander begun to comprehend his destiny."

"Ah." Sander was starting to understand some of this situation, at least. "And your Talent told you that Corran and I would be here?"

"Precisely." Poth gave him a dazzling smile. "So we knew just the right moment to turn up and recruit you."

"Recruit me?"

"Both of you," the Seer explained. "We have need of your Talents."

"Mine?" Sander was confused. "But you're a Seer - much stronger than my limited Talent. I have to touch someone to see their future. You see much more."

"Yes, but the problem is that I see the big picture." Poth gestured, throwing her arms wide. "I see only what will happen as a result of what *has* happened. So, for example, if Corran there was to decide to walk out of here by the left path, I can see what would happen on that path. But I couldn't tell what was there *until* he decided to take that path. You, on the other hand, tell what *will* happen, regardless. If you touch someone, you see what must inevitably happen. In my case, let's say that Corran decided to take the right path instead of the left, then I wouldn't be able to know what was there - because my Talent was used on a choice that he eventually didn't take."

Sander was starting to comprehend. His ability was more limited, but more accurate. Hers was far stronger, but also far more general. "So you need me to fine-tune your plans," he said.

"Exactly," Kander agreed. "I've got the outline all worked out, but there are some pesky little details that just won't stay straight. I'm not sure why, but I think it's because those blasted dragons of yours."

"They're too *alien,*" Poth explained. "I can't quite get a grip on them. The closer they are to events, the fuzzier the future is to me."

"Ah..." Unlike Poth, Sander was getting a clearer picture. "And until they left us, you really couldn't see where we were, or what we were doing."

"Right." Poth spread her hands. "But now they're gone, I can see you both much more clearly. Everything's firmer."

"Until they return," Sander pointed out.

"Yes. Once they're back, my predictions will start getting unclear again - but yours won't."

"I see. And Corran?'

"He has the Talent to be Unseen," Kander answered. "That's always very helpful when it comes to combat situations."

"You expect to see combat?" Sander was taking this gently - there was something very disturbing about Kander, and he didn't think it would be advisable to push matters.

"Of course. With my plans, fighting is inevitable. But we shall come through together!" The Burning God laughed again, and then turned his attention back to the cowering villagers. "Now, the question becomes - what sort of punishment is appropriate for worshippers who fail me?"

Tomar dared to raise his head and stare, aghast, at his god. "How have we failed you, Lord?" he asked, terrified. "Have we not done all that you have asked of us?"

"No, you have *not* done all I've asked of you!" Kander yelled. He sent a blast of fire scorching along the ground, barely missing the old man. "You've failed in everything I asked you to do! Where are your men with the prisoners I told them to bring me?"

"I do not know, Lord." Tomar cowered again, clearly expecting to be blasted.

"No, you don't, do you?" his god yelled. "Do *any* of you wretches know?"

Magga gave a gasp. "That slave claims that they are all dead," she wailed. "I thought he was lying -"

"He's not lying!" Kander howled. "They *are* all dead. And do you know *why* they are all dead? Because they failed me, that's why! They didn't obey my orders." He stalked closer to Tomar, who winced at the pain from the flames, but who didn't dare retreat. "Do you recall my instructions when I sent the Raiders off to that village in Stormgard three years ago? Do you?"

"Yes, Lord," Tomar whimpered. His skin was turning red, as if through sunburn. He was trying not to show either pain or panic, and not managing well at either. "They were to find the girl and to bring her back here to you."

The girl? Sander scowled. "You sent them after Melayne?" he guessed.

"I sent them after Melayne," Kander agreed. "I ordered that they she brought to me here, unharmed." He stood over Tomar, whose skin was starting to wrinkle from the terrible heat. "And what did I say about her parents? What were my instructions?"

"That they were not to be harmed, Lord," Tomar gasped out. He was trying to shield himself from the fierce fire of his god, and failing.

"That they were not to be harmed," Kander repeated slowly, in a deadly voice. "And those morons *killed* them! Killed

Melayne's parents! I told them - I told them, anyone else - fine, kill and enslave whomever they wanted. But not her parents! Not *my* parents! And they ignored my explicit instructions, and murdered them."

Now Sander understood what he had seen in the cove by the farm. "You discovered what they had done," he said, slowly. "And you killed them."

"Indeed I did," Kander said, with evident satisfaction. "I killed all of those responsible once Poth informed me what had happened."

"She can't be much of a Seer if she didn't know the Raiders were going to kill Melayne's parents," Corran said, mockingly.

Poth gave him a venomous glare. "I couldn't see what they were going to do until they decided to do it," she snarled. "And by then it was too late to save the old couple. All I could do was tell Kander, so he could punish those involved. And he did." She stared at the prostrate villagers. "And still will."

"Yes," Kander agreed. "I still will. My vengeance has not reached its limit yet." Abruptly, he threw off a bolt of fire that fell onto Tomar. The old man had time for a single scream before his body was one large flame, and then ashes. "So much for your leader - fool."

Sander was stunned. Kander had acted too swiftly for him to even react - though how he could have stopped the Burning God he had no idea. He couldn't get within ten feet of him without suffering severe burns. Kander was only a Talent and not a god, but it was easy to see why these villagers were so terrified of him that they would confuse the two attributes.

Now Kander turned to Magga. "And the other ships," he prompted. "The rest of your moronic men-folk. What were my instructions to them?"

The woman couldn't answer at first. Her mouth worked, but nothing came out.

"She's terrified of you," Sander pointed out. "You'll get nothing from her like that."

"She *should* be terrified of me," Kander replied. "I am their god, and they've really annoyed me. Now I hold them accountable for their failures, and will mete out appropriate punishments."

"Appropriate?" Sander asked. "Do you think burning someone to death for events he had no control over is *appropriate*?"

The burning figure turned on Sander now. "I am their god!" he yelled. "Whatever I decide is appropriate is, by definition, appropriate!" He held out one blazing hand, and Sander could feel the power of the fire he contained. "Right now I am being nice to you because you could be useful to me - and because you're married to my sister. But don't push your good fortune. If you annoy me much more, Melayne is going to be a very young widow." He whirled back to Magga. "Answer me, you wretch! If you don't use that tongue of yours, I'll burn it out of your stupid mouth!"

"You, you," Magga croaked. "You told them to go to the Far Islands and to bring back this Melayne you speak of."

"Yes," purred Kander. "I told them to go to the Far Islands and bring back my sweet baby sister." He bent down slightly, and Magga winced at the pain of his heat. "Look around, you stupid bitch - do you *see* Melayne here anywhere?"

"No... no," Magga gasped. It was impossible to tell if she was answering his question or just begging for relief from his heat.

"No, you don't," Kander agreed. "And neither do I! This is completely unacceptable, you know." He moved away from the stricken woman a few feet. "I am your god, and it is your duty to do my bidding. Twice I've sent your men off on tasks for me, and twice they've failed to do as I instructed. And twice they've died as a result of it." He glared at the prone villagers. "And if I were to be a merciful god and spare the lives of all of you, you'd raise more moronic men-folk who can't do as they're instructed in even the simplest of matters. So there's only one thing I can do with you failures..."

Sander started forward in horror, but two of the Talents grabbed him roughly by the arms and held him in place. A third had Corran by the throat. Poth laughed, and leaned to look into Sander's horror-stricken eyes. "Silly man," she purred. "Did you think I wouldn't see *that* coming?"

"He's going to kill them all," Sander gasped.

Poth shrugged. "They're idiots; they deserve it."

"There are children!"

"There *were* children," she murmured. "Now they're toast..."

Bright as Kander had blazed before, now he was brighter than the sun in the sky. The heat, even at this distance, was searing. The villagers suddenly understood what was happening. Some of them tried to scramble to their feet and run for their lives, but most had no chance. Streams of fire flowed from Kander as he threw his flames. Screams of fear and agony were swiftly cut off as the fires caught all of the stricken people. There was a horrible stench of burning flesh, and Sander felt sickened.

Abruptly, it was over. Fire still burned on the ground and in the buildings where people had been, but there was little sign of there ever having been anyone alive here. Most of the people had been incinerated almost instantly, so hot had the fire been. There were still a few twisted lumps of charred flesh, and a few pieces of bone, but nothing else.

The villagers - down to the smallest baby - had been annihilated.

Sander's legs went weak, and he wanted to cry for the murdered people. They had been harsh and unkind, but they had been people. Now they were all dead, burnt up in one terrible moment. He felt dizzy.

Kander abruptly put out his flame. He was completely unscathed - even his clothing hadn't been harmed. Sander didn't know how this was possible. He stared at the murderer - Melayne's brother! - in horror. "Well," the would-be god murmured, "that's all finished with." He shrugged. "Don't you just hate incompetence?"

"Not as much as you obviously do," Sander gasped.

Kander laughed. "True, true," he agreed. "But we gods can't tolerate sloppy worshippers, can we?"

"You're not a god," Sander growled. "You're just a man. A Talent, true, but still just a man."

"A man?" Kander looked bemused. "Could a *man* do what I just did?"

"No," Sander replied. "A man would not be so callous."

"I was talking of my power," the would-be god said, sighing. "No mere man can control fire as I do."

"You're just a Talent," Sander said. "There are many who are Fire-Casters."

"I am not just a Talent!" Kander yelled. "Fire-Casters! I've seen Fire-Casters, and there's not one who can do that! Not one! None who can stand among the flames unharmed, and control the raw element as I do."

"So you're a very powerful Talent," Sander said. "Melayne is powerful, too - but she doesn't try to hurt or create fear. She is kind and considerate."

"She's been sheltered," her brother said. "She's a sweet little thing, too young and naive to understand the ways of the world. But I'll teach her. With her on my side, we will rule this whole world."

"She will never agree to help you," Sander told him. He glared at Poth. "Ask your pet Seer - surely she can tell you that much."

Poth laughed cheerfully. "I can indeed see that," she agreed. "Little sister is a goody-goody. She *loves* everyone, even sweet little bunny rabbits." Poth smiled widely. "But you do have another use, you know."

"Yes," Kander agreed. "I think even my sweet, gentle sister will have second thoughts about joining me if the alternative is to see her husband turned into a living candle - don't you?" He smiled again. "But I'm sure it won't come to that, brother-in-law. I'm sure she'll understand, and there will be no need to toast you."

"You're crazy," Sander said, sickened.

"Now, now, name-calling isn't nice." Kander smiled. "But I don't hold grudges, and to prove it, I'll even give you a present." He gestured at Poth. "She'll be more than happy to warm your bed tonight - not using real flames of course."

Sander was reeling at this change in mood. "I'm married to Melayne," he said. "I don't allow other women to take her place."

Poth moved closer, and put her arms about his neck. "I can see we'd have great fun in bed together," she said. "I'm a Seer, remember - I can see the outcome."

"Then you can surely see I will never cheat on my wife," he snarled.

Poth sighed, and kissed the end of his nose. "Yes, I can see that you think you're being all good and noble. But she's not here, and I am. I can wait - I can be very patient. It will happen - I can see that."

"Then you're as crazy as he is." Sander knew she was either wrong – or lying.

"My, aren't we the feisty one," she cooed, and then laughed. "I think it would be a good idea to keep him and the brat tied up tonight - I can see all sorts of plans to escape are bubbling in his brain." She shook her head at Kander. "Silly man - and we would have had *so* much fun. I can still see it..."

"Well, run along now, then," Kander answered. "You men, do as Poth suggests. You know what will happen to you if either of them manages to slip out tonight. I'm not a very forgiving god, you know." He surveyed the blasted clearing. Flames still danced at the edges of the charred ground, and several of the houses had caught fire. "I'm just going to enjoy the fruits of my powers. In the morning, we start our journey."

"To where?" Sander asked, as the men holding him started to drag him away, toward one of the intact houses. "Where are you taking us?"

Kander smiled cheerfully. "To Dragonhome, of course. That's where Melayne is heading right now. Oh, don't family reunions give you a warm, warm feeling in your heart?"

Chapter Twenty

Ganeth felt as if she was finally awakening after a very long sleep. Her mind came back into something like its customary focus, and she stared around, wondering where she was, and what she was doing here.

"Here" appeared to be a rocky crag. There was snow further up the peaks, and it was quite chilly where she was - certainly colder than she normally liked to be. She raised her flexible neck and slowly studied everything she could see. Rocks, mostly, and mountain peaks. In the distance she could make out the ocean. Her senses told her she was somewhere to the south of the last place she could clearly recall, but she wasn't at all sure where that might be.

There were two things close that were not rocks. One she recognized immediately as the sleeping form of her brother, Brek. He looked as exhausted as she felt. The other was a second dragon, completely unfamiliar to her. She was larger than Ganeth, and clearly older. She was also wide awake, and using her front claws to clean her scales along her neck.

"Who are you?" Ganeth asked. "Where am I? What has happened?"

The female stopped grooming herself and glanced, amusedly, at Ganeth. "Ah, so you're back with us. How do you feel, little one?"

"I feel... strange." Ganeth stretched, and discovered that parts of her neck were sore, and felt as if they had been injured slightly. Also parts of her belly and further back toward her tail. "I ache. And I cannot remember how I got here, or what I have been doing. Or how long I have been here."

The other dragon snorted, amused. "It's often like that the first time. Intoxicating, they say, though what exactly that means I do not know."

"The first time?" Ganeth couldn't understand this dragon. "The first time for what?"

The female laughed, gently. "Mating, of course. What else? Why do you think you're so sore - and so happy?"

Mating? Now that her companion mentioned it, Ganeth was starting to recall something about a male dragon that wasn't her brother... But it wouldn't come into focus. "I have been... mating?" she asked.

"Oh, yes, you've been mating. That brother of yours, too." She looked rather pleased with herself. "Considering it was the first time for either of you, you acquitted yourselves rather well. At any rate, you certainly pleased my brother. And I have no complaints with Brek."

"Your brother?" Was that who the other male dragon she vaguely recalled was?

"Oh dear." The other female shook her head. "I suppose I was like this the first time, too. It was quite a while ago, though, and I don't really know."

"I don't understand." Ganeth's mistiness was clearing a little. "I can remember there was an odd scent in their air that we felt compelled to follow. And something about a dragon..." She shook her head, but it wouldn't clear. "There should be more, but I can't quite understand." She knew that there was something she was forgetting, something important - but it refused to come into focus.

"It's the mating dance," the other dragon explained. "It can overwhelm any dragon - but the first time, it can be all-consuming."

"The mating dance?" There was a vague memory in Ganeth's fuzzy mind of flying with another dragon high above mountain peaks...

The other female sighed. "I suppose I'd better explain the facts of life to you, dear - a bit late, now, mind you. Didn't your mother ever tell you about this?"

"We have no parents," Ganeth said, sadly. "They were killed shortly after our eggs were laid."

"Then how were you raised?" The older dragon seemed quite surprised.

"By humans."

"Humans?" She shot upright. "That *can't* be! Humans *kill* dragons! That's why we fled to these cold southern lands centuries ago."

So that was how these dragons had escaped the general slaughter! "Most humans do seem to hate dragons," Ganeth agreed. "But there was one family that didn't. They kept our eggs safe until we hatched. A human named Sander fed us - dead meat."

"Dead?" The female gave a shudder of disgust that passed down her entire body. "Oh, you poor things! However did you survive like that?"

"We were fortunate - a human came who could speak with us, and who could understand us. Her name is Melayne, and she saved our lives. She found us living flesh, and she saved us when humans wished to kill us. Now we share lives with our humans."

"Share? With *humans*?" The other dragon gave another repulsed shudder. "You poor things! It's a good thing, then, that you found my brother and I! Having to live with humans..."

"It's not so bad," Ganeth assured her. "My human is one who was recently hatched, and is as young as I am. His name is Corran, and I'm very fond of him." There was something else she should know about him, but she couldn't quite wrap her mind around that yet.

"Well, we'll soon cure you of *that* madness!" the other dragon promised. "You are fortunate, then, to have found us."

"I suppose so." Ganeth stretched out in the sun, which made her feel better. The warmth was bringing life back to her body. "But you were going to tell me why I have trouble remembering what happened to me. And you still haven't told me your name."

"I have, in fact, several times over the past few days." The other dragon laughed a little. "I'm Kata. My brother is Hagon. He's off hunting right now, but he'll be back soon." Now that the names had been spoken, they *did* sound rather familiar to Ganeth. "It's the mating madness," Kata explained. "When we prepare to mate, all kinds of changes take place in our bodies.

Chemicals we produce flow through us, heightening our senses and responses, but they tend to affect the brain. It's like a sort of temporary madness. You get used to it after a while, but for the first few times it completely possesses you, and you can think of nothing else - you *must* mate, and everything is centered upon that. As you get older and more experienced, the madness fades to merely pleasure. The first times are overwhelming, though - and very, very nice." She gave another barking laugh. "My brother is very taken with you. And I have to confess that Brek is most pleasant to be with."

"We've been mating?" There was something definitely familiar about that, but she still couldn't recall it at all well.

"For several days," Kata replied. "And we'll continue for a while longer." She shifted slightly. "I think my eggs have already been fertilized, but why stop when you're having fun? How about you? Are you fertile yet, do you think?"

Fertile? "Ganeth sighed. "I don't know how to tell."

Kata laughed again. "Well, you and Hagon have mated quite prodigiously, so I would imagine you must be seeded well by now. And if you're not, yet, you soon will be. It is so good having fresh dragons here again. It's been a while since I laid my last clutch, and they hatched."

"How long?" Ganeth asked.

"A long time. Years and years. Luckily, we dragons live for quite a while, and stay fertile almost all our lives."

"Yes, I suppose so," Ganeth said, absently. She glanced at her brother, who showed no signs of stirring. "We found you, then?"

"Yes, several days ago." Kata scratched absently behind one ear. "When we're in heat, we dragons give off strong scents. The ocean winds must have carried them to the two of you in the north. You came flying in here, half-crazed. That's why you're having trouble remembering things - those scents have strange effects on the mind. Maybe that's why you're hallucinating about being around humans."

"Hallucinating?" Ganeth tried to focus, but her mind kept slipping away from something important. "No, no, I'm sure that's real. I remember my human very well - and Melayne. She's *very* clear in my mind."

"Then you've had a very strange upbringing. Those of us here have never even seen a human." Kata's muzzle twitched. "I've seen ships, of course, out at sea, but we stay very clear of them. One thing every dragon learns is to avoid people. They're treacherous and murderous."

"Some are," Ganeth had to agree. "Perhaps even most. But there are some you can trust."

"Not that I've ever found."

Ganeth felt a little annoyed. "Well, you wouldn't find that if you spent your whole life avoiding them."

"There's no point in arguing about humans," Kata said. "You're here, now, and the humans aren't. We can lay our eggs and hatch our babies here in safety. Few humans come this far south, so we're quite safe."

That sounded... oddly appealing and alarming at one and the same moment. Ganeth couldn't understand why. What was this urge of hers to fly away? She couldn't fathom it. She and Brek had flown here in the first place to look for mates, hadn't they? That much she could recall with certainty. And now they had found them. So what was the problem?

"There are others!" she exclaimed.

"Of course," Kata said. "Many others. There's at least a hundred of us in these cold southern lands now."

"No, not here," Ganeth said, excitedly. "Back home. We have another brother and two sisters. They're waiting for us to return and tell them if there are other dragons." That must be what she'd been trying to recall!

"Oh. Well, that's good news. Maybe you can fly back and fetch them here - I'm sure they'll be most welcome. And there will be others in heat soon, so they can mate as well. We'll have such fun together now - and they'll be better off without humans."

"I'm not sure they'd agree to come on those conditions," Ganeth told her. "Tura, especially - she's Melayne's, and the two of them have bonded closely." Again, something scratched at her memories, but she couldn't quite identify it. "Anyway, she was wounded by a band of dragon slayers, and she won't be fit to travel for a while."

"Dragon slayers?" Kata was alarmed now. "They still exist?" She shuddered. "When I was a hatchling, my mother brought me and my kin here to escape the slayers."

"That was two hundred years ago!" Ganeth exclaimed.

Kata shrugged. "I told you we'd been here a while. But I still remember the terror she felt. Those humans had specialized in killing dragons. I'd have thought they'd have died off without anything to hunt. Humans don't live that long, do they?"

"No - their lives are relatively short," Ganeth explained. "But they pass their skills and knowledge down to their own hatchlings, and those to their hatchlings in turn. These dragon slayers are long descended from the ones who attacked you - and, thankfully, they lack practice. That's how we were able to survive their attack - well, that and the humans we live with, who fought for us."

"Humans fought *for* you?" Kata was clearly amazed. "What kind of humans are these?"

"They're good, and kind, and love us," Ganeth said. "And we love them. I couldn't give up my...." Her voice trailed away as she suddenly remembered what it was that had been eating at her. "Corran!"

"What's a Corran?"

"My human!" Ganeth exclaimed. "I knew there was something about him that was important! I was supposed to meet him - oh, *days* ago! And I abandoned him! He may need me - he's very young, and almost without power. I have to go to him!"

"Go to him?" Kata hissed, annoyed. "You're with *dragons* now! You don't need humans. You will stay here with us and be happy."

"If I abandon Corran," Ganeth assured her, "I will never be happy again. I must go to him - he must think I've deserted him! I must -" She broke off, and looked at her brother. "Brek!" she cried, sharply. "Brek! Awake, you lazy creature!"

"What?" Brek opened one eye, blearily, and looked very confused. "What? Mating time again?"

"Stop thinking of mating!" Ganeth cried, urgently. "Start thinking about Sander!"

"Sander? Who's Sander?" Brek yawned and stretched, and then caught sight of Kata. "Ah! My delicious one! It's time to have fun again?"

"It's time to *remember*!" Ganeth exploded. "Brek, you *must* remember Sander! We left him and Corran days ago! They may be in trouble now, needed our help."

"Yes, yes, all right," Brek grumbled. "We'll get to... what was their names again? Well, we'll go soon. First, though, more mating."

"You're hopeless!" Ganeth growled. "We *must* go to them! Now!"

"I'm sure it's nothing serious," Brek said, dreamily, staring at Kata all the time. "There are more important things in life."

He was obviously still under the influence of the mating scents. Ganeth didn't know what to do about him. She knew how powerfully she had been affected, and how hard it was to recall anything else as mattering. But he would come around eventually, she knew. Perhaps the best thing was for her to head out alone and look for Corran and Sander. Brek could follow when he'd recovered sufficiently.

"Ah!" Kata said, with evident satisfaction in her voice. "Here comes Hagon now - *he'll* manage to talk some sense into you, I'm sure."

Ganeth glanced up into the sky. Skimming low over the waves, she could make out a dark shape. Her heart beat faster, and she felt herself starting to become aroused. Now that she knew what was causing it, she could smell, even at this distance, the mating scent that Hagon was exuding. Her body was starting to respond, and she was having trouble recalling what had felt so urgent a moment ago.

No! Corran! She *must* remember Corran! It was important! More important than... More important than... She shook her head to try and clear it.

It was no use. The scent overwhelmed her, and her rational mind slipped away. With a cry of passion, she spread her wings and rose in the air to meet her beloved.

Nothing else mattered. Nothing.

Chapter Twenty One

"Why don't we try and escape?" Corran asked his father as they sat together eating their noon meal.

Sander shook his head. "It's no good," he explained. Poth was handing out some large, rather sticky fruits to people, and he nodded in her direction. "She'd see your plans as soon as you did, and she'd be able to stop you."

"But I can be Unseen!" Corran said. "If I'm careful, she won't be able to detect me."

"I wish that were so, but it isn't," Sander replied. He tried to think of a way to explain it. "Her Talent and mine seem similar, but they're not really. I see what *will* happen to a person - one vision each time of something that *must* happen, no matter what. Poth sees what *may* happen, and it's fairly general. For example, if she thinks about you, she can tell what you're planning to do right now - but not necessarily what you'll be planning to do tomorrow, if you decide on something different. She can see what *might* happen *if* I decided to join Kander's band of plotters - but she can't tell whether I ever *would* join."

"Then she should be easy to escape," Corran said, sniffing. "If I just *act* and don't *plan*, then I could lose her."

"Doesn't work like that, kid," Poth said. She'd managed to get closer while they were speaking - and, of course, she knew what they were speaking about. "Your father's right - you couldn't escape me." She hefted the three fruits she had left. "Tell you what, why don't we test it? You go Unseen, and I'll try and get you with these fruits. If you're right, you'll be able to escape and go for help. If I'm right, you'll need to take a wash. Nobody gets hurt, but you might learn a real lesson."

Sander could see no possible harm in allowing this, so he nodded to his son - who promptly vanished from sight.
Poth gave Sander one of her entrancing grins. "I like this kid," she admitted. "If you want more children I can be very cooperative. I could even predict whether they'd be boys or girls. And we could have such fun making babies together..."

Abruptly, she whirled and threw a fruit. It seemed to vanish in mid-air. "Well, he needed to wash his face, anyway."

"I don't know why you're so interested in me," Sander said. "You must know I'll never cheat on Melayne."

"She may not be alive forever," Poth said, grinning. "I, on the other hand, can see precisely what to do to live a long, healthy life. And my Talent tells me that of all the men I like, you're the one I'd most enjoy being with." She whipped off a second shot, which disappeared in flight. There was a faint "Ouch!" "It would be lots of fun," she promised. "Imagine it - making love to a girl who could see everything that would *really* please you... and be willing to do them. I see we'd be very compatible, and I can see myself having a wonderful time in your bed..." She closed her eyes dreamily and threw the last fruit. It vanished also. "Enough!" she called out. "That's three for three - are you convinced now that I can find you?"

Corran reappeared, fruit juices running down his face and neck. He looked very crestfallen. "I guess so."

"Your father's really smart," Poth told him. "You should listen to him more. Come on, I'll help you get clean." She put an arm across his shoulders and led him away.

Sander studied her, thoughtfully. There were times when she seemed very pleasant and considerate - when she wasn't acting completely insane. Perhaps there was a way he could use that? Maybe pretend to play up to her obvious desire for him? Poth turned around and grinned at him, and he sighed. Of course not - she'd *know* if he were faking it. She was a very difficult foe to face, because he didn't really want to hurt her. On the other hand, Kander was clearly completely insane. He glanced at the man who styled himself the Burning God, and scowled. It seemed like all of Melayne's relatives were going to be major league trouble. He was wondering how she would take the news that her older brother was alive - and totally mad. Melayne! He missed her so much! He kept trying not to think about her, but he couldn't. He wanted to hold her, to comfort her, to love her. He wanted to be with the children she'd birthed to him, and just stay locked away forever with her.

It was impossible, of course. They couldn't just go off alone and live their lives - too many people depended upon them. People - and dragons.

Where *were* Ganeth and Brek? Maybe Poth could... But, no - she'd already mentioned that she couldn't see dragons. Their minds were too hard for her to wrap her thoughts around. He couldn't help worrying about Brek, though. What *could* have kept him from returning? Powerful he might be, but he was still young and inexperienced.

And what did Kander have in mind for them? Sander wished he had some insight into his brother-in-law's plans, but the Talent leader was being very close-mouthed. Stress was taking its toll on Sander, and he knew it was only going to get worse.

If only Melayne were here! She was naive, and often very simple-minded, but she was so brave and supportive and wonderful. Somehow, being with her made all things seem right, no matter how bad they were. He missed her terribly.

There was a sudden, gentle pressure on his shoulder, as two firm hands began to massage him. His first reaction was to jump up, but his second was to enjoy the feeling. He went with the second.

"I told you I could be wonderful for you," Poth breathed in his ear. Close-up, she smelled like berries, or the forest. He turned slightly to stare into her deep blue eyes, and she grinned again. "I *know* the exact spots to rub to make you feel better. If you like this so much, just imagine what making love to me would be like." Her grin widened. "I could tell you. Better yet, I could show you..." She gave a gentle tug on his hands.

He shrugged free of her hands. "Poth, I..." He shook his head, and then gestured toward Kander. "Why aren't you after him? He's your leader, and you seem absolutely loyal to him."

"Kander?" Poth shook her head firmly. "He's my *god*. I would *never* even think he'd be interested in me."

"He's not a god," Sander replied. "He's just another Talent."

"Oh, no, not just another Talent," she said. "He's very, very unique. You've seen what he can do - have you ever seen a Fire Caster like him?"

"So he's very powerful," Sander argued. "He's still a Talent, like us."

"Like Melayne, maybe," Poth said, thoughtfully. "She's really powerful, too. It seems to be something that runs in the family."

"Yes," Sander said. "When I checked Melayne's old home, I discovered a very large dragon buried there. And Talents are caused by chemicals from dragon's scales. But Kander never lived at that farm... so that can't be how *he* got to be so powerful."

"It's simply who he is," Poth replied. "Gods don't need mortal reasons." She cocked her head to one side, thoughtfully. "I wonder if that means Melayne is a god, too?"

"Melayne is very wonderful, but she's no god," Sander informed her. "And she'd be the first person to tell you that. Speaking of whom..."

"You're wondering how she is," Poth said, clapping her hands in delight. "I could See you were going to ask me to check up on her." Then she frowned. "But I can't. I don't know her."

That was interesting... "You have to know the people you See about?" he asked.

"Mostly." Poth sighed. "I mean, I can See you getting back together with her after all this is over, but it might not be true."

"Right." That made sense - she could See he *intended* to be back with Melayne again, but a lot of things might interfere with his plans, things she couldn't predict. So she was only seeing a potential future. Unless she knew Melayne and could See her future, also, then Poth couldn't predict accurately what would happen to both Melayne and himself.

Plus, there were bound to be dragons involved, and *they* would mess up Poth's visions completely. Which was perhaps an advantage he had - if the dragons ever came back.

He looked at her again, and she pouted. "My Talent is good and it's useful," she said. "But it's not infallible. Yours is! So why don't you take those silly gloves off and touch me? Maybe you'll see that we're meant to be together, after all."

"Maybe," he agreed, humoring her. "But maybe I'll see your death. I saw my first wife's that way."

"Oh, you think I might be your next wife?" Poth looked very eager.

"That's not what I meant," Sander growled. "I meant that I can't control my Sight. I see what I see - and it may be for good or for evil. I don't know. If I touch you, we'd both be taking a very grave chance."

"Okay, let's forget that idea for now," Poth said. "I got Corran cleaned up, and it's about time to start moving again. Kander can get very impatient. Gods don't like to be kept waiting." She glanced across at him.

Inevitably, as she'd known, Kander called out: "It's time to move on again, people."

Corran sighed, and moved to his father's side. "I hate all this walking," he complained. "I wish the dragons were here - it's so much more fun to fly."

"But not as good exercise," Sander told him. He looked at Poth. "If we are walking the whole way, it will take us quite a while to reach Dragonhome."

"We're not walking the whole way," Poth replied. "Kander has things planned, don't worry." She ran her hand through Corran's hair. "Just a couple more hours, then you can ride." She grinned. "I'll let our method of transportation be a surprise."

"Why are we going to Dragonhome?" Sander asked her. "If Kander wants to meet Melayne again, she's in the Far Isles."

"Maybe she *was*," Poth replied, looking a little distracted. "But that's not where she *is*. I can see that if he went to the Far Isles, he'll meet up with her again in a few months. But by going to Dragonhome, he'll see her in a couple of days."

"But why would she be there?" Sander asked, puzzled. "She's pregnant - or, rather, she was - she must have had the baby by now. She wouldn't take a newborn on such a journey, and I can't imagine she'd leave a baby behind."

"I don't *know,*" Poth growled. "I can't See why she does anything. I told you, I don't know her. I can just See that Kander's best way to link with her is at Dragonhome. I don't know why she'll be there, but she will be." She gave him a lingering look. "It's your best chance of seeing her again, too. Mind you, your life is intertwined with hers much more strongly." She pointed south, "Weeks out in the ocean, there are rocky islands. If, for whatever reason, you decided to go to one of them, you'd still meet with Melayne there - in about six months. I can't say why, just that it would happen. No matter what your choices are, you're bound to run into her again. It's just a matter of time."

"We love each other," Sander said simply. "We couldn't bear to be apart."

"So I gathered," Poth agreed, off-handedly. "It's a shame you don't feel that way about me."

"You know I can't."

"I know you *don't.*" Poth gave another of her wicked, attractive grins. "But if you *couldn't,* then I wouldn't be able to See the two of us together."

Sander scowled. "You're an attractive woman," he admitted. "And I'm only human. Of course the thought crosses my mind from time to time that you're... interesting. But that's all. I'd never seriously consider cheating on Melayne with you, and you know that."

"Things may change," Poth said. "Even I can't see all the possibilities." She moved away, walking forward to join Kander.

Corran looked at his father, worried. "I don't think I like her," he confessed. "I don't know why you do."

"I don't, really," Sander said. "But she's the only one of Kander's people who is willing to talk to us, and she's telling me lots that we may need to know."

"She scares me," Corran admitted. "She can see me when nobody else can."

"But she's not infallible," Sander pointed out. "For example, she saw that Kander's best chance of meeting Melayne was to send the Raiders to her farm after them. But Melayne escaped. Partly, I think, it was because Poth can't see Melayne's powers because she's never met Melayne. Poth knows Melayne has the ability to talk to animals - but she doesn't know that's only a part of Melayne's Talent. As a result, she underestimates Melayne. Also, she didn't See that the Raiders would disobey Kander and kill his parents. And she didn't See that the Raiders Kander sent to the Far Isles after Melayne would fail. Poth can't See the dragons, and that's a huge blind spot. So, since she can only See Melayne partially, and the dragons not at all, we still have an advantage here. And, added to that, she can only See you once you've decided to go Unseen. If you were to do it on the spur of the moment while she was occupied on something else, she might not be able to See you." He held up a warning hand. "But I don't want you to test that! Keep it in mind as an option if we get really desperate."

"You don't think things are desperate now?"

"No." Sander mused a moment. "Kander doesn't want us dead, or he could have fried us when he destroyed that village. He's still after Melayne, and my bet is he wants us around as hostages, to force her to do something. In that case, he won't dare harm us. He might even treat us nicely, hoping we'll be on his side when we meet Melayne again."

"Are we going to be?" Corran asked.

"No." Sander smiled down at his son. "Kander is insane - literally. His Talent seems to have affected his mind, and he really believes he's some kind of god. The thing is, his Talent is very strong indeed. No other Fire Casters can set themselves alight as he can without burning themselves to death. This seems to have convinced him he's really special. And his followers certainly believe it. Poth worships him, quite literally. And she's also at least on the edge of madness. Perhaps her Talent affects her mind, too. Seeing all those possibilities in her head might make the real world seem - well, almost dull in comparison. We can't really trust either of them, because if we cross them, they might harm or kill us out of anger or madness. But as long as they think they may win us over or be able to use us against

Melayne, well, then, we're fairly safe. So we'll be careful and try not to annoy them too much."

"Maybe you should pretend you like Poth, then?" Corran suggested. "Girls love it if you flatter them. She might be nicer to us if you did."

"You're a bit young to be so manipulative," Sander commented, raising an eyebrow. "But I'm not going to do it. She'd be suspicious, even if it is what she wants. And if she thinks I'm trying to manipulate her, it could turn her against us. No, we're safer being honest with her, I think."

The march continued. The other Talents stayed away from the captives, and talked only amongst themselves. Sander didn't have any idea what their abilities might be, but clearly they were Talents that Kander felt were useful to his purpose - whatever his ultimate aim might be. Kander didn't approach them, either, and didn't speak of his plans. Poth dropped back from time to time to chat, but she said little of any significance. It was mostly flirting; she seemed to be obsessed with Sander.

Sander was tempted to try and play her up a little - but he was certain his instincts were correct, and that this would be a mistake. Poth *seemed* to be fairly rational, but there was an undercurrent of madness in her mind that worried him. "Why do you follow Kander?" he asked her at one point.

She frowned, as if that was a stupid question. "He's the Burning God."

"You *know* that's not really true," Sander said. "He's a Talent - a powerful one, but a Talent. And he's quite, quite mad."

Poth glared at him. "How can you say that?" she asked, annoyed. "You've seen his power. You've heard his words."

"I saw him slaughter a helpless village," Sander replied. "That proves he's insane. There was no need at all to do that."

"They were evil people," Poth replied. "Surely you saw that while they held you as their slave. We could have rescued you earlier, but Kander wanted you to see what sort of people they were. If Kander hadn't destroyed them, they would have raised their children to become Raiders, and they would have killed and enslaved many more people. So, killing them off helps everybody in the end. Besides," she added, almost as an afterthought, "they really annoyed Kander by messing up his orders. Since he was their god, they should have been more careful to do as he told them."

"That's the real reason he killed them," Sander said. "Not because he was trying to save their future victims, but because they annoyed him."

"It's a bad idea to annoy a god," Poth pointed out. "They should have known it would result in trouble."

It was no use trying to convince her; she believed what she believed, and like most people, she wasn't going to change her faith very easily.

They trudged on through the woods in silence. Poth went back to rejoin Kander, leaving Sander alone with Corran. As always, the other Talents kept away, talking only amongst themselves. Perhaps Kander had issued orders, or perhaps they simply didn't like outsiders. There were about twenty of the Talents, and they all had the hard-eyed, grizzled look of being former fighters. Sander knew that Kander had been taken from Melayne's family to fight, so he imagined that the Fire Caster had met up with most of his followers during that period of service. They had undoubtedly faced battle together - there was little other explanation for Kander's horrendous scarring - and that gave them a strong bond of loyalty to one another. Only Poth seemed to be gentler and more vulnerable. There were eight other women in the Talents, and they all had that alertness and wariness of having seen combat. Poth was the only one who seemed able to smile. Sander couldn't imagine what these Talents had been through, or how many deaths they had seen - or caused - all for the sake of the fake wars. He could sympathize with their wanting something better from life - and even revenge on the people who had given them up, or those in power who had sent them off to die. But was that what Kander was planning? If so, why did he seem so desperate to get hold of Melayne? Was it simply that he believed she was his only living relative?

But she wasn't, of course - there was also Sarrow. Yet Kander had never mentioned his brother's name once. Was it possible that he didn't even know of Sarrow's existence? Kander had been very young when he had been taken by the King's Men, and he might not even know he had a brother.

And if *he* didn't, then Poth didn't, either... Sander had to hide a smile. Poth certainly wasn't infallible - and they were heading for Dragonhome, where Sarrow held sway! That was a factor that she couldn't possibly account for in her predictions - which meant that, whatever Kander's plans were, there was going to be a monumental failure in his future. Sarrow and his power of Persuasion could break Kander and his team apart... And even if Kander did know about Sarrow, he still couldn't know what his brother's talent was... It hadn't manifested itself properly until three years ago.

There was certainly hope, then. Sander didn't know what Kander had in mind, but it was almost certainly doomed to fail. In that case, he and Corran would have to be prepared to take advantage of whatever happened. And Poth couldn't predict what Sander would do because he didn't have a clue himself what he was going to do - except to seize whatever opportunity presented itself.

Perhaps things weren't as black as they seemed.

A short while later the woods started to thin out as the band was approaching a steep rise. The party moved on a little slower, and then they broke out of the trees altogether and into a meadow. Sander stopped, surprised by what awaited them there.

It was a sailing ship, sitting out in a sea of grass - no water anywhere for miles around. How had it managed to get here? It looked to be in perfect condition, and there were a half-dozen more Talents aboard it, obviously waiting for Kander and his party. This was making absolutely no sense at all.

Poth saw his confusion and laughed, bright and cheery. "Puzzled, aren't you? I told you, Kander is a god - he plans... in interesting ways. Come on, we'd better get aboard."

"But... there's no water for it," Corran protested.

"It doesn't sail on water," Poth told him, her face crinkled in amusement. "Come on, kid, you're going to love this." She clapped her hands together. "Oh, this is such fun!"

The Talents already on the ship threw out rope ladders so that the party could come aboard. As the others started climbing, Sander looked at the ship, confused. "It's perfectly vertical," he said to Poth. "Shouldn't it have fallen on its side?"

"That would damage it," Poth told him. "You want to go first, or shall I? That way you could watch my backside - I've been told it's rather cute. Though not by you." She pouted.

"I'll go first," Sander decided. He didn't want her thinking he was looking at her body. He scampered up the ladder, followed by Poth and then Corran. Sander helped his son aboard. They were among the last on deck, and the Talents started to haul up the ladders.

"Get us underway," Kander ordered, and then went below.

"Watch this," Poth said, grinning again. "It's excellent."

The ship was some forty feet long, and had two vertical masts and one thrusting forward. The sails were all furled, and a couple of the Talents started up the two main masts, clearly preparing to unfurl them. What on earth was going on?

There was a shudder and then the ship gave a lurch. Sander, caught unawares, staggered. Poth grabbed Corran to prevent him from falling, her grin still huge. Sander grabbed hold of the rail that ran about the side of the ship and held fast. As a result, he was staring directly overboard as the ship gave a finally shudder and launched itself.

Into the air.

Sander watched the ground dropping away below their vessel, and whirled around. "How is this happening?" he demanded.

"Lifters," she explained, pointing to two men and one woman who stood beside the wheel. The three of them had looks of furious concentration on their faces. "Their Talent is rather like that of Flyers - only instead of just raising themselves from the ground, they can Lift quite heavy weights into the air. They're raising the ship and keeping it up."

"It looks like quite a strain on them," Sander remarked, worried. "How long can they keep it up?"

"Several hours, actually," Poth replied. "Then we have a second team who will take over from them. It's the best way to travel - flying!"

Sander gazed overboard, and saw that they were a couple of hundred feet in the air already. The air-sailors in the rigging released the sails, and the stronger wind at this height caught the materials, billowing them out strongly. The ship began to move along with the force of the wind.

"This is so..." Corran said, looking pale.

"Terrific?" Poth asked, happily.

"Scary," he said, and ran to the rail. He was promptly sick over the side.

Poth looked unhappy. "But he likes to ride the dragons!" she protested. "I thought he'd love this."

"It's too unnatural," Corran gasped. "Dragons are fun. This is..." He threw up again.

"It's going to be a long flight," Poth muttered to herself.

Chapter Twenty Two

"It's no use," Ysane said, sighing. "I can't help but worry."

Bantry smiled fondly down at her as she nursed Falma and Melayne's still-unnamed son. "Well," he said, "maybe you'd better try. We don't want the boys growing up on worried milk, do we?"

"Oh, you idiot," Ysane said, affectionately. "I'm sure they're both doing well. Trust me, they're both drinking eagerly." She glanced down at the boy firmly slurping at her right breast. "Mind you, I can't help worrying that he *still* hasn't made a sound."

"He's making a lot now," Bantry said. "Sucking noises, mostly."

"You know what I mean." Ysane gave her husband a mock frown.

"Well, he's much too young to strike up a conversation," Bantry pointed out. "And, other than that, everyone who's examined him - and there've been plenty of *those* - say there's nothing at all wrong with him." He shrugged. "Maybe he's just a quiet child."

"No children are *this* quiet," Ysane replied. "Trust me - I helped raise most of my brothers and sisters. I know babies are meant to cry."

"Maybe he's just terribly polite," Bantry suggested. "I had an uncle once, who was so polite he'd apologize to a stone if he tripped over it."

Ysane laughed at his nonsense. "Well, you at least keep me steady," she said. "It's impossible to be too serious with you around."

"All part of my job, my love," he told her, kissing her forehead. She could clearly see the affection in his eyes. "And that's one job I don't mind doing at all. Beats mucking out the stables, trust me."

She knew he was acting silly in an attempt to cheer her up, and it was, to a large extent, working. But with both Melayne and Sander missing, and both of them off looking hard for trouble, Ysane's mind wouldn't be quieted. "They could be in danger," she sighed. "They could be dead."

"That pair?" Bantry shook his head. "They're both as tough as they come. Trust me, I've known Lord Sander longer than you, and he's hard and firm in his purpose. Besides, he's got two dragons looking out for him, and there's not a lot that will get by two dragons. And while I will concede you've known Melayne longer than I have, I think you'd be the first to admit there's not much she can't handle if she wants to. Why, I'd back the pair of them against a whole army, I would."

"I'm sure you would," Ysane said. "And, I suppose, so would I. But it's the not knowing anything that makes me worry so." She gestured at the baby at her breast. "Will he ever get to see his mother and father again? Will they have a chance to name him, finally?"

"I hope so," Bantry said, cheerily. "He can't go through his whole life being called *hey, you*. That would be embarrassing."

"You know what I mean." Ysane sighed again. "It's a shame none of the Talents that Devra brought along is a Seer. That would set my mind at ease."

"That Healer of hers is worth more than twenty Seers, my love," Bantry replied. "He's being kept busy, too - it's amazing the ills people discover they have once a Healer turns up. Folks as won't take medicine a physician prescribes will line up to have hands placed on them by a Healer."

"Yes," Ysane agreed, absently. "But I would still give a lot to know what's happening."

"So would we all," Bantry said, serious for a moment. "But since that's not likely to happen, we mere mortals have to cope the best we can."

Ysane gave him a strange look. "Do you ever wish you were a Talent?" she asked him.

"Me?" He laughed. "What would I do with a Talent? I'm just a plain, simple soldier. I do what I'm told when I'm told it, and fight when I must. Besides, with my luck, I'd end up getting a Talent to turn cheese into milk, or something."

"Oh?" Ysane tried to give him a ferocious glare. "And I suppose marrying me was the booby prize too, eh?"

"Marrying you, my sweet," he told her, "was the one single most smart thing I've ever done in my entire life. Or ever likely to do." He kissed her forehead again affectionately. "What about you?" he asked her. "Do you wish you had a Talent?"

"I never used to," she said. "I was always so thankful I was *normal*. Now... Well, I realize I was wrong to think that way - that it's just as normal to have a Talent as to not have one. And seeing what Melayne and the others can do... Well, yes, I'll confess I'm a little bit jealous of them. I'd love to have a Talent - even if it was just to turn cheese into milk! I'd feel more useful then, not helpless as I do now."

"Helpless? You?" Bantry shook his fist in her face. "Don't *ever* even think that, my girl. Look at you, taking care of two babies - and a foolish husband. You're hob-nobbing with kings and queens, now, too - aye, and lords and ladies. You're no simple farm-girl now, my lass - you're *somebody*. Melayne relies on you, and trusted you with her most precious possession - her boy. *She* knows how far from useless you are. So let's have none of this nonsense, hear?"

He had such a way of comforting her; no wonder she loved him so much. "All right," she agreed. "I'm not useless. But I can't help feeling that way sometimes."

"No more can we all," Bantry replied. "There's times I feel a downright hindrance to the whole world. I know I'm not smart - I'm a soldier, born and bred, and I take orders well, but I can't plan and plot like Lord Sander. Sometimes I feel I'm use to neither man nor beast." He held up a hand to stop Ysane saying anything. "And then I realize - Lord Sander places his trust in me, and he's nobody's fool. So if he trusts me, then I had better trust me, too. And the same goes for you - Melayne trusts you, and she knows what she's about, that one. So you trust *her* trust, even if you don't think you're up to much." He scowled. "Did anything I just said make any kind of sense?"

"All of it," she assured him. "And you're no doubt absolutely correct." *But,* she added to herself, *I can't stop worrying...*

Darmen stroked his wife's hair, and sat down beside her in her small sewing room. Perria liked to busy her hands as often as possible, and, even though she had ladies' maids, enjoyed her work. It might be beneath her dignity, but Darmen would never complain, as long as it pleased Perria.

"Are you happy?" he asked her.

She patted his hand. "As happy as I can be, with our friends missing and possibly in danger. I'll be happy once they return - if they return."

Darmen frowned. "You think they may be killed?"

"That's always a possibility," Perria admitted. "But somehow I doubt it. Melayne is more than capable of facing most dangers. No, that's not quite what I meant." She glanced oddly at her husband. "Do you ever regret that I wanted to give them sanctuary three years ago - despite the dragons?"

"Regret?" Darmen was genuinely surprised. "No, not at all. I love Melayne, too - she's like the daughter we never had." Despite everything, they had never been able to have children, though not through lack of trying. Even though Perria was beyond childbearing age, they still enjoyed trying as much as they had when they wed thirty years before. "And Sander is a strong, wise man. Taking them in was clearly the right thing to do."

Perria nodded. "As I thought. Were you... thinking of suggesting them as your successors one day?"

That was something Darmen had never shared with anyone, but it didn't surprise him that his wife had guessed his plans. "It had crossed my mind, yes. They're very capable, and they love our people. It seems like a good match."

"But it may not be in *their* minds," Perria said, gently.

"What do you mean?" Darmen asked, puzzled.

"Melayne has gone to confront her brother in Dragonhome - and that is, by right of marriage, her inheritance.

If she defeats Sarrow, then she might decide to move back there, you know. She only fled three years ago because the dragons were young and weak, and in need of protection. Now... well, they're quite sizeable, and capable of fighting for themselves. They might prefer to return home."

Darmen considered the idea. "I hadn't thought of that," he admitted. "But, as always, what you say has a lot of possibility in it. They *may* prefer to go home, if they now can. I'd be very sorry to see them go, but it's their decision, of course. And I would wish them the best of luck."

"Oh, so would I," Perria said, cheerily. "But then we would be without heirs, wouldn't we?"

"We'd be no worse off than we were three years ago, before they came here."

Perria shook her head. "We'd be three years older - three years closer to death. And there is a possibility - if you're willing, and if Melayne and Sander will consider it."

"And what might that be?" Darmen asked, curious.

"We could adopt one of Melayne's children as our heir."

Darmen stared at her, astonished. "Do you truly think she'd give up a child, even to us?"

"Oh, I shouldn't imagine it would occur to her," Perria said. "But if we were to ask, to point out that we desperately need an heir... She has a good, generous heart, and she's obviously capable of bearing further children." She chuckled. "The way she and Sander bed one another, I'd think that would be quite inevitable. She might be willing to help us out - especially since she hasn't as yet really bonded with her son."

"You aim to ask her if we can take her child?" Darmen shook his head. "I think that might be a bad idea. If she were to say no, it could poison our friendship. And if she were to say yes... it would mean losing a child. I don't believe she'd be happy with either eventuality."

"Perhaps not," Perria agreed. "But do we have any other options? Much as I love our people, I can't think of any who would be capable of ruling. And who else is there? Again, I love

Ysane and Bantry, but they're followers, not leaders. I really can't see any other way out of this dilemma. Can you, my dear?"

To be honest, Darmen couldn't. But to ask Melayne to abandon her child... "She would be able to see him as often as she wished," he mused. "It's not as if he would be a stranger to her." He shook his head. "But this is all simply theory. We do not know yet that Melayne and Sander will not return. In that case, *they* could still be our heirs."

"Of course," Perria agreed. "But a wise ruler prepares for *all* eventualities - and no one knows how wise you are like I do." She patted his hand again. "It is simply something to think about."

"Yes," he agreed, slowly. "It is..."

Tura was feeling a lot better now, thanks mostly to the ministrations of the human healer, Hovin. She flexed her wings, fanning him with the strong breeze that created. It was a shame she couldn't communicate with him in words, but he understood her meaning well enough.

"Not yet," he said, grinning. "I know you're feeling a lot better, but those flight muscles are very complex. If you try to use them too soon, you could end up damaging them again. And if you're flying at the time that might prove fatal." He stroked her head in a reassuring manner. "Another week, I promise, and you will be as good as ever. I know it's hard on you to stay here in this courtyard while Melayne is away, but you won't help her by injuring yourself again. Wait."

"The human is correct," Loken agreed, nuzzling her sister. "Another week, then fly."

"Melayne is likely in trouble," Tura complained. "And I have abandoned her simply so that I may rest."

"That is nonsense, and you know it," Shath growled. "Your task is to heal. As the human said, you'd be no use to anyone if you spasm while flying and fall to your death. Hard as it is, you must practice patience."

"But I feel so useless," Tura said, sulkily.

"We are not useless," Loken argued. "We guard the Far Islands, as Melayne wished. These humans are so frail, and we may need to be able to fight for them at any time. It is what Melayne wished; would you refuse her request?"

"Yes," Tura grumbled. "She set me the task only as an excuse for me to heal. It is not what she truly wished of me."

"It is her request," Loken repeated. "And it is sensible. You're behaving more like a human than a dragon. You know the wisdom of what has been said; why do you fight it?"

"Because I am worried for Melayne. You know how naive and trusting she can be, and she is facing her brother - always a weak spot in her emotions."

"A human failing," Shath agreed. "But Melayne is stronger that she appears - you are bonded with her, so no one knows that better than you. She has help from her human friends, so she is not helpless."

"She needs *me*," Tura growled. "And I her. It is... painful being apart from her. I feel as though one of my legs were missing - incomplete, and crippled."

"It isn't easy for you, I know," Loken agreed, sympathetically. "But you *must* heal up completely, or you could make matters worse. Killing yourself to get to Melayne will aid no one, and we should lose a sister. It is not acceptable."

Tura hissed. "You would *stop* me if I tried to leave?"

"You know we must," Shath replied. "It is for your own good. If you are not sane enough to recognize that, perhaps more than your wing has been damaged."

"Betrayed by my own siblings?" Tura growled. "I had never expected that."

"That you would call our concern *betrayal* shows you are not thinking clearly," Loken snapped. "If you will not rest because it is the logical and right thing to do, then you will rest because you cannot fight your way past the two of us."

"And if you try," Shath added, clicking the claws of his right foreleg together, "you will most certainly be damaged. That would mean even longer before you recover fully and are able to go after Melayne."

Tura bowed her head. "What you say is true," she agreed. "I will comply. But I shall not like it."

"And don't even think about slipping away while we are occupied in guard duty," Loken informed her. "We shall have one eye on the sea, and one on you. You are becoming almost human yourself, and I cannot put lying past you now. It is a shame that you have sunk so low."

"I have said I will stay and rest," Tura snapped, angrily. "And I will do as I promise. If you are so suspicious, perhaps I am not the one becoming too human."

"We accept your word," Shath said, smoothly. "But you will understand it if we still check up on you from time to time. It is... family concern."

"Liar," Tura said. But there was no anger in the word. She understood their actions were born out of concern for her. How could she not feel affection for them? "But I shall worry the whole week."

"Yes," Loken said, sympathetically. "So shall we all, even if it is not in our nature to worry about what we cannot change. You may be the one bonded to Melayne, but she is our friend. We cannot help but be concerned about her. But we trust that she knows what she is doing, and that all will be well."

"Perhaps it will," agreed Tura. "But I should feel better about matters if I were by her side."

She looked down at the human healer, who had been watching the conversation without being able to understand it. He appeared to be worried for her also. Tura smiled, inwardly. He was only human, but he cared. She nuzzled him gently with her snout to reassure him that she would behave. Then she settled down to impatiently wait out the week...

Chapter Twenty Three

Melayne squinted upward, shielding her eyes from the glare of the midday sun. Kaya, the falcon, was nowhere to be seen. He had refused to go off alone when offered the chance following his freedom, and had decided to follow Melayne instead.

"Maybe he's gone, finally," Greyn offered, hopefully. "Realized he's not needed."

"He's an extra pair of eyes," Melayne pointed out. "And he can see quite a way when he's aloft. Besides, I don't think he *wants* to leave us. He's too used to being around people."

"He's just a chatterbox," Greyn complained. "I think he's just glad he's found somebody to talk to. He hardly shuts up when he's around you."

"That's a bit harsh," Melayne said. But there certainly was some truth in it - the falcon's reports *did* tend to be on the long-winded side of things.

"We don't need him," the wolf objected. "My pack can see as far as he can, and we're a lot more use in a fight."

"I'm hoping we won't get into a fight," Melayne replied.

Greyn gave one of his barking laughs. "You always say that, but it never happens. Ever since I've known you, you've been in one fight or another. You seem to stir up trouble just walking about."

Again, there was some truth to what he said. Melayne sighed. "I wish it would all just go away. All I wish is to settle down in peace with my husband, and my children and my friends. All this fighting and struggling is too wearing."

"But you don't give up."

"If I did, then we'd none of us be safe." Melayne sighed again. "Much as I hate it, I *have* to keep on with my path."

"That's life," Greyn said, philosophically. "One great fight for survival, in the hope that things are better for the next generation. Me, I'd like to see a world where wolves are safe, and prey is plentiful. But, of course, my prey would like a world where *they* are safe and wolves have been hunted to extinction." He laughed again. "You can't please everyone, you know, much as you may try."

"I know." Melayne looked up as Batten rode up to join her. "Speaking of not being able to please some people..."

The Seer reined in his steed as he came level with her. There was a grin on his lips and in his eyes again. "Why are you wasting time with your animals?" he asked her. "I'm a much better predictor of trouble. All you have to do is to ask me."

"You know how I feel about that," Melayne said.

"That you don't trust me," he replied, still amused. "That you think I'll tell you only as much as I want you to know. That I'll try and manipulate you to act in ways I wish."

"That about sums it up, yes," she agreed.

"You could always use your Talent to force me to tell you the truth."

"But not *all* of the truth. I can make certain you don't lie directly - but it's always possible to slant things any way you please."

Batten laughed. "Are you like this with your husband, too?" he asked. "I understand that he, too, can predict the future. Won't you allow him to, either?"

"I couldn't stop him even if I wished," Melayne answered. There was a sharp pain in her heart as she thought again of Sander. How much longer before they could be together again? "And his Talent differs from yours - his works by touch, and he sees only a single sharp vision of what must be - not a fuzzy picture of what may be."

"And he clearly touches you a lot," Batten said. At her sharp glance, he laughed again. "You've had two children - you wouldn't have them if he didn't touch you now and then. So, how do you handle that? Does he have to stay fully clothed in bed, or do you just refuse to let him tell you what he sees?"

"I don't see that my personal life is any of your business," Melayne said, blushing slightly. She missed Sander's touch so much...

"Maybe it isn't," Batten agreed, shrugging. "I was simply wondering how you handle his predictions, and if that has any bearing on why you're so reluctant to accept mine."

"His predictions with me are always the same," Melayne answered. "He simply sees us together. He makes virtually no predictions concerning us. Certainly, he did not foresee our separation."

"Or so he said," Batten argued. "Maybe he *did* see it, and simply didn't tell you about it, knowing how you are."

"Sander would never lie to me," Melayne said, sharply. "Not even for my own protection. Our relationship is based on trust."

"Fine," he said, shrugging. "Then ask him about Poth when you meet up again, and see what he has to say about her."

Melayne glared at him. "I was quite clear that I don't want any of your Seeing. And you can't make me suspicious of Sander. I trust him."

"That's your affair - or his." Batten laughed. "I could tell you about her, if you like - all about her."

Melayne scowled. "You know, I've always thought that we Talents were like a family. I've never disliked one - until now."

He shrugged. "I guess I'm the black sheep of the family, then. But remember that name - Poth. You'll know her when you see her - she's a very attractive blonde. I can't really blame Sander for -" He broke off as there was a menacing growl from Greyn. "Oh well, maybe I'll save the rest of the story for later." He wheeled his horse and rode off to join the others as they readied the midday meal.

Greyn looked up at Melayne. "I could tear his throat out for you," he offered. "It would probably taste vile, but I'd endure it for your sake."

"No, thank you." Melayne sighed. "You're right - he *is* poisonous, and I know he's trying to manipulate me. He's a fool, though, if he thinks he can make me doubt Sander. I just wish I knew what his ultimate aim is, though."

"Probably the same as all of us," the wolf suggested. "Safety, a mate and a full belly."

"Life is simple for a wolf," Melayne said, wistfully.

"It could be simple for humans, too," Greyn replied. "Except they insist on complicating matters, don't they?"

"It's a talent we have," Melayne said, sadly.

"You should just give up on them," advised Greyn. "Come and live with the pack. You'd never have to worry about us."

"But I have my family, and my friends." Melayne straightened up in the saddle. "Responsibilities."

"You're too human," Greyn told her, and laughed again before he ran off.

There was some truth, as always, in everything the wolf said. But Melayne knew that the answer to her problems wasn't to try and retreat from them. Her life was a constant struggle, but the fight was worthwhile. If she could only leave the world a slightly better place for her children, it would all have been worth it. Probably.

Their party was stretched out a bit - the wolves and the falcon were off on scouting duty, and the humans in small clumps. Right now she rode alone. Ahead was Batten, also alone. About thirty feet ahead of him were Corri and Margone, deep in conversation. And in the lead, where she preferred to be was Devra, alone.

A slight smile crossed Melayne's lips as she studied Corri and Margone. The Talent and the ex-Slayer seemed to be spending a lot of time together... Maybe something was brewing between the pair of them. Corri was cute, attractive and bubbly, while Margone was quiet, intense and handsome. They did make an interesting couple. She'd have to talk with Devra about it - for all her cynicism and just plain grouchiness, Devra was Corri's best friend, and she'd know about it if there was anything to know.

Melayne laughed gently. It felt so normal, like she was a girl again - is *she* dating *him*? Are they an item? For just a moment she could forget the urgency and peril of their mission and enjoy simply speculating about whether friends were coupling up. It was a shame all of life wasn't like that, instead of this constant struggle. But it was wonderful to be lost in such simplicity even if only for a short while. Then Batten moved between Melayne and the couple, and she was forced to think on darker matters.

She didn't trust the Seer. It was partially because of his sneering attitude toward everyone, and partly simple gut-instinct. It must be part of her Talent to be able to grasp people's natures, and she *knew* that Batten was devious and scheming. The problem was, she simply didn't know whether he would mislead or betray them, or simply try to use them for his own ends. Either way, though, she had to be wary of him.

Perhaps Greyn was right, and they'd be better off sending the Seer away. But she knew that wouldn't stop whatever it was he had in mind, and it felt safer to keep him closer at hand. If nothing else, if he tried to betray them, then Greyn could kill him.

She *hated* having to have plans to hurt people, but she simply couldn't take any chances. There was too much at stake not to be careful. The thought of being responsible for anyone's death really troubled her - but what other options did she have? She hated the choices she was forced to consider, but she simply *had* to consider them. For better or for ill, she was in charge. She had never sought it, and she certainly didn't want it, but the way circumstances had worked out, she was now Lady of Dragonhome, with all that might entail.

True, at the moment, the title meant nothing much, since she was technically in exile, and her unstable kid brother had actual possession of the castle. But that might change - in fact *had* to change. Three years of exile had been hard. Oh, Darmen and Perria had been truly wonderful, and they were good friends. But Melayne knew that when her husband stared off into the distance at night, his mind was on Dragonhome. It had been his home and his family's home for a dozen generations. Melayne had never felt truly at home anywhere until she had entered Dragonhome. It was partly for Sander's sake, and partly because that was where the dragons had been hatched and she had first met them, but it was the closest that anywhere in this whole world felt like home to her.

She wanted it back. Not just for Sander, and for Corran, who was heir to Dragonhome, but for herself, and for Cassary and the so-far-nameless one. The children had never seen the castle, but it was their heritage, and they needed to be there. They all did.

And she was grimly committed to getting it back - whatever the cost.

She could only pray that this didn't include hurting Sarrow. For all of his faults, he was still her younger brother, and she loved him. Somewhere deep inside him, he must love her, too. The problem was that he was so scared that he was using his Talent to protect himself at the expense of others. That had to cease. But she hadn't really thought much beyond that about what to do with him.

What could she do with him? Could she even really fight his Talent? How many people did he already have in his thrall, and what were his instructions to them? He had given orders to the Slayers that he'd sent to kill her. Kill her! How could he have done that? He was still a child, and panicking, defending himself the only way he knew. He didn't *really* want to hurt her, she was sure - he was simply so powerful and so scared he wasn't thinking straight. She would be able to sort his mind out.

She hoped.

She knew that Devra didn't believe it was possible. Neither did Margone. Corri - well, Corri supported her, whatever decisions she made. That was Corri's nature; things were very simple for her. She had faith in Melayne, and that was that. So, Melayne wondered, who was right here? Was she being realistic or overly optimistic? There was no real way to know until they reached Dragonhome and confronted Sarrow at last. She was looking forward to it and dreading it at the exact same time.

If only... if only...

She shook her head to clear it. Wishing was not a Talent, and it didn't make things come true. If things were different, she'd be happier. But they weren't, and so she'd simply have to be strong enough to deal with whatever came. Whatever the outcome, whatever the price, she would endure.

She heard a cry in the sky, and Kaya came wheeling down to pace her. The falcon seemed quite pleased with himself.

"I followed your instructions," he reported. "I flew and flew, and watched and scouted. The farm dwelling you spoke of is there, and there are only peasants about. No soldiers, no nobles, just peasants. I can't imagine why you're interested in it, but it seems to be safe enough. Now there's a castle not too far from it, and I checked that out, also, as you requested. Now *there's* a place! Soldiers everywhere, and men in finery. There is the smell of roasting meat and the flesh of hunted animals. And there's activity all over it - the humans appear to be making their nest stronger, with stone and trees and mortar. We should go there - much more our sort of place, if you ask me. Peasants? Pah!"

"Thank you, Kaya," Melayne said, as he paused momentarily for a breath. "We will indeed be going there, though I doubt we'll have a civil welcome. But we're heading for the farmhouse first. I've friends to see, and news to relate. Now, why don't you rest? Or have lunch?"

"Rest?" The falcon gave a sharp laugh. "I am Kaya, supreme among falcons. I need no rest! But a snack would be quite acceptable." His mind on that, the falcon wheeled away.

Melayne urged Fleetfoot on, until she drew level with Margone and Corri. Corri grinned at her, but seemed a trifle distracted. Perhaps she and the ex-slayer *were* getting interested in one another. "We're close now to the farm," Melayne informed them. "We'll take a short break there before moving on to Dragonhome." She felt a twinge of nervousness as they drew closer to their target. No matter how she had tried to prepare herself for this, Melayne was dreading her confrontation with her brother.

"Sounds good," Corri agreed. "I hope they're as nice as you claim - I could do with some food that Devra hasn't cooked."

"You'll like them, trust me," Melayne promised. She moved ahead to join Devra. The Talent gave one of her usual scowls. "We're almost there."

"Wonderful," Devra growled. "And close enough to Dragonhome for them to smell us."

Melayne grinned. "Maybe you should take a bath at the farm," she suggested. "Then there'd be nothing for them to smell..."

"Are you saying I stink?"

"Of course not," Melayne replied with a straight face. "But the wolves *are* staying upwind of you..."

"Damned cheek," Devra growled. She sniffed at her sleeve. "It's just my clothing."

"You don't smell," Melayne said, unable to restrain her laughter any longer. "You're just so serious all the time, I couldn't resist teasing you."

Devra glared at her. "You'd better watch out," she warned. "I have been known to extract bloody revenge from time to time..." She gave a tight smile. "You figure out if I'm joking or not."

Melayne felt a lot more cheerful. Her mood brightened further as they approached the fields and saw the large house in the distance. As always, there were several men hard at work with the crops, and several young women bustling about the yard and house. They all saw the small party as it drew closer, and they came together warily. Melayne saw that a couple of the older boys held their hands hidden behind their backs - carrying weapons, obviously. Had things become that bad, then?

As they approached the house a large, well-built woman came out, alerted by one of the younger children. She was wiping her hands on a towel, obviously caught mid-cooking, and studied the approaching riders. Melayne waved, and the woman's face cracked into a huge smile.

"It's Melayne!" she cried, happily. "Look lively, all of you. Falma, go fetch Father. Polim, get some more water boiling! Tey - where the devil is Tey?"

Melayne reined in and slid from Fleetfoot. The woman grabbed her in a huge, happy hug. "Melayne, you're so welcome!" She peered at the other riders, and there was disappointment on her face.

"Ysane couldn't make it," Melayne said, apologetically. "She's looking after the children."

"Children?" Ysane's mother's eye went wide. "How many has she got?"

"Just the one," Melayne replied. "She named him after Falma. But I have two, now, and she's looking after them for me."

"News later," the mother decided. "Refreshments first. Now, who are your friends, Melayne? You're all welcome here if you're with Melayne," she added. "Come in, come in. Rest. Drink! Eat!" Her nose wrinkled. "Maybe take a bath."

"That's it," Devra growled. "I'm going to hurt somebody..." But she allowed herself to be dragged into the farmhouse by two of the younger children. Margone, Corri and Batten followed.

Cups of steaming tea were handed around, and chairs found for the visitors. The children dashed about, some on errands and some just for the obvious pleasure of running around. It was chaos, but of the best possible kind. Melayne felt almost as if she had come home. She missed her own parents still. They had been quiet, solemn people, not like this disorganized rabble. But Ysane's family were good folks, and genuinely happy to see Melayne again.

Somehow, the news managed to get passed around, and Falma thrust his chest out with pride when he heard that his sister had named her first-born for him. It was obvious he was going to boast about this for months. Ysane's father - a tall, weather-beaten man with large muscles and a larger heart - gave Melayne another hug that left her almost breathless, and then repeated the action with the other girls. Devra tried to avoid it, and failed. Margone, to his obvious relief, escaped with nothing more than a bone-crushing handclasp.

Then came the food - a veritable feast of meats and pastries and vegetables, followed by fruit pies, until even Ysane's father could eat no more, and they could all settle back. Falma had seen to the stabling and feeding of the mounts, and darkness had started to settle comfortably about the house as they all gathered in the main room in front of a well-stacked fire to relax after their meal. Ysane's parents sat closest to the fire, with their five guests about them. The children - who couldn't sit still for any length of time - were in constant motion, so Melayne was never certain how many there were. They were excited and chatty and happy.

Melayne delivered all of the news she could think of concerning their sister. Comments like "Fancy *her* married!" and "A boy! Think of that!" flew about.

"A couple of travelers brought us news," Ysane's mother said. "So we knew she was well, but it's good to hear first-hand from you, Melayne. And you're looking very well yourself. Two children, you say?"

"Yes." Melayne felt another pang of pain thinking about them, but forced it aside. "We'd asked the travelers to pass on the news for us. We didn't dare return before this, considering the feelings locally about the dragons."

That set off another round of excited questions from the children, who wanted to know everything about the "monsters", including how many people they had eaten. They were a little disappointed when Melayne informed them that the dragons had never eaten even a single person. But they thrilled to every last word when she and Corri took turns relating the battle with the Raiders. Margone sat through it all withdrawn and silent, clearly uncomfortable to he had taken part in the fight for the wrong side. Batten was in a corner on his own, nursing a drink and saying nothing, his face completely blank. He was the only one not enjoying this.

Finally, though, Ysane's parents ordered the children to bed - even Falma, to his disgust, and there were just the seven of them left in the large room. The firelight cast a warm glow across everyone, and Ysane's father spoke up for the first time in a while.

"You're not here for a social visit," he observed. "Oh, I know you're happy to see us and all, but we're not the real reason you're here, are we?"

"No," admitted Melayne. "But I couldn't ride by and not stop in and visit."

"I should think not!" Ysane's mother said, indignantly. "Father and I would never have forgiven you if you had. But what is the real reason you're back?"

"Dragonhome," Devra said.

"Ah." Ysane's father nodded, and sat back in his chair. "I thought as much. There's been a lot happening at the old castle - mostly rebuilding and re-arming."

"Re-arming?" Devra asked, sharply.

"Lots of soldiers coming in," the farmer explained. "We've been selling a lot of provisions to the castle - quite a bumper year for us, it has been."

Melayne was relieved in one way - she'd been afraid that Sarrow would simply have ordered the local farmers to hand over their crops. They would have been forced to obey, and that would have ruined them. It was quite a relief to hear that he was paying for the supplies. But it raised another question. "Where's Sarrow getting the money for all of this from? It can't be cheap, paying workmen, hiring and feeding troops."

Devra glared at Melayne. "Is that all that bothers you?" she asked. "Who cares how he's paying for it? What matters is that he's got lots of troops there. And we're just a handful. We're *very* outnumbered."

"That might matter if we were planning to fight him," Melayne agreed. "But we're not, so it's hardly relevant." Devra threw her hands up in despair, and settled back, muttering under her breath. Melayne turned back to Ysane's parents. "Do you know how he's paying for all of this?" she asked.

"With good gold," Ysane's father answered. He took a piece from off the mantel, and showed it to her. There was the likeness of Juska on it. "King's gold," he added, unnecessarily. "Several nobles have thrown in with him."

Corri frowned. "I don't understand."

"It's fairly obvious," Batten said, the first time he'd spoken in a while. "I don't even need my Sight to get the point. There are a lot of nobles who aren't happy with Juska, but individually there's none strong enough to stand up against him and win. If they joined together, they could overthrow him, but they lack the courage to take that step. Then along comes your brother, and he starts to rebuild Dragonhome. The nobles see this as an act of defiance against the king - it was his father who attacked and wrecked it initially, years back. He'd been afraid of the power of the Lords of Dragonhome, and aimed to make a point of his power to the lords. It worked, too. So, when Sarrow starts rebuilding, the lords can only interpret it one way - that he feels stronger than the King, and ready to take him on." Batten shrugged. "Individually, the lords are cowards, but once the lead is there..."

"They all jump aboard," Devra said. "And we probably helped them decide!" She glanced at Melayne. "When you faced Juska down and won, I'll bet that prompted a lot of the lords to switch sides."

"It's nothing to do with me," Melayne said, irritated. "Anyway, none of those lords we met could have beaten us here - we travel faster than they could. These are nobles who decided in advance. And they're bringing in troops and money for the cause. I wonder if Sarrow is *really* thinking of overthrowing the King?"

"It would make him safe," Margone said, quietly. "If he were King, then the lords would be forced to protect him, wouldn't they?"

Melayne sighed. "Politics!" She looked at Batten. "I'm not really a cynic, but that's not likely to happen, is it? If Sarrow *did* lead a revolt against Juska, how long would the lords stand behind him?"

Batten grinned. "You're learning, Melayne," he said. "The lords who back Sarrow would no doubt be thinking that as soon as Juska is overthrown, it would be a lot simpler to overthrow a boy. And I don't need my power to See that, either." He concentrated. "It *is* what Sarrow is planning," he said. "Being

King would make him feel very safe. And, as you suspect, the lords would then attack him." He shook his head. "There are too many variables to be certain what would happen in that case, but I think we could all agree it's not likely to end very well for anyone involved."

"So, to save your brother's life," Corri said, "we have to stop him."

"Yes." Melayne sat back, sighing. "Why is it that just when life looks to be so complicated it's impossible to get through, it then gets worse?"

"Because life's like that," Devra said. "As I constantly try and impress upon you. But you never listen to me."

"I'm listening now," Melayne said simply. "Use your Talent - tell me, what's the best way ahead for me?"

Devra concentrated a moment, and then swore. "The way you're going," she admitted. "But that doesn't mean you'll win - just that it's your best option."

"I can tell you more," Batten said, eagerly. "My Sight is pretty clear. If you meet your brother, and nothing else changes, then you will convince him to stop his plans."

"If nothing else changes?" Margone asked. "What does that mean?"

"It means that the future is very complicated," Batten snapped. "If it's just Melayne and Sarrow, face to face, then she will convince him to stop. But there are too many other factors to be certain that they *will* be alone. There's the individual lords - if one of them decides to interfere, then the picture gets complicated. If two or more decide..." He shrugged. "And if there's any outside influence, then I can't say for sure."

"Outside influence?" Corri asked.

"Like the King deciding to put down this upstart," Devra said. "I'm sure he must have heard about the growing rebellion by now, and he might just decide to send troops in to stop it."

"You're getting the idea," Batten said, approvingly. "I can only predict the outcomes of things as I see them. It's possible that things I don't know about might interfere."

"In other words, you're not much use at all," Margone said bitterly.

"I'm better than nothing," Batten snarled back. "I can at least give advice and warnings."

"If we can trust what you're telling us," Devra pointed out. "You have no reason to be loyal to Melayne, unlike the rest of us here."

"I have no reason to betray her, either," Batten said.

"None that we know of," Devra corrected him. "I'm sure you're playing all sorts of mental games with these potential futures, looking to see in which one you'll come out the best."

"Of course I am," he agreed, grinning again. "I have to look out for myself. But it so happens that my best bet is to stay on Melayne's side. So for that, if no other reason, I can be trusted."

"So you say," Devra repeated.

"So, indeed, I say," he agreed.

"This will get us nowhere," Melayne broke in. "We only have Batten's word for anything he tells us, so how much we accept what he says depends purely on how much we believe his word. After that, we're just talking in circles."

"You're in an unenviable position," Ysane's mother said. "What do you aim to do about it all?"

"What I've intended all along," Melayne answered. "Rest tonight, and then in the morning I'm going to Dragonhome to confront Sarrow. After that, our fate is in the hands of the gods. I can do only that, and trust matters will work out well." She looked at her friends - and Batten. "None of you needs to accompany me."

"You're not getting rid of me that easily," Devra said, firmly. "You need someone to watch your back, even if it is a hopeless fight."

"And I'm coming," Corri said firmly.

"And I," Margone stated.

Batten grinned. "I *have* to come - I've Seen it."

"If we didn't have the farm and family," began Ysane's father, but Melayne cut him off.

"I wouldn't dream of it," she said. "You *do* have responsibilities, and I'm not planning on fighting, anyway. This will simply be a small family reunion, and I shall reason with Sarrow."

"Who has not, to date, shown himself to be particularly reasonable," Devra muttered.

"It's all we can do," Melayne said.

Devra sighed. "Yes," she agreed. "It's all we can do. And pray that there's nothing going on that we don't know that might ruin things for us."

Chapter Twenty Four

The flying ship had landed for the evening, and the meal prepared. Sander sat with Corran - neither was bound or even obviously watched, but Sander knew that they were still prisoners. He sat by the fire, brooding.

Flying had been an interesting experience - it wasn't as smooth and natural as riding the dragons, and was actually quite like sailing. Winds had buffeted the craft about in the air much as waves might have tossed it. But comparing the experience to riding dragons had made Sander worry about Brek and Ganeth again. What could have happened to them? Were they somehow dead? He couldn't imagine the rest of his life without Brek. He had really bonded with his dragon.

He had originally looked after the five dragons simply because he saw it as his responsibility. While they were hatchlings, he'd fed them - poorly, as it turned out! - and worried over them, keeping them as secret as he could. But since Melayne had come along, he had learned to love the dragons, as she did, unconditionally. And especially Brek, of course. The day he had first "heard" Brek speaking inside his mind had been one of the best days of his life.

It was interesting how all of the best days of his life revolved about Melayne. And he felt a thrill and a chill knowing he was to meet her again soon. Being separated from her was torture - but he dreaded what would happen when Kander found her.

Poth came over, with steaming bowls of stew for him and Corran. Corran eagerly attacked his; Sander was slower, but just as pleased to get food in his stomach again. Poth walked away, without a word, but swinging her hips deliberately and grinning over her shoulder at Sander. Even Corran noticed this.

"Why does she do that?" he asked his father. "Doesn't she know that you love Melayne?"

"Yes," Sander replied. "But I have a theory. Poth has used her Talent to look into her own future, and she's seen that her best chance at happiness is with me. Best, mind you, doesn't mean likely. So, despite the fact that it almost certainly will never happen, she's become fixated on this *perfect* future of hers that we share together. She won't admit it can't happen, and she won't allow herself to consider losing it. She's convinced herself that it *will* happen, simply because she wishes it so."

"Silly woman," Corran muttered.

"I suppose she is," his father agreed. "But I can't blame her overmuch for wanting it. She seems to have had a very rough life."

"Do you like her?" Corran asked.

"I *could* like her, if I wasn't already committed to Melayne," Sander admitted. "She's very pretty, and she tries hard to please. In another world... But we aren't in another world, we're in this one, and I love Melayne. It's that simple. Her plans will never work out."

"Not as long as Melayne is alive," Corran said, slowly. "Do you think Poth is fond of you enough to be planning to kill Melayne?"

A shiver of horror passed through Sander. "I had not even considered that," he admitted. "How could I have been so blind?" He shook his head. "But Poth doesn't seem to be the type to commit murder." Though she hadn't been too bothered when Kander had done so… Was it a very large step from approving of murder to committing it yourself?

"Not even if she thinks her entire future happiness depends upon it?"

Sander couldn't say; he really didn't know Poth that well. She *seemed* to be pretty gentle in nature, if left to herself - but she seemed to think that the murder of the raider villagers was nothing to be bothered about. He, on the other hand, couldn't forget the pain and terror. And Corran had a very good point. She *was* obsessed with the idea that she could only be happy being married to Sander... Was she so obsessed that she might plan to kill Melayne?

And she did have Sight... so she could work out a perfect way to kill her rival without making it look like her fault, so that Sander wouldn't hate her forever for the act...

He almost wished that Corran hadn't brought up the possibility. He didn't want to think about it. But he *had* to - he had to protect Melayne from Poth. If he could...

What he needed to do was to touch Poth with his bare hands, so he could see what lay in her future - and pray that it wasn't Melayne's death. Touching her would be simple enough - all he had to do was to romance her a little. She'd be eager for his touch that way...

Of course, if she were innocent of any lethal intentions, he'd be leading her on, only to upset her badly when she realized she'd been tricked. But what else could he do? He *had* to protect Melayne!

Poth returned a short while later, but, unfortunately, not alone. Kander accompanied her, his eyes almost glowing.

"We reach Dragonhome tomorrow," the fire caster said. "And then all of my plans and schemes will begin to come to fruition."

Sander fed another dead branch into the fire. "Are you going to share those plans?" he asked. "I do seem to have some part to play in them, after all."

"I don't see why not," Kander said, agreeably. He was in an outgoing mood for once, obviously charged by the closeness he was to his goal. "I must join with Melayne."

"Join?" Sander was puzzled. "In what way?"

"In whatever way seems best," the would-be god replied. "It is to fulfil a prophecy made almost twenty years ago, when she was born."

"A prophecy?" Corran's eyes widened. "You mean like Poth gives?"

"No, more like your father's, boy." Kander smiled. "I remember the details distinctly. It was when my parents and I lived in Hollow Lake, in Stormgard. It was a small village, but friendly. There was a Seer who had managed to hide her Talent from the King's Men, and she'd stayed with the village. It was a tradition that when a child was born, the Seer would touch the child and foretell the future for it. Well, when Melayne was born, the woman came around and touched her.

"And then she had been filled with her vision. It transformed her completely. "This child and her brother," the woman said, "will do great things in another country. They will change the way of the world, and overthrow injustice." Then she turned to my father and said: "You must leave here as soon as the girl can travel. There is a small farm, on the coast, that you must work. It is your destiny, and hers, and her brother's." So my father did as he was told." Kander's face darkened slightly. "But, just before we were to set off, the King's Men came around, and they discovered I was a Fire Caster. I was dragged from the family, and sent off to train for war. I have never seen my family since that day. But I can never forget that prophecy - it is burned deep within my soul." He came out of his memories, and stared hard at Sander. "So, you see, it is my destiny to join with Melayne and to change the world. I am the Burning God, and she will be - whatever is required of her to complete our conjoined destiny. I have been working at it since I was taken from my family."

Poth stirred, finally. "He led a rebellion in the ranks of the Talents," she added. "He shared his vision with us, and I could see great things to come, which is why I joined him. We have been working since to make the vision come to pass. And tomorrow - all will be revealed."

It was starting to make a crazy kind of sense now. Sander was understanding what Kander had planned. But there was one huge problem that the insane god *hadn't* foreseen - and Poth couldn't have done, since she'd never met Melayne.

Melayne had *another* brother...

Kander was no fool. His eyes narrowed. "What is it?" he growled. Sander shook his head, not knowing what the revelation might mean. Kander was insane, and hearing an unpleasant truth might serve to overbalance him completely. "Don't try to stay silent," Kander snapped. He reached a hand out toward Corran. "I need you, but the brat here isn't necessary..."

Sander wanted to attack the Talent, but he knew that would be useless. The Fire Caster could burn him to ashes in seconds. The only way to beat him was to knock him out before he realized he was being attacked, and there was absolutely no chance of that while he was so alert. Sander hesitated, and Kander allowed flames to flow along his arm and across his fingers. Sander did not dare take a chance with his son's life. "Melayne has another brother," he admitted, slowly.

"So?" Kander was puzzled, but Poth understood immediately.

"Maybe *he's* the one the Seer was prophesying about, and not you," she said.

Kander looked completely blank. "How could he be?" he finally asked. "I am the one with destiny. This other brother cannot possibly have power like mine."

"In some ways," Sander said, cautiously, uncertain how far to push matters, "his power is greater than yours."

"How can it be?" Kander screamed. Fire played across his whole body now, burning hot, but not consuming him. Sander, Corran and Poth were forced to step back from the Burning God. "How can anyone match the power that I control?"

"His is not like yours," Sander said, shielding his eyes from the blaze. "He has the ability to Persuade. People have to do as he asks them."

"That's a useful Talent," Poth muttered.

"But not as good as mine!" Kander howled. "Not as strong as mine! I shall prove it tomorrow - by killing him." He whirled on Poth. "Is he at Dragonhome?"

Poth concentrated. "I can't see him through you," she said. Then she glanced at Sander. "But I can through *him*." She focused. "Yes - *he* is the reason that Melayne is going to Dragonhome."

"So," Kander growled, "my sweet sister is attempting to meet up with her brother? Is she planning on fulfilling the prophecy herself then?"

"How can she be?" Sander asked. "She doesn't even know about it. Your parents didn't tell her about it, I'm sure – or she'd have mentioned it to me. Whyever she is meeting with Sarrow, it can't be to fulfill anything."

"She could always be doing it unwittingly," Poth said. "Prophecy *must* come to pass, whether the people involved are conscious of the prophecy or not. Trust me, I'm an expert in the field."

Kander's fires had died down a lot. Now there were just thin flames running the length of his body, nervously, mirroring his inner turmoil. "I will kill this Sarrow," he stated. "Then there can be no doubt as to who is meant in the Seer's vision. My sister and I will bring in a new order, a new rule, a new power to tame this whole world." He glared at Poth. "You can see that, can't you?"

Poth squinted. "I see *something* like that," she agreed. "If you and she come together, then there will be monumental changes in Farrowholme. The King will be overthrown and you and she shall rule." She glanced at Sander. "But my Sight is only conditional, Kander. There are many, many uncertain factors here. I didn't know about Sarrow until a few moments ago, and there may be other things I don't know about that could mess everything up. *He* can see what *must* come to pass - have him use his Talent."

Kander nodded, thoughtfully. "Yes," he agreed. "It is time my brother-in-law made himself useful around here. Sander, you will read the future for us."

Sander winced; he had not wanted to do this. Partially it was because he was afraid of what he might See - he hated to look into any future, knowing that it *must* happen. Since he had met Melayne, he had always been desperately afraid that one day he would see her death. As a result, he dreaded touching her naked skin almost as much as he adored touching it. Each time they made love, he was afraid of what he might see. Thankfully, so far, he had seen only good things with her.

But now? Kander was very, very dangerous, and just as unstable as a wildfire. Whatever Sander saw might unhinge the lunatic fatally. On the other hand, perhaps he might even see a way to defeat him...

"Let's start small," Kander decided, seeing Sander's uncertainty. "Poth, let him read you first. I'm sure you'd love to know if you really have a future with him."

Poth smiled at that. "I can See us together all of the time," she admitted. "But my Sight is only what could be... To See the real future... Yes!" Eagerly, she reached for Sander.

Sander had no choice. It was what he had wished, anyway. He needed to see if Poth was planning harm for Melayne. Swiftly, he drew the long glove off his right hand, and reached out to stroke Poth's cheek. She purred at his touch.

He jerked back, appalled.

He must have gone white, because Poth looked at him in alarm. "What is it?" she asked. "What do you see?"

"Nothing," he choked out. "I see... nothing."

Kander gave a roar of anger. "Don't try to play games with me!" he screamed. "We saw your reaction - you can't expect us to believe that you didn't see anything!"

"You misunderstand me." Sander was badly shaken, and he had to fight to focus. "I don't mean I didn't See anything. I Saw very clearly. And what I Saw was - nothing!"

"You mean she dies?" Kander howled. Poth was stunned, her fingers clenching and releasing.

"No, I don't think so," Sander said. "If she were to die, I would see that event. I see... nothing. A complete blank where she should be. She is not dead, she is not alive. She is simply... not." He shook his head. "I've never seen anything like it, and I don't understand it at all. And, to be honest, it scares me." He was shaking, and couldn't stop.

Poth reached for him, holding him, comforting him. "My poor boy," she murmured. "My poor love." She seemed more upset over his feelings than his terrible Sight.

"I don't know what happens to you," he breathed. "I don't know."

Kander gave another growl, and pushed Poth aside. "Enough of that," he decided. "Now it is time - you will read me." When Sander hesitated, still shaking, Kander held up a burning hand. "Read me, or I fry your whelp right now."

Sander pulled himself together. "I have no control over what I see," he said. "It may be what you wish; it may simply be something inconsequential. I cannot tell."

"Read me!"

Sander removed his left glove as well, and placed both gloves through his belt. He hesitated for a moment and then reached out and grasped Kander's wrists firmly. Mild fire was still playing over them, and he flinched.

And then he Saw...

He cried, dropping to his knees, but not releasing his hold.

"What?" Kander howled. "What is it that you see?" His skin was heating up now, as his urgency grew.

"Fire," moaned Sander. "Just fire..."

"You see fire?" Kander glared down at him. "Then *feel* it, too!" Abruptly his arms were fully ablaze.

Sander screamed in pain, releasing his grip on the Burning God's arms. There was the stench of burnt flesh, and nothing but pain from his hands. He thrashed about, wanting to stop the pain, but unable. Corran, sobbing, dropped to his knees beside his father, wanting to help, but uncertain what to do.

Poth was not so helpless. She smacked Corran across the shoulders. "My bag, over there, beside the fire," she said, urgently. "There's a jar inside it - bring it to me." When Corran hesitated, she yelled: "Now! Do you want your father to suffer?" Corran leapt to his feet, sprinting for the bag. Poth moved to cradle Sander's head. He was still howling in pain, holding his hands in the air. They were red and black on the palms where the fire had seared them. Poth could imagine how he must be feeling. "A minute," she crooned, sympathetically. "Just a minute. I can help with the pain. I can."

"He's useless," Kander spat. "He either sees nothing, or else he won't speak the truth. Of course he saw fire for me, because that's what I *am*. It tells me nothing!" He stalked away in disgust. Everyone kept well out of his way.

Then Corran was back, holding the jar. Poth released her hold on Sander, and unsealed the small pot. There was a thick cream inside it, and she began to gently lather it onto Sander's damaged hands. He screamed, and flinched away as fresh pain filled his body.

"Hold him," Poth ordered Corran. "This ointment will help him. But it must go on *now*, or his hands might be permanently damaged."

Corran did as he was bid, holding his father's forearms tightly. Sander flinched, but didn't drag free. Poth continued to splash on ointment, and then she ripped a length of cloth from her long skirt. She used this to bind Sander's right hand, and then a second strip to bandage his left.

Finally, wonderfully, the pain began to abate, and Sander could begin to think rationally again. His hands were still a mass of pain, but he could start to focus his thoughts again. "Thank you," he gasped to Poth, through pain-filled eyes.

"It's happened to us all from time to time," she said. She pulled her blouse from her shoulders, and Sander's blurred eyes could see she had red hand imprints on both shoulders. "He... forgets himself sometimes when he's in deep emotions. That ointment will dull the pain eventually, and then start the healing process. But you won't be able to use those hands for at least a week." She gave a wicked grin. "Don't worry, I'll help you if you need to pee."

He managed to smile slightly. "I think Corran had better do that," he said, softly. "I wouldn't want to raise your hopes..."

"I'd like to raise something of yours," she murmured.

"I'm still a married man," he reminded her. She had been telling the truth - the pain was already dying down to merely unbearable.

"I like a man with some experience." Corran resealed the jar, ready for the next time it would be needed, and wiped her hands on what was left of her skirt. "Why did you not tell him what he wanted to hear?"

"I spoke the truth," Sander said. "All I saw was fire." He shook his head. "I could not lie about my vision. And I do not know what it means. Simply fire, consuming everything."

"And you don't know what your Sight about me means, either," Poth said, sadly. "You don't know much, and that's a fact."

"I know we're in serious trouble," he replied. "Tomorrow is not going to go the way he's planned it. And I don't know why." He glanced down at his son, and saw the tears in his eyes. "If Kander hadn't burned me, I might have been able to read Corran's future, and gotten some clue as to what is going to happen. Now..." He held up his ruined hands. "Now I cannot use my Talent at all. Perhaps even never again. I do not know if my hands will heal - or, if they do, whether I'll be able to use them for my Talent again." He gave a wan smile. "Well, I never did want to see the future, anyway. It seems that it is too often bad."

"You'll be seeing Melayne again tomorrow," Poth informed him. "I am certain of that. No matter what else changes, that stays constant." Her eyes were still cloudy with tears. "I'll lose you."

"Poth," he said, gently, "I was never yours."

"You were in my mind," she growled fiercely. "I could almost believe it would happen. But when Melayne is back - what chance will I have? She's all that you or Kander wants! There's no room for Poth in either of your lives!"

"You're my friend," he told her, honestly. "I like you. You're kind and funny, and cute. But you can never be more than my friend. Melayne is my life."

"That's not enough for me," Poth said, sadly. "I can't be content with it. I will always want more - at least, in whatever time I have left. Something is clearly going to happen tomorrow, and it's going to be very, very bad for at least a few of us." She sighed. "I've been looking into your future, Sander," she added. "I see you reunited with Melayne, whatever else happens. But there's a shadow of evil over everything. Nothing seems to be working, no matter which way I twist the options. Something is going to go very, very wrong."

Sander sighed also. "Why doesn't that surprise me?" he asked, rhetorically.

"It's the story of our lives," Poth said, sadly. "I don't think we are all going to live through this reunion."

"Neither do I," Sander admitted. "Neither do I."

Chapter Twenty Five

Melayne opened her eyes blearily and looked up at Devra as she was shaken awake. "What's the matter?" she asked, tiredly. It seemed as if she'd only just closed her eyes, and she desperately wanted more sleep.

"He's gone," Devra growled.

It took her sleepy mind a moment to process this information as Melayne struggled to wake. "Batten, you mean?" she asked.

"Who else?"

Melayne shrugged. "Well, I can't say I'm exactly surprised. We knew he was going along with us only to further his own plans. It doesn't make any difference."

"No difference?" Devra shook her head. "Melayne, there's only one place he could have gone, and that's to Dragonhome. And there's only one reason he could have gone - to betray us to your brother. I *knew* I should have kept a better watch on that rat. Sorry, I'm insulting your friends the rats."

Melayne was fully awake finally. She yawned and stretched. "Devra, stop talking like this is a problem. If you'd intended to keep a better watch on him, he'd have known about it, and worked out a way around it. He's a Seer, remember. If he wanted to leave us, he was going to do just that. As I said, it's not a problem."

"Not a problem? He's only going to betray us to Sarrow, and that's not a problem?"

"Of course it isn't." Melayne stood up. "We've not exactly been hiding ourselves, and Sarrow had to know we were coming anyway. We're not here to fight him, but to talk - so it doesn't matter if he knows we're coming, does it?"

"You're missing the point," Devra complained. "Batten is a Seer, so he *knows* who the winning side is, and he's gotten onto it. So that means Sarrow is going to win today."

"Devra, I love you, but you worry too much about the wrong things," Melayne said. "Is there any water around here? I want to wash my face."

"Over there, in the pitcher," Devra said, pointing to a table. "And stop changing the subject. I'm worrying about the *right* things."

"No, you're not." Melayne used the ice-cold water in the pitcher to clean herself, and then rubbed her face with the fleecy towel provided. She was starting to feel human again. "Batten can't See everything - we know that. He can't see factors he doesn't know about, so there's always the chance of something going wrong. He also can't See the actions of animals, so there's another thing he's blind about. So, yes, he *thinks* Sarrow is going to win, because as far as he can See that's what will happen - but it's not inevitable and it's not unchangeable. Besides, as I keep saying, we're not here to fight, so we can't even really talk about winners and losers."

"In other words," Devra said, slowly, "you're willing to trust your blind optimism over his ability to See the future."

"It's not blind optimism," Melayne said patiently. "We're in the right, and we have several assets neither Batten nor Sarrow understand. All I have to do is to Communicate with Sarrow, and everything will be fine. I don't believe that at heart Sarrow is evil - he's just a scared boy, trying to survive as best he can."

"Hello!" Devra yelled. "And one way he tried to survive was to send armed men to kill you! And now you're going to walk right into a castle where he has lots more armed men... Melayne, I love you, but you're insane. And I mean that."

Melayne laughed. "Devra, you're such a pessimist."

Devra growled and threw up her hands in disgust. "I give up," she snarled, and stormed from the room where they'd slept.

Corri, in the meantime, had woken from her makeshift bed in the corner of the room and washed her own face. Now she raised an eyebrow and looked at Melayne. "Well, the day's starting off perfectly normally - you and Devra having a fight."

"We just see things a little differently, that's all," Melayne answered.

"Very differently," Corri agreed. Then she rubbed her hands together. "Do you think Ysane's folks are planning on feeding us this morning? I'm starved!"

They were indeed planning just that. Melayne and Corri left their shared room and instantly smelled fresh bread and bacon cooking. Melayne, as ever, felt a tinge of regret for the poor pig who had given his life for the meal, but found the scent of the fresh loaf irresistible. By the time they had reached the kitchen, semi-organized chaos greeted them. The younger girls were helping their mother with the cooking. The boys and Ysane's father were presumably out doing their early morning chores. Devra was helping to set the large table, still muttering to herself.

"Can we help?" Corri asked, cheerily.

"You can get the plates," Ysane's mother suggested, without looking up from her cooking. One of the girls showed Corri where they were kept, and she and Melayne started to lay them on the table.

"Morning." It was Margone, entering from outside. "I thought you girls were going to sleep all morning. I've been up for hours."

"Show-off," Corri muttered, but with a grin. She gave him a kiss on the cheek. Melayne raised an eyebrow, and Corri blushed slightly. So it looked as if Melayne's guess about the pair was accurate... Well, at least *some* good was coming out of all of this.

Ysane's father and brothers came in now, and the next thirty minutes was a raucous mixture of eating and talking, followed by clearing the table and scraping the very few scraps to feed to the pigs. The menfolk vanished back to their chores, and Melayne, Corri and Devra helped with the cleaning up. Finally, though, everything was finished, and there was a moment of stillness.

"We have to go now," Melayne said. "Thank you all for your kindness. And for the food."

"You take care now," Ysane's mother said, her eyes tearing up. "I don't know what you have planned, but it seems to me like there's danger ahead. We would love to see you all back here again, very soon."

"We'd love to be back," Devra replied. "And you're right about the danger. But Melayne seems confident we can handle it."

"Well, that's all right, then," Ysane's mother replied. "She knows what she's about, that one."

"I sincerely hope you're right," Devra muttered. "I'm starting to feel like I'm the only person in touch with reality here."

Melayne hugged everyone, and the other girls followed her lead. Then they left the house. Outside they found that Margone and Falma had their horses saddled and waiting. Ysane's father was there also, looking grim.

"We're ready to go with you, Melayne," he said, producing a long-bladed knife from behind his back. "Falma and I will fight alongside you."

"No!" Melayne exclaimed, in true horror. "We are not going to fight," she explained. "And, anyway, your family needs you both here. But I truly thank you for your willingness to help."

"Are you certain?" Falma asked. He looked a trifle disappointed. "Or is it that you just don't want us along because we're not soldiers?"

"That's not it at all," Melayne assured him. She gave him a hug. "We'll be back soon, and you'll see that everything is fine. We don't need any soldiers. There isn't going to be a fight."

"She hopes," Devra muttered. "But it takes two to make peace - and only one to make war." Corri punched her on the arm. "See what I mean?" Devra complained.

"Stay here with your family," Melayne said, swinging up into the saddle on Fleetfoot. "We *will* be back, I promise, when all of this is over. We're in no danger." Ysane's father and brother didn't look convinced, but they nodded, and remained watching when the party rode off.

"Smart move," Devra agreed, as they started on the pathway to Dragonhome. "They would have been a liability in a fight."

"I meant what I said," Melayne answered. "There won't *be* a fight."

"You just keep right on thinking that," Devra said. "I'll be the realist, as always."

Melayne shook her head; there was no changing Devra - and maybe that was a good thing. Devra was right in one way, at least - Melayne *was* always convinced that things would go the way she wished. She needed someone like her friend to ground her more in reality, and she appreciated it. Even when she ignored the advice.

Devra understood Melayne's mood, and nudged her horse ahead to ride with Corri. As a result, Margone fell back a little to join Melayne. "This road must hold many memories for you," he said, gently.

"Yes," she agreed; he had somehow sensed what she was thinking. "The last time I traveled it, I was a young girl, scared, with a brother to protect and no helper in the world. I was heading to an unknown fate that would change my entire life..." She shrugged. "Not much difference, I guess."

"Except this time you have helpers," Margone pointed out.

"Yes," Melayne agreed. "Since those days I have been blessed with many good and loyal friends." She reached out to touch his hand. "And I believe that you are one of them."

Margone paused, and then said, reflectively: "The last time I rode this road, I was so sure of myself, so certain I'd found my destiny. I had trained all of my life to slay dragons, as had my father, and his father. And I had received the call that there were dragons in the world again. Suddenly, my whole life seemed to have purpose. I felt so full of myself, so cocksure..." He laughed, ruefully. "I was so wrong. I had been raised to believe a lie, that dragons are dangerous to people, and in need of slaughter. Thanks to you and your friends - and the dragons - I know I was completely wrong then. So here I am, now, riding back along this same path, but for a completely different purpose, and to a very different destiny. And it's one I believe in with all of my heart. Melayne, I have to make my life *mean* something. I can't let my legacy be a mistake. And I believe that I am now on the right path to my true destiny."

Melayne smiled, sadly. "I hope you're right. But I suspect that none of us really knows what our true destiny is. We learn that as we go through life. Perhaps even on our deathbeds we cannot truly know what we've accomplished with our lives. It's only with what we leave behind for those who follow that the pattern of our life unfolds, I suspect."

"*You* have done so much already," Margone said. "It seems to be your destiny to help others find theirs."

"I'm not doing it consciously, then," she replied. "I'm just trying to survive, to do the right thing for those I know and love. This is for Sarrow, and Sander, and my children, and the dragons. It's not about me at all."

"That," he said with a gentle smile," is probably why it's *all* about you. You never seem to think of yourself at all. You don't seem to see your own importance."

"I'm not important!" she protested. "I'm just a Talent doing her best for her family." She missed them all again - Sander and Corran, Cassary and the unnamed one, and the dragons - especially poor, wounded Tura. Her heart ached, but she steeled her will, knowing that what she was doing was for them all. And for Sarrow himself, no matter how little he might currently appreciate it. She couldn't allow him to continue the way he was going, because it would hurt too many people - Sarrow included.

"Well, whatever you believe, I know what I believe. And what Corri believes, too." Margone was silent a moment. "She's the most amazing girl I have ever known, and I want to get to know her better when all of this is over. She has such a light in her eyes, you know..." He shook his head. "But you don't need to hear about my silly crushes, do you?"

"Of course I do - and it's not silly!" Melayne was glad of something to lighten her mood. "Corri is a wonderful girl, and I suspect the two of you would be a terrific couple. But that's probably just the matchmaker in me talking. You know us women - we love to see happy couples."

He had actually blushed. "My point was," he said, slowly, "that Corri has implicit faith in you. She'd follow you into the Underworld if you told her it was necessary. Even Devra, I suspect, isn't as much against your plans as she claims."

"Devra feels very protective," Melayne explained. "To the Talents and especially to me. She believes I'm not smart enough to look after myself. She wants to be my mother, I suspect."

"Well, whatever she feels, she trusts you. As do I." Margone grinned. "I may think you're a little foolhardy, but I'll follow you anyway. Let's face it, my judgment so far about my own life hasn't been very good."

"You trusted what others told you," Melayne said. "But you've learned to find your own answers. That's important for us all. And you have matured." She grinned. "Besides, you've fallen for Corri, and *that* strikes me as extremely good judgment."

Changing the subject - probably to avoid further embarrassment - he asked her: "Do you have any plans? I mean, ones that Batten might not be able to See?"

She shook her head. "He was with us for a while. He probably knows me well enough now to be able to predict pretty much everything I will do. And since I always planned simply to ride in to Dragonhome and talk to my brother, I don't have a problem with that. But I *do* wish to have a few tricks up my sleeve, and Batten told us he can't See the actions of those he doesn't know, or animals."

"He was with us long enough to know me - and Corri and Devra," Margone pointed out. "Probably even Ysane's family, too. So there's nobody there to be able to surprise him."

"There's always *somebody* to surprise him," Melayne argued. "None of us can ever know *everything* that might happen. So I suspect he'll get a few shocks. And I am hoping to provide a few of my own." They were a fair distance from the farmhouse now, so she called out: "Greyn!"

The wolf slipped out of the woods to pad along beside Fleetfoot. "I was starting to think you'd forgotten about me," he said, laughter in his bark.

"How could I ever forget about my first true friend?" Melayne asked him. "I simply didn't want to upset Ysane's family by having a pack of wolves around their livestock."

"It would have been... tempting," Greyn agreed. "So, what plans do you have for mischief and fun today?"

"I *can't* have plans," Melayne informed him. "If I do, then Batten will know them."

Greyn's snout flared, and he bared his teeth. "*That* one passed this way hours ago. His stench lingers. He is going to betray you - as you predicted."

Melayne's lips twitched. "I have a small talent for Seeing myself, it seems. He does what he must, and events will unfold as they must. I give you and yours no orders, and make no requests of you. But I ask you to watch, and to use your best judgment. You are to be my secret weapon, for the Seer cannot begin to guess what you might do. So don't tell me any plans you make - simply do what you feel is best."

Greyn barked his laugh again. "I understand. You won't see me, my friend - but I will see you, and I will do what I can to aid you." He bounced off into the undergrowth again, and vanished from her sight.

"So," she said, sighing, "I lay my plans as I am able. Greyn will be one thorn in his side that Batten cannot See, and there may be others. I do not know what will befall us today, but I believe that, here and now, it will end."

Margone smiled. "Melayne, nothing ever ends - there is always tomorrow, and its crises."

"Then we shall meet them tomorrow. There are more than enough problems for one day."

There was a cry from the air, and then Kaya was wheeling down from the sky. Melayne smiled at her newest friend. "And what news do you have for me?" she asked.

"The men at the castle are very busy," the bird reported. "Something has them worked up."

"My impending arrival, no doubt," Melayne answered. "Are there many men?"

The falcon, of course, didn't understand how to count. "Many, many. Lots with weapons, and they're the ones rushing the most."

"It sounds as if Sarrow is preparing for our arrival by having his soldiers readied," Melayne informed Margone. "Hopefully, it's just a defensive maneuver."

"Perhaps he doesn't mean to give you a chance," Margone pointed out. "He prepared the slayers to kill you on sight - his soldiers may have the same orders."

"They might," Melayne agreed. "But I can't bring myself to believe it."

"Just because you can't imagine it doesn't mean it isn't true."

"I know." Melayne sighed. "I looked after Sarrow since he was a baby. He depended so much on me, and, I thought, he loved me. I find it difficult to accept that he's lost all of that love."

"Perhaps it never was love on his part," Margone said gently. "Perhaps it was simply need."

"It was love, I'm sure of that. But after three years - who knows what he may have come to believe? His love might have evaporated, while mine is unchanged." Melayne came to an abrupt decision. "Everyone, gather around," she called. When Corri and Devra pulled alongside them, she informed them of Sarrow's activities. "It's getting to be too dangerous for you all," she finished. "I want you all to wait here for me. I'll go on alone."

Devra snorted. "I don't care what you want," she replied. "You're too naive to allow you to go on alone. I'm staying with you."

"You might get killed," Melayne protested.

"So might you," Devra said. "You need me, and I'm going with you whether you like it or not."

"So am I," Corri said, defiantly. "Anyone who threatens you threatens me. Besides, what's to say that if he intends to attack you, he won't simply send men after us anyway? He knows we're here - Batten is bound to have told him. We're just as likely to be attacked whether we're with you or not. So I'm staying."

"As am I," Margone added. "Aside from the fact that I've sworn allegiance to you, I'm not leaving Corri's side. If she's with you, then so am I." He gave the blonde girl a wide smile.

Devra groaned. "Can we save the mushy stuff for later? If there *is* a later. Or, if you've got to do it, do it out of my sight."

"Why?" Corri asked, mischievously. "Jealous because you don't have a boyfriend?" She blew a kiss at Margone. Laughing, they rode on ahead together.

"Those two are annoying," Devra growled.

"Maybe you *are* jealous?" Melayne said, her lips twitching.

"If I wanted a boyfriend," Devra pointed out, "I could simply use my Talent to Find one, couldn't I? But I'm not crazy enough to want to share this kind of a life with any man. If we could be killed any moment, I wouldn't want to be distracted by thinking about a lover."

"There's no better time," Melayne said, gently. "Everything I do, I'm doing for Sander, or my children, or my friends."

"Well, try doing something for yourself some time," Devra said. "Like trying to preserve your own life. Or, if you insist on risking it all the time, at least think about Corri, Margone and myself - we'd kind of like to get through this alive, you know."

"I know," Melayne replied. "And I'm almost certain we'll all survive this."

"It's that *almost* that worries me," Devra said. "And now I'm going ahead to annoy Corri some more. I have to have *some* fun today if I'm at risk of being killed." She nudged her steed on to move forward, leaving Melayne alone with her thoughts.

Melayne appreciated the time alone. Her mind was in such a whirl. Was she risking her friends' lives? Well, yes, obviously - but would Sarrow *really* want them all dead? He had never really been *evil* - he was simply doing the best he could to protect himself. The problem was that he was only a boy still, and he wasn't very good at considering other people when making decisions. He was as selfish as most children were, and he acted out of that and fear. She was *almost* certain he was no killer.

But, as Devra had said, there *was* that "almost".

She sighed. She had made her plans - such as they were - and this was the worst possible time to second-guess herself. She simply had to go through with what she had decided long ago, and that was that. She would have to trust to her luck and the good God, and do what she felt was right.

Whatever the outcome, it wouldn't be long now. She recognized this road from her first trip to Dragonhome, and they were getting quite close to the castle. The last time she had traveled it, she and Sarrow had been fugitives, desperate for a place to hide, and without a friend in the world except for Ysane and Greyn. Now - how things had changed in three years! She had loyal, stubborn friends, and she was seeking resolution, not refuge. But she was still trying to do her best for her younger brother.

What else could she have done?

Her heart ached for Sarrow. She hated that she had been forced to abandon him three years ago, but at the time there had been no other viable solution to their problems. With baby dragons to look after, she and Sander had been forced to flee. And for the past three years, Sarrow had done anything he wished, with no one to rein him in, or to offer him advice. It can't have been good for him to grow up like that. Children needed limits set, and someone to teach them how to behave in society. Sarrow had had none of that.

What kind of a monster might he have become? She would discover the answer to that in a very short while...

As they drew closer to Dragonhome, she noticed the road had been well-traveled. There were deep ruts, created by the wheels of heavily-laden wagons. There were hoof marks everywhere, and evidence that the underbrush at the side of the road had been hacked back to widen the way. Everything spoke of a great deal of activity.

And then she had her first glimpse of the castle in three years, and she stopped, gasping slightly. Her companions reined in beside her, and they studied the view ahead.

The first time she had seen Dragonhome, it had been in fairly good shape, but sections of the walls and towers had collapsed. Sander had not been able to afford workmen and materials to repair it, and even if he could, he didn't dare allow them into the castle with five baby dragons howling for food all of the time. Sarrow had made up for lost time and opportunity. The walls were firm and strong, the towers restored. It seemed almost a different place - stronger, fresher, more vital. But the great gateway had not changed, and that was what made the castle unmistakable. It was in the shape of a dragon's head, jaws wide. To enter the castle, you had to walk through the jaws, down a passage like a throat and then into the courtyard. The great stone head looked fresh and clean, but it was quite unique. This was Dragonhome - Sander's ancestral home, and her own heritage now.

Except, of course, it was still being held by her crazed brother.

There were people everywhere - stone masons working on the walls and towers, other craftsmen entering and leaving the main castle. It was a flurry of activity that at another time would have warmed her heart. There were soldiers, too - some practicing their arts - archers, swordsmen, lancers, riders - and the general staff needed to run such a castle. She could hear the baying of hounds, the squawks of chickens, the neighing of horses, the braying of donkeys. It was a complete contrast to the place she had grown to love - but it meant that Dragonhome was whole again.

Sarrow had done a stunning job of work. It was all most impressive.

"Interesting," Margone observed. "Plenty of soldiers, but they don't seem to be waiting for us. They're all practicing their skills, not lurking in wait."

"They ones we see aren't," Devra pointed out. "That might be calculated to put us at our ease and not prepared for an ambush later."

"Perhaps it just means that Sarrow is letting us know he's not our enemy," Melayne suggested.

Devra shook her head. "He's had plenty of warning we were coming. If he wanted to be nice, he'd be out here, waiting for us. I don't see him anywhere. He's rather unforgettable."

"I don't see him, either," Melayne agreed. "But perhaps he's waiting in the courtyard for us."

"Right," Devra growled. "Maybe he's baked us a cake and wants to surprise us."

"Well, we can't just sit here," Corri pointed out. "Maybe I should fly over the castle and have a look at it?"

Melayne shook her head. "They might take that for an attack," she said. "I think the best thing is for us to ride on down and then walk in the front door."

"The best thing for *who*?" Devra asked. "Us or him?"

"Please," Melayne said. Devra shrugged, and urged her mount on.

They rode the remainder of the way to the gate. The workers looked up at them and then returned to their work. They were clearly not worried by the new arrivals. That meant they were either used to such visits, or else that they'd been warned and told to behave naturally. From the scowl on Devra's face, it was easy to guess which she believed. Melayne wanted to believe the best of her brother, though.

She slid from Fleetfoot's saddle at the gateway. It had been rebuilt so that it was too narrow to ride through - horses now entered and left the castle by a second gate, kept locked and barred when not in use.

"Be careful," her steed muttered.

"I shall," Melayne promised. "Wait for me here."

Corri, Devra and Margone moved afoot to join her. Screwing up her courage, Melayne walked toward the great stone jaws of the dragon. The "eyes" were sentry posts, but she saw no one manning them. She walked into the dark passageway that led from the "teeth" as if down a throat toward the courtyard. It was bright ahead, and there were more workers scurrying about there. It all looked rather peaceful.

And then there was sudden activity. Hidden doors in the walls swung open, and armed soldiers rushed out. Melayne half-twisted, but there was no time for any of them to react. The burly men grabbed each of the travelers, holding them firmly. More men waited beyond those, swords drawn.

"What -" Melayne started to say, but them one soldier jerked her head back ungently and rammed a cloth into her mouth. She tried to struggle, but two more held her arms firmly. The one behind her wrapped a cloth over her mouth and tied it off. She could breathe, but not speak.

"I hate being right all the time," Devra growled. She, too, was being held firmly, but without a gag. Melayne glanced around, and saw Corri and Margone were captives, their weapons removed from their sheaths.

"Well," said a very familiar voice. "If it isn't my sweet sister. How are you, Melayne?" Sarrow came from behind her, laughing. "Oh, I'm sorry, you can't speak, can you?" His eyes narrowed. "Like me, your Talent expresses itself through your voice. If you can't speak, then you can't convince anyone to turn against me, can you?"

Melayne tried to speak, but could only make faint noises. She wanted to tell Sarrow that she wasn't here to harm him, that he had nothing to fear - but couldn't.

He was taller now, having had a growth spurt in the past three years. He was almost as tall as she was, and his hair was long and well-groomed. But he was still the same old Sarrow - almost.

Batten stepped out of the hidden room behind the youth, grinning. "Didn't I tell you they'd be here?" he said.

"Oh, I knew she'd come," Sarrow said. "How could she resist it? I see that none of my assassins managed to get to you, my dear sister. I really didn't think that they would. But I knew you'd never be able to stay away after such an attack. I knew you'd take it as an invitation to come and visit."

"Stop taunting her, you bastard," Devra growled. "You must know she came here to make peace with you, not to attack you. I was in favor of attacking."

"And you'd have had even less chance of surviving that way," Sarrow snapped back. "I remember you, Devra - my sister's willing little toady. I haven't quite decided what to do with you yet. Or the others." He glanced at Margone. "I see you switched your allegiance quite painlessly."

"She freed me from your Persuasion," Margone answered. "And I came to see that she is a good, kind person."

"Oh, spare me your justifications," Sarrow said. "I can make you obey me anytime I can be bothered to do it."

"I don't think so," Margone replied. "I suspect that Melayne's influence of freedom is stronger than your chains of commands."

"You may be right, there," Sarrow said, off-handedly. "I'll have to experiment on you and see which of us is the stronger Talent." He then looked at Corri. "Well, at least you're still as pretty as ever, Corri," he said. "How would you like to become my lady?"

"I'd sooner become your scullery girl," Corri answered.

"That can be arranged. You men, hobble her, and tie her hands together. She's a Flier, and I wouldn't want her to be able to get away from us once we're out in the open again." Sarrow turned back to Melayne, grinning. "But where are my manners, dear sister? Welcome home again. I'll bet you've married Sander by now, haven't you? You always did know how to get ahead. Smart move - except it won't help you in the slightest." He gestured to his men. "Come along, all of you. I have a special surprise ready as a sort of welcome-home gift." He walked ahead. The soldiers forced Melayne and her friends to follow. Melayne had never felt so helpless. She could do nothing - especially not speak. Sarrow had planned this well, indeed. She was pushed out into the courtyard.

Most of the people there went about their business, ignoring the little spectacle. One man, however, did not. He was tall and muscular, with an unpleasant face, warped by a scar that went from above his left eye, across his nose, and down his cheek. Someone had evidently tried to slice his brains out at one time, and almost succeeded. He was standing by a brazier, and the coals within it were glowing red-hot. Several long-handled instruments had their ends buried in the coals.

"This is Charka," Sarrow said. "He's a very skillful specialist." He grinned at Devra. "Want to guess what he's good at?"

"Scaring babies?"

"Oh, more than babies, I assure you," Sarrow replied. "He terrifies anyone left with him." He glowered at Melayne. "You'll be spending a little time with him, sweet sister. His main task today is ripping out your tongue so you'll never be able to use your Talent again."

Chapter Twenty Six

Melayne struggled, but she was unable to break free of the soldiers who held her. With the gag in her mouth, she could only make soft, urgent sounds.

Devra wasn't so constrained. "Leave her alone, you sadist!" she growled. "How can you even *think* of doing that to her?"

"I'm being merciful," Sarrow announce, smugly. "I can't have her using her Talent against me, so it's either removing her tongue or her life. Would you rather I simply kill her?"

"She would *never* harm you!" Corri cried. "She's your sister - and despite everything you've done, she loves you."

"Well, we'll test how strong her love for me is, then, won't we?" Sarrow said. "We'll see if she still loves me after I've had her tongue ripped out. Charka, get ready. You two -" he addressed the soldiers holding Melayne "- bind her arms so she can't struggle out of your grips. The rest of you keep very good hold of her friends."

"If you harm her," Devra snapped, "I swear I'll kill you."

Sarrow whirled on her. "You're not related to me at all, so it won't bother me in the slightest to have Charka torture you to death. Keep provoking me, and I swear you'll die. Eventually."

Melayne wanted to plead with her brother, to reason with him - but he'd ensured that would never happen. All she needed was to talk to him - and she would soon never be able to do that again. The soldiers forced her, painfully, to her knees, and then bound her hands tightly behind her back. Sarrow watched narrowly.

"I'm sure you're thinking that as soon as they remove the gag, you'll start talking," he said. "Don't worry, I've thought of that. When Charka's ready for you, you'll be knocked senseless. It'll be kinder that way, too - you won't feel the pain. I've no desire to torture you, Melayne. It's not that I don't love you. But I cannot take chances. You *must* be rendered powerless."

Charka was working with his brazier, using a bellows to send the flames roaring. He was examining the instruments he had in the coals, determining when they would be ready to mutilate her. Melayne could think of nothing to do to escape from her fate. It seemed so horrible and insane that her quest would come down to this - having her tongue ripped out of her mouth, to be forever mute. Never to be able to tell her children that she loved them. Never to be able to whisper endearments to Sander. Never to be able to talk to her animal friends again. She wanted to scream - but that was, of course, denied her too.

"I'm ready," Charka said, in a gravelly voice that sounded as if it issued from within a crypt. "Prepare her."

"I'm truly sorry about this," Sarrow said. He raised a hand, and then scowled. "What is *that*?"

He was looking beyond her, into the air. She didn't know what he was referring to. Held as she was, she couldn't turn to see. Her friends could, and she saw looks of utter astonishment on their faces.

"Sir?" Charka asked, his hands on his instruments. "Shall I proceed?"

"No - wait a moment." Sarrow grabbed Melayne's face roughly and glared into her eyes. "Is this one of your tricks?" Melayne tried to ask him what he meant, but could only mumble. Sarrow let her face go, and snapped at the guards: "Let her rise."

Their heavy grips loosened, and Melayne struggled to her feet. Then she turned and looked upward. Was it Kaya? But why would that surprise everyone so?

It wasn't the hawk. Nor was it her second thought - one of the dragons.

It was a ship - a flying ship!

It looked like a large Raider vessel, in full sail - but it was gliding through the air toward Dragonhome, not afloat on a river. Figures lined the sides of the ship, and there were sailors furling the sails, preparing the ship to come to port. And all over a hundred feet in the air!

"I've never seen anything like that," Corri breathed. "And I practically live in the air."

"Is this one of your tricks?" Sarrow screamed at Melayne. She shook her head. She had no idea what this meant.

Batten stepped forward. "Sir," he said, "she knows nothing of this - if she did, I would have Seen its arrival. It's a complete surprise to her, too. None of your prisoners know anything of this."

"Then what is it?" Sarrow yelled. "I need to know! I can't chance any interference with my plans. And I can't believe this... thing is arriving here by simple coincidence. It *has* to be something to do with her, no matter what you say. She has a real gift for messing up people's plans."

Melayne almost wished he were correct. But he was right that this couldn't be some simple coincidence. Yet she had no idea what it meant, or how such a strange phenomenon could have anything to do with her.

The ship was lower now, and everyone in the castle had stopped whatever they had been doing to stare up at it. Whoever was captaining the ship clearly knew what he or she was doing. The sails were coming down, and the vessel was dropping down toward a perfect landing in the courtyard. Anyone in the way hastily moved back, and a space large enough to hold the ship was rapidly cleared. Now it was down to sixty feet, and dropping gently.

Melayne could begin to make out the figures as people now. She recognized none of them until –

She wanted to cry out in joy. It was Sander! Sander! Against the odds, her husband was here, somehow, prepared to rescue her. Her heart beat faster, and she wished she could make more than weak mewing sounds. How good it was that he was here - this must be his doing, somehow.

Then she saw Corran beside him, and her step-son didn't look happy. Surely if this was a rescue, he would appear pleased to see her? Why was he so glum?

Beside her two loves, she saw a tall, beautiful blonde woman - that had to be the Poth whom Batten had mentioned.

For a moment she felt a pang of jealousy - she *was* gorgeous, and any man would be tempted by her. Perhaps even Sander... And then she saw soldiers on the decks, and two of them had weapons covering Sander and Corran.

They were prisoners, too!

So this *wasn't* a rescue attempt. It was something else. Things hadn't gotten better - they had become much, much worse. Not only were she and her friends prisoners, but so now were her husband and step-son.

But who was their captor? It obviously wasn't anything to do with Sarrow, because the sight of this ship had startled and panicked him.

Just what was going on here? And was there any way that she could turn this development to her advantage? At least it had stopped her mutilation - for the moment. Charka was as startled by this as everyone else.

The ship came in for a gentle landing, and now she could see the whole deck. There were two dozen or more men and women all gathered behind... Her skin crawled as she saw the dominating figure on the ship. He was tall, slim and his exposed skin was crawling with scars. That was bad enough. But there was a... stench, really was the only word for it - a stench of twisted, warped malevolence emanating from the man.

And there was also something horribly familiar about him, though she was certain she had never seen anyone like this before.

Sarrow jerked his eyes from the ship to Batten. "What will happen?" he cried, almost pathetically. He was clearly realizing he had somehow lost the upper hand here. "You must See! You must tell me what will happen!"

And, on the ship, the scarred man cried out to Poth: "See! What will occur now? Is my destiny achieved? I must know!" Both Batten and Poth focused -

And both become absolutely rigid, their faces completely blank.

Sarrow whimpered. "Batten! Tell me! Tell me!"

But Batten clearly could not speak. He seemed to be barely even breathing. He was locked into place, staring into nothing, seeing nothing. It was as if his mind had somehow switched off...

On the ship, the hideous man raged: "Poth, curse you! I *have* to know!" He looked as if he were about to strike the frozen woman.

"It's what I Saw," Sander barked. "The blankness - remember? I saw *nothing*! It's what she's feeling - nothing. She's trapped inside her mind."

"Why?" the scarred man raged. "How can this have happened? I need my Seer now, more than ever before."

Melayne saw understanding dawn on her beloved's face. Sander smiled grimly. "That man down there is also a Seer," he said, gesturing at Batten. "Two Seers, both attempting to predict the future, but on different sides..."

"What of it?" the captain snarled.

"Both of them are attempting the same thing - to See how to defeat their opponent. But when their opponent can do the exact same thing... They're locked together, each trying to out-predict the other - and completely unable to do it. They're frozen because neither can see a way out of their dilemma."

"This is not the time!" the man screamed. Then, to Melayne's shock, flames burst out all across his body. She expected him to be burnt alive, but that didn't happen. There was no stench of burning flesh, and the man seemed to be unaffected by the blaze that had enveloped him. "I must know what will happen now that I am reunited with Melayne!"

Reunited? But she had never seen him before, of that she was... And then the truth began to dawn on her.

She *did* know a Fire Caster - or *had* known one. Her older brother, Kander, whom she barely remembered. He had been taken by the King's Men to fight in the wars, and, as a result, her parents had fled, taking her with them while she was still a child. They had wanted to protect her, knowing that she, too, was going to be a Talent.

Could this, then, somehow - against all odds, against terrible fates - could this be her *brother*? If only she could speak! Yet this was certainly not the kind and gentle boy she vaguely recalled. If this were Kander indeed, he had been changed in the years he had been away.

Sander had finally seen Melayne, and his face lit up with joy. "Melayne!" he cried, and moved to leave the ship. The guards closed in on him, and he was forced to halt. "What have they done to you?" he cried.

"That's your husband?" Corri asked Melayne. She nodded. Corri's eyes widened. "Wow, you really married well - he's so *handsome*." Melayne wished she could tell her friend everything else that Sander was, but couldn't.

Sarrow started to pull himself together. His plans had been demolished by the arrival of the ship, but he was beginning to get control of his terror. After all, he still had his Talent, and he should be able to control even these new arrivals. Melayne could see awareness of all of this flash across her brother's face. He stepped forward. "Who are you?" he called out. "And how *dare* you arrive like this?"

The blazing man glared at Sarrow, and then turned to Sander. "Who is that little fool?" he demanded.

"Your brother," Sander said.

Melayne stiffened in shock. So she *had* been right! Somehow... somehow, this was Kander. Alive - but not well. And not, apparently, very sane either.

"So," Kander breathed, the flames wreathed about him growing stronger. "You're the little snot I have to kill to achieve my destiny?"

"Kill?" Sarrow went white. "No, you *can't* kill me. I won't allow it. You can't kill me - you hear me?" Melayne could feel him putting all of the force of his Compulsion into the order, feel it wafting out across all of the new arrivals.

"You little brat!" Kander yelled. "You think I care what you want? I have to kill you, to achieve my destiny."

"Stop him!" Sarrow ordered. He was panicking now that his Talent had failed him. His worst fears were coming true.

"Stop him!" The command wasn't directed to anyone in particular, so nobody moved.

Except for Corran. With a sly grin, Corran walked to the side of the ship, and then gripped a rope, lowering himself overboard. To Melayne's astonishment, the guards who had been watching him and Sander quite carefully a moment ago seemed to be paying no attention to her step-son at all. She couldn't understand it.

Reaching the ground, Corran walked casually across the courtyard until he stood beside Melayne. As far as she could see, nobody was paying him any mind whatsoever. She stared at him, and he grinned even more widely.

"I've discovered my Talent at last," he told her, softly, as he proceeded to untie the gag from her mouth. "I can be Unseen - people can't notice me, no matter what I do."

The gag came free, and Melayne gasped in a breath. "But I can see you," she whispered back.

"Because I let you. I didn't want to scare you by taking off your gag and ropes invisibly." He looked very proud of himself. As soon as he freed her hands, Melayne gave him a huge hug.

"I am *so* glad you and your father are here," she said.

Corri, standing next to her, suddenly realized that Melayne was free. "Hey!" she muttered, not wishing to draw attention to them. "What gives?" Then she gasped as invisible hands started to untie her also.

"Quiet," Melayne whispered. "I suspect things are about to get very interesting..." So far, neither the guards nor Sarrow had noticed that she was free. They were all too intent on watching Kander.

Still blazing away, he had leapt lightly from the deck of his ship to the ground. Now he was making his way across the courtyard toward Sarrow. Sarrow, panicking, gestured to one of his soldiers with a bow. "Shoot him!" he screamed.

The soldier obeyed, loosing a shaft and then whipping another from his quiver to prepare a second shot. Though he saw it was pointless, he had no choice but to obey Sarrow's orders, and kept firing arrow after arrow.

None of which reached Kander. They burned up before impact, and only light ash fell to the ground.

Sarrow turned to more men. "Use your swords!" he ordered. "Hack him to tiny pieces!"

Three men started forward, swords at the ready. Kander merely laughed, and reached out a hand. His fingers moved, and fire shot from him, hitting the first soldier, and burning him alive. There was a stench of charred flesh, and a scream, mercifully cut short, as the dead man fell to the ground. The other two guards looked as if they wished they could run, but they were compelled to follow Sarrow's orders. Kander gestured again, and this time the bolt of fire caught the next man's upraised sword. The metal blade simply melted, and white-hot iron flowed down the unfortunate man's arm. He, too screamed, and fell down, writhing, his arm a festering wreck. Kander simply burned the last man down as he charged.

Sarrow was almost gibbering now. Melayne had been too appalled to act before, but the stink of burnt bodies roused her anger and pity. "Stop!" she called, and stepped forward.

Sarrow's eyes narrowed. "How did you get free?" He began to turn to the men supposedly guarding her, but then he recalled Kander, and hesitated. He couldn't decide what to do, which menace was the greater to him.

"Melayne?" Kander halted his implacable advance and stared at her. "Is that you, my sweet sister?"

"It's me," she confirmed. "Kander - what have you become?"

"A god, dear sister - a god." He blazed even brighter, and everyone had to shield their eyes. "I am the Burning God now - but you are still my sister, and we shall go from here to achieve our destiny together."

Melayne had no idea what he was talking about, but she knew she couldn't allow this to go on. "You're killing people, brother," she said, gently.

"They mean nothing." Kander simply shrugged. "They're unimportant."

"They're human beings!" Melayne cried, appalled. "They *aren't* nothing! They aren't unimportant!"

"Stop him," Sarrow begged. "He's going to kill me next! You've got to stop him, Melayne!"

"You rat," Devra growled. "You were going to torture and mutilate her, and now you expect her to *help* you?"

Melayne laughed. "Sarrow, you're my *brother* - of course I'll help you. And then we'll talk about what *you've* been doing." She stared at Kander. "Why do you wish to kill your own brother?"

"The prophecy," Kander explained. "It says that you and your brother will do great things, will change this world forever. It *must* mean me. I *know* it means me. But, to be certain, I have to be your only brother. Then it couldn't mean anyone else, could it?" He made it all sound so simple, so obvious.

Melayne shook her head. "Kander, how could you think I'd agree to do *anything* with you if you killed our brother?"

"You'd have to," Kander said, slightly sullenly. "It's the prophecy. You have no choice." He sounded like a child who was being punished.

"I *always* have a choice," she said. "And I chose the path of peace - whenever I can. I will not allow you to harm Sarrow." She stepped between the two brothers. Sarrow gripped her shoulder from behind, his fingers tight and terrified, cutting into her skin.

"Be reasonable, Melayne," Kander begged. "You know I can't harm you, or the prophecy would be broken. But I have to kill that little weasel. Anyway, you should thank me - he was going to hurt you."

"Yes, you seem to be forgetting that part," Devra complained as she moved to stand beside Melayne. "I think the little stinker *should* get barbecued." She grinned. "I'd be happy to do the job myself."

"Don't be silly," Melayne said. "And you might be safer away from me - I don't think my brother's prophecy covers you, too."

"It does not," Kander said. He raised his hand, preparing to strike.

"Don't you dare touch her either!" Melayne yelled. "Whatever has happened to you, Kander? You were always so kind, so gentle! How can you kill people so casually?"

"Because I have been transformed," He replied. "I am no longer mortal, but a god. In the war, I saw so much pain and suffering - and all for *nothing*. It was all a game that the kings were playing, a game to rid themselves of Talents - because they were afraid of us. We have abilities they can never have, and they're afraid that we will take over and rule instead of them. There was never any other point to the war. I realized this as I fought for my king... Victories were meaningless, nothing was ever resolved. The war *had* to be eternal, because fresh Talents were always being born, and they always had to be disposed of.

"I came to see the futility of it all, and I left, taking Poth and the rest of my men with me. We were the strongest, we were the best - we were those who survived. And I knew that I needed a purpose in life. That was when I remembered the prophecy, and began to see that I had to find *you*."

"And that is when he went insane." Sander stepped forward, and Melayne's heart sang. It was so good to see her husband again! And then she saw that his hands were wrapped in bandages. The guards were still with him also.

She felt a great chill draw through her body. "What has happened to you?" she asked him, her voice filled with pain.

"Kander... burnt me a little," Sander explained. "Poth helped me." He held up the bandaged hands. "I'm afraid I'm not much use at the moment - I can't touch anything."

"Then I owe Poth," Melayne said, her voice a low growl. "And I owe Kander, also." She turned back to face her brother. "You have hurt my man," she said. "And you have killed people who did not deserve it. I had never thought to see you again alive - and now I wish I had not."

"Melayne!" Kander cried. "I did all of this for you. We are meant to be together. None of the rest of it matters!"

"*All* of the rest of it matters!" Melayne screamed back at him. "If you can't understand that, you may be beyond my help.

You can't just go around acting as if you're a god and everyone else is an insect."

"I'm not *acting*," Kander said. "I *am* a God."

"No," Melayne said. Her heart was breaking, but she now knew what she had to do. "No, you're not - your mind has gone. You've seen too much, done too much, suffered too much. You're no god - you're barely even a man any more." She felt her Talent growing within her, and she focused it all on her lost brother. "I'm sorry, Kander - I don't know what this will do to you - but you must *see* what you have become." She let her Talent flow with all of her force, washing over her brother. Her gift was Communication, and she had to make Kander once more see what he had done. He had to communicate with the lost soul within his crazed mind.

"No..." he whispered, falling to his knees. He held his head in his hands, shaking. "No!" His head bowed, his body shook. Flames raced across his skin, and everyone was forced to step back from him.

"What's happening?" Devra hissed. "What did you do?"

"I've forced him to see what he's become," Melayne answered, grief wracking her. "I've made the Kander I knew return - to confront what he has become. He is at war with himself." Tears rolled down her cheeks.

"Now!" Sarrow cried, stepping from behind Melayne, where he'd been cowering for her protection. "Now we can kill him. Guards!" He turned to give the order, orders they would be compelled to obey. Melayne gave a strangled cry, but she couldn't form coherent words. She was lost in the waves of pain that were wracking her older brother.

Devra grinned and stepped forward. Her right fist lashed out, catching Sarrow firmly on the jaw. With a startled look on his face, he simply collapsed to the ground. "I've been wanting to do that for a long time," Devra muttered with a great deal of satisfaction. "I think we'll all get along better without his interference."

Melayne felt another pang of pain for her younger brother, but she could hardly focus. She could feel the agony washing through Kander as though it were a tangible object. He had stopped screaming at least, but he was on his knees, his body wracked with emotional pain and grief. She was becoming lost in it all.

Corri gripped her shoulders and shook her, hard. "Melayne!" she called out. "You have to break the connection with him! He's sucking you in somehow. Melayne!"

She heard the voice, but the words didn't register. Her whole word was pain now - the remorse and guilt and horror at her own actions, all of the evil she had done, all in the name of her - his - destiny. The depths to which she'd sunk, the lives she'd taken... Her parents, the raiders, that whole village that had irritated him, the soldiers, the innocents, the -

A stinging slap across her cheek made her head ring. Bemused, hurting, she blinked and looked at Corri. The blonde girl whipped her hand back again and gave a stunning blow against Melayne's other cheek. "Break free!" she screamed.

Her whole face hurt, but the emotional pain was gone. "I am free," she mumbled. Her cheeks stung badly. "Stop hitting me."

"Oh, thank the good God!" Corri threw her arms around Melayne, hugging her tight.

"No fair," Devra grumbled. "How come you get to punch Melayne, and I only get to smack the brat?"

"Thank you, Corri." Melayne gingerly touched her stinging cheeks. "As soon as I can talk properly, I'll thank you better."

Corri jutted her chin up. "Take a punch back at me," she suggested.

"Idiot. I don't want to hit you. You may have saved my life." Melayne looked at her brother, still lost in the depths of his own mind, and her heart almost broke. "I was getting drawn into his madness."

Sander moved to stand beside her. The men who had been guarding him didn't move, confused by everything that was happening. "My love," he murmured. He held up his hands.

"I wish I could touch you, but it's not practical." Instead he kissed the tip of her nose. "You can't imagine how much I missed you."

"Believe me," she assured him, "I can. I felt it myself." She threw her arms about him, hugging him tightly to her. It felt so wonderful to have him with her again.

Sander grinned at Corri over her shoulder. "I don't know who you are," he said. "But - thank you."

Corri grinned. "You're welcome. Formal introductions later, I imagine, my Lord."

"Oh, yeah," Devra grunted. "I forgot - we should be calling Melayne *my Lady* now, and not *you idiot*."

Melayne released her husband and looked from one brother to the other. Sarrow was unconscious, and Kander was lost in a world of pain. "Some family reunion," she muttered. "What do we do now?"

Chapter Twenty Seven

There was the sound of a sword being drawn from its sheath. "Now," growled an angry voice, "I think we get some payback." Melayne turned, and saw that the Talents who had accompanied her brother on his wild flying ship had moved forward. Two of them were drawing blades, and one of them - a tall, dark, and muscular man - had spoken. He glanced at Kander, who was still on his knees, sobbing. "Your brother promised us wealth and power, but he doesn't look much like he's going to be paying off on his promises - and it's all your fault."

"That's right, Rinter," one of the others agreed. "Let's take what we can from here - it looks like they've got more than a few coins to rub together in a pile like this."

Sander moved to shield Melayne. "There's no need for us to fight," he said, gently. "Kander's plans have fallen through, but I'm sure we can come to some agreement."

Rinter pretended to think it over. "Fine," he said. "Hand over all the gold in this place, and we'll leave."

Sander gestured down at where Sarrow was still unconscious. "I think the gold belongs to him. I know I didn't have much when I ran the place."

Rinter shrugged. "Well, he's in no shape to hand anything over. I guess we'd better just take whatever we find - and anyone who gets in our way will take whatever we dish out."

There was the sound of further weapons being drawn. This time it was caused by the dragonslayers. "I don't think we can allow that," one of them said. He was another tall man, dark and with a scar on one cheek. "We're owed some money ourselves."

Rinter laughed. "You think *you* can stop us? You're not Talents, and you'll not manage to get close to us with those weapons, I can tell you."

Melayne could see things were going to get out of hand very quickly, and that blood was bound to be spilled. She moved out of Sander's shadow. "Perhaps they can't," she agreed. "But I can stop you."

"Girl," Rinter growled, "you don't seem to be able to do anything but talk. And that can be stopped pretty simply with cold steel."

"Stay out of this, dragon-lover," the slayer agreed. "We're not so easy to stop as this freak imagines. We're trained slayers."

"I will not allow bloodshed," Melayne said, firmly, moving to stand between the two groups of armed men.

"You can't stop us, girl," Rinter snapped. "Parron - get her!"

Melayne gave a shriek of astonishment as she felt herself suddenly rising into the air. Parron must be one of the Lifters, who had helped to keep that ship in the air. It was a simple matter, obviously, for him to Lift a mere slip of a girl fifteen feet straight up.

This seemed to be the signal for the fight to start. Slayers and Talents clashed, while Melayne hung helplessly above the battle. Sander was unable to do anything, his hands useless. Rinter was a Fire Caster, it turned out, and he used his ability to make his sword blaze. Sparks flew, and there was the song of metal on metal as his weapon met that of the slayer.

Melayne couldn't follow what happened next at all clearly. She saw Corri launch herself through the air toward the ranks of the Talents, and Devra drew her own sword and, with a loud yell, threw herself into the fight. Margone followed the girls, his own sword out. Then Melayne went spinning through the air. She was too dizzy to focus for a moment, and then she felt herself falling.

Wiry arms grabbed her, and she caught a glimpse of Corri's laughing face. "Parran should never have tried his Talent on me," she said. "I can fly rings around anything he can do." She brought Melayne in to a landing, and then was off again.

It was absolute chaos. All three groups were attacking one another with everything they had. And, as if that were not insane enough, Melayne heard a snarl, and three large, dark wolves sprang into action.

"Did you think I'd miss all of the fun?" Greyn growled, as he ripped at one of the Talents.

Melayne simply couldn't get anything straight - there was too much happening. She'd lost all control over anything now - that much was clear. The Talents and the slayers were both driven by greed to get whatever they could from this degenerating situation, and were laying into anyone around them with a will. Melayne could see Devra fighting one of the slayers, and laughing. The wolves were harrying anyone they reached. There was no sign of Corran - presumably he'd gone completely Unseen to help out. Sander, unable to fight, was crouched over Sarrow, who was still unconscious.

Could matters get any worse? Melayne was completely out of her depth, and didn't have any idea what she could do to stop all of this. Despite her will and her Talent, people were already injured and dying.

Sarrow's guards had joined in the battle also, though some of them seemed to be a little confused as to who exactly they were supposed to be battling. Two remaining Lifters were sending fighters spinning through the air. There was one Talent who could fly, and he had tackled Corri thirty feet about the castle. Others were using swords or other Talents Melayne couldn't immediately identify.

And then she heard the sound of beating wings.

She looked up, and saw Brek and Ganeth. The two dragons were spiraling down from the sky. For a moment, it seemed as if the battle was suspended as all eyes turned upward. The leader of the slayers stepped back from Rinter. There was a startled, happy expression on his face. "Dragons," he breathed, entranced. "At last - we have our purpose..."

Melayne winced; it was as if fate were playing every trick on her that it could. *Now* the dragons had to show up? Beside her, Sander gave a start.

"Oh, no," he groaned. "Brek's been missing for days, and now he decides is the right time to return?"

The fighting had fizzled out as more and more eyes turned upward to see the approaching dragons. The slayers all had eager, expectant looks on their faces - well, they had trained all of their lives for just such a moment as this. Melayne had wanted the fighting to stop - but not so that the slayers could tackle her dragons.

Taking advantage of the lull in fighting, Greyn slipped to stand beside her. There was blood on his muzzle. "Well, this should complicate matters even more," he commented. "About the only thing this battle was lacking was dragons..."

"A truce for the moment?" the leader of the dragon slayers offered Rinter. "We have more important things to worry about now. These dragons are *hers*." He gestured toward Melayne. "They will undoubtedly fight on her behalf."

Rinter eyed the dragons, then Melayne and finally the slayers. "Agreed," he said. "We'll carry on our... discussion after the damned dragons are dead."

The slayers and the Talents separated, the Talents drawing back toward the castle walls, allowing the twenty or so slayers the maximum space. With fierce grins, the men readied their swords, axes and other weapons.

"I imagine you'll want us to stop them?" Greyn asked. "The remainder of my pack is approaching, and we can take on the humans without much of a problem. We're not big and clumsy like dragons."

Don't you dare! Ganeth called down, as she beat her wings to come in for a landing. *These men are *ours*!*

Melayne was startled to hear a measure of pleasure in the dragon's voice. "They've been trained to kill dragons," she objected. "You and Brek can't possibly defeat them alone."

They are not alone, said an unfamiliar, powerful voice.

We've brought... friends, Ganeth explained.

Melayne looked around, and then gave a jerk of surprise. On the largest of the towers, another dragon was perched. But this was no youngster, like her own two friends. It was larger - much larger - with powerful wings and muscles. It had to be at least forty feet in length, and its claws alone were three-foot rapiers. Melayne could feel the self-confidence oozing from the beast.

Friends? Melayne slowly glanced around. There was a second, huge dragon on the gateway - this was clearly female, but just as large and old and powerful. There was something about this new pair of dragons - but she'd have to wait until later to sort out what was going on here.

The large male seemed to grin somehow. *I've heard of slayers,* he commented, and it was quite clear that, somehow, all of the humans could hear this dragon talking. *If you want us dead, come - try it.*

Devra had managed to sneak up beside Melayne. "Why are they provoking the slayers?" she asked, softly.

"Because they're certain they can take them," Melayne replied. "These new dragons are very brash - and they're infecting Brek and Ganeth." Her own dragons were also tensely awaiting an attack by the slayers.

"Should be interesting," Greyn observed. "Are dragons good to eat? I only ask in case they don't survive this fight. No point in wasting good meat. And there's plenty of meat on them..."

Melayne was at a loss. Should she try and stop this impending fight? She knew the dragons wouldn't thank her if she did - and neither would the slayers. They had trained all of their life for just such a moment as this, and to have it ripped from them when it was within their grasp would infuriate them. She would never be able to convince them to make peace if she frustrated them now.

"I think," Sander said softly, "that, for once, you're just going to have to let events take their course. This battle *will* happen, whether you wish it or not."

"But Ganeth could get injured - or killed," she protested, feeling helpless.

"I know. And you know I love her dearly. But it's *her* choice, Melayne, and we have to respect that decision, whatever the outcome." He laid his hand around her shoulder. "You can't force everyone to do your will - and you wouldn't, even if you could. You're not your brother. Sometimes you must let them do what they wish - whether it's the best thing, or even whether it's the dumbest thing."

Melayne felt tears welling up. "I feel so *helpless,*" she protested. "And I hate it. I should be able to do something, to stop this."

"You can't control everything," Devra said, agreeing with Sander. "Even you have to let things be sometimes. I know you hate losing control, but this battle is beyond you."

Margone surprised Melayne by moving forward himself, partially blocking the slayers. "Bavin," he said, urgently. "You know me - we've trained together. Listen to me!"

"Listen to you?" The slayer's leader shook his head. "I don't know what that witch has done to you, but she's turned your mind somehow. There's nothing you can say we want to hear."

"She did nothing to me," Margone said, not entirely truthfully. "But I've come to realize that dragons aren't the evil we've been taught to believe. They're no danger to humans. There's no need to slay them!"

"It's what we are," Bavin growled. "It's what we do. If we allow dragons to live, we deny ourselves, our fathers, and everything we stand for."

"Then deny it!" Margone cried. "It's wrong - deny it!"

Bavin shifted his grip on his sword slightly. "Once we're done with these dragons, we'll come after you - spineless traitor! Now - out of our way, or die first!"

Margone made a move to draw his sword, but Corri gave a cry and held his arm. "No, Margone - you can't stop them. Only the dragons can do that. Let them pass - it's what they all wish."

Reluctantly, Margone moved aside, his face stone-like. Corri breathed a sigh of relief. Melayne realized that her friend must have come to care for the ex-slayer very much indeed.

Then there was no time for thinking. With a roar, Bavin led his followers forward. Three of them had used the delay to arm themselves with long lances, whose honed points glittered keenly in the sunlight. The others only had swords - and their attitude. Melayne realized suddenly that they were ill-equipped to battle dragons here, in Dragonhome - their giant arrow-throwers were not ready, and the slayers had had little time to formulate any sort of a plan. They were in the worst possible position, fueled by anger, desire to kill and their own adrenaline-laced excitement at finally seeing the creatures they had trained all of their lives to slaughter.

They had absolutely no idea what they were up against.

True, Ganeth and Brek had never been in a fight for their lives, either - but they were growing dragons, and their hides were very tough scales. And the other two dragons were huge - and, presumably, experienced. This was unlikely to be a quick, simple fight.

The large male spread his wings and dived down from the tower he had been perched on. His wingspan was almost fifty feet, and he kicked up quite a wind as he dropped the hundred or so feet toward the courtyard. The three slayers with lances prepared to meet him, grounding the blunt end of their lances on the ground, and raising their points to be ready. The dragon laughed, and swooped low over them - but above their points. As he flew past, one great front claw lashed out. There was a scream, and one of the slayers fell back. The claw had raked him open from face to groin. Blood and entrails spilled from him, as he fell to the ground, his useless spear clattering across his dying body.

Bavin, meanwhile, had reached Brek, lashing out with his sword. Somehow the dragon managed to twist and avoid the blow, but he couldn't quite retaliate. Bavin swung again, and this time connected. Brek gave a growl, and Melayne saw bright blood flowing from a wound to his shoulder. But Bavin had come in too close for this blow, and before he could reverse his swing, Brek reared up, and then stabbed down. Bavin tried to roll under the lunging dragon, but Brek's claws raked across his back. They weren't deep enough wounds to kill Bavin, but they tore a cry of agony from the man. Still, he managed to elude a second blow, and stumbled to his feet. Both combatants were injured, but neither was prepared to give up. Growl and howl mingled as the two joined battle again.

Melayne didn't know which way to look. Two more of the slayers had reached Ganeth, and were probing at her with their swords. She was lashing out, trying to get past their defenses. Meanwhile, the large female dragon had also swooped down, and was attacking a group of four slayers from the air. They were hacking and slashing at her, but she had the advantage of being airborne, and one swift lunge wrapped a claw about one of the men. He screamed as he was lifted into the air, and slashed at the foot that held him, drawing blood. The dragon screamed, and her head snapped forward. She bit the slayer's head, tearing it from the man's shoulders and spat it aside. Then she let the blood-streaming corpse fall to the courtyard below.

The battle was insane, and almost impossible to follow. Melayne had impressions, mostly - men lunging, dragons snapping, all of them crying out, either in anger or pain or anticipation. There was a sharp tang of blood - both human and dragon - in the air, and she felt sick. Whoever won this battle, there would be plenty of corpses at the end.

Rinter seemed to be content to simply watch and wait, and his men were following his lead. Most of them were grinning, enjoying the battle. Melayne's party had gathered close to her, possibly to ensure that she didn't do anything foolish in trying to help the dragons. Greyn was slightly behind her, yipping his enjoyment of the fight.

One of the lancers managed to get in a blow at the male dragon when he flew back to attack, stabbing him through the shoulder. The great creature fell from the sky, one wing injured and dragging. But he was by no means out of the fight. Ignoring the pain, he lashed out at his attacker, skewering him on one long claw. The slayer screamed in agony, and the dragon simply closed his claws about the man, slicing chunks from his body. He then let the corpse fall to the ground and spun about to attack another of the slayers.

Melayne felt sick to her soul. This fight was so unnecessary! But there was nothing she could do to stop it. She simply had to watch as her friends Ganeth and Brek fought gleefully for their lives. All four dragons were now bleeding quite profusely from the blows they had suffered, and yet none of them appeared to have been slowed by any of their injuries. There were the bodies of at least eight of the slayers on the ground now, but the remaining dozen or so seemed to be heedless of their losses.

Ganeth had managed to back Bavin up so that the castle wall was now at his back. *Slayer,* she growled, *it is time to pay back for all of my kind that your kind has murdered in the past.*

Bavin couldn't understand the dragon's words, of course, but he comprehended the intent. "It's time for you to die, monster." With a roar, ignoring his wounds, he rushed forward.

Ganeth's front foot lashed out. Bavin's sword sank deeply into it - Bavin's final, fatal mistake. As he tried to drag the sword from the dreadful wound, Ganeth's other foreclaw whipped out. The razor-sharp claws slashed easily through flesh and bone. Bavin didn't even have a chance to scream as his head was sent flying. For a second or so, his neck spouted blood, and then his torso crumpled to the ground.

Then Ganeth fell forward, her foot still pierced by the dead man's sword. She keened loudly, and then Melayne saw Corran for the first time in quite a while. He had slipped through the warring factions, and now approached his dragon. Carefully, he reached out and withdrew the sword, throwing it angrily aside. Then he clutched Ganeth about her sinuous neck and hugged her tightly. Melayne understood perfectly, but she gasped as another of the slayers moved across the courtyard, intending to attack the wounded dragon. "Corran," she gasped, helplessly.

There was a gray blur of movement, and the slayer belatedly realized that he had been targeted by something a lot smaller and furrier than a dragon. He started to turn, but Greyn leapt, sinking his teeth into the man's sword-hand. The slayer screamed in pain, and his weapon went flying away.

"Arrogant dragons," Greyn laughed. "Thinking only they can fight."

Melayne was truly grateful to her old friend, but glad to see that he sped out of the way of the battle now that Corran was safe. He returned to her side, grinning happily. "I hope your cub has sense to stay down now," he commented. Melayne ran her hand through the thick fur on the back of his neck.

"Thank you for saving his life," she murmured.

"It's not over yet," the wolf said.

But, mostly, it was. The dragons had taken on their old foes - and won. With Bavin's death, the other slayers had lost a lot of their confidence. Six of them were dead, and another half-dozen or more wounded or dying. The few left standing were all slowing in their attacks.

The large male, however, was not done with them. Hissing and snarling, he plowed into the remaining slayers. He employed teeth and claws indiscriminately, lashing out with powerful limbs and jaws, ripping and shredding.

Moments later, there was not a single slayer left on his feet. The dragons had won, but none of them was unscathed. Ganeth was still bleeding badly, and unable to stand. Brek was bleeding from a number of cuts, some quite deep, but he was on his feet and unbowed. The large male was covered in blood - mostly human, but with copious amounts of his own mixed in. He was roaring in triumph, and obviously very pleased with himself. The larger female was hurt, limping gingerly on her front left foot, and she, too, had any number of smaller wounds. But all were alive, and quite likely to remain that way. Melayne was overjoyed, and she ran to Ganeth as her husband went to see to Brek.

"She'll be okay," Corran told Melayne. "She just needs some attention and rest."

"And love," Melayne said, ruffling his hair. "Which she'll get plenty of, obviously." She hugged Ganeth. "I am so glad that you're both still alive."

"Thanks to Hagon, and his sister, Kata," Ganeth said. "They were amazing, weren't they?"

"Yes," Melayne agreed. "Wherever did you find them?"

"In the southern seas," Ganeth replied. "There is a small colony of dragons out there. Brek and I scented them while we were helping to hunt down the raiders with..." Her voice trailed off. "Oh, Corran, I am *so* sorry! We abandoned you, and forgot about you - until this morning. Then, once we had come to our senses, we came after you, to make certain you were well. We didn't mean to abandon you. It's just -"

"Time for talking later," the older male - Hagon - said. "Now it is time to finish what we've begun. It's time to kill all of the humans."

Chapter Twenty Eight

Melayne froze, staring at the huge, imposing creature. "You can't do that," she gasped. "We mean you no harm."

"Humans!" Hagon spat - saliva mixed with a good deal of blood. "None of you can be trusted. The only way dragons will ever be safe is if we kill you all. The warriors trained to slay us are all dead or dying, so it should be a simple matter to finish off the rest of you pathetic losers."

Melayne moved to protect Corran. "We won't be as easy prey as you seem to think," she vowed. "I have no wish to harm you, but I shall if I must."

"Harm me?" Hagon barked his laugh out. "Prey, you can't harm me."

"She will try," Ganeth said. "And she is surprisingly able. She will not go easily into death. And I shall stand by her side - if you attack my humans, you have to go through me."

"You?" Hagon stared down at Ganeth. "They are *humans* - and humans kill dragons."

"Not these humans," Ganeth said. "They would never hurt us. I am bonded with the boy, and the woman is my friend. I will fight you rather than allow you to harm either of them - or any of their friends."

"You will fight me?" Hagon echoed. "Child, you will lose. You will die. Don't you understand that?"

"Yes," Ganeth said, simply. "But I would rather die than abandon my friends."

Melayne felt a deep surge of pride in the dragon, but she hoped that it wouldn't come to that. There had to be a way she could take out Hagon before he could attack them. It was just a matter of thinking it through - if she had the time.

Abruptly, startlingly, Hagon gave another of his booming laughs. "Did I not choose my mate well?" he asked. "She fought humans bravely, and bears a wound. And she would even fight *me* to protect her friends! Ha! *This* is a dragon!" He lowered his muzzle, and gently licked her. "I am proud of you, my mate."

Melayne was astonished. "You're not fighting us?"

"No." Hagon stared at her. "If Ganeth calls you friends, then so do I. Maybe there is some good in humans, after all. If she is willing to die to protect you, then I accept her judgment."

Corran was still struggling to get past another word. "Mate?" he asked.

Ganeth sighed, happily. "I am with eggs," she said. "Hagon and I mated."

"Frequently," Hagon added, sounding quite pleased with himself.

Brek had approached now. He had clearly been prepared to fight alongside his sister had it been necessary. Since it wasn't, he went back to licking his wounds. "Kata and I also," he added. "It is why we were gone so long. Dragons in heat get quite... intoxicated."

"So do humans, sometimes," Sander said, laughing. He grinned down at Melayne. "I've missed you, my love."

"And I you," she told him. "We'll get... intoxicated with each other later, I promise you."

"Be gentle," he said, holding up his hands. "I am unable to defend myself."

"Poor darling." She stroked his forearms. "Does it hurt much?"

"Not since Poth treated the burns." He glanced at where the Seer stood, still locked in immobility, at the rail of the ship. "I feel terrible about what has happened to her."

"We'll worry about her later," Melayne said. "There are still other matters to be resolved. She gestured toward Rinter, and then at Sarrow's soldiers. "There are still two more factions for us to face and defeat. Only the first battle has been won."

Perhaps, Brek said. *But now you have dragons to fight on your side.* He eyed the human soldiers warily. *I think they may be less inclined to attack you now.*

Greyn laughed. "These dragons think they're really something, don't they? Why don't you tell them that it's enough having wolves on your side?"

"Because I'd rather have both wolves *and* dragons," Melayne said, laughing. "But you do both have a point." She walked back to where Rinter was still observing her. "You've seen what we're capable of," she informed him. "I have dragons and wolves willing to fight with me. Do you still wish to fight? Or are you willing to talk now?"

Rinter glared at her from hooded eyes. "Girl, you're a real pain, you know that?" He glanced at his men, and then shrugged. "We're used to winning every battle we fight, but I can see we might have... problems with this one. I'll speak with my men, and let you know our decision."

"Good idea," Melayne approved. Then she walked to where the leader of her brother's soldiers stood. "Now, how about you lot? Do you want to fight, or to make peace?"

The soldier glanced from Melayne to the dragons to the wolves. Then he looked at where Sarrow still lay unconscious. "We've been ordered to protect our lord," the man said carefully. "But he appears to be in no immediate danger."

"Nor will he be, if I have any say in it," Melayne assured him. "He is my brother, and I love him."

"Then we shall wait and observe," the soldier replied. "As long as you are telling the truth, we have no quarrel."

"Good." Melayne nodded to the man, and the turned back to her friends. "Well, the fighting seems to be over for the time being - now it's time to try and wage peace instead of war."

"And how do you propose to do that?" Devra asked. "There are too many people here with different agendas - we can't accommodate them all."

"I'm not interested in appeasing them," Melayne said. "I simply want to resolve matters." She sighed, and thought for a moment. "Right, first off - Kander." She walked over to where her long-lost brother was still sobbing, lost in his own inner world. She knelt down in front of him and gently touched his cheek. "Kander," she said, gently. "Brother. Talk to me."

Slowly, he looked up and his eyes focused on hers. "Melayne?" He still appeared to be very confused. "Sister?"

"I'm here," she said, softly. "I'll always be here for you."

"I've done evil things," he said.

"None of us are perfect."

"That's not what I mean." Kander shook his head. "It's my fault that our parents are dead - I sent the Raiders after them with orders to capture them. But the fools killed them instead. They had orders to bring you to me, but they chose not to pay attention. So I killed the guilty ones."

"That's understandable, in some ways," Melayne replied.

"Then I sent more Raiders after you," he said, as if he hadn't heard her. "And *they* tried to kill you, too. In the end, I slew them all."

"That's true enough," Sander said from where he was standing beside Melayne. "He used his Talent to murder the whole village. Women, old men, children, babies - he killed them all."

"I know." Kander bowed his head. "I was angry with them for failing me. And I believed myself to be a god. Whatever I did *had* to be right - didn't it?" He looked up, his eyes agonized. "But since you spoke to me, I've begun to understand. I was... warped. Twisted away from the truth. I was living an insane lie. I had fooled myself, and duped my people. I lost sight of what I should have been because of what I thought I was. There is no forgiveness for what I have done."

"There's *always* forgiveness, if you're truly sorry and wish to make amends," Melayne assured him. "I forgive you."

"That's not enough," he told her. "I can hear the voices of those I've killed. I can hear our parents, accusing me. And they're right, all of them. I'm a murderer, and unfit to be alive."

Melayne felt a shock. "Kander," she said, "that's -"

"Insane?" he finished for her. "Yes, I know it is. I've been insane for the longest time, and I don't think I will ever recover. But I'm sane enough now, thanks to you, to be able to comprehend the evil I've done in the name of my destiny." He staggered to his feet, and backed away from her. "Melayne, I'm truly sorry for all that I've done, but I can no longer live with myself or my conscience. Goodbye, sweet sister."

Melayne jumped to her feet. "Wait!" She tried to move forward, but Devra and Sander grabbed hold of her, tightly. Sander gave a moan of pain, but wouldn't loose his injured hands.

"No!" he snapped, firmly. "You don't know what he can do."

Melayne wanted to fight, to argue, to lash out - but not at her husband and friend. Instead, she was forced to stand still, tears streaming down her cheeks.

Kander had staggered back, his head in his hands. Abruptly, flames shot up, all over his body, blazing with intense heat, forcing people to stumble away from him. As Melayne watched, Kander seemed to grow brighter and brighter.

"He's overdoing it," Devra gasped. "He can survive his own flames normally, but..." She glanced around, desperately. "Parron!" she screamed to the Lifter. "Take hold of him! Get him out of here before he kills us all!"

Parron had been speaking with Rinter, but looked around when his name was called. He grasped the problem in a second and nodded. Then he concentrated, and the blazing ball of incandescent light that Kander had become rose swiftly into the air. It was already a blaze to rival the sun, and growing stronger by the second. Parron staggered slightly, but kept on Lifting the Burning God.

There was a sudden, overwhelming blast of light and heat far over their heads that sent them all reeling. When Melayne could manage to see things again, her older brother had vanished completely.

She gave a cry of pain and would have collapsed if her husband and friend had not been holding her. "Kander," she gasped, sobbing.

"Killed himself," Devra said. "He couldn't live with the true knowledge of what he had done."

"It's my fault," Melayne cried. "I made him face himself."

Devra shook Melayne, hard. "Listen to me, you idiot!" she snapped. "It is *not* your fault. *He* made his choices. *He* killed people. *He* proclaimed himself a god. None of that was your doing. All you did was to wake him up to reality - a reality he wasn't strong enough or brave enough to face. I know you like playing the martyr, but this isn't your fault. His death was a result of choices that he made."

"Devra is right," Sander agreed, gently. "Melayne, my love, you did what you had to do - he was intending to kill everyone who disagreed with him. Especially Sarrow. You stopped a massacre."

"By killing my own brother," she gasped.

"By showing him what he had become - not a god, but a monster." Sander held up his bandaged hands. "I got off lightly - I will heal. Many, many others did not survive him. What you remember of your brother was lost a long time ago - buried under madness and hatred and egotism. You have to let go of your own feelings of guilt, because you did nothing wrong."

"And, besides," added Devra roughly, "we still have other problems to deal with - your living brother, remember? Sooner or later he's going to wake up, and then he'll try to mutilate you. You *do* remember that bit, right? The red-hot tongs, the ripping out of the tongue?"

Melayne forced herself to stop sobbing. She nodded, shaking. "You're right," she agreed. "I can fall apart later. Right now, we have other problems to resolve." She drew in a deep breath and let it out slowly, then wiped the tears from her face with the back of her sleeve. "Okay, let's get on with it."

She walked to where Sarrow lay, and examined him. His breathing was regular, and he appeared mostly unharmed. There was a bruise starting to form where Devra had punched him, though. His jaw was going to hurt when he awoke. She glanced up at Devra. "That's some punch you have."

Devra grinned. "That was the first part of your plan I actually enjoyed. The brat deserved it. I think I skinned my knuckles, though."

"We have to wake him now," Melayne said.

"Fine." Devra picked up a bucket and walked to the nearest water trough for the horses. She slopped up half a bucket of water, and then threw it at Sarrow. He jerked awake, spluttering, and shaking his head. Then he touched his jaw.

"What's going on?" he asked, confused. Then he looked around. His eyes widened as he took in the dragons, the ship and all of the bodies scattered about.

Melayne couldn't chance him using his Talent. Concentrating her own, she bent to look her young brother in his eyes. "Sarrow, you must focus," she said, firmly. "You have to understand what you have been doing - and that your fear is irrational. You need never be scared of me - and you know I will never allow anything bad to happen to you if I can prevent it."

Sarrow was still groggy, but he seemed to grasp what she was attempting. "No!" he gasped. "I won't let you influence me! I won't listen to your lies!"

"They're not lies," Melayne assured him. "And it isn't *my* voice you're hearing but your own. I am merely loosing the bonds of madness that have crept into your mind. See through your fears, and past your terrors. I am your sister, and I love you." She concentrated hard, striving to break through the barriers of his fears.

Sarrow started to scowl, and his mouth opened. Then he shook his head again, sending a fine spray of water everywhere. He seemed to be fighting a battle within his own mind. Melayne was exhausted – she had done all she could with her Talent. Now it was up to her brother. Would sense or fear win out in his young mind?

"Melayne?" he finally said. "Melayne, are you all right?"

"I'm fine," she told him with great relief. "Mostly. How about you?"

"My mouth hurts," he complained, still rubbing it.

"I hit you," Devra said. "And I'll be happy to do it again if needed."

"No," he said, hastily. He blinked, and looked at Melayne in confusion. "I was going to have your tongue cut out, wasn't I?"

"Yes." Melayne studied him, trying to see what he was thinking. Her Talent only enabled her to Communicate, and not control. She had tried to erase his fear of her, but only he could ultimately do that. The next few seconds were crucial - he could either order his men to capture her, or else change his mind. She had no further way to influence him. Devra stood ready, fiercely prepared to defend her friend, but Melayne prayed this would not be necessary.

"I'm sorry," Sarrow whispered. "I was just so scared..." His eyes started to tear.

"I know," Melayne said, clutching him to her, hard. "I know." She was almost overwhelmed with emotion. "But it will be fine, I promise. I will protect you."

"You always protect me," Sarrow said. "I don't know why - I've been so horrible to you."

"You're my brother, and I love you," Melayne told him. "That's all that matters." She allowed him to get free of her ferocious hug. "We're together again now, right?"

He nodded, and then grinned - the clear, pure smile of love. "Right. Together again."

The captain of the guards moved over to join them. "Do you have any instructions, my lord?" he asked, his face neutral.

"Yes," Sarrow said, firmly. He glanced at his sister, and then the others around them. Finally, he gestured to one of the bodies. "I think we'd better start cleaning this place up. And I think a feast of celebration of some kind is definitely called for. I've come to my senses at last." He stroked Melayne's hair. "Oh, and one last thing - I'm not the lord here - he is." He pointed to Sander. "You take your orders from him from now on. Understand?"

"Yes, my.... sir," the captain said. He turned and marched off, calling to his men.

"All's well that ends well?" Corri asked. Melayne noticed she was gripping Margone's hand very firmly - and that the ex-slayer seemed to be pleased with events.

"Not yet," Melayne said, wearily. "Corri, maybe you had better talk with the Talents who worked with my brother. Any who want can stay with us. Any who wish to leave - well, arrange for them to get provisions, will you?"

"Fine." Corri tugged at Margone. "Come on, make yourself useful."

There seemed to be plenty of movement by now, but Melayne knew here chores were not quite finished yet. There were still the dragons to take care of, Greyn to be seen to... But first...

She walked across to where Poth and Batten were still standing, frozen, facing one another unseeing. Again, she was struck with how beautiful the young blonde woman was. "We have to help these two now."

"That may not be the best idea you've had," Sander said. "Both of them seem to have caused a lot of trouble with their visions of the future."

"We can't leave them like this," she argued. "We need to wake one of them up, and then get rid of the other one."

"Which of them do you want awake?" Devra asked.

Melayne considered. "I *know* we can't trust Batten," she said.

"But waking Poth might be a really bad idea," Sander pointed out. "Love, she's got this crazy idea that she wants to marry me. She might be... inclined to try and hurt you."

"I'll take my chances," Melayne said. She looked curiously at Devra. "How do you intend to wake her up?"

"It's really simple," Devra replied. "They're both comatose because each of them is trying to out-predict the other. All I have to do is to take Batten out of the problem..." Her fist whipped out, connecting with Batten's unmoving jaw. He collapsed immediately, and she rubbed her knuckles. "I'm really starting to like your plans."

Poth blinked abruptly, and then her eyes opened wide. Her whole body shook, and she might have fallen if Devra hadn't grabbed her and supported her. Poth smiled her thanks, and then turned to look from Sander to Melayne.

"You've found one another again," she said. "I knew it would happen."

"I told you that I loved Melayne," Sander reminded her.

"I know, I know." Poth sighed. "But a girl can hope, can't she?" She looked at Melayne. "I can See what he sees in you," she said. "And I mean that very literally."

Melayne employed her Talent again. "I hope we can become friends," she said, gently. "And that Sander won't be a problem."

Poth shook her head. "I know when I've lost." She glanced around the courtyard. "And I seem to have lost a great deal. What happened to Kander? I can only See the future, not the past."

"He's dead," Devra said, quickly. "And most everything else seems to be resolved. The only question left is - are you going to stay with us, or move on?"

Poth looked surprised. "You'd allow me to stay?"

"If you wish," Melayne said. "As long as you understand that you have to be with us, and not plotting your own agenda." Poth looked from her to Sander to Devra. Then she shook her head. "I have to admit, I don't really understand you, Melayne of Dragonhome. But I'm happy to agree to your terms. I would really like to have a place to live. And I can make myself useful - I'm sure you'll have a lot of need for my particular Talent, given the way you act."

"What do you mean?" Sander asked, anxiously.

"There's trouble ahead," she replied.

"What a surprise," Devra growled. "Melayne seems to attract it like dung draws flies."

Melayne punched her gently on the arm. "You might have come up with a more flattering description," she complained.

"Hey, I tell it like I see it." Devra grinned. "I could have said sh-"

"Enough," Melayne decided. She was starting to feel a little better. She'd lost one brother, but regained the other. And the problems with the Raiders must surely be over, which meant that the Far Isles - and her children! - were safe. The dragons were back, and had found others of their kind, so they had a good chance of survival. Her friends had come through the battle mostly unharmed, and - perhaps best of all - they were back in

Dragonhome. "We're home now," she said, firmly. "And dragons are back in Dragonhome. Never to leave again, I hope."

"Not everyone will like that," Sander reminded her. "Most people are still terrified of them."

"They'll have to get used to them, then." Melayne was starting to feel a lot better. She still missed her children, but they could be brought here now.

They were *home* at last!

Devra glared at her. "Melayne, stop looking so smug," she growled. "There's still trouble to come, remember?"

"But we can face it," Melayne insisted. "Together." She saw Devra's expression, and sighed. "Fine." She turned to Poth. "All right, what's the trouble ahead?"

Poth looked worried as her Talent came into play. "What do you want to hear about first?"

"*First*?" Sander echoed. "There's more than one problem?"

"Oh, yes."

Melayne sighed. "So what else is new?" she groaned. "Well, let's start with the most urgent problem - tell me about that..."

Epilogue

"He's getting worse," Commander Krant said, slamming a fist into the open palm of his other hand. "Much worse. This morning he was ranting on about the fleas being *her* spies, and wanting the entire palace checked for mice saboteurs."

Aleksar growled. "He's completely lost his nerve. That arrogant Talent bitch has him thoroughly terrified."

"Yes," the army commander agreed. "His mind is completely gone - he can think of nothing but her now. He just sits in his bedchamber, cowering at any sudden movements." He gave Aleksar a sharp glance. "This can't go on - the kingdom will crumble."

"Don't you think I know it?" the Lord replied. "I'd have acted before now - but I wasn't certain which side the army would be on."

"We're practical men," Krant stated. "Things are getting worse, and that's bad for any country. We will stand behind anyone with the strength and will to do what must be done. We've talked it over, and it seems to us that you're the best candidate for the position."

Aleksar nodded. "I agree." They had been walking toward the King's personal suite as they had been talking, down corridors that seemed gloomier and more depressing than usual. There were guards everywhere, but very few servants - the reverse of how Juska usually arranged matters. He loved to have the servants around to fawn on him, and to scurry off to do his smallest whim, and he hated anyone around with a weapon, no matter whose side they might be on. Outside the door to Juska's sleeping chamber was a single guard, who saluted his commander.

"How is he?" Krant demanded.

"As before, sir," the guard replied. "He's hunting for fleas on his hands and knees. I had to promise to allow no rats or mice to enter his room."

"Pathetic," Krant growled. He glanced back at Aleksar. "I'll await you here."

"Good." The Lord rapped once on the door, and then entered the king's bedchamber. For a moment, there was no sign of the monarch. Aleksar carefully closed the door behind him. "Juska?" he called, peering about the room.

There was movement behind the great four-poster bed, and then Juska's frightened face popped up on the far side. "You didn't let anything in with you, did you, Aleksar?" he asked, frantically. His eyes darted about the room. "No vermin? No insects?"

"Nothing, sire," Aleksar said, smoothly. "I am alone."

"Good, good," the king babbled. "You can't be too careful, you know. They're all her spies - I know it. And she has pigeon assassins - did you know that?"

"No, sire, I didn't." Aleksar moved gently across the room, not wishing to disturb the raving man any more than possible. In his current mood, there was no predicting what the madman would do – and some crazy people possessed great strength.

"It's true. I've ordered the guards to kill all pigeons on sight. It's the only sane course of action to follow, wouldn't you say?"

"I completely understand, sire," Aleksar said. "And I've come to you to tell you that all of your fears are over. There's no need for you to worry about Melayne any longer."

"Is she dead?" Juska asked, pathetically eager. He grasped as Aleksar's tunic. "Is the bitch dead?"

"No, sire," Aleksar said. "You are." He slid his long knife in between the king's ribs, directly into the heart. Juska showed a second of surprise on his face, and then keeled over, spraying blood over the bed sheets. Aleksar was glad he'd trained to use either hand in battle – his right hand was a mangled wreck thanks to Melayne and that treacherous hawk. He carefully wiped his bloody blade on an unmarked section of the sheets, and then looked down at the pathetic form huddled dead at his feet. "Coward," he hissed. "You were never worthy to be king - but this? To allow that slip of a girl to frighten you so?" He turned his back contemptuously on his late monarch, and walked back, flinging the door open. Krant was waiting, watchful.

"The king has suffered a... heart attack," Aleksar said. "Have the servants remove his body and prepare him for a state funeral. And have them clean up the blood, and replace the sheets. I want this room tidy for when I sleep here tonight."

"Yes - sire," Krant replied. He gestured at the guard, who saluted and hurried away. "And - further orders?" he asked.

"Well, there has to be a coronation, of course, with due ceremony." Aleksar smiled without humor. "That can be worked out in the next few days. I don't think there will be any other claimants for the throne, will there?"

"None that I can think of, sire," Krant said. "Oh, Juska did have one bastard son by one of the ladies in waiting. I've already given orders for both of them to be killed - just to be sure."

"Most wise. Krant, I think we will get along very well - we seem to think along the same lines."

"Thank you, sire."

"There is one more matter, and this is one you will have to see to personally. Who are we at war with at the moment?"

Krant thought for a moment. "Morstan and Pellow, I believe. I'll have to check to be certain."

"Do that - then recall the army. I'll write to the kings letting them know what we're doing, so they can declare war on Vester and Farrowholme instead of us."

"You think you'll need the army here?" Krant asked, puzzled. "I assure you, Aleksar, my men are all on your side."

"Not *here*, no - I have a task for them to do. One only our devoted Talents can do." Aleksar's brow furrowed as he considered matters. "I'm not frightened by the tricks of that stupid bitch Melayne of Dragonhome. She can cause trouble, but nothing we cannot handle. It seems to me that the best person to kill a Talent is another Talent. And we have far more of them on our side than she has on hers. I want every last Talent in the army sent to Dragonhome - and I want her killed, and the place brought down into ruins. Then I want the ground salted so nobody can ever live there again. Melayne has written her own doom..."

Next:
The Siege Of Dragonhome

About the Author

John Peel was born in England and moved to the U.S. in 1981 to get married. He and his wife live on Long Island with their pack of miniature pinschers. He has written over a hundred books, including the "Diadem" series and "2099", along with tie-ins based on "Doctor Who", "Star Trek" and "The Outer Limits". You can find him at:
www.john-peel.com
and on Facebook at: www.facebook.com/JohnPeelAuthor

About the Artist

Nicole Lane did the reverse - she was born in the U.S. and moved to England. She lives in Bristol with her parner, two little girls and her artwork. This is her first book cover, but definitely not her last. You can see more of her work at:
www.nicolelaneart.com

CPSIA information can be obtained
at www.ICGtesting.com
Printed in the USA
BVOW06s0147010517
482792BV00007B/97/P

9 780615 567082